RECONCILED

BOOK THREE OF THE ASUNDER TRILOGY

CURT LOCKLEAR

We invite you to download your complimentary MP3 album of Americana music inspired by the *Asunder Trilogy* at: www.reverbnation.com/splinteredsongsofthecivilwar

PRAISE FOR
CURT LOCKLEAR AND
THE ASUNDER SERIES

"**Asunder** *is a book full of passion ... for a
good story, for history and for the Civil War.*"

– ROBERT HICKS, *NEW YORK TIMES* BEST-SELLING AUTHOR
OF *THE WIDOW OF THE SOUTH* AND *THE ORPHAN MOTHER*

"*Mr. Locklear has a particular talent for stringing
words together, which makes for very lovely prose.
And his word pictures are exquisite. As a researcher
myself, I also enjoyed the detail used in creating this
historical world—especially during the heavy battle scenes.
Extremely engaging. Overall, a very rewarding read.*"

– MICHELLE ISENHOFF, BEST-SELLING AUTHOR

"*Cyntha's ability to spin a fine story when she's stopped
by soldiers on the road, the efforts made by siblings parted—
sometimes forever—by the war ... and the decisions made by a
host of characters operating well outside of their comfort zones
make* **Splintered** *a riveting saga that's hard to put down.*"

– D. DONOVAN, SR. REVIEWER, *MIDWEST BOOK REVIEW*

"**Splintered** *by Curt Locklear is one of those novels
that demand your attention because of its well-crafted
and well-developed plot line. Everything was connected so well,
every character was so perfectly drawn and described
that I felt at one with them. The story itself was very
engrossing. You can feel the emotion right from the get go
and you will find it till the very last word of the novel.*"

– 5-STAR REVIEW, TABIA REVNEER, *READERS' FAVORITE*

Reconciled
ISBN: 978-1-7339945-6-9 (soft cover)
            978-1-7339945-7-6 (hard cover)

Cover by Karen Phillips http://www.phillipscovers.com

Warren Publishing
www.warrenpublishing.net

Printed in the United States of America

Reconciled *is dedicated to those who endeavor to keep American history alive. Rather than tearing history down in an attempt to rewrite it, true historians work diligently to tell the whole story. History has beauty as well as warts, but attempting to hide or rename the ugly parts of our past does a disservice to all Americans—and to our descendants.*

God bless America.

Do all things for the greater glory of God.
–1st Corinthians, 10:31

HISTORICAL FACTS

Fact 1: Before the war, Robert E. Lee freed the slaves he had inherited. He was married to Mary Custis, the great granddaughter of Martha Washington.

Fact 2: Ulysses S. Grant, who's real name is Hiram Ulysses Grant, received the Ulysses Simpson name in a clerical error at his registration to West Point. His family kept their slaves before and during the war until passage of the Thirteenth Amendment. His wife Julia Dent Grant had an African American slave maid, Jule, given to her as a gift at her birth. Jule traveled with Julia when she regularly visited her husband at his Union army camps.

Fact 3: Before the battle of Shiloh, General Albert Sydney Johnston considered turning over the army to General P.G.T Beauregard, but President Davis declined.

Fact 4: At the Battle of Pea Ridge, General Earl Van Dorn had forgotten that he had ordered the ammunition wagons to get out of the way of the army on their march around the Union army, then failed to order up the wagons, thus with ammunition low, it lead to the defeat of the Confederates.

Fact 5: Mary Todd Lincoln listened to the advice of Elizabeth Keckley, a freewoman and seamstress who worked for her in the White House. Mrs. Keckley, a widow who lost her only son at the Battle of Wilson Creek (the battle in the first book, Asunder) advised Mrs. Lincoln to seek out spiritualists to help her speak to the spirit of her son, Willie, who died of Typhoid Fever in February, 1862.

Fact 6: Though Nettie Colburn was Mrs. Lincoln's favorite, Charles Colchester, a friend of John Wilkes Booth, was a regular visiting spiritualist in the White House, holding a number of seances. At one séance, his ruse was discovered, and he quickly left and then vanished from Washington, DC. President Lincoln himself attended a few seances.

Fact 7: Many attempts were made to assassinate President Lincoln, most notably, one in which a shot was fired at him on his way to the Old Soldiers Home (Asylum), and the bullet went through the top of his hat. The actual event occurred in 1864.

Fact 8: The Washington Monument was being built during the Civil War.

Fact 9: During the war, Washington, DC quickly became overrun with runaway slaves and with brothels.

Fact 10: More American soldiers died at Shiloh than in all the American wars up to that point.

Fact 11: The home of the President was not called the White House until President Theodore Roosevelt named it so. Throughout the Civil War, the mansion was referred to as the Presidential Palace, the President's House, Presidential Mansion, and Executive Mansion.

ONE

TERROR AND FLIGHT

MARCH 7, 1862, 12:30 P.M.

ONE MILE NORTH OF LEETOWN, ARKANSAS, NEAR PEA RIDGE

S ara lashed the reins on her roan mare's sides, making sharp
turns through crowded trees. Bullets zipped past her like
angry wasps. On all sides of the horse, blue-coated soldiers
rushed, their eyes wide in terror. The men were herding together,
running, then slipping on the ice-laden ground, falling, and
scrambling up again. Each man sprinting as if he had to out-
pace the entire world. Those on foot rushed in zigzag fashion,
glancing off the tightly knit trees like marbles slung around in
a bucket. Others rode their horses, colliding with tree and man,
knocking many soldiers to the ground, trampling some under the
horses' hooves.

An Iowan soldier, a minié ball piercing his back, stumbled
in front of Sara just to her left. He did not yell, just a guttural
fleeing of air from his mouth, and then he tumbled prostrate.
Sara pulled up Esther and looked down at the man, already dead.

"Hee yaw!" She dug her heels into Esther's sides and sped on,
weaving among the melee of soldiers.

A whirlwind of smoke from nearby cannon fire engulfed
Sara and the fleeing men. Bullets shot from behind her chipped
off bark from the trees and sent twigs and branches cascading.

Farther behind her, a regiment of Cherokee braves who had aligned with the Confederates whooped their abysmal war cries. They had ambushed these Iowan cavalrymen and were merciless, hacking and slicing even the wounded soldiers with tomahawk and knife. Now these Cherokee mercenaries under the command of Confederate General Albert Pike chased the routed Yankees.

Their belligerent cries rose.

Cannons boomed to Sara's left, followed by a strident whooshing in the sky. Far behind her, more cannons thundered. Just beyond the crowded trees, the shells exploded, tossing dirt and fire high into the air.

Sara drew up Esther sharply, the mare's hind quarters squatting and skidding against the force of the forward motion. In front of her, a jumble of rider-less horses jostled together in front of a wide half-circle clump of vine-woven bushes. The horses bucked and reared, their ears pinned back. They were trapped against the tangled wall of foliage.

Then, as if called by some ghost's bugle, the entirety of the horses scattered into the crowded trees, save one dapple gray that leapt, shrieking, into the bushes and became entangled in vines and sharp branches. In a moment, it kicked its way free, crushing much of the foliage in its escape.

A Yankee officer, riding at a mad pace immediately behind Sara, could not stop. His mount jerked sideways and sent the man flying head-first into a stout oak. Sara heard his skull crack. The horse, its feet twirling and slipping in the melted snow mire, flipped on top of the man. Its legs pawed at the air like it was beating at some invisible drum. Then it rolled off the soldier and scrambled to its feet to race away.

Sara looked at the dead officer. He had a comely, young face, rosy-cheeked, but his eyes were bulging, and a pock of cream-colored flesh and blood spilled from the hole in his head. Then she saw the deceased soldier's revolver, still holstered.

She jumped down, snatched the gun, and climbed back into her saddle.

The Cherokee war whoops were drawing closer.

She could not turn back.

Before she could decide on a new direction, a dozen soldiers raced past her and began plowing through the foliage at the spot smashed down by the horse. They hacked the branches with large knives and sabers, even pulling the branches out with their bare hands. Sara gasped at the realization that the soldiers, instead of slicing at the enemy, had used their war tools more as farmers would to hack at brush as if clearing land for plowing. In moments, they had gained a narrow channel through the undergrowth.

While Sara held Esther's reins tight, the group grappled its way through the opening. Another soldier limped after his comrades, blocking her from the avenue of escape. His arm dangled at the elbow by mere tendons, the blood gushing. His face was blanched gray, and he was holding his arm together with his spare hand.

How can he still be alive? Sara recalled the battle of Wilson Creek, its horrors and sorrow. Brave men dying for what cause? Despite her trepidation for her own life, her heart ached for that soldier who was sure to die.

Then she heard the screeches of Cherokees, immediately behind her. The sound was like a thousand wolves chained together—a repellent, chilling howl. She glanced back and saw a mob of Indians afoot, surging toward her, rifles in one hand and raised tomahawks in the other. In that split element of time, she wished she had *not* regained her lost hearing, for their screams seemed to her like the screeching of death angels she had read about in the Bible's "Revelation."

Before she could coax Esther through the gap in the brush, she glimpsed, in her peripheral vision, a muscled brave wearing a red turban, but with no shirt even in the icy wind. He burst through the brush and planted both hands on her mare's rump and leapt behind Sara, riding tandem. Esther reared. The Cherokee put one arm around Sara's waist, and grabbed her hair, wrenching her head back. Barely maintaining her seat in the saddle, she turned her head enough and beheld the brave's face, painted and fierce, his matted hair swept upon her cheek. His furious eyes, seeing her, took on a bewildered look for an instant.

Esther's front hooves came down, stutter-stepping.

The Cherokee regained his bloodthirst, jerked her hair and pulled from his gritted teeth a broad hunting knife. Sara smoothly swung around the revolver and was in the act of discharging it, but a Union soldier's bullet split the Indian's neck, his blood spurting. His expression turned again to surprise, and he tumbled dead from the horse, yanking some of Sara's blond strands in his fall.

Sara figured whoever shot him was a considerable talent. A sharpshooter.

She drove her heels into Esther's sides, and the animal rushed through the spare opening of the brush and into a grassy glen. A portion of the morning sun, split in two by a narrow cloud, sent spears of light that glanced off the snow-speckled ground, causing her eyes to water. Shading the glare with her hand, she saw before her a line of Federals formed along a rail fence and in front of a clinch of trees, their rifles and pistols raised. One soldier hugged the pole of a fluttering flag with the word "Illinois" stitched in gold letters. She reined Esther to a stop and surveyed once more behind her. She saw no Indians but was not going to wait.

"Jump, Esther!" Sara punched the mare's sides with her heels, and her mare tore straight at the Yankee line. The men dove out of the mare's way. Esther leaped the fence and over a prone man, and bounded through more forest, then out into a wide, snow-drowned farm field. A good hundred yards away, a long line of Federal soldiers was filing along at a trot, their rifles and gear clanking. They halted and turned north toward the battlefront. Sara trotted her horse the distance of a hundred yards to the assembling regiments, swung around the end of the line and drew up well behind the three-line deep formation of Union infantry.

She, like they, could only see the field, then the long stretch of trees with smoke rising above.

Her heart continued racing, and she was choking at every breath. She fully expected the violent Indians to burst through the foliage like an unrelenting tempest. But, after several minutes, when no attack occurred, Sara began to calm herself. *Slow breaths, slow.*

About fifty yards to Sara's right, an artillery crew unlimbered cannons and set them to roaring. Off to her far left, the remnants of the routed Union cavalry regiments cowered in a hollow surrounded by trees, well away from the fighting.

Her fear subsiding some, she became aware of excruciating pain in her leg that she had broken weeks before in Fayetteville when the arsenal blew. Having pushed hard with her un-splinted and unhealed leg to coax Esther, she wondered, "Did I break it again?"

No matter how hard she tried to halt them, tears flowed copiously.

Then the terrors of what she had just witnessed cascaded into her mind. Had she really seen a Cherokee brave carve loose the scalp from a soldier's head? The sound of the skin peeling like a deer's hide pulled from the carcass hung in her ears. Had she seen another soldier's head cracked open? Had she almost killed an Indian who was intent on butchering her? She was living the worst of nightmares. Her body trembled. She looked up at an opening in the smoke cloud at the midday sun in the brilliant blue sky and immediately felt dizzy.

Rolling her hands round and round in nervous repetition, she realized she had come no nearer to Joseph, the man she loved. And, once again, war, just like at the Wilson Creek battle, had encompassed her. Her soul felt as if it had been cored out by some ragged drill.

She slid from Esther and landed hard on the sun-bright, icy field, her legs extended out before her, the revolver in her lap. Her brow was awash with sweat. Her leg ached, though the icy ground soothed it some.

Esther bent her long neck and nuzzled Sara's shoulder. Sara reached up and stroked the long blaze and velvety muzzle on the stout animal's face. "How can you be so calm, Esther?" Sara bowed her head. "Dear Lord," she prayed aloud, her eyes closed, "please let this be the last battle. Let men no longer be about killing one another. No more death, please."

She could not hear the last words of her prayer, for the cannons bellowed again.

TWO

PREPARE FOR WAR,
ROUSE THE WARRIORS
— JOEL 3:9

MARCH 7, 1862, 1:30 P.M.
ONE MILE NORTH OF LEETOWN, ARKANSAS

Paul McGavin lay on his back in a shallow pile of snow-frosted, brown leaves. When he roused to consciousness, the first thing he realized was that he was shivering and that he lay on frigid ground. His breathing was strained; his chest felt as if it was a cooper's barrel, clamped with metal bands. He had no idea where he was or what he had been doing. Casting his gaze to look back, he saw blue sky with tatters of clouds and the bleak, scraggly tops of trees, mostly barren of leaves.

Drifting back into unconsciousness, he dreamed he was riding hard at the Texas creek where his brother, Asa, had ordered him to chase the fleeing horse herd, leaving his brothers and friends to fight the Comanches, and he could not help them. That dream then blended into the more recent incident—at Fort Smith—when his friends had shot it out with the slave bounty-hunters. In torrents of red and black washing the dream, John Coincoin was fighting to save his and his wranglers' lives in a whirlwind of twisting, flailing bodies.

He awoke from the nightmare, flinching, sure that the bounty hunters' bullets were flying at him. Gathering his senses, he calmed his breathing, slowly growing aware of his predicament, lying amid snow and decaying leaves.

His left eye was blurry with a pinkish film. He raised his left hand to his eye to wipe it and felt intense pain in his arm and in the middle of his back, like he had been strapped across a railroad tie. He rubbed his bleary eye, and then his forehead, and felt a profuse wetness. He brought his hand before his eyes. The palm was covered in blood. *Have I been shot?* He knew that head wounds bled disproportionately to the severity of the wound. He gingerly touched his forehead near his dark brown hair again and found a deep gash and surmised that the wound was from a cut, not from a bullet.

Fierce cannonading, which had been stilled when he first awoke, spouted loud, echoing booms, followed by intense shrieks, the cannonballs slicing the sky.

Paul sat up, his body tense. *I'm in a battle.* He fumbled around in the leaves and snow and found his spectacles and put them on, then looked out into meadows, surrounded by trees.

His thoughts remained muddled. *How long have I been out?*

Twisting a little, a throbbing pain rose in his chest like he had been slugged with a hammer. He lay down again and put fingers to his chest where the ache was. He felt a metal square box in his shirt pocket, and he recalled that Sara had given him the small, silver case at General McCulloch's headquarters on that snowbound night. The night she put her hand to his cheek. *Probably that box was the most valuable thing she owned.* He felt a surge of ardent admiration for the strikingly beautiful woman, not just because of her comely appearance, but her intriguing charisma and depth of character.

He tugged the box from the pocket and studied it. It was smashed flat, and a bullet, a minié ball, was lodged tight in it. The awareness that he actually *had* been shot, and that Sara's little gift had saved his life, gradually sank in. "Thank you, Sara." He thought long about her sweet smile and bright eyes, then said, "Thank you, God, for her."

Paul heard a horse snort and the clop of hooves. He turned his sore neck to his left and saw his mare just a few feet away, still tied to the tree he had climbed. He looked up at the leafless elm and saw his binoculars hanging by the strap from a bare branch. Then, his memories returned. He had been up in the tree observing the Yankees when he saw the line of skirmishers firing.

He surmised that one of their shots hit him. He had tumbled from the tree, landed on the back of his horse, which broke his fall and gave him the ache to his back, and he rolled a few feet away. *Lucky, I'm not worm meat.*

He bent his neck to his right. Immediately, he spotted General McCulloch's body almost covered with the abundant dead leaves that flitted about in a stiff breeze. In the distance, the general's white stallion grazed placidly. Taking a deep breath, he stuck the bent jewelry case in his jacket pocket, then struggled to his feet, clutching his bruised chest. He wiped his bloody hand on his pants, and then tore the tail of his shirt into a strip and bound his head wound.

A few bullets thudded into the trees beside him. He ducked. Then, half crawling, half walking bent over, he made his way to General McCulloch's body. He pawed open the general's coat where an inch-round tear was evident, directly over the heart. The shirt was covered with dried blood, a darkened spot in the center of the stain.

Paul clutched the general's wrist for a pulse. He felt none. General McCulloch was dead.

General McCulloch's eyes were closed, and his face had a placid expression like he was dozing. Paul knew that death was almost an inevitability in war, but losing his close friend accented a harsh reality for which he had not been prepared. He knelt silently by the body, occasional bullets whizzing by. He placed the general's hands together across the chest. Then, in a second gesture, he slid the general's binoculars, which had been lying in the grass, into one of the general's hands. He bowed his head and said a poorly fashioned prayer. "I have no good words, General. Only my heartfelt thanks to you and to God for your friendship."

Great volleys of gunfire were erupting from the line of trees just beside where his horse was tied. The rebel army was firing on the little advance group of Union skirmishers, but they were firing back. Paul looked out past where the general lay, and past his horse. Hundreds of Indians were sprinting away from the battle. He saw General Pike turn his carriage and was chasing after them.

"The Indians ran away. I guess we'll have to beat the Yanks without them."

Paul, because of the fall, felt like every sinew, joint and muscle was bound with tight tethers. He gathered enough strength to grab his hat from the ground, limped back to his horse, untied it and slowly mounted it. He cantered back into the tree line until he came upon a company of soldiers, most of them sitting on fallen logs or rocks, a few standing, a few kneeling, some of them occasionally taking shots at the distant Union soldiers. Their horses were tied to trees farther back. The soldiers looked weary beyond reckoning.

One man had a ragged upper arm wound, his torn jacket blossoming red, but he kept saying he was all right. Paul felt no compunction to address the man or get him help. Filled with too much sorrow over General McCulloch's death to care, he just looked at the man who was grinding his teeth and beating his chest to show his toughness.

Finally, a fellow soldier scolded the wounded one, helped him remove his jacket, revealing a dainty flower-print shirt. He made him lie down and made him apply a cloth with pressure to the wound. Then he gave him a swig from a canteen.

Paul, barely able to lift his left arm because of the pain where the bullet had slammed against the box in his pocket, rode deeper into the interior line of McCulloch's army. He came upon Colonel Armstrong and told him the sad news. "Frank, he's at peace. Get some help to retrieve his body."

Colonel Armstrong cantered his horse west through the trees, enlisting a few Alabaman soldiers to follow him. Paul continued east, not telling any other officer he met what had happened.

"What's the old scout want us to do, Captain?" a lieutenant called. "What does General McCulloch have planned?"

Paul pushed his glasses up on his nose and journeyed on toward where Brigadier General James McIntosh was positioned.

He would tell only General McIntosh, the next officer in charge after McCulloch. Paul continued through the line a mere two hundred yards and finally ventured upon General McIntosh standing on top of his horse near a thin tree, feet planted on the saddle, with one hand grasping the tree trunk, the other hand holding binoculars to his eyes.

"General McIntosh! A word, please," Paul called.

The general waved at Paul, then leaped to the ground and sprinted up beside him. "New orders from the general?"

"A private word, please, General McIntosh." He leaned over toward the stout officer with bright eyes, black hair, and a burly beard that he wore in an attempt to belie his youth. The general removed his hat, so Paul could whisper in his ear.

When the message was told, General McIntosh's face showed, at first, disbelief, then wonder, then anger. "There will be revenge!"

"I believe Colonel Armstrong has begun garnering a party to retrieve his body. The Yanks are keeping it pretty hot over there." He pointed in the direction where General McCulloch's body lay.

"Nonsense. I shall take my entire brigade, recover his body, and sweep the enemy from the field. We'll send them scampering

back to their rat dens! There will be *revenge*, Captain McGavin."
Calling his officers of the Second Arkansas brigade together, he
informed them of their general's death and strategized with them
in a small huddle. Each man removed his hat while the general
led a lengthy prayer. At its end, replacing their hats, the officers
scattered and began ordering the soldiers into battle formation.
The soldiers who had been hiding in the initial cannon barrage
were scattered like so many fleas in the uneven contour of
the forest.

"Shall I tell Colonel Hebert or any of the other colonels?"
Paul yelled at General McIntosh, who was striding with alacrity,
shouting orders. He mounted his steed, yanking hard on the reins
and spinning the horse around toward the Yankee army.

The general ignored Paul, so intent was he on his endeavor.

Paul watched, almost with alarm. Half the soldiers who had
gathered in small conclaves or were checking the loads in their
weapons were unprepared when General McIntosh unsheathed
his sword, pointed it forward, and called, "Advance! On the
quick step!"

His junior officers hastened their men, shouting epithets
and encouragements, but only a few elements of the regiments
stumbled out past the tree line.

Paul could see the impatience in the general's face when
he wheeled his horse around to face his men. He was yelling
something at the men and at his officers, but the cannonading
drowned out his words.

General McIntosh's face had turned plum-colored. To
Paul, the man seemed to have lost his bearings on proper
military comportment.

"Wait! The men aren't ready!" Paul yelled at the general
who had trotted his horse several dozen yards in front of the
line, angling to the right, somewhat in the direction of General
McCulloch's body.

General McIntosh leaned back, lifted his sword once more and yelled, "Forward!"

In short order, the jumble of soldiers progressed quickly toward the forest that stretched between the soldiers in gray and those in blue. Their officers barely mounted on their own steeds, calling orders all the while, buglers sounding mixed calls, confusing the soldiers even more. Paul dismounted his horse and leaned against a tree to watch. He did not expect what happened next.

THREE

That Which Is Attained, That Which Haunts

MARCH 7, 1862, 1:30 P.M.
LEFT FLANK OF THE CONFEDERATE ARMY, ATOP LITTLE MOUNTAIN,
NORTH OF LEETOWN, ARKANSAS

With the battle swelling to his right, Joseph Favor leaned against a narrow pine. His blond hair had grown long during the last weeks and hung past his collar. He stood beside other members of the Third Texas Cavalry in a tight copse of trees atop the small knoll on the extreme left flank of General McCulloch's army. No bullets had yet pierced their hilltop. He, like all the soldiers, knew nothing of General McCulloch's death.

A few yards away, Colonel Elkanah Greer paced noisily, punching his gloved fist, often stopping to curse at the Yankees, then yell at the Confederate army, then cursing his luck. "I am the war's cuckold!" he shouted. "I came here to fight!"

Colonel Lane, his next in charge, stalked a similar route farther down the line.

Joseph raised his hand to look at it, the skin folded tightly over knuckles, lithe sinews that grasped weapons to tear a man loose from his soul. He had used the tanned hand to raise a sword and strike at soldiers in blue. He looked at his other hand that had fired his revolver indiscriminately at men he had presumed were his enemy. Shuddering, he stuck his hands in his jacket pockets. Unlike the colonels of his regiment, he was not predisposed at all to fight.

Most of the cavalrymen, their horses tied to trees, had taken a knee or sat down on a rock or a fallen log. A few still perched in their saddles. Many had produced pipes from dirty pockets, filled the pipes from pouches of tobacco, lit the pipes, and chewed on the tips, wordless, with thoughtful expressions. None seemed to Joseph to be anxious.

One older fellow with a puckered brow and a stringy beard said, "War with Mexico. About like it." Joseph knew the man who rode a horse with one stirrup shortened, and had to use a cane to stand upright—a hero of the war that America had heaped on Mexico in order to grab more of the land of the Southwest. He had read articles that it was nothing more than an attempt to extend the boundary of slave states clear to the Pacific. His remembered hatred of slavery was boiling up in him.

A sharp breeze blew up the slope. He stepped beside his sorrel horse, using it to block the wind. Beyond him and his comrades, out in the farmers' fields, the panoply of the battle expanded. Far to the south, thin streams of smoke drifted up from the chimneys of a small town. Joseph held his monocular to his eye.

A long tract of barren trees stretched closer, and he could make out several scurrying squads of Union troops in the shadows. In front of the trees perched a small farm. Beyond the tract, he could see three cannons in another field, their muzzles raised high, spouting fire and smoke. From the number of blasts coming from that direction, he knew there were more cannons out of his line of sight.

Closer still were a considerable number of Union troops ducked in tight behind rail fences that zig-zagged out into the snowy meadows. Neat lines of blue. Easy targets for any sharpshooter. Joseph watched a Yankee take a hit from a Confederate bullet and collapse. He wondered what the man's life had been like up to that moment when his existence had been so abruptly cut short. What was that man's history? *At least he has a history. I have lost so much of mine.*

A few minutes earlier, he had watched the Confederate cavalry overwhelm a small Union cavalry detachment and a three-cannon battery, not far from a farmhouse and barn. The victors then milled about the place, instead of pursuing the routed enemy. Soon, the churning mass of cavalry was joined by howling Indians, the mercenaries bartered for by General Albert Pike. They had raced from a far cluster of trees and into the midst of gray-clad soldiers. Joseph thought that they were behaving in feral fashion, like a pack of coyotes. Some stood on the cannons, others danced what he guessed was some sort of war dance. The officers could not prevail on them to settle down.

Then, fresh cannonading began from the Union guns beyond the dense line of trees behind the farm. The cannister exploded and rained down around the cavalry and Indians. The cavalry withdrew in an orderly fashion to a safe distance from the explosions, but the Indians fled in a disjointed fashion to the north and quickly were out of sight.

"Must be from the Jack Rabbit tribe, runnin' off like that," Colonel Greer announced, watching them with his binoculars. He turned to a courier and sent him to find General McCulloch and get further orders.

The skinny private, probably not older than sixteen, rose in his saddle and trotted away. "Hurry!" Colonel Greer hollered after him.

The private kicked his heels into his horse's sides.

"We should be at the front of the fightin'," Colonel Greer announced, "not holed up in the rear!"

In this cove of trees away from the fight, Joseph felt as if he was in a walled-off castle, surrounded by a moat filled not with water, but with his tears of grief and regret. He was remembering much more of his earlier life. The memories fell into his mind like books tumbling from shelves, each book revealing more of his past. He knew now for certain that he had served in the Union army and had trained at Camp Keokuk, Iowa, that he had ridden on a crowded transport down the Mississippi to St. Louis, then disembarked. He had marched to a battle, though most of those details remained unfathomable. Officers had barked orders. Smoke was everywhere. Men were screaming in pain.

He remembered that, though he was married, their union had produced no children. He remembered waiting by the altar of a church for his bride to enter from the rear, but he could not recall her image. His memory of his wife was hazy, and shafts of some interior, tangential light seemed to hide her countenance.

He had a vivid memory of the young, trim, dark-haired woman fetching up for him a beefsteak that she had garnered from a neighbor and served to him on a plate dyed with blue and white scenes of an English countryside. The plate overflowed with greens, slathered in grease, fried potatoes, and the steak glistening in the light of a candelabra. Her offering was for an important event. He strained to recall the cause of her generosity, but could not capture it, nor her face. He scowled, trying to remember.

He began to feel like his secret thoughts were becoming exposed, like he had been turned inside out, and the other cavalrymen knew it and were staring at him.

His anxiety grew over what course he should take next. He was frankly glad the Third Texas was not in the fight. He was certain that he could not now raise his sword against a Union soldier. He began hoping that they would be drawn into battle at close quarters where he could surrender to a willing Yankee and re-enlist for the North.

"The First Iowa Volunteers." The idea had raced into his mind, and he said it out loud.

Several cavalrymen gave him a look like he had lost his grounding.

Ebie, his always buoyant Englishman friend, stepped up beside Joseph. "You doing alright? That fuzzy blond head of yours jumping like a toad frog?"

Joseph drew a smile across his lips. Ebie, an Englishman, having landed in America a few months before the war, who had no business fighting for either side, had saved Joseph's life in the battle outside Bentonville, Arkansas. He was a good man, and a funny one. In fact, Joseph had grown to admire most of the men in the regiment and maintained great admiration for Colonels Lane and Greer.

"Sharpened me rapier last night. Honed to a razor's edge," Ebie announced, smiling. "I'll be a bold deceiver. I intend to rob some Yanks of their family jewels." He pointed and twisted his saber in the direction of Joseph's man parts and grinned mischievously. "You know, I don't think very many British care for them Yanks after they rebelled in seventy-six. Not much at all." He stuck his saber straight up into the air and swung it around like the baton of a drum major.

Joseph found it ironic that a man from England would be so ardently in support of rebels. He shrugged his shoulders and gave a slight smile.

Of a sudden, a tumultuous movement of soldiers broke to the right, among the trees in the valley below them. Joseph held up his own monocular to watch.

The center of the Confederate line was a roiling pit of soldiers rushing and bumping into each other. Soldiers gamboled out of the trees in squads and in no semblance of an organized line. An officer was riding about amongst the trees, standing in his stirrups, waving his arms and shouting, the horse's reins hanging loose. A second officer was trying to mount his steed, both horse and man spinning in a circle while the officer kept one foot in a stirrup, the other dancing on the ground.

Abruptly, the motley line of soldiers in brown, gray, tan, and beige jackets, and wearing a hodge-podge of hats, stumbled out into the field toward the trees that hid the Yankee cannons. Joseph recognized the flag of the Second Arkansas mounted infantry. They faced a long stripe of Union soldiers, hunkered down behind the rail fence.

Then, far ahead of the Confederates that were hurrying to prepare an attack, Joseph recognized Brigadier General McIntosh astride his dark horse, his saber raised. Joseph knew it was he by the feather plume in his hat. The youthful general kept looking back over his shoulder at his brigade.

Behind him, the brigade attempted to catch up, many of them at a run.

The Yankee skirmishers at the fence opened fire, then broke and ran back through the narrow forest.

General McIntosh was not struck. Behind him, two Confederate captains who had been speeding to catch up with their general had their steeds shot dead, the animals plummeting like heavy boulders into the field, and the men tossed onto the icy ground.

Both men jumped up, momentarily dazed. One took out his revolver and shot his dying horse in the head. Then the captains trotted after their commanding officer. General McIntosh halted, turned his horse, and met the dismounted officers.

The running infantrymen caught up, attempting to maintain the semblance of a line. When they arrived beside General McIntosh, he again brandished his sword and pointed it toward the trees where the Union skirmishers had fled. In a moment, the general, with his brigade jogging a good distance behind, entered the dense grove of trees.

The men of the Third Texas cavalry began cheering.

"If I was a Yank with a gun," Ebie commented to Joseph dryly, "I'd shoot the fellow on the horse first."

Colonel Greer, who had stepped away to the far side of the hill to send out more couriers, jogged up beside Joseph. "What's happening, Corporal?"

"Looks like General McIntosh has been ordered to take the battle to them, sir. That's the Second Arkansas," Joseph said. His tone was sad, for though he was fast losing his allegiance to the Southern cause, he held General McIntosh in high esteem and hoped he would not be killed, nor for any more soldiers to die. He felt no compunction to continue fighting.

A few minutes later, rifle fire erupted beyond the trees. Joseph and his companion cavalrymen stood on tiptoes or shinnied up the trees attempting to see something, anything, of what was transpiring. Smoke curled above the trees and spread out like a second sky.

"Ah need someone to find General McCulloch," Colonel Greer announced. "That fool Ah sent earlier should be back by now."

Several soldiers volunteered to perform the deed. Colonel Greer pointed at three of them. "Go!"

"Should we begin an attack ourselves, the Third Texas, that is?" Colonel Lane asked.

"No, General McCulloch knows how to handle this. We'll await his orders."

A new sound of rustling leaves and tramping feet. All around the bottom of the hill, Colonel Hebert's brigade was snaking through the forest at a jog.

Ebie stepped up beside Joseph again. "Ha' ya noticed the ghosts, Joseph, me lad?"

Joseph turned to see Ebie's face was not its usual ebullient appearance.

"Do you see the ghosts, Joseph?" Ebie asked pointedly. "Do you sense them?"

Joseph gave him a quizzical look.

"They're here now, wandering about, lost, trying to figure where they are ...." His voice drifted off, and he stared into the vast blue sky.

Joseph was unsure what to say. "What are you talking about, Ebie?" he whispered, trying not to draw attention to either of them.

Ebie had now hunched his shoulders, and his eyes darted back and forth. "I'm not a ghost, am I, Joseph. Am I dead?"

Joseph humphed. "Of course not. I'm alive, you're alive, we're all alive." He had never seen Ebie behave this way.

"I'm from England. You know that, don't ya?"

Joseph nodded. "Keep your voice down, Ebie. The men are gonna think you're crazy."

"England is full o' ghosts. So many wars. A hundred years war. Wars against the Scots, against the Catholics, against Napoleon. Against Spain. Roundheads and Cavaliers. Lopping off heads. Acres and acres of gravestones." He slumped, almost into a standing fetal position, then crouched to his knees.

Joseph thought hard for a moment, regarding his English friend. "Yes, Ebie, of course, there's ghosts, but they'll find their way to their final resting places. They won't bother the brave Third Texas Cavalry." He looked down expectantly at the man, hunched, and with a bothered look on his brow.

Ebie stood abruptly. "Well, the ghosts have moved on. Finding their way, they are." He smiled.

Not sure of any other course of action, Joseph hugged the man and patted him on the back. After the hug, Ebie strolled away into trees, twirling his sword and whistling "Dixie."

A half hour later, the battle shifted into the trees to the south of the little hill where the Third Texas bided their time. Colonel Hebert, the next officer in line after General McIntosh, launched his own attack on the Yankees' right flank.

FOUR

TEARS OF AN ANGEL

MARCH 7, 1862, 1:30 P.M.
THE BURNED-OUT REEDER HOUSE ON A HILL
NEAR WILSON CREEK, MISSOURI

Reverend Edward Felder awoke with a start from a troubling dream, his heart pounding. The soft silence of the snowbound morning seeped into the burned-out remains of the Reeder house where he slept, half naked, with his arms around Constance Carver. The silence pounded in his ears. He could hear his own breathing and that of Constance's tranquil dream breaths.

The fire in the fireplace had dwindled to embers.

He eased his arms from around her, slunk as noiselessly as possible from under the blankets and Constance's bearskin coat. He slipped on his long underwear and trousers. Then he put on his dilapidated shoes and his patched, threadbare coat. Finally, he donned a sock cap and crept out the back door of the remaining outer wall of the Reeder home. The door creaked on its hinges.

In the yard, he turned for a moment to watch his breath rise and to eye the mostly burned-out home. He realized he had been fortunate to find even this partial shelter after being chased out of Springfield, Missouri by Union Captain Philip Sheridan for his outspoken comments about what he called "the plundering jackal army." His own home caught fire and burned to the ground in the battle when the Yankees drove General Price's Missouri Guard out of the town, then his church was torched by some *brigand*, as he termed whoever it was, in the night.

The events had been like lightning strikes. His comfortable life of guiding his flock was cast into the sharp war wind, which then blew him into this icy hell.

He trudged out across the ice-topped, crunching snow. He stopped several yards from the house and gazed out into the nothingness of the early morning, taupe-shaded snow that blended into a vast grayness of forest and then into the somber, ashen sky. The stark trees surrounding the farm were like mourners gathered to mark his impending death.

He was dismally cold, but he did not care. He was more concerned for the welfare of his soul. Making love to that brash woman who called herself Juniper Watson was a dire sin. She had caught him in a moment of weakness. She seduced him like a harlot. He was figuring on methods of atonement for his sin when he heard the squeak of the door hinge, and the door slam.

He did not turn to watch Constance approach. He just listened to her footfalls on the crunching snow.

"What ya doin' out here?" Constance stopped at Edward's side and leaned around to look at his face. "Eddie, you're gonna catch your death out here in this bear weather."

Bear weather? What did she mean by that? Reverend Felder closed his eyes, feeling a tear that had collected in his eye roll down his cheek.

"Did ya hear me, Eddie?" Constance stepped around to face him. She wore her floppy hat pulled low, and her big bearskin coat that almost swept the ground. Her dark cheeks were infused with rose from the cold. "This is bear weather. About the only animal that could stand it is a bear. And they're smart 'nuff to hibernate. Now get inside where I've stoked up the fire." She grabbed his arm.

He pulled his arm back. "No. I'll not spend another moment with you, Juniper, a brazen woman." He turned his back on her.

Constance gulped air, then she grabbed his shoulders and spun him around to face her. "First of all, Eddie, my name's not Juniper. It's Constance Carver. That was my farm, one place over, that was burned to the ground, worsen this one. I'm sure you seen it when you was comin' here to the Reeders' place."

"I wish we had met under other circumstances. You caught me at a weak point in my life. I must ask the Lord for forgiveness, but not with you around." His voice was rising. "I have denied myself all the years of my ministry. To live a chaste life ... and ...."

"Ask the Lord for forgiveness? You must be falarkin'." Constance matched her tone to his. "You have one time in your life to enjoy one of the few pleasures in this life, and you want to ask for forgiveness?"

Edward looked piercingly at her, but said nothing.

"Edward," Constance lowered her voice to a whisper and stepped closer to the man, who did not back up. "Do you think I'm pretty?"

Edward cleared his throat. Finally. "Yes, I find you markedly becoming."

"And do you find this pretty, as well?" She opened the coat revealing her naked body, the goosebumps rising on her skin, her nipples erect.

Edward turned his head, then looked at the ground, then backed up. "Be gone. Do not tempt me!"

"Don't go tryin' to sound Biblical on me. Just answer my question!"

"Yes, yes. Now leave me be. I must go now." He swirled to head back to the house where his horse was tethered under the lean-to shelter. "Be gone from me. You are brazen. You are a demon sent from hell," he hollered over his shoulder, storming away, his coat tails flapping behind him.

"No, I ain't. I'm an angel sent from heaven to save you!" Constance's voice was as congenial and sincere as any Edward had ever heard.

He stopped. Constance jogged up to him, holding the bearskin coat tight around her. Once more, she took hold of his shoulders and spun him around. His eyes glowed moist.

"How long you denied yourself a woman's softness and the joy of love-makin'? Ten years?"

Edward looked down. "Eleven."

"Don't you think with all this war around us, it's time we started carin' for one another? Some of us, at least."

Edward looked up and nodded. He truly found her appearance and her forthrightness appealing. In his current state, the words she spoke now were like golden honey to sweeten his barren, crumbled life.

"Look! I ain't in the habit of proposin' to a man, but I'm apt to do it now. I need to have a good man, and I can tell you're a good man. You wouldn't cheat. You wouldn't lie to me. Hellfire, my former husband. Yeah, that's right, I was married before. Not in a church with a ceremony, we just lived together."

"You took no vows?"

"No, we didn't take no vows. I was just fifteen, didn't know no better. We lived together five years. Most painful years o' my life. He drank too much, gambled too much, was lazy, cursed at me all the time. As it was, I did most of the plowin' and chores. One time, he chased me with a red-hot andiron. I have a scar on my backside. I'll show you if you'd like."

"Not necessary. What about your children?"

"Ain't got none. Look, I know I've been ramblin'."

"Yes, you have." Edward smiled. "But where is your husband?"

"Off to the war. Might be dead for all I know. Ran off and left me trapped by the Yankees, and ... Why, in the name of heaven, did he abandon me?" Tears plunged from Constance's eyes. She tried drying them with the coarse bearskin coat sleeves, but did little to stop the flood. "Damn it, Reverend. I'd be a good wife to you. I'd do what you told me. I'd even go to your church and try not to fall asleep when you're preachin'. I just need someone who, for once in my life, loves me." Her last words were choked out between sobs.

Reverend Felder looked up at the steel sky. Long before Constance arrived at the burned-out house, he had considered the likeliness of his surviving even the next few days and found it severely wanting. Time and again, digging in his mind for succor from Bible passages, he unearthed only despair. It seemed that God had somehow abandoned him. He knew nothing of farming, only of preaching, and had been counting on that ministry for his livelihood. This woman, who lacked basic, formal comportment, did understand farming, and she knew how to use a gun for food. The night she arrived at the Reeder house, he ate the first real meal in weeks. *Perhaps she is the answer to my prayer. Who am I to question God's will. Together, we just might survive this war. And she sure did pleasure me last night.*

Revered Felder, the austere, iron-rod-for-a-backbone preacher, reached out and took Constance in his arms and held her tight. "What if your husband comes back?"

"I don't care. He abandoned me. And we never took no vows."

"Can you read?"

"Of course, I can read," she snuffled.

"Will you read God's holy scripture?"

Constance stopped crying and looked up at the injured, but handsome, face of the dark-haired man with the widow's peak in his forehead, and deep, piercing, lonely eyes. "Is that a proposal?" For Constance, the cave of loss and nothingness had kept her closed in so long. She had had to press down her feelings of anguish of a farce of a marriage, of unfilled dreams, of a sort of hell. Now, a glimmer of light twinkled in a chink of the cave wall.

"Answer my question, Angel Constance."

"Yes, I'll read it every day and twice on Sundays."

"Then, Constance Carver, that is your real name, isn't it?" Edward lowered himself to one knee before her.

"Yes." Constance was bawling. "I'm sorry, Eddie, I ain't cried in front of no one in so many years. Go ahead. Please say it."

"Constance, perhaps the angel I've been praying to God for, will you marry me?"

"Yes, I sure will, yes." She helped him to his feet, and they kissed long, their lips pressed hard, their tongues finding the pleasure of desire and relief, of longing at last fulfilled.

After the kiss, she pulled him by the arm. "Let's get back in bed and make some more lovin'."

"No," Edward insisted. "Not until after we're married."

Back under the warm blankets by the fire, it did not take him long to surrender readily to her entreaties. They spent the rest of the day, naked, together, making love twice more and rising only to add wood to the fire.

In late afternoon, the sun split the clouds, and the weather warmed. Edward sat up in bed and listened to the melting ice dripping from the eaves. He awakened Constance. "I know a family south of here, the Martins. Pastor Martin is retired, but he can still perform the vows. I feel he will take us in and marry us. I'm sure they'll let us bide with them for a period of time. What do you say to that?"

"Sounds wonderful, Eddie." Constance ran her long fingers through his shaggy hair. She had not felt such ease since the war had begun. She appreciated the gentle manner he showed her and hung on his words, for the tone of his voice was like slow-poured molasses, smooth and sweet. She had seen him in the Wilson Creek valley a few times, standing on a tree stump or a wagon bed, and had heard that same voice ring like a clarion, and she had balked at the fierceness of his harangue on sin and hell. It was like he was two men rolled into one, and she felt excitement at getting to know him—this worthy man.

"Then, as soon as it warms a bit," Edward continued, "we'll head south to Tennessee. I know a little Methodist church there by the river. Good farmland. The pastor may need an assistant. What do you say to that?"

"I say thank you for askin' my opinion. I ain't used to that. Surely, our lives will get better and better, away from the war. What's the name of the church?"

"Its name is a Hebrew word for peace. Shiloh."

FIVE

No Safe Haven

At Elkhorn Tavern, the gunfire had ceased for a few minutes. Ben McGavin stood in almost complete darkness beside Cyntha Favor in the cramped cellar which was about as wide as a couple of grave plots. It smelled of dirt and root and mold. Cobwebs laced the rotted timber ceiling. Slivers of light filtered through the cracks of the ceiling, the floor of the tavern. Ben held the twin cellar doors just open. Behind them, Anthony Atkinson and his wife, Jeanette, stooped below the low ceiling beside the Cox family, flickers of sunlight through the cracks dancing on their faces.

The little group had watched a handful of advance Confederate cavalry launch a spirited attack on the Union Missouri battalion stationed around the tavern to protect the Union wagon trains. The small cavalry force retired a short distance up the Telegraph Road after a sharp fight. Then the Union cannons and soldiers swept up from their encampments. Federal soldiers filled the tavern, and a thousand bluecoats amassed around the tavern. Ben, Cyntha and the others had taken shelter in the cellar. Only Josiah Reynolds stayed behind, caring for injured soldiers who could not move, and Cyntha was beside herself with worry for his safety.

"What is to become of my home?" Polly Cox wailed. "I so wish my husband was here." No sooner had she said this than a crash of dinnerware sounded above them. She put her hands to her pallid cheeks.

Her elder son, Joe, hugged her, and her sobs were like a wounded fawn. Joe's wife, Lucinda, and the younger Cox boys huddled in the far reach of the cellar. Above, dozens of Yankee soldiers' feet clomped stampede-like on the tavern floor.

"Looks as though there will be a fight right here," Anthony said flatly. He hugged Jeanette Atkinson tight with one arm, and his six-year-old daughter, Clara, in the other arm. The child he had adopted upon his marriage to the widow, Jeanette Bennett, clung to his neck and whimpered.

"Perhaps they've driven the rebels away," Cyntha said loudly. "Perhaps the rebels have moved on."

"I doubt it," Ben said. He leaned on his left foot, keeping the weight off his splinted right leg. "I think a big rebel army is comin' here. They been spoilin' for a fight, and ..."

Cyntha swept past him and threw open the doors of the cellar, the bright noon-day sun hurting her green eyes. "I must see to Reynolds. He's my best friend." She hurried into the house.

"Your best friend? That old nigger? That sounds ..." Ben stopped, hoping that Cyntha had not heard his outburst. He had come to admire the freeman. *Shit. He's a friend of mine, too.* He hated his ambivalence about slaves. He had learned early on in his life the teachings of some White men who saw the Negro as a sort of offshoot of natural human beings—human, but less so. But Josiah Reynolds defied that description. Ben realized he had ignored the sound reasoning of a different set of White men who wholeheartedly saw all men as equal, regardless of their color or heritage.

Reynolds had saved his life and was about the smartest, wisest man he had ever met. He shrugged his shoulders. *Most important, I don't want to set Cyntha against me.*

Now that the cellar doors were open, Ben limped up the rough-hewn rock stairs and glowered at the rushing Union soldiers. Not a one was standing still. He rounded the corner of the house and saw numerous cannon and caissons rumbling north down the Telegraph Road, and a few of the cannons were already being unlimbered. The cannoneers unhooked the chains and leads, released the horses, and then hastened the teams back behind the tavern. Other cannoneers pushed on the cannon wheels, lifted the train, and shoved the cannons into position.

An officer sprinting by Ben stopped and stared a harsh eye at him, his hand on his holstered revolver.

"Injured soldier." Ben pointed at his splinted leg. "Long story." He was not about to reveal he was a Confederate.

The officer nodded and sped along his path, hollering and waving one arm like it held a flag.

Ben slowly surveyed the area and saw that the majority of Federals were moving north, farther up the road. Others moved east on the Huntsville Road. In his weeks of scouting Union General Curtis's troops in northern Arkansas, he had taken great care to learn the look of most of the regimental flags. He recognized the Fourth Iowa, the First Iowa battery, and Missouri and Minnesota regiments.

A noise above him caught Ben's attention. Looking up, he saw a soldier occupy a position on the upper porch of the tavern. Ben recognized the Whitworth rifle the man held. A sharpshooter. He called to the man, "What brigade is this? Who's the officer?"

The man never looked at Ben, lining his sight out into the trees. "Colonel Carr's the commander." Abruptly, the man fired his rifle, smiled briefly, then began reloading. He looked down with a condescending smirk that made Ben feel like a mendicant, begging for alms. "That's his majesty there." The sharpshooter pointed at a bewhiskered colonel in his late thirties seated on a black horse. "He's sharp, but don't ever cross him."

"Thanks." Ben looked piercingly at the colonel who was speaking to a driver of a caisson.

"Say!" the sharpshooter called, finishing the loading of his rifle. "You Union? Where's your uniform?"

Ben took a moment to formulate an answer. "They had to tear it up to mend my leg." He pointed at the splint. "This is what they gave me."

The man nodded and looked again at the trees, searching for a target.

Ben momentarily considered sneaking up and killing the sharpshooter, then dispatching the Union colonel, but thought better of it. *Too many Yanks, like vultures at a corpse.* He devoted his thoughts to figuring some method of escape. He figured there was some strategic action he should take but was confounded as to what it should be. Every horse he saw had a rider. The artillery horses had guards who looked as nervous as foxes trapped by hounds and ready to squeeze the trigger on anyone who came close.

Ben rubbed his hands about his shoulders, for a damp breeze blew, and he had left his jacket upstairs when the fighting began. *Best not wear a gray uniform. I need a blue one.*

Directly, he saw Cyntha helping Reynolds walk out onto the long front porch. Reynolds was coughing like he had the fits. Cyntha sat him in a vacant porch chair where Reynolds continued to cough. At last, the gray-haired former slave grew quiet while Cyntha rubbed his back, took a wool blanket from under her arm and slung it over his back, then kept her hands resting on his shoulders.

A somber silence ensued across the entire stretch of land. Save for an occasional snort of a horse, or the rattle of harness chains, or a few calls of officers down the road, there was no noise. Ben looked into the blue sky split by clouds the color of hammered pewter. A flock of geese in their V formation honked noisily above, soaring in their northerly trek. He noticed the measured distance between each bird and the unison of wingbeats. They climbed higher behind a cloud and were gone from sight. He wondered how the birds knew the weather would be warming, for, at that moment, he felt chilled.

He limped by Cyntha and Reynolds, nodding briefly at them, and entered the open door of the tavern, forcing his way past two soldiers pointing their guns out into the yard. Looking around the company of soldiers, he found what he wanted, a Union soldier's jacket on the floor under broken dishes. The jacket was probably from one of the injured men who had been recuperating in the tavern in the previous weeks. He made his way confidently to the jacket, picked it up and put it on. It fit, and he buttoned it closed.

He made his way out the back door to where the artillery horses, standing in their traces, were guarded now by six soldiers. He scanned the faces of the soldiers, all of whom looked younger than he. *Maybe I'll just stroll away down this gully and escape behind the trees.*

He hobbled down the trench behind the house, deeper into the woods, the incline becoming steeper. His leg ached like it had been speared by a railroad spike. He abruptly came upon a long line of Union infantry with sword-bearing officers. Their backs were to him, but he saw no way he could escape going that direction.

The instant he turned around the air exploded with the sound of cannon fire. Above the booms and wails of the cannons' blasts, he made out the shrieking yells of the Confederate army. He looked back and saw a throng of gray-coats struggling up the ravine, the Union army pouring fire on them.

The attack was short-lived, for the rebels, who looked to Ben to be a much larger force than the Federal defenders, gave up the charge and retreated, tumbling and sliding down the slippery, steep gorge.

Cannon fire then erupted to the north of the house, down the Telegraph Road. Volleys of rifle fire followed. One volley, then an ensuing silence, then another volley, then another, then silence. After a space of time, the cannons roared again.

Ben rounded the southern side of the house and met Anthony, who was just limping up the stairs of the cellar. He left the doors open. "Stay down there," Anthony called to his wife and child and the Cox family, huddling below. "I'll see what's going on, check on my sister, and get us some water. I'll be back."

Ben could scarcely discern, in the opaqueness of the cellar, the pale faces of women and children nodding at Anthony.

Anthony turned to Ben. "Do you know what's happening?"

The cannons continued to roar. Ben yelled his answer. "Well, that's Yank cannons a shootin'. Ain't no cannon comin' up from the Southern boys. Just shootin' their rifles. I imagine they ain't had time to unlimber their artillery yet."

"Do you know whose Confederate army it is?" Anthony yelled.

"Nope, not an idea. Hope it's McCulloch. Might be Pierce's Missouri Guard. Think I'll take a look-see."

"Well, I know there's a tanning yard down Telegraph Road, at the bottom of that long ravine. If the Confederates are coming up from there, they've got a hell of a climb."

"Wish I knew how many Southern boys they was a comin'."

The two men walked together to the front porch. Anthony stopped beside his sister and Reynolds, who was breathing heavily.

"What's wrong with Josiah?" Anthony asked Cyntha.

"I can't tell you now. Not now." Tears had welled up in the corners of Cyntha's eyes.

Ben hopped up on a porch railing, trying to see anything down the road. Just smoke engulfed the leafless trees. A few Yankees ran here and there.

Of a sudden, a lieutenant, his sword clacking at his side, sprinted up to the door of the tavern. "You men, grab blankets and quilts and bring 'em down the road. We've got wounded!"

In a moment, the entire company of Yankees rushed out the door, holding blankets, sheets, quilts, even towels, and then followed the lieutenant. When the last soldier, a slight fellow with a hawk-shaped nose and small eyes, came through the door carrying a measly piece of bolt cloth, Ben yanked it from his grasp. "Give that to me. You stay here." He shoved the soldier back into the house, flicked the soldier's nose, took his cap and placed it on his own head.

Though mostly hopping on his good left leg, he traipsed off after the other Yankees. He hollered back to Anthony and Cyntha, "I'm gonna take me a look-see."

Cyntha attempted to bring Reynolds inside.

"No, sister," Anthony demanded. "In a few minutes, this house will be filled with wounded. Take Reynolds down to the cellar. If the Confederates sweep through here, the cellar is the safest place."

Cyntha nodded, and, supporting Reynolds by the arm, she helped him to the cellar. In another few minutes, Anthony came down the cellar steps with a wooden bucket of water, a ladle, and some cornbread, wrapped in a greasy, swaddled bag. He pulled candle stubs from his pocket and some matches. "This will have to do."

He closed the cellar doors just when more Union troops jogged up the road from the south and the gunfire down in the ravine and on Telegraph Road broke in a fury.

Anthony hugged his new wife and daughter. Was a cannonball going to end them all?

SIX

HOPE AND DECEIT

MARCH 7, 1862, 2:00 P.M.
FREDERICKTOWN, OHIO, MRS. CLEGG'S BOARDING HOUSE

In the early afternoon, John Coincoin made it a point to sweep the floor of the hall just outside the Fox sisters' door. He did not want to be told he was dawdling in his work by the boarding house owner, a sour-faced widow named Astrid Clegg, whose continual pursed lips gave the impression she had just sucked a lemon. He knew she would fire him in a minute if she thought he was not working as hard as two men. But his curiosity was too much. He had been hoping each day of the four days the Fox sisters had stayed in the boarding house that he would have an opportunity to speak with one of the sisters should she emerge from their room.

He stopped a moment at a hall mirror to judge his dark brown body with brawny shoulders. He straightened the collar of his worn shirt, swept the sweat from his bald scalp. *At forty-five years and now free, I'm twice the man I used to be.* He felt a brief surge of pride.

He thought that, perhaps, if he was polite enough, the sisters might give him a private séance and let him speak to his dead parents, or to his old master whom he loved so much, or even to Asa McGavin, that Texan horse wrangler who had promised him his freedom. Because of his older brother's pledge, Paul McGavin had granted John his freedom. He wanted to thank Asa, since he had not been able to before Asa died in that quicksand hole. He shuddered thinking of it.

John's wife, Miriam, was down in the kitchen, cleaning up after breakfast, which the Fox sisters had not attended. His oldest son, James, was chopping wood in the back yard. The remainder of his children stayed in a simple house, a mile outside of town, and fended for themselves. Each day, long before the sun arose, John, Miriam and James made the trek to the boarding house in pleasant weather or inclement.

John began dusting a vase with his bare hand. The vase teetered on a little pedestal, and he was about to give up waiting when, quiet as the tread of a mouse, Maggie Fox stepped out of the room, still in her nightgown and a kerchief tied around her black locks. She was barefoot.

John took a deep breath and strode up to her, his broom shouldered like a rifle. Maggie halted and allowed him to approach, making no attempt to slip back into the room.

"I need to make use of the outhouse," she said, "but I've forgotten how to access it. Can you point it out to me?" She swayed back and forth. John thought she looked a little like a sapling bending in a stiff breeze.

She leaned in toward him, her bosom showing form in the gown. Her breath smelled noxious of liquor.

John ignored her question and made his own entreaty. "Miss Fox, ma'am." He cleared his throat. "I'd be right interested in havin' you help me speak to some dead folks what're special to me. Could you do that some time? I'd be most grateful."

"You would." She giggled. "How grateful?" She inched closer to him, smiling.

"I could pay you. I got sixteen cents in my pocket now and ..."

"Sixteen cents," she cackled and then put her finger to her lips and shushed herself. "Shh, shh, shh."

"I got my life savings stowed away, but I can't touch that for nothin'."

Maggie's eyes glanced left and right, then followed John's gaze at his storage closet. Then she whispered, "I tell you what. How about you and I find an empty room and let me see that big old thing you have." She moved against him, placing the notch between her legs against his trousers, and rested one hand on his shoulder. She stuck a finger of her other hand in her mouth and sucked on it.

"No, ma'am!" John backed away, almost knocking the vase from the stand. He caught it and held it in both hands, letting the broom clatter to the floor. "I's married." He worried that any other boarders might come out in the hall to assess the situation. Then he remembered that all the remaining boarders had left earlier. "I'll just 'scuse myself." He turned to leave.

"Don't go." Maggie's voice sounded as forlorn as an un-weaned calf who had lost its mother.

John turned around.

"I'm sorry, sir." She had her mouth turned down in a frown like a child might use who was denied a licorice whip from the candy jar by her parents.

John wondered. *She called me sir.*

"If you can get me some whiskey, I'll talk to your folks, as you called them."

"I don't know if I rightly know where I can get some whiskey. The owner won't allow none even on the porch."

"I'll bet you can find some somewhere." Maggie took on a dejected look, pouting again like a child.

John wondered if all her facial expressions were just acting, yet he so wanted to speak to his parents and to Asa, at least. "All right. You allow me to talk to my folks, I'll find you some whiskey. But what about your sisters? Don't you need them to do de talkin'?"

"Not hardly," Maggie snorted. "Kate is asleep, and Leah went to check on the next train out of town. She'll be gone for hours."

"So is the hall a good place? I can't take no chance of goin' in a room wid a White woman."

"The hall is fine. Give me your hands."

John put down the vase and slowly placed his hands in hers.

"Ummm, nice, strong hands," she said, purring like a cat. "But never mind. What's your name?"

"John Coincoin."

"Coincoin. All right. Who do you wish to speak to first?"

"My mam and pap."

"What's their names?"

"Mary and Lothorio Ames. I was sold to Mistress Coincoin. She was a colored woman, like me."

Maggie blinked unintentionally at his telling of his history. She stared at him for a long time, finally rolling her eyes up, followed by tilting her head back and lolling it round and round. She began to sway and moan. After she had done this for a full two minutes, John cleared his throat, thinking that perhaps things were not going to work out. The only sound was the clock at the end of the hall chiming noon.

"Mary and Lotho Ames." Maggie groaned, at last.

"Lothorio."

"Of course, Lothorio. Are you there? Your son wants to know. One tap for yes, two for no."

John heard the loud crack against wood. He never thought to look down at Maggie's bare feet.

"Do you love your son?" Maggie whispered.

Snap went Maggie's toe.

John smiled. "I love you, too, Mam and Pap."

"They know, John. What do you want to know?"

"Are they happy."

"Are you happy?" The pop of the toe joint echoed. "They have indicated they are quite happy, and they are free. Lots of hoecakes and sausage and grits, as much as they want. Lots of liquor trickling in little streams that you can cup at any time, and it never runs dry." Maggie smacked her lips, then opened her eyes. "They're gone. Who else?"

"But."

"They're gone. They're happy. Who else?"

"My old master. I loved him dearly. He treated me like a son."

"Very well. His name?"

"Mr. Jameson."

"Was he your master? Did he have lots of slaves?"

"Yes'm, he had a passel of slaves for a while, then the farm went down, and I was his only slave left."

"Hmmm. Hold my hands again." She took John's hands and rubbed her thumb seductively between his fingers. Seeing no response from John, she tilted her head back and moaned. "Mr. Jameson, can you come forth? One tap for yes, two for no?" Her pronunciation was markedly slurred.

Tap. Tap.

"No!" John blurted. "I's sorry, ma'am, to break you concentration. Why for he can't come out?"

"Why can you not come forth, Mr. Jameson? Is it because of your sins of owning slaves?"

The loudest snap echoed on the floor and up the walls.

"He is burdened by his many sins of owning slaves and not giving them their freedom. He is trapped and can't get free." Maggie smirked a little.

Tears welled up in John's eyes. "But he was a good man. Befo' he died, he set his slaves free. All of 'em. Even me, but I stayed to take care of him 'cause he was ailin' so."

Maggie open her eyes and saw the tears trailing down John's face. "Oh, oh. Wait. Mr. Jameson, are you soon to be set free from your burden?"

A loud snap against wood. John turned his gaze to the floor.

"Look at me, John Coincoin."

He raised his eyes, his cheeks moist.

"John, your old master will soon be free to be in paradise. He is gone now to pay his final dues, so he will be as free and joyous as your mam and pap."

John pulled his hands from her and wiped his face. "That's won'ful news. Now, Asa McGavin is de last one."

Maggie stretched and yawned. "You must understand. Talking to the dead wears me out. I'm done." She put a finger to his lips. "No buts. I will be revived if I have some whiskey. Are you going to get me that swamp water or not? Isn't that what you darkies call it? Swamp water?"

John stood with his mouth agog. He closed his mouth. "Yes'm." He turned to go. "I be back directly." He gathered his broom and trudged down the stairs. He knew an old man who made moonshine. He figured he could get a jug on credit.

When he returned to the Fox sisters' room with a small crock of homemade brew, Leah met him at the door and told him to take it away. He smelled the fetid stench of vomit but did not see Maggie passed out on the bed beside her sister. Slipping carefully down the stairs, hoping his employer did not see him with a liquor crock, he could hear Leah's shrill voice screaming at her sisters.

SEVEN

SCATTER THE NATIONS
WHO DELIGHT IN WAR
– PSALM 68:30

MARCH 7, JUST PAST 2:00 P.M.
EIGHTY YARDS NORTH OF LEETOWN, ARKANSAS

Outside Leetown, the Union cannons fired in an uncoordinated fashion, sometimes the entire row blazing in unison, other times shooting randomly, the flame and smoke belching from the bores like volcanoes. The explosions of the Confederate return cannon fire landed within yards of where the Yankees were lined up. They knelt on one knee along the last rows of the farm field. At each explosion that tossed sludgy mud at them, the men ducked.

Then the cannons' firing ceased for a prolonged silence of several minutes.

Sara sat in the field far to their left, facing the vacant snowy, sloppy field. Grasping the reins of her horse, she pulled herself up from the snowy ground, her leg like a useless, painful peg. She had raced from farmer Foster's barn so quickly, she had forgotten her cape. She was cold, and the melted snow she had been sitting in dampened her dress, which clung to her skin like a soiled, clammy rag. Her leg ached so much, she yearned to tear it off.

Upon rising, Sara heard a rifle volley from the direction of the Illinois skirmish line along the fence that she had ridden through in her escape from the Indians. It was followed a few minutes later by a second volley. Besides those firings, the battlefield had fallen quiet.

A Yankee officer barked some orders, and one of the Yankee regiments that stood in front of her marched away rapidly at an angle in the direction of where the skirmish line was established. More volleys arose that way, rifle fire going in both directions. Sara could see only smoke and hear the gun's clicking, like a nest of angry rattlesnakes.

She decided to move farther away from the fighting.

With difficulty, her leg throbbing, she mounted Esther and trotted the animal several yards directly behind parallel lines of Yankee soldiers, stretched at the back of the field and extending perpendicularly to a narrow road that ran north. She knew it was Leetown Road, for Mr. Foster who had taken her in the night before had told her that much. *I hope the Foster family are all right.*

She knew how armies, like a swarm of hornets, seemed to care little for the families caught in their caustic wave of slaughter or in their wake after they passed. The Fosters were innocent of owning slaves, innocent of promoting the war, and she had no idea if they had even chosen a side. Maybe their crime was being in the way of two great armies while trying to eke out a living and stay away from war. She uttered a small prayer on their behalf.

Backing Esther in among an evergreen grove, she looked behind and saw smoke dribbling from chimneys of a forest village. *Leetown, perhaps.* She prayed, "I entreat thee, Lord, grant safety to these families."

The weather was warming fast, and the snow and ice in the field was quickly melting, muddy puddles standing in the fields, reflecting golden and silver under the sun. And where she had halted, the melting ice dripped from the trees, plopping on her shoulders and arms and down her neck. She shivered but was too weary and scared to search for another spot. She felt like she was a cornered animal. She hoped she was well away from the Indians. *Why are the Indians even here? I don't understand. This is a White Man's war! An Indian almost killed me.*

She noticed a low, sorrowful moan emanating from somewhere, and then realized it was her own voice.

Her terror had overwhelmed her. She had heard of persons subjected to so much fear and death that they lost their senses, babbling and screaming for no cause, and then being sequestered in an asylum. She took several deep breaths. *You can survive, Sara Reeder.* She began praying fervently for her own well-being.

Occasionally, the Union soldiers would turn their heads to look at her, their eyes burning through her. *They're wondering who I am. Can they tell I want them to lose, to go away?* They would turn their heads back like some sort of machine piece on a swivel, to stare at the bleak, nearly leafless forest across the field. Although she sat on her horse two dozen yards behind them, she smelled them; sweet like molasses and coffee, but also rank like pig swill. The jingling and clanking of their metal accoutrements and guns never ended. Each one shifting his hold on his rifle, changing a foot placement, straightening a leather strap. She imagined herself rushing between any two of them to warn the soldiers in gray to stay away. *Don't come here. There is death here.*

The volleys to the left ceased. In the burdensome silence, she felt as if a cord was tightening around her chest. She berated herself in that she had not been vigilant enough to watch that Joseph might have marched through Fayetteville, past the very café where she worked. Why had she let her tired body force her to stop the night previous to this day? *I should have pressed on to find him.* Now, with her ability to hear having returned, the suffocating silence was equal to the cannonading.

A couple of soldiers started joking and laughing, elbowing each other. Soon, others in the line were enjoying some soldier's joke, and the mirth spread up and down the line. One fellow stepped out in front of the others and danced a jig, then returned before any officer spotted him. The whole line became chattering magpies.

Sara thought they were behaving like a crowd at a circus might do while waiting for the ring-master to march out in his tall hat and his red vest with a megaphone in his fist to announce the next act. She almost expected a troop of circus performers to appear in the beige and white field. A dancing bear and his trainer, perhaps, or a set of dappled horses prancing in a ring, with a lady wearing a pink dress and a masquerade mask and standing on a horse's back. She had never attended a circus but had studied pictures in her father's books in their home at Wilson Creek.

She was startled when muffled shooting began off to the north, beyond the wide band of trees across the field. A few Yankees scampered from the forest, then more followed, sprinting and falling in the open land, some carrying their rifles, others without their weapon. Along with them came a herd of deer. Men and animals leaping and cavorting. Sara thought—*the circus act.*

Deep within the trees beyond the field, a sudden swelling of voices rumbled like far-flung thunder. The deep rumble seemed to have no body, a phantom storm. Then, a dense gray shadow filled the forest, blocking any light. Stark, leafless, trees, like spears, were smothered in a cloud of gray.

The Confederates were attacking, and it sounded to Sara like an immense number by the roar that spilled out from the trees. The deep-throated yell changed to a menacing screech. Yipping, whooping, and howling.

The Yankees stood, a blue picket fence between her and the field, shuffled their feet and began cursing and making worried comments. A few soldiers tried to turn and run, but sergeants, with grim faces and revolvers held tight in their fists, forced them back into line.

"If your gun's not already loaded," a Captain announced while he strolled in front of his regiment, "now's the time to do it."

The regiment to the far left that had headed toward the Illinois skirmishers swung their line, their rifles aimed toward the oncoming Confederates. Then, not one hundred yards away from where Sara sat on her mount, as if he was the only charging soldier, an army unto himself, a mounted Confederate officer emerged from the band of trees. He sported a dense, dark beard on his face. A feathered hat adorned his head. Alone, screaming like a banshee, he galloped his horse toward the Union soldiers, his saber raised. He was initially the only Confederate in sight, though the wide gray shadow of soldiers hastened out past the edge of the trees behind him.

The Yankees on the left opened fire. Sara watched the fire and smoke from the guns, then heard the clattering reports a moment later. The charging officer's plumed hat flew off, and he lurched backward. In Sara's mind, she perceived the muffled sound of the bullet plunging into his chest. Thump. And heard his body, dead even as it was falling, landing like a sack of oats on the earth.

In a moment, the wave of Confederates flooded into the field, shouting, and a few of them shooting at the Union line. Three Yankees near Sara took hits, groaned, and crumpled to the ground. Comrades near them kneeled to their aid. Each wounded man twisted in contortions, holding his stomach.

As if on a cue from some unknown source, the entire Rebel line halted, secondary lines plowing into the backs of those in front. Two officers afoot rushed to the dead officer. His horse stood by the body, its head down, nose to its master's chest. Moments after the officers reached the body, both men shouted over and over, "The General's dead! General McIntosh is dead!"

The Confederate army's yells turned to anguished moans and angry threats. Sara heard the cacophony of calls and wails, and livid, foul curses hurled at the Yankees rising above the moans and howls.

Union officers in front of her raised their sabers almost in unison. "By rank! Fire!" was repeated down the line. Volley after volley vomited from the rifles, and Rebel soldiers collapsed, dead or wounded, the others ducking or fleeing.

Below the rifle smoke, rising rapidly in a new breeze, Sara saw the officers, with help from some privates, lift the Confederate general's body and hastily carry it back into the trees. General McIntosh's horse plodded after its dead master, seemingly oblivious of the bullets zipping around it.

After a few more erratic volleys from both sides, the shooting stopped. The Confederates were no longer visible, having shrunk back into the trees, and the Union soldiers began re-loading their guns.

Slowly at first, several began cheering, raising their caps and waving them. Soon, the whole Union line was rejoicing.

Sara began to weep. Her sorrow was too deep. She remembered briefly seeing General McIntosh at the house on her journey two nights previous. They had not met, but she understood the impact on an army losing a leader. Her father, Lucas, had spoken of the dismay and confusion of soldiers whose officers died in battle.

Wiping her tears on her sleeve, Sara noticed a bleeding notch cut on Esther's ear. Had the animal obtained the wound when Sara rode her through the tangled brush? Or had a bullet come that close to striking her? A Confederate bullet!

She gritted her teeth. She hated war.

Her thoughts were broken when she saw a swarm of blue-coats wading through the trees on the opposite side of Leetown Road. *What now?*

EIGHT

WRATH HAS A FACE

MARCH 7, 1862, 2:00 P.M.
GENERAL CURTIS'S HEADQUARTERS, CROSS HOLLOWS, ARKANSAS

General Curtis was vexed. He said the word to himself several times. "I don't understand Van Dorn," he said to his subordinates, circled around him. "Osterhaus is out there, fighting a huge force, he says, and calls for reinforcements. And Carr?" He opened the tent flap and looked out at the pure blue sky. He could hear the rumble of cannons from the northwest and from the north.

He turned back to the little circle of officers. "Where was I?"

"Carr, sir," Colonel Jefferson C. Davis said.

"Yes, Colonel Carr has sent word that his men are holding, but cannot hold forever. I cannot believe that Van Dorn marched his whole army around us. What an idiot! In a snowstorm, no less."

"Yes, sir."

"He must have the advantage in manpower, or he would not have done such an obstreperous move." His next sentences were mumbled to himself, looking at his volumes of pages describing each regiment.

"Colonel Davis." He turned to the officer who had the same name as the Confederate president. "Take your regiment to assist Osterhaus. On the double now."

Colonel Davis saluted and disappeared out of the tent. He climbed on his horse and galloped northwest to gather his regiment for a quick march.

∞

MARCH 7, 1862, 12:30 P.M.
LEETOWN, ARKANSAS

B. Franks Richards rose from the bed where he had lain beside the woman whose name he had forgotten. It was midday of the day after he had arrived in Leetown. The clanking and stomping rush of an army passing through the town had awakened him from his drunken sleep. His head pounded. His nose felt pinched into his skull. Brushing back the dark, stringy mop that clung to his face, he slung his feet over the edge of the bed and pulled on his britches. Standing, he wobbled a little, and with his suspenders hanging down, stepped across the frigid floor and pushed open the window shutters. Though the sunlight stung his eyes, he witnessed, intermittently through the dense growth of trees, throngs of blue-coated soldiers rushing in an uncoordinated fashion, heading north along the narrow town's single road.

"What the hell are them Yanks doin' here?" he muttered. "Curtis's army is supposed to be back at Sugar Creek." He let his mind be baffled awhile. Then he heard the unmistakable thump of cannons, and the popping and snapping of rifle fire. Listening to the burgeoning battle developing a couple of hundred yards north of where he stood in the woman's house, he wished for liquor.

He turned to gaze at her. She looked jaundiced in the sunlight flashing through the window, one breast lying flaccid above the sheet. She turned in her sleep, pulling the sheet and blankets up to her shoulders, drool lying on her chin. She was in her late forties, some grey strands in her hair, hardly a youthful beauty anymore, though he surmised she had once been.

He had used her and felt pleased that he had. Looking at her now, she did not appear particularly becoming, but, when he had ridden into town the day before, she had made the mistake of looking at him twice.

He had been searching for a wagonload of whores who had been following the Union army, but had not found them. So, he forced his attentions on her, though she attempted half-heartedly to evade him. He was persistent, and after plying her with whiskey that he had pilfered, she succumbed to his animalistic, violent urges. He did not care if she enjoyed it. She was a vessel for him to exploit, to dump his manhood into. He used her like a hunter used a hunting dog. If the dog was not good in the hunt, the dog was cast off. If she had not been good for his aggressive advances, he had no need for her.

He liked using people, the sense of inordinate power. That is what he wanted most—power over people. He prided himself on his big plans. Make a name for himself, run for a political office. Have his way.

The woman, Mrs. nameless woman, had said that her husband and son were off to war. He forgot which army. North or South. "It don't matter," he had told her. "I don't give a shit for either side."

The cannons growled fiercely. His head felt like great iron balls rolled between his ears, front to back. Stumbling to her bureau, he searched for laudanum or any pain reliever. He kicked the whiskey bottle on the floor, stooped, picked it up and allowed the dregs to dribble into his mouth, though much of it fell on his thatch of a beard.

He threw the bottle out the doorway into the parlor. It shattered.

In the parlor, three fellow marauders lay, just stirring, sitting up, slouching in their long-handled underwear and their vomit, shirts bloused out, wakening from their drunken stupor. Each of them groaned and yawned and wiped the vomit from their faces, then wiped their hands on whatever furniture was nearby.

The night before, when the woman had passed out from drink, he invited his surly cohorts to have their carnal way with her, which they did, inebriated as they were. Out cold, she never knew what was happening.

Richards sat stiffly on the bedside, then lay back asleep for more than an hour despite the rancor of battle mere yards from the house. He finally awoke and struggled to put on his socks and boots. "Get the hell up!" he yelled at the three sots. They stirred slowly and began dressing. He hated these men who lacked any couth, and who devoutly followed him, but he needed them to accomplish his goals.

Looking once more out the window, he observed glimpses of additional bluecoats filing out of the woods and onto the barely visible snow-clad field. He hated the Northerners, the *invaders*. When the war started, he had enlisted with a Missouri Union regiment, ready to punish the South. On the first day of drill, he got so crosswise with his sergeant, every man of the regiment revolted against him, and the colonel sent him packing. *They think I ain't good enough. I'll show 'em. Someday, they'll bend their knee to me.*

He hated the South more, and anyone from the South. His father had owned a small plantation with slaves in Georgia, but when his pa found out he had been bedding every female slave, he gave him a portion of his inheritance and sent him away. "Make your own fortune," his father told him in their parting. "But don't come back here 'til you're a man."

After Richards had squandered the money trying to sell whiskey to the Indians, he sought work on a large plantation and was hired as over-seer. The plantation owner, a Mister Meacham, was a pleasant man who doted on his slaves, to both the chagrin and joy of his wife, often throwing parties for them. He gave them whiskey and invited them to dine with him and his wife on the plantation house porch of an occasion, and often joined them in the fields, gathering the cotton into a long, trailing sack.

Richards enjoyed the whiskey and the parties, but he cared not for the benevolence the man showed the Negroes. He considered it his duty to be harsh toward them, especially the field hands. He took to whipping them or tying them up and tossing them in a ditch for half a day.

After he beat one slave almost to death, word made its way to the plantation sire, who called in the sheriff and had Richards cuffed in manacles, then stretched him naked, tied to a tree.

Mr. Meacham strode up beside Richards, who, instead of begging for mercy, spit at his employer.

"I ain't never taken the lash to no one before, especially not a slave," Mr. Meacham said in a steely tone, "but I'll take pleasure in peeling your hide." With that, he whipped Richards fifteen strokes, raising large, bloody welts on Richards' back. One of his swings went high and struck Richards on the face, leaving a gash that ran down his cheek. Then he and Mrs. Meacham personally applied a soothing salve to the swollen stripes before sending him to bed in his quarters.

He gave Richards a day to rest, then drove him away at gunpoint. Down the road from the plantation, Richards stole a horse, reins and saddle, and vowed revenge on the entire South.

The three marauders in the parlor began calling out and cursing each other. The woman he had bedded awakened, and seeing his scarred back for the first time, was alarmed. "What happened to your back?"

"Fell in a briar patch," Richards barked, then threw on his shirt, and pulled up his suspenders. "I got work to do." He never looked at her, but gathered his coat, pistol and rifle and other accoutrements and walked stolidly out of the house. His companions followed him.

The woman watched them go, her mouth agape. Then she turned to the window and flinched at the thuds of cannon fire.

Richards walked out onto the porch of the simple home and donned his leather jacket.

The town, embedded in a tight grove of trees, had one dirt road still covered with crusty snow. Melting ice dripped from the trees and eaves of the few homes, a church and a smithy, and a few shops. Townspeople had already gathered along the street, surprise and dread showing on their faces.

Most of the men who were too old to enlist in an army had clustered in front of the Masonic hall. A burly blacksmith in his apron, tongs in hand, was addressing them. He stood atop a wagonload of barrels, gesturing wildly with his fire-scarred hands. He flung the tongs in the direction of the battle. It clanged along the street. "Damn the Yankees!" he bellowed.

"Damn the Rebs, too," Richards muttered.

The women and children crowded together on the simple church's porch steps, the reverend attempting to comfort them. He had his hands extended, often patting the women's shoulders and the children's heads, extolling them to trust in God.

A shopkeeper and his wife and children were hurriedly loading the shop's wares into a wagon, preparing to escape. "They'll come in here and take everything!" he yelled to no one in particular.

Richards watched one young woman with long blond curls helping her crippled father climb falteringly into a carriage, and he immediately thought of Sara. "That sesech!" He grinded his teeth. She had escaped his grasp twice, once at her home that he had burned, and when the old Confederate private got the drop on him and sent him running. The second time, he thought he had her, and she had thrust a gun against his chest. *If I ever find that sesech again, I won't make any mistakes, and she'll be mine until I use her up.* He licked his lips.

The battle noise was increasing. Union soldiers were racing through the bare semblance of a road and threading their way up to the long, snow-covered field. Richards watched the gathering troops and the dense black smoke of cannon and rifle fire.

"Shit." Richards took a Bowie knife and carved a chunk of tobacco from a plug he kept in his pocket and shoved the chunk in his mouth. He spit. "I came up here to avoid the stinkin' sesech and the stupid abolitionist Yanks, and they followed me. I ain't gonna get found."

He looked again at the worried townsfolk and watched the young blond drive the carriage away south with her father. Tobacco ooze dribbled down his beard. He went to his horse, saddled it and mounted. *That old cripple couldn't save that morsel of a girl if I was to want her.* He considered the prospect of pursuing the carriage that was fleeing the battle but decided instead he would turn west, then north and lead his men to new pickings. *Go abroad of the fight.*

NINE

THOUGH I WALK THROUGH THE VALLEY OF DEATH

– PSALM 23:4

MARCH 7, 1862, 2:00 P.M.
ELKHORN TAVERN, ARKANSAS

Cyntha Favor had seen considerable calamity in the world. She prided herself on her capacity to deal with tragedy and sorrow. A neighbor losing a child to illness, a cousin dying in childbirth. Whole families torn apart with rancor toward each other. And she had been there to help the families heal their wounds and come to an understanding. Even her daring nighttime escape from Springfield with Reynolds and Constance Carver, despite her fears, she had forced herself to be strong. She had prevailed in hoodwinking Colonel Mezaros in the Union cavalry camp. She felt a depth of gratification.

But she had never been in a cellar, hearing hundreds of boots stamping a few feet above where she stood, the clomping mingled with the moaning and screaming of wounded and dying men. Cannon fire made the timbers and walls of Elkhorn Tavern tremble. With each explosion, the canning jars on the meager wooden shelves tilted and clanked, a high treble to the concussive bass of the cannons. Constant rattle of rifles, explosions that punched her ears. She felt she was at a boxing match, like the one outside her husband's camp at Keokuk. She had been encouraged by friends to attend. She had watched, at first out of curiosity, then with horror, though she could not tear her eyes away from the fists landing at first on two men's faces, then in a riot of many soldiers. The pummeling and bone-cracking sounds had echoed in her mind for days afterward.

Now, she felt as if she herself was in that dirt ring, surrounded by shouting onlookers, taking the jabs and hooks, and many fists beating her ears and even her body. She bent over, controlling her desire to vomit, then glanced around at her companions in the dank hole in the earth, her fellow sufferers' faces illuminated by flickering candles on little tin plates. She saw the horror on Polly Cox's face and her daughter-in-law, Lucinda's, face. The younger Cox boys were balled up in the farthest corner with their eyes closed and hands clamped over their ears. Lucinda's young husband, Joe, tried to be comforting to his mother, wife and brothers, but utter dismay and futility filled his eyes. In the candlelight, he looked like a helpless, decrepit old man. To Cyntha, all of them were crammed together like penned animals.

She saw glimpses of light through the several cracks in the tavern's floorboards above, which would come and go when the soldiers' feet shuffled and rushed along the floor. Covering the gap, then, a moment later, letting the spare light gleam into their underground vault.

Her brother, Anthony, struggled to maintain a sitting position on the rock steps under the cellar doors. The end of his wooden leg sat in a dark, viscous fluid on the floor. Jeanette, sitting beside him, had buried her face in his shoulder while he held secure the ropes squeezing the twin doors closed. Several times, heavy brogans and rifle butts had banged against the door, and harsh voices demanded they be let into the hole, a place to crawl away from the devastation transpiring in the yard and in the crowded trees surrounding the tavern. Anthony had held tight, and each assailant departed.

His daughter, Clara, only six, clung to him, whimpering, her little freckled face pale and moist with tears.

Cyntha unconsciously rubbed the shoulders of Reynolds, her dear friend, not thinking of what she was doing. She had garnered a chair from the porch and brought it down into the crowded cellar, for he could not stand, the coughing fit having worn him out. His head bobbed up and down, and she could see breaths did not come easy for her freeman companion and employee. Drool sat on his gray beard.

The blanket around his shoulders slipped to the earth. When Cyntha reached for it, an oily drop of liquid splashed on her face, followed by another. Placing the blanket around Reynolds's shoulders, she felt it had become damp. She wiped her face with her wrist and attempted to look at the moistness. She could not tell what it was, and, so, picked up one of the candles, and held it close to her skin. The liquid smear was blood. She held the candle aloft and scanned the floorboards above and saw more blood, dripping through the floorboards.

Holding the candle high in a sweeping motion, she beheld that Polly's dress was splotched red where blood had drizzled down upon it. Polly, seeing the blood on her dress, gasped and leaped backwards against the wall. The remaining Cox family members shrank from the blood trickling like raindrops into the cellar. Polly and Lucinda screamed. Cyntha looked at the floor where the blood, now a small red stream, flowed along a little trench, and ended in a puddle at the edge of the stairs where Anthony's wooden leg dipped in it.

Anthony lifted his leg from the pool of blood and grasped the ropes holding the doors secure.

The cellar doors banged multiple times.

"It's me! It's me!" a tenor voice was hollering, barely audible above the roar of gunfire. Anthony pulled tighter on the ropes, hoping this new soldier would leave like the others. He looked up and, in the crack between the doors, saw lips and elements of a tanned face. "It's me! Ben McGavin!"

Anthony released his hold on the cords, the doors flung open, and Ben stumbled inside, careening against Anthony and his wife, barely missing stepping on Clara. He landed in a heap on the dirt floor. "Ow. Dang it!" He clutched his ankle, the shattered bones beginning to mend since being smashed by a Yankee bullet a week earlier. He gritted his teeth and tightened the splinted boot wrappings. Breathing hard, he sat up in the dark, for Anthony had again closed and secured the doors.

After grimacing with his eyes shut for some moments, Ben finally looked at all the faces staring at him, each one stricken with fear. He gave a small laugh. "Well, don't all y'all say at once that you're glad I'm alive."

No one laughed. The Cox family stayed close together. Anthony glowered at him. Cyntha's expression was of deep worry. The old former slave slumped in his chair like a dead man, his head on his chest.

The battle sounds outside abated and began to dribble down to spare, solitary rifle shots.

Pressing his back against the cellar wall to push himself up from the ground, Ben felt the board plank splinters pricking him through his Union jacket. With effort, he stood. "Just so you know, I been down in the thick of it. I was watchin', tryin' to get a feel for what's comin'. Lots of gray coats down in that ravine. Lots of smoke, too. So much smoke; twice, I walked right into a soldier 'cause I didn't see him. Then, some Yank officer orders me to go fetch this or that. I go, and then switch to another spot. Some other officer with bric-a-brac on his sleeves tells me to get my rifle, get back in line and shoot some 'Sesech' he calls 'em. I pick up a Springfield from the ground. Must've been from some poor Yank who got scared and run off without it. And I considered shootin' the officer, but I don't. I just go off and watch which way the battle's goin'. Scoutin'. That's my job. Lots o' men dyin'. Lots of 'em hurt bad. And I ..."

"The ladies and children," Anthony interrupted, "don't need the details, Ben."

Ben looked at each individual, starting with the cowering children. He breathed in their terror breath, and could almost feel their panic, their hearts pumping hard. He looked last at Cyntha and could not help the torrent of empathy and tenderness he felt for her. "I ain't tellin' nothin' bad."

While new explosions sent dust cascading down on the denizens of the dank cellar, he gazed a long time at Clara and the Cox boys. Finally, he smiled. "Aw, nobody was hurt really much. A few little cuts. Like I was sayin', I spent most o' my time duckin' and hidin' behind trees. Like I was playin' hide and seek. Those bullets were flyin' up from that ravine. Zip, zip, zing." He made arm motions like bullets whizzing by his head. "I know the Yanks was shootin' back, but if I was countin' the whistlin' bullets flyin' by my ear, them blue-bellies is outnumbered bad."

Cyntha drew in a deep breath, her hands still on Reynolds' shoulders. "Do go on, Ben. You said there was whistling." She sensed his distracting tale of his adventure above ground and the wild gyrations of his arms were allaying the entire group's apprehensions.

"Yeah, the bullets were whistlin'. And you *have* to hear this. Some little Yank band off in the field toward the Huntsville road was tootin' and bangin' away on wild tunes. I even heard 'em play 'Dixie.' Most unusual." He was pointing and jerking his thumbs this way and that, waving his arms in grand motions and pretending he was beating a drum.

His devil-may-care attitude and singsong telling of his wayward jaunt among the Federals brought smiles to the adults. Each child grinned gently when he pretended to play a fife with his fingers by his lips, twirling them in the air. "Tweetley tweet."

The gunfire abruptly ceased completely, like a vacuum had sucked all the guns away. Lightly, drifting on the air, the bare semblance of a tune played by reed and horn trickled down into their underground cell. A jaunty tune played with an accompanying fiddle and backed by a banging drum.

Her eyes closed, Cyntha began humming along with the melody that she recognized. *The Arkansas Traveler.*

Ben lowered his voice and continued his telling, forgetting his young audience. "I came up to the tavern and saw all the wounded. I was surprised at the number. They're in the house, laid out in rows. Bunches of 'em in the yard. Some are covered with blood. That old sawbones who looked at my leg a few days ago and told me I couldn't ride anymore. He's there in the kitchen. He was cuttin' away on a leg when I walked by."

No sooner had he made the pronouncement than a man in the house let out a loud shriek. A gruff voice in the house yelled, "More chloroform, damn it."

Reynolds' next action was not expected. He had been sitting like a man asleep but straightened like he had been infused with a new spirit in him. In the dim glow of the candlelight, he looked filled with a youthful vigor. "Come on!" he demanded. "There's hurt boys in the house, and we could be helpin'."

Despite Cyntha's effort to keep him seated, he stormed up the steps past Anthony and threw the doors open, strutting, his big arms pumping. Gunfire resumed. First, a few cracks and thwacks. Then, like a volcano disgorging, the Rebels yelled their screeching wail from down in the vale. Bullets began hitting the house. The Confederates were charging.

Cyntha, trembling like a leaf about to be blown from a tree, took a deep breath and followed Reynolds up the stairs and was out in the smoke and the zinging bullets. Anthony hobbled up next, then Ben.

"Stay here, Joe!" Ben hollered, "and watch after the children and women."

Joe Cox nodded.

"I'm not staying here to die in this rat hole!" Jeanette was on her feet. "At least, I'll die being of some help in the clear air." She directed Clara by the shoulders and placed the child's tiny hand in Polly's, and followed Ben, who was hopping on his good leg, up the steps and out.

After Jeanette exited, Ben closed the doors of the cellar.

When the group caught up with Reynolds, the Union cannoneers were rolling their artillery back from their forward position in the trees above the Tanyard ravine to a few yards north of the Tavern. They unlimbered the cannons there, aiming down the road, and began loading the muzzles with grapeshot. One of the artillerymen held a rusty bucket of nails.

"Come on." Reynolds rolled up his sleeves. "Let's see if we can save some lives."

Ben considered that, when the Confederates did force their way up the hill, he better not look like a Yankee. He tossed off his blue kepi and jacket and limped slowly inside the tavern with the others.

Anthony spotted a wooden bucket with a ladle, half-full of water, in the arms of an obviously dead soldier, his pupils fixed. He closed the corpse's eyes, lifted the bucket and carried it into the tavern.

Men in bloodied shirts, sleeves torn to tatters, hastened throughout the tavern. Some struggled at carrying the wounded men upstairs, ones that were already bandaged. Some of the wounded yowled in pain, some cried, others appeared to be out cold.

In the back of the kitchen, a single surgeon sawed with vigor on a soldier's leg, a high keening screech with each stroke. A heavy barn muck basket sitting to the side of the kitchen table already contained a half-dozen appendages.

Cyntha came up beside him. "How can I help?" she asked.

TEN

BATTLES ARE LOST IN THE SAME SPIRIT IN WHICH THEY ARE WON

– WALT WHITMAN

MARCH 7, 1862, 3:00 P.M.
ATOP LITTLE MOUNTAIN, ONE MILE NORTH OF LEETOWN, ARKANSAS

Paul had watched the drama of the death of General McIntosh unfold, the soldiers degenerating into a useless mob, yelling at each other, some fisticuffs starting up. Likewise, he saw Colonel Hebert's brigade funneling back from battle around the small hill. Defeat and despair showed on their faces, sure as a rash might show. Some carried wounded comrades to the handful of surgeons who were just clearing areas to lay the men. There were no tents for the surgeons. All medical tents and stretchers had been left behind on the supply wagons. No wagons meant no operating tables made from the wagon beds. The men were simply laid on the moist forest floor.

He heard Hebert's men calling, "Colonel Hebert's captured! Major Tunnard's captured!"

The Second Alabama had recovered General McCulloch's body and brought him through the trees. Paul watched the body borne on a make-shift stretcher along the small path, and the soldiers removing their hats and bowing their heads. Many of them tried to hold back tears. They brought the stretcher to where General McIntosh's body lay. They positioned McCulloch's body beside his fellow general.

After several moments of mourning, the men drifted away. Some of them went to their mounts and rode out to where General Pike was trying to gather the men for a retreat to Twelve Corner Church and await orders from General Van Dorn. Paul knew few men would follow Pike. He was a general, but the men figured him too much akin to an Indian, a savage by contact, like the ones that had run away from the fight.

Paul had even heard grumbling among the captains and lieutenants that there was no condition under which they would follow his orders. *No one left to lead them. It falls on Colonel Greer now. Hope he's up to this.*

He beckoned for one of McIntosh's couriers. "Get fire in your britches and find the hospital wagons. The surgeons can do little with no tables, stretchers or surgery equipment. Ride out now!"

"Yes, sir!" The corporal scatted through the throngs of men as fast as he could coax his horse.

∞

Joseph had watched the rushing Rebel army, McIntosh's brigade, and presumed that they would sweep the smaller Union force away. If he had considered himself aligned with the Rebel State's cause anymore, he might have found the progression of soldiers with brilliant flags fluttering a thrilling spectacle, like a parade. He felt, instead, an abject disturbance penetrating his soul.

The Confederates lurched hastily into the span of trees that hid the Union forces and their cannons. Their yells echoed up onto the low hill where he stood beside a white oak, and the whines and yelps made him cringe. He propped himself against the tree, not out of boredom, but because his own thoughts were so jumbled, he could not muster a will to even move. He realized now that he had enlisted back in June of the previous year into the First Iowa Volunteers. He remembered, too, that he opposed the slavery supported by rich plantation owners in the South as well as by most people in the North; or, at least, they turned their heads.

He hated the fact that the Southern plantation owners, who filled and controlled the state legislatures, conspired to take their states out of the Union in order to preserve their personal economy and affluent way of life on the backs of other humans. He further understood from his many conversations with virtually all the Confederates in his regiment that the typical soldiers fought not to preserve slavery, but to defend their homes or their own state's sovereignty, and, admittedly, to whip a few Yanks, whom they saw as a blot on the ideals of freedom.

The common Southerner and the Southern plantation owners were at cross purposes.

He felt more anger at the Northern mill owners and factory workers who countenanced slavery, for it spurred their own wealth. He remembered heated arguments with several Iowans who had no desire to free the Negro. "Job robbers," they called them. He wanted more to smite them than even the plantation elitists.

The slaveholders felt they had a right to own other people. *But people in the North should know better. Slaves do not drive their economy. No slaves are conspiring to take their jobs. The slaves only wish to be free, like my friend, Josiah Reynolds.*

Josiah Reynolds. His thoughts rushed to the able, prudent, and, indeed, sagacious former slave. His wife and he had bought his freedom. Reynolds was not a property set free, like an aged horse, sent out to pasture. He was, in Joseph's heart, a godsend companion.

Dear Reynolds, I pray that you are well and taking care of my wife, keeping her from harm.

The impression of Cyntha's face had sprung to his mind that day, and he nurtured that remembrance in his mind, yet her name eluded him. *Confound it!* He pounded his fist against the tree, barking his knuckles.

The tumultuous noise in the stretch of trees where General McIntosh's troops had marched abruptly stopped. The firing from the Federal cannons stopped. With a burst, the entire Rebel brigade rushed back out from the trees like they had enraged some monster who was fast upon their trail. In the midst of the throng, he recognized the general's stallion with an officer's body draped over it. One man led the horse, another paced beside it, holding the general's broad hat, the purple plume dragging the ground.

The thousands of soldiers rushed in clumps, crowding, then dispersing, like individuals fleeing from a flood. No yells of emboldened, valiant men now, but, instead, men weeping and wailing and cursing, even as they ran. Occasionally, soldiers would turn and discharge their rifles back at the stark beltline of trees.

The men of the Third Texas rushed to the edge of the hill and slid halfway down the slope, attempting to see what was unfolding. For Joseph, the cause of the event was evident. General McIntosh was dead. He could feel their sorrow and dismay.

Colonel Greer walked down the hill to stand beside Joseph. Through his binoculars he stared at the curious, disjointed spectacle. "Ah cannot believe it. We have lost an able leader. McIntosh was a good man."

At that moment, a courier galloped up to a few feet from Colonel Greer and Joseph and yanked his mount to a shuddering halt. "Colonel Greer," the courier said, "it is with great sorrow that I inform you. I have spoken directly with Colonel Armstrong, General McCulloch's aide. He bids me tell you that General McCulloch is no longer in this world."

Colonel Greer stood as motionless as a statue, his face torn with anger and dismay like a church's gargoyle. After a good minute, the colonel finally said, "God help us!" He plodded back into the woods and was soon out of sight.

Joseph turned his gaze into the flat valley at the curious procession of mourning soldiers retreating north and, ultimately, into the densely packed woods behind Ford Road. He knew that Colonel Hebert was next in command after the two fallen generals. He further knew that Hebert's brigade had traversed around the knoll on which he stood, heading south through the vine-tangled, dense woods that surrounded the hill. He could only wonder at what would occur next.

In minutes, Hebert engaged his brigade with the Union army. Horrendous rifle fire and smoke belched from the woods, swelling up like an immense bellows had blown into a great furnace. The woods looked ablaze, and the wild calls and shrieks of men told him that a great many men's lives were ending. Joseph smelled the smoldering, wet wood mixed with the acrid black powder tang.

ELEVEN

MEN'S DAYS LIKE FLEETING SHADOWS

MARCH 7, 1862, 3:00 P.M.
ONE HUNDRED YARDS NORTH OF LEETOWN, ARKANSAS

With her back to the hamlet of Leetown, in a cove of a dense growth of trees, Sara sat on Esther. She watched the entirety of Union soldiers that stood in front of her wheel to the right and hasten across Leetown Road where a dense forest was filling with smoke and fiery flashes of guns. She followed the advancing troops, several yards behind them.

I can't go there. I can't watch. Despite her admonitions against herself, curiosity overwhelmed her, and she prodded Esther hesitantly forward.

In the clustered spike-like trees, like hundreds of pitchforks flung together, woven with tangled brush, the battle roared, a hidden tempest with waves of sound breaking against invisible crags. Amidst the smoke, great bursts of fire from thousands of rifles zipped like seams of lightning. First on the left, then on the right, spreading back and forth for two hundred yards. Yelling burst from the forest, often high-pitched like shrieking winds, other times growling like fierce beasts, sometimes muffled. Hidden by the smoke's veil, the joint bellowing of hundreds of voices rushed here and there, followed by isolated angry threats, or the tormented wails of men in incredible pain.

The Yankees and Rebels were in close combat, for even the sound of bodies hurled against each other often spilled out of the gloom. Sara could tell nothing of the progress of the struggle, save, twice, a horde of Union soldiers fleeing pell-mell out of the woods, then re-forming with a new line of arriving troops and wading back into the smoky cavern of trees.

For Sara, the scene was too familiar, yet hauntingly different. Fire and smoke. Conflagration and canister. Agony had taken root on earth. Hell had opened a hole in the land, and the men had been swallowed up into the abyss itself.

Perhaps because her mind needed to take her away from what she was witnessing, a passing remembrance floated into her mind, one of sitting on the porch of her old home atop the hill beside Wilson Creek. In her remembrance, she was a mere child of ten. The sounds of battle seemed to dwindle; the chaos went away. She was safe in her mind's recalling.

The memory was sunny and glowing and warm. She had plopped herself down on the steps with her legs splayed out, blowing dandelions' puffballs and watching the filaments float about and disappear in a stiff, but warm, breeze. The age-old cottonwoods and red cedars swept their shadows back and forth across the yard—rustling. In the meadow with the burned tree stumps, one of her father's milk cows was lowing, and a calf was mewling.

At that moment, she had looked past the yard and down the trail that lead away, crowded by sugary-smelling honeysuckle bushes and vines, and then at the vast oak that spread above the little family graves behind the picket fence. Her brothers, all three of them, were buried there. She had known them before they died. The one nearest her age died a slow, lingering death of disease. The older boys died when bitten by rattlesnakes after they fell in a nest of them while wrestling in boyish play. She had knelt beside them when they died.

Her mother's body lay beneath the ground under the oak. She had never known her. She died when Sara was a baby.

At that moment, with the world stretching out before her, she somehow understood death, particularly her own death that would someday come to her. Her own mortality had become evident. Eternity stretched before her. She did not grasp it fully, but something in her began to burn to know more.

What was death? What was this ending? That epiphany of that long-gone day blended into many of her thoughts as she grew up. Love and its ecstasy. Death and its sting. What were they? Questions too large for even the wisest to understand. Was she in love with Joseph? *Yes.* She was adamant about this element. But why was she so curious about this war, this wholesale killing and maiming?

Bursting from the trees and stumbling, three men carried a fourth, who was bleeding from his chest. The soldiers laid their wounded comrade down a few feet from her. Two of the men rushed back under the canopy of smoke while the third stayed close to the man on the ground. He knelt and clutched the fist of the wounded man.

"Is it rainin'?" the wounded man said. "There's water on your cheeks, brother."

"Yes, yes, it's rainin'. Coolin' us all off. Keep the fever from you."

He said his brother's name several times, but Sara could not make it out, for the words, in his sorrow, turned into blubbering.

In a moment, directly in front of her, dozens of men were being carried from the battle and down the road toward the village behind her. Dozens of others were falling and scrabbling in the dirty snow in their retreat. Their yells of agony, fear and despair filled the forest. She recognized one of the men as the jokester who had stood in line in front of her earlier.

Unknowingly, so intent on her thoughts, and watching the bloodbath unfolding, she rode directly up beside two officers standing in ankle deep, sludgy water, each pointing at a map. The men glanced at her briefly, then resumed their study of the map.

"Yes, Colonel Osterhaus," the shorter one said, "this is Morgan's Woods. I'll send a courier to General Curtis for reinforcements."

"Good. Now, go to Colonel Ashboth! Colonel Davis's men and ours can only hold so long," Colonel Osterhaus said. Sara recognized his long mustache and his bearing from having seen him at the Foster farmhouse earlier in the morning.

When the shorter man mounted his steed and sped away, the colonel slogged to his horse, tied to a tree and jigging at the constant barrage. He rose upon the steed and trotted away. Sara might as well have been a timid forest creature, for he paid her no heed.

While Sara watched the smoke-filled Morgan's Woods and the rifle blasts blazing, Richards and his marauders galloped a few dozen yards behind her, hidden by the trees, traveling west on an old hunting trail toward the Bentonville Detour Road.

TWELVE

∞

FEAR AND HOPE
STRADDLE EACH OTHER

MARCH 7, 1862, 3:30 P.M.
EIGHTY YARDS NORTH OF LEETOWN, ARKANSAS

S ara had considered retreating to the protection of the small
village which the soldiers called Leetown but gave up that
notion. The Federals were sending their wounded there in an
unending stream. Quite simply, she had ventured too close to the
battle that was concealed from her view by the tightly packed woods.

When stray bullets began whizzing out of the forest, she turned
Esther and rode back to where she had originally stationed herself
after fleeing the Indians. She backed Esther behind a sturdy oak.
The invisible seesaw battle seemed to go on and on.

The afternoon had wound down to nearly evening when she
witnessed a group of about a dozen Confederates on foot who
had been taken prisoner. The unarmed soldiers were encircled by
a guard of twenty Union troops.

Colonel Osterhaus, accompanied by aides and couriers, trotted
up to the prisoners and halted.

"Captured us a Rebel colonel," a spindly-legged Yankee captain
announced. He pointed at a Confederate colonel in his thirties who
stood next to a Confederate major within the prisoner group.

The Confederate colonel raised his head. He had a bright, serious face, though begrimed from gunpowder. His head was bare, revealing a receding scalp. His pristine uniform bore a red sash around the waist and an empty scabbard where his sword had been.

"And with whom do I have the pleasure, sir?" Colonel Osterhaus asked.

The colonel in gray saluted with his white-gloved hand. His other hand's glove was bloodied. "I am Colonel Louis Hebert. Confederate States of America. Your humble servant."

"It is an honor to make your acquaintance, sir." Colonel Osterhaus saluted. "I would stay longer to converse with you, but I have a battle to win in the woods yonder."

Colonel Hebert straightened. "Sir, you may have much more to do to win it. I am the officer in charge of the brigade, and I am proud to say my men have not wavered even once under your army's fire. They fight for their country. Something that you invaders cannot say. And ... were it not for the smoke and the confusion, we would not have wandered into your men's clutches. We were close to breaking your line. Our Louisiana Pelicans outfought you three to one, sir. You have here their dogged major."

"I am honored, sir." Osterhaus nodded at the lean, muscled major, also bereft of his hat.

The major, who looked as fatigued as a wrung rag, squinted up at his captor. "Ah am Major W. F. Tunnard. Third Louisiana Pelican Rifles. The honor is mine. When our men have won this battle, perhaps we can join at table for coffee ..." He seemed to want to say something more but shut his lips and looked down.

Sara gasped, for she instantly recalled the major's kind gesture when he was but a captain at the cantonment at Cross Hollows. He was the officer who was grieving his dead wife and had the wherewithal to donate his wife's never-worn dress to Sara. There he was. *Such kindness he showed me despite his grief. And now a prisoner.*

"I am sure you are proud of your men." Colonel Osterhaus sounded conciliatory. He leaned over his horse's neck and spoke to the Union captain in charge. "Take them to Leetown. Secure them in the Masonic Hall." He turned once more to Colonel Hebert. "With your permission, sir." He saluted and galloped off.

When the Union guards led the group of captives away, Sara recognized a friend walking along the edge of the group— Sergeant Rabaneaux. His purpled nose, his wide girth and his obvious limp, she remembered him as well as if she had a tintype of him. His head was down, the cap lost in battle. He held no weapon, but clutched in his fists, like it was his greatest treasure, was the little music box with faded brown ivory that Sara had gifted him.

Sara turned Esther to follow the captives being led away, hoping to speak to her dear acquaintance. "Sergeant!" she called, but the Louisiana prisoner did not turn.

"Sergeant Rabaneaux!" she screamed again at the top of her lungs, though her yelling was lost in the rancor of battle thunder. She coaxed Esther forward, but then drew up.

Three Yankee guards had spun around, their rifles trained on her, both fear and anger on their faces, a sort of wanton despair bound up in confusion. They seemed surprised to see a woman so close to battle, but adamant to fulfill their orders against any intruder.

"Where'd you think you're goin', miss?" one of them barked.

"I ..." Sara thought quickly. "I live there. It's my home." She pointed toward Leetown.

"Sure, you do," the soldier said sarcastically. "Be gone, southern bitch."

Sara knew that the shock showed on her face, and she considered pulling the pistol she had taken from the dead Yankee and shooting them all, but she slowly guided Esther away and rode off into the wide field. She looked back, but they were still watching her.

The battle's bangs and clangs and booms and yells of agony and strife bombarded her ears. She could hold her tears no longer.

Unable to get near Sergeant Rabaneaux, she began to consider a new strategy. *That Colonel Hebert is not in charge of the Third Texas. The general that I watched being shot and killed was not General McCulloch. The Third Texas is under General McCulloch. Perhaps the Third Texas is just up the road. Not yet engaged. I'll not hold to intemperate hope, but I shall hope.*

She slapped the reins on Esther's sides and raced the horse west toward the road that ran along the farms and led north. *I will not give up.*

She headed through the same belt of trees where the Cherokees had routed the Iowan cavalry. Her mind swept like a whirlwind from fear to hope to anger to remorse. She forced herself not to think of the "savages." That was what newspapers and books called them. At last, galloping out of the trees and across slogged farm fields, she gained the narrow road and headed north. She saw clumps of Confederate soldiers backed into the forest behind the Ford road. *Those are McIntosh and Hebert's men. McCulloch's men and the Third Texas must be farther up this road.* She could not fathom the intricacies of command. Her mind was too muddled.

The farther she rode, the fainter the battle noise, though the rattle of guns and explosions of artillery spilled out into the broad sky in undulating waves, rolling and echoing. She would pray for the good Louisiana sergeant and all the prisoners, but if the Third Texas cavalry were within McCulloch's army, she was determined to find Joseph. *I'll not be deterred.*

She rode along the Bentonville Detour Road, heading unknowingly around Pea Ridge's Big Mountain toward Elkhorn Tavern. A bare half mile ahead of her, Richards and his gang galloped at a vigorous pace.

THIRTEEN

ENEMIES ON MANY FRONTS

MARCH 7, 1862, 4:30 P.M.
TWELVE CORNER CHURCH ON THE
BENTONVILLE DETOUR ROAD, ARKANSAS

Richards and his men came upon the line of three supply wagons parked by the little church at Twelve Corners on the Bentonville Detour Road. Two dozen Confederate soldiers were positioned around the area, most of them asleep in or under the wagons. When the marauders rode into view, five of the Confederates, three of them Negro drivers, raised their variety of weapons—muskets, shotguns, and revolvers.

At twenty yards behind the rear wagon, Richards held up his hand, and the gang halted.

A burly sergeant with three revolvers stuck in a belt the size of a razor strop stepped down from a wagon seat and stood with hands on his hips. "Ya best state yor reason for bein' here, or I'll order ya shot where you stand." He made a motion to his soldiers, and five rifles cocked.

Richards licked his lips, eyed his companions, then removed his hat in a sweeping motion. "Beggin' pardon, sergeant. We didn't mean to spook you. We're just local boys lookin' to join up. Fight for the South."

His words hung unanswered.

He shifted in his saddle. "Look, we have our own weapons, and we have a notion to whip some Yanks. Ain't that right, boys."

Murmured yeses and nods came from his three cohorts.

The sergeant continued his grimace, but he flashed his eyes right and left into the bare trees. "This all o' you?"

"Yes, sir." Richards made a lame attempt at a salute.

"Head back the way ya came. We ain't takin' no green recruits to slow us down."

"I see." Richards eased himself slowly out of the saddle.

Every rifle turned toward him. He took his revolvers from the front of his belt and lay them on the ground, then strode forward a few paces.

"Take one more step, and I'll have you shot! I've a fever to do it now!" the sergeant barked.

Richards stopped and held his empty hands out to the side. "All right, but we're pretty hungry. The damn Yankees stole everything from us. Have you got anything for us to eat?" He made the sorriest expression he could muster. His men rubbed their stomachs and attempted to look hungry.

"Now, I see why you want to join up, just to get free grub. Well, we ain't got anything in these wagons except hospital tents, stretchers and medicines."

Richards looked down at his guns.

"For the last time, get on your horse and turn around."

Richards had no intention of returning the way he had come. He took a long look at an opening in the trees to the left of the road, a path of sorts. "All right." He backed up. "So why are these wagons here on this road? Ain't the battle over yonder?"

"We just follow orders. General Green has most of the wagons with food and ammunition back at the crossing at Sugar Creek. General Van Dorn thought the wagons were slowing down the army's progress. We're just waiting to be called up. That's all you need to know."

When Richards bent to pick up his guns, the sergeant said, "You're no account, low-lyin' marauders. I ain't stupid. Leave them Navy Colts where they lay."

Richards straightened and slowly mounted his horse. He whispered to each of his men, then slowly pulled a third revolver he had stuck in the back of his belt, then he laid it across the saddle horn. He and his men wheeled their horses slightly as if heading back.

"Now!" Richards yelled. He flapped the reins and dug in his spurs. Simultaneously, he let fly two bullets, each one hitting a soldier, both men collapsing. His gang also shot at the soldiers who returned fire. Richards and his gang sped into the path that angled into the trees beside the road. More gunfire erupted when additional Confederates who had been sleeping inside the wagons raced out and shot at the gang vanishing into the forest. One of Richards's men took a hit in the back and tumbled from his horse.

"Leave 'im!" Richards called. In a moment, he and the remaining two had slipped behind the trees and were winding their way north, hidden by the clumps of dense vegetation. The soldiers fanned out along the road, loading, and then aiming their weapons into the gloom, but they saw nothing to shoot.

The sergeant, clutching a laceration to his hand, ordered, "See to our wounded. Then check on that dead 'un. And be wary. That varmint might not yet be dead."

While the wounded soldiers were lifted into an ambulance wagon and aided by a nurse, the sergeant summoned a corporal on horseback. "Ride back and find General Green at the Sugar Creek crossing and tell 'im we ain't got no orders. He must know that *if* General Van Dorn wants these supplies all the way over at that tavern, he best send for us now or it'll be too late."

The corporal galloped south toward the long ammunition train on the Bentonville Detour Road near Sugar Creek.

"If'n they ain't got no ammunition," the sergeant muttered, "they done lost this battle."

∽

When Sara rode up to the three wagons about five o'clock, two soldiers pointed their guns at her, then immediately held them down. "Where ya goin', miss?" a spindly-legged lad said.

Sara drew up Esther and, though her leg pained her awfully, smiled at the two men, both as young as she. "Are you with the Confederate army?"

"Yes, we are," the spindly-legged one said and tipped his hat.

"That's good."

"You look about chilled to the bone, miss. Why don't you stop and warm yourself at our fire?"

Sara looked at the inviting campfire by the road, where three soldiers stood warming themselves. "I entirely wish that I could, but I've important business up the road."

"And what might that be?" The sergeant appeared from behind the wagon, his pistol drawn. He stared at Sara, waiting for a response.

"I'm ... to give a message to ... Captain Paul McGavin. He's a scout for General McCulloch."

"A scout, huh?" The sergeant frowned. "I do know the name, but what business would he have with a young lady delivering the message in the middle of a battle." He stepped closer to Sara. Esther stutter-stepped when Sara abruptly pulled back on the reins.

"All right. Here's the message. One of our generals is dead, and Colonel Hebert is captured. I believe I can trust you not to share it."

"So, you know something of the battle down yonder?" the private piped.

"Yes, it isn't boding well for our army. Now please let me go."

The sergeant reached up and gathered a handful of the horse's reins. "I ain't convinced you are helpin' out the good captain ... or General McCulloch. What's yor name, child?"

"Please let me go. I must find Captain McGavin." She could not find any more story to devise in her tired, muddled mind.

"There ain't nothing up that road except more of the weary soldiers what dropped by the wayside, worn out by cold and hunger." The sergeant was smiling now. "Whatever business you claim to have up that road, you ain't gonna find it with the dark comin'. You look like you could use some rest yo'self."

The sergeant turned toward the privates. "See to it that this woman is taken prisoner until I can question her further." In turning, he released his grip on the reins.

Sara punched her heels into Esther's haunches. The horse reared, the men falling away from under the hooves. Sara brought the horse down and raced alongside the wagons within inches of the tree branches. Reaching the campfire, she skirted it.

In a moment, she was off the road and in the trees. She could hear the men cursing and yelling. A lone shot echoed, and the bullet hit a tree near where she rode. In a few more strides she was behind a wide oak.

Safe. Not hardly. Now I have my own Confederates shooting at me. Her thoughts wandered to Paul, and she yearned to see him, find him. She pulled up. "No, wait. I want to find *Joseph*. Not Paul." Confusing thoughts pitched and bounced in her brain. *Why am I wanting to find Paul?*

She trotted Esther back onto the road and looked back at the wagons in time to see a courier gallop up to the sergeant and holler, "Bring them wagons quick. We got wounded and they's in bad need of hospital tents and stretchers. We got two dead generals." The wagoners jumped into the wagons and turned them down the Ford Road toward the battle.

In a few minutes, Sara could no longer see the wagons heading east.

"Two dead generals?" Sara said aloud. "Lord! What more calamities can there be?" She continued around Pea Ridge's Big Mountain on the Bentonville Detour, though she had no idea where it led, hoping that this route would lead her to the man who had stolen her heart.

Twilight began settling, the stars spilling out on the darkening canvas of sky, and the dropping temperature tore at her slender frame. The farther she traveled, the more hundreds of Confederates she saw curled up under flimsy blankets or leaning against trees or hunching over spare campfires and blowing on their hands. Sara called Joseph's name over and over, but no one answered.

One soldier came out from where he had been sitting and offered her a greatcoat. "My friend won't be needin' this no more. He froze to death. You take it."

Sara gratefully flung the long coat over her shoulders and secured the button at the neck. "Thank you. I'll pray for your friend. Are you sure he's dead?"

"Yep. I watched 'im die." He turned away and spoke over his shoulder. "Nothin' I could do.

"I'll pray for you, too," Sara called after him.

Into the long night she traveled, driven by the compulsion she did not fully understand. She stopped once to let Esther gobble some spilled corn and drink from a bubbling spring.

Behind her but a mile, Richards and his gang had regained the road and plodded along, stopping occasionally to rob some poor, sleeping soldier of his gun or accoutrements. Richards wore a victorious smirk on his face. He had determined that with one stolen wagon, he could prosper just dandy stealing soldiers' items and reselling them.

FOURTEEN

Of Blood and Forgiveness, Courage Against Power

MARCH 7, 1862, 4:30 P.M.
ELKHORN TAVERN, ARKANSAS

The surgeon paid no attention to Cyntha. Never looked at her, though she offered help twice more.

When the leg fell loose, he immediately broke off the ragged femur edges with a bone snip, and then began tying the arteries closed with thread. Finally, he released the clamps that had held the arteries shut and handed the clamps to a weary-looking nurse, his hands slopped in blood.

Cyntha, fetching up all her courage, gingerly took hold of the discarded bloody limb from the table and laid it in a brimming basket. She closed her eyes, fighting to keep from vomiting.

When the gray-haired surgeon had finished, he grabbed a jug of liquor, took a long swig, corked the jug, and then sat on a three-legged stool. Another man, perhaps a less-qualified surgeon, looking no older than his mid-twenties, grasped a file and rasped down the jagged bones; then he secured the piece of flesh that had been saved from the discarded section of leg over the wound with thread. He sewed a ragged stitch and applied a gooey plaster around the perimeter of the wound. This surgeon's apron was streaked scarlet, and his face was spattered with crimson speckles, as though he suffered from measles.

The table glistened deep maroon. When the nurse and orderlies lifted the amputee from the table, blood poured off onto the floor in sheets.

The air smelled like iron mixed with putrid, spoiled meal, and even a pungent pong, like overdone meat, almost sweet. Cyntha looked around to see the source of that peculiar odor. In the corner by the window, a soldier slumped, his face and hands red and black and with white blisters; some were popped and oozing. His eyelids had been burned away, yet he was still alive. His lips were peeled. When Cyntha bent down to speak to the soldier, she realized his skin was the source of the smell. Anthony appeared and knelt beside the man and offered him a ladle of water. The man slurped voraciously, then Anthony gave him another ladleful. Cyntha looked at her brother's face, the brother she so loved, but toward whom she had borne so much anger. She saw he was weeping. Her anger melted away from her like long-frozen ice off the eaves of a roof. She tenderly patted Anthony's back, remembering the courageous, kind heart of her brother.

The burned man, though his eyes were wide open, staring, appeared to fall asleep. His chest rose and fell rapidly.

"I better get some more water." Anthony stood and trudged out the door, bucket in hand, to the well.

Cyntha rose and regarded the rest of the home's lower floor. In the parlor, she saw Jeanette, Anthony's wife, kneeling, patting the hand of a wounded man, bloodied from chest to abdomen. The youth was giving a brave smile to Jeanette, though her eyes told of her anguish. Reynolds had taken hold of a comatose soldier's legs and was helping another fellow, who bore the unconscious soldier by the shoulders, carry the man upstairs.

To Cyntha's amazement, Ben was stanching a soldier's wounded leg, pressing a cloth against the shredded flesh with both hands.

Other men lugged a dead soldier, pale as the snow, to the yard. Cyntha looked out the window and saw them lay the body on the ground alongside a row of other dead soldiers. Her heart tore at her. Had someone ... anyone, on the battlefield of Wilson Creek, tried to save her husband's life? Or was he just rolled into a mass grave for the unnamed? Tears flooded down her cheeks.

Only when bullets began striking the house on all sides did she pull herself away from her sorrow.

When she turned back to the kitchen table, a new soldier had been placed there, and the older surgeon was tying a tourniquet to the man's mangled arm while the younger doctor held the forearm up to control the blood loss. Cyntha saw that the soldier's hand had been blown almost completely off. He groaned and called for his mama over and over.

"Where's my scalpel?" the old physician bellowed, looking around.

Cyntha saw the sharp instrument lying partially under the wounded man's leg. She grasped it and handed it to the surgeon, handle out to him.

"Good," he said. "Stay here, woman. I need the help."

Cyntha remained by the surgeon and did whatever was commanded of her. In the period of a half hour, the front of her dress was splattered with blood. After each surgery, the surgeon commanded she take up a pencil and his medical journal, and she recorded the terms and descriptions he dictated of each surgery.

About three o'clock, the gunfire and cannon blasts from the Confederates increased. With shrieks and whoops, the Rebels were pushing up the ravine behind the house. Bullets struck the house in a wild stridency, like a tempest hailstorm. So many bullets that they sounded like a great wind was buffeting the house.

Cyntha peeked out the window just as a Rebel artillery blast smashed a hole in the chimney's rock. Canister balls came next, cutting a swath of holes in the wall. Some balls tore through the north wall and struck an orderly in the neck. He did not even have a breath to yell in pain, but plummeted to the floor.

Cyntha felt strong arms suddenly surround her, bearing her to the floor. She knew her brother had grabbed her to keep her safe. He rolled to the floor beside her, his face pressed to the boards. She peered around and saw the doctors and nurses all clinging to the floor. They stayed pinned down until, at the end of a few minutes, the Confederates had swarmed the tavern and the grounds.

A Confederate battery rolled into position just in front of the tavern and let loose a thunder of grapeshot at a final line of retreating Yankees. The Union soldiers raced headlong in flight, south along the Telegraph Road and into a serried field, pulling their cannons and caissons with them. Most of the jubilant Rebels, clustered in large groups and small, hollered joyously and fired their rifles into the air while officers tried in vain to get them to fall back in line. Not all the Confederates in gray or mustard brown or homespun white were filled with joy. Some sat crying in the yard. Others leaned languidly on the fences, exhaustion showing in the entirety of their demeanor.

Inside the tavern, the surgeon called a halt to all efforts and ordered lanterns lit. When Cyntha and Anthony rose, they saw the wounded soldier who had just had his arm amputated, lying on the table, dead. Canister fragments that tore through the walls had ripped his stomach apart. Three orderlies lifted the body and carried it to the back yard.

Anthony stared out the smashed window panes. Cyntha, slipping at each step on the blood-laden floor, came up beside him. He pointed to the cobalt sky, ebbing to dark. "Stars are already out."

Cyntha took his arm. "I love you, brother. I'm sorry I've not even considered a wedding gift for you and Jeanette. Will you forgive me?"

"You are forgiven a thousand times over. I hope you can do the same for me."

"I have. Where is your wife?"

"Jeanette has gone down to the cellar seeing to the welfare of our daughter and the Coxes. My heart is pained for them. Their house is ruined."

After the orderlies lit several lanterns, the little troop of volunteers and doctors continued their meagre efforts at a job too large. Cyntha remained at the window. Her Union army appeared defeated. *How could any good come from this? I fear this horrible war will go on and on, and the Negroes will never be free.*

Of a sudden, a cadre of gray-coated officers trotted their horses up to the front porch and dismounted. While some of the lieutenants held the horses' reins, two generals entered the tavern with several adjutants close behind. Doctors with medical bags entered next, crowding into the parlor. One of the adjutants kicked the legs of a wounded Yankee, forcing him to move out of the way.

An obese general in a light gray uniform waddled in. His face was ruddy, framed with wide sideburns down to his chin. His arm bore a bloody bandage, the jacket torn at the elbow.

A tall, slender general strolled in next, scuffing his muddy boots on the floor. Cyntha thought the taller general had a rather arrogant look to him. Around his mouth, he bore a goatee and a long, snaking mustache, waxed and curled at the ends.

The fat general shoved a wounded Yankee from a chair, the man falling in a heap. The general pinched his bandaged arm, attempting to slow the bleeding. He dropped into the chair, grimacing.

Most of the Yankee nurses and orderlies stood, hands by their sides. Two nurses at the rear door held the basket filled with sawed-off limbs, ready to carry the appendages outside and dump them upon the pile of other amputated limbs.

The tall general, his hand resting on his holstered revolver, was sweating profusely, his pallor pale, and deep shadows dwelt under his weary eyes. "Ah am General Van Dorn, and Ah hereby take all the Yankee filth in this home as prisoners. Major, see to the removing of any armaments they may have." The general pointed at the wounded, and the major, along with other adjutants, waded into the room, stepping over the bodies, as they began gathering any weapons.

"Take those who can walk outside to the back and set a detail to guard them," General Van Dorn commanded.

The adjutants rousted a handful of wounded Yankees, plus the nurses and orderlies, and escorted them out the back door, where the day's light was quickly diminishing.

General Van Dorn, seeing a Union colonel among the wounded, saluted him. The officer returned a poor salute.

"Ah am commander of this brave Confederate ahmy," the tall general said. "This brave officer beside me is General Sterling Price. This home is now our temporary headquarters ...." He looked down at the blood-soaked floor and furniture. "Or rather, our hospital." He coughed, his face turning a deep burgundy.

After his coughing fit, General Van Dorn turned toward the kitchen and eyed Cyntha. He swept off his hat with a flourish and made a slight bow. "Mah pardons, ma'am. From your appearance, it looks like you have been caring for the wounded. Ah admire your verve. Now, you are allowed to care for our Southern wounded."

Cyntha bit her lip, rather than incur any wrath from someone she considered her personal enemy, especially a general.

The gray-haired doctor, his arms swathed in blood, as was his apron, leaned his head into the doorway. "You best give us a minute to finish up the wounded we have now before you bring in more."

"You needn't worry, doctor, we have our own illustrious surgeons who are up for the task. Even now, soldiers are setting up a hospital tent behind the house. We are not here to let men die; we are merely here to drive the Yankees from our homeland. We shall make short work of the invaders, as is our destiny."

One of the Confederate surgeons was busy applying a new bandage to General Price's arm. General Price turned to his fellow general. "I'll be ready to launch the attack presently."

General Van Dorn nodded, and then whispered some remarks to several adjutants, who immediately left and mounted their horses. General Price stood and thanked the surgeon and nodded at General Van Dorn. He rushed out the door and called out a number of orders to the soldiers milling about the yard.

Soon, a stream of orderlies bearing the moaning and wailing wounded on stretchers and blankets stormed into the house. They laid them on the floor shoulder to shoulder where the Union soldiers had been. Some soldiers limped in with leg wounds, others wobbled in with a head or arm wound. The soldiers laid the wounded on the parlor floor with no attention given to the severity of their wounds.

General Van Dorn found himself forced to step into the kitchen by the torrent of wounded men being brought in. From the influx of men, he became pressed up against Cyntha who had backed against the wall. He smelled of fusty cologne mixed with menthol and had pungent onion breath.

He smiled. "Mah lady," he whispered, leaning to her ear. "By your dress and coiffure, Ah can see you are a woman of exquisite taste. Ah would imagine you would appreciate a break from this inhospitable place, perhaps to retire for a dinner sometime, when all this unpleasantness is past, or perhaps for a nice ride in the country ... chaperoned, of course."

Cyntha stood still as stone, no smile. She held her breath.

Ben, appearing suddenly, stepped up beside her, and then wedged himself between her and the general. "This woman is my wife, sir." His voice was as menacing as a badger's growl. He placed his hand on the general's chest.

General Van Dorn leaned back and gazed admiringly at Cyntha, a toothy grin on his face. "Or perhaps not for now. I do have a battle to win. By your leave, ma'am." He doffed his hat and made a low bow. He gave a stern look at Ben. "Mind your station, soldier."

Ben held his tightened fists behind his back. Slowly, he drew his right hand out and saluted.

Cyntha was trembling. Time was not moving. Breathing seemed to be unattainable.

General Van Dorn turned abruptly and stepped outside, then mounted his horse. Soldiers, who were forming into long, wavery lines, cheered him. He rode out of sight into the gathering dark. Cyntha listened to Rebel officers yelling orders, the clank of gun and saber, the tromping of soldiers' feet. *The battle and the killing is not over.*

Ben momentarily took her hand in a gentle squeeze, then returned to assisting the Confederate wounded.

Cyntha slumped against the wall, shivering. The surgeon finished plastering the amputee's leg and glanced back at her. "I've heard tales of that Van Dorn. Fancies himself a lady's man." He took a huge breath and sank onto his stool. "If the Rebs win the day, by tomorrow, you best find a way to be hidden from here. Do you have some place to go?"

"No, I don't. This is my cousin's home. It was to be a place of refuge. And now ...."

The Confederate army began treading south in two long parallel lines toward the barren field, some two hundred across until reaching a bank of trees. Union soldiers and massed cannons waited there.

Stars twinkled in abundance now, the temperature plummeting.

Cyntha stood, took a cloth from a box and tried to wipe some of the blood from her dress. She looked around the parlor, where a few of the injured soldiers' agonizing screams were reaching fever pitch. She spied Reynolds on the bottom step of the stairs, his head leaned against the wall. He was asleep. She left out the back yard. "Oh, no. Where is Ben?"

FIFTEEN

WHEN PATHS CROSS, WHAT PAIN OR COMFORT MIGHT THERE BE?

MARCH 7, 1862, 10:00 P.M.
ELKHORN TAVERN, ARKANSAS

W ith the moon not yet risen, and long before she could see Elkhorn Tavern, Sara heard the yowling and pleadings of men under the surgeons' knives, losing their limbs. She knew the sound well, and reckoned it as a sign that hell had again broken the sod of the earth and sent its demons up to increase man's suffering. She had heard it too often at Wilson Creek.

When she came into view of Elkhorn, its walls gleaming in the flickering firelight of hundreds of campfires, she was ready to tumble from the saddle. She rode Esther through the camps of the exhausted Confederates that stretched up the Tanyard ravine along the Telegraph Road. Most slept on their arms, meagre blankets about them. A few drank from wooden canteens; others sat, staring into the starry firmament. Despite feeling pain and weariness coursing through her body, her first concern was for her horse. She dismounted and led Esther to where horses were tied on a stringer a hundred feet from the tavern. Water buckets sat in the muddy shadows under the stringer. While her mare drank, Sara removed the saddle and let it fall to the ground.

Standing beside Esther, she began to feel she had lost her will; no compunction to do anything at all, save sleep. Not to look for Joseph, nor even for Paul, nor to stay alive a moment longer. Just collapse and never rise again. Everything that she had driven herself to do for the last several days had been for naught. She was, once again, surrounded by war and bereft of hope.

She could see silhouettes of surgeons and nurses along the wall of the well-lit hospital tents. The many silhouettes moved swiftly, as in a waltz. The ragged yellow flags, which designated a hospital, draped limp on staffs. The calls of a man about to lose an appendage emanated from one tent, first pleading that they not cut it, then urging the surgeon to get it done quickly, then hollering, "Cut the damn thing off. Faster. Faster," then finally shrieking, "Kill me, kill me, please!" Then she heard the surgeon and nurses trying to rouse the man with calls and demanding he "stay with us." Then all was quiet.

Moments later, shadowy figures carrying a dark burden exited the tent and laid it among other similar forms under the trees.

Someone standing near the line of the dead bodies called into the dark, "I hope you don't 'spect us to bury 'em all tonight. Ain't gonna happen."

She heard smatterings of conversations from a group of soldiers about an attack they had made in the coalmine darkness across the field that lay beyond the tavern. From bits and pieces of their dismal dialogue, she learned they had been driven back by massed Federal artillery.

"We'll get 'em tomorry," one soldier mewed, his voice as bold as a cat that had cornered a mouse. The others murmured agreement, though she could sense their weariness.

Sara decided to tie Esther with the other horses, leave the saddle nearby. Her heart demanded she help the wounded. What else could she do? She had learned a great deal about caring for battle-shattered men from Dred Workman. His nursing skills far outmatched any she had ever seen, so perhaps she could use what she learned from him to be of assistance up at the tavern.

She had the desire in her heart, if she could just find the energy. Her leg tormenting her, she limped up a path through a wide expanse of campfires with only a few soldiers even taking a glance at her. Their raw, powder-smudged faces in the firelight's glow exhibited a variety of emotions—exhaustion, sorrow, despair, horror, and even trance-like expressions.

She stopped her stride long enough to observe a weary-looking general, seated on a stool by a fire. He wore a goatee and a mustache, choked deep throaty coughs, and drank frequently from a bottle of some liquor. She knew his rank from a quick look at the shoulders of his coat. She stood awhile, observing the many young men crowding around him while he scribbled messages on foolscap. He handed the notes, one after another, to the couriers, who then ran to mount their horses.

Opposite the goateed general, another general, rotund and gray-haired, sprawled on a blanket, leaning on an elbow, somnolent, his eyes shut.

She yawned, fighting against the sleep her body yearned for, then bolstering her resolve, she limped to the tavern. On the porch, one soldier stared at nothing. A wounded soldier sat, leaning down on his arms, his head bound with a blood-stained bandage, his hair matted like a wet sheep. He slept with restless dreams, thrashing his arms in the air. At the door, soldier after soldier sped into the tavern while others plied their way out, some with items in their hands, all of them rushing like hell was on their heels.

At the end of the porch, a single private stood with the butt of his rifle planted on the boards, but his head faced south, peering out into the black-as-pitch field where pickets fired occasional shots, flashing like fireflies. He never saw Sara. She thought, *Fine guard he's makin'*.

She walked inside and saw the floor stained red from one end to the other, and she nearly slipped on a slick spot. The smell of raw guts and spilled blood almost overwhelmed her. Soldiers sat against the walls, some holding bandaged ribs, some rubbing the nub of sawed-off legs, others with their heads bound in bloody cloths.

"Ya best mind your footing on the floor," a bald-headed nurse looked up from a surgery. "Yes, sir," Sara replied.

"Why're ya here?"

"I'm here to help." As true as her words felt, her mind dwelt in a cloud.

"Then take this bolt of linen and tear it into three-inch wide strips," the bald man said. He tossed the bolt at her, and she almost dropped it. "Do it quick! Then roll the strips and place them in the box here." He pointed at a wooden crate beside the operating table. He threw a pair of dull scissors on the floor at her feet. "Quick! Or don't do it." He returned to helping the surgeon bind up a head wound on a soldier whose skin was the pallor of a white marble column.

She went outside and found an unoccupied chair near the door, sat and began cutting the cloth into strips.

A shadow blocked the light from the doorway. Sara looked up and beheld a woman in a fine satin dress that at one time had been cobalt blue, but now bore considerable splotches of maroon. The woman's hands shone crimson-stained in the gleaming light.

"Here, let me help you," the dark-haired woman said. She sat on the porch at Sara's feet and helped keep the bolt of cloth from folding while Sara cut the strips.

"My name's Sara Reeder." Sara paused from her cutting.

"I'm pleased to meet you. My name is Cyntha ..."

Horses pulling a caisson clattered by, covering Cyntha's words completely, so Sara did not hear her last name, and she was too tired to ask it.

After the caisson passed, Cyntha said, "I've been working much of the day. It's nice to sit down for a while."

Sara studied the face of the woman with dark hair that had once been tied in a bun, but, now, numerous strands hung about her face; her cool green eyes, and her piteous attempt to maintain a smile on her blood-stained cheeks. A conjecture from somewhere deep inside her flew to her lips. "Have we met before?"

Cyntha shook her head no. "I don't think so, but I'm so glad you're here."

Sara made the best smile she could engender and extended her hand. "Pleased to meet you, Cyntha. Is this your home?"

Cyntha shook Sara's hand. "No, it's my cousins' home, the Cox family. My brother and his wife are here with their daughter, too. This house ... this house was supposed to be a safe-haven, but ..."

Sara pointed to Cyntha's wedding ring. "Where is your husband? Is he off to war?"

"My husband was killed in a battle. My hope now is to free his soul from torment."

Sara gave a questioning look, then she grasped Cyntha's meaning. She set to cutting the fabric again, trying not to look at Cyntha's eyes. She was somehow astonished by this demure woman who seemed similar to herself in depth of heart, yet more calm, more confident, but who was suffering the wound of a sword of sorrow through her heart for the loss of her husband. In a way, this new companion's agony mirrored her own.

The young women worked together in silence, cutting, folding, and rolling the strips. Moans of the men inside and outside the house interweaved continuously with bangs and clangs of men working with artillery and horses galloping on the outer reaches of the army. Occasionally, the rumble of war subsided enough that they heard the weary Missouri Guard soldiers snoring. A single fiddle player somewhere in the dark eked out a hymn, "Oh, Sinner Man."

"War is horrible." Sara cut the last strip and rolled it and looked piercingly at Cyntha. "A bane on mankind. Men ride off to battle, and we women have to bear the brunt of mourning for their deaths."

Cyntha closed her eyes. She felt her body would melt for weariness.

"I'm looking for my future husband," Sara blurted. "He's in McCulloch's army."

"Oh," Cyntha's eyes widened. "I thought that you lived nearby and would have heard. Several officers were talking. General McCulloch died, as did General McIntosh. The whole army is split in half. No telling where the rest of the soldiers are."

"Surely, no! I was hoping to find my fiancé here amongst these soldiers." A lump grew in Sara's throat, and she stood, her fists tight by her sides, which was her habit when under duress and desiring to determine a new direction.

"I believe, by tomorrow," Cyntha continued, rising as a rheumatoid woman might, "the Rebels will have won the battle. You will have time to find your soldier then." She turned and looked at the moon rising, spreading a spectral luminance onto the battlefield. "So much carnage. By tomorrow, a great many women will have letters written to them by an officer, telling them of the passing of their husbands or brothers or fathers or sons, and they will learn to mourn like me. I don't see the point of this fighting anymore."

Sara reached out and hugged her, and the two fell on each other's necks, weeping. Finally, releasing their embrace and wiping their tears, they looked up into the indigo sky.

"My father," Sara stated, "was a major in the army. General Taylor gave him a telescope as a gift of gratitude for his bravery in the War with Mexico. In October, marauders raided and burned our home, stole our livestock, and ruined our lives. In the commotion, my father's telescope was destroyed."

"I'm sorry ..."

Sara put her finger to Cyntha's lips. "You have enough tragedy in your life. No need to add mine."

At that moment of suffocating quiet, several Confederates, wrapped in shadow, trotted their horses up near the two generals seated by the campfire several yards north of the tavern. Two of the soldiers alighted, their backs to the tavern, and began speaking to the generals. Neither Sara, nor Cyntha could hear their conversation. In the firelight and torchlight, they could tell that one of the soldiers who had dismounted was dark-headed and taller than the blond soldier who was with him. They watched them take a note from the thin general, and with their faces obscured in shadow beneath their wide brim hats, they mounted their horses and sped north into the vast, swallowing night up the Telegraph Road.

The women moved inside to attend the torn and battered men until the moon rose to straight above them. Though intent on the assistance she was giving to the surgeons, Cyntha worried about Reynolds, who had been upstairs when he collapsed. She hoped he would rebound. Her concern about Ben being missing increased. She had a desire to be near him, though she considered the fondness she held for him inexplicable. She steeled her thoughts. *It'd be better if he is gone. Good riddance.*

SIXTEEN

∞

THE OPPORTUNITY LOST

MARCH 7, 1862, 8:00 P.M.
LEETOWN BATTLEFIELD

Hours had passed since General McIntosh's and McCulloch's deaths. Paul was concerned that nothing was being done in McCulloch's Army of the West. The regiments floundered in disarray. *Where is General Pike? He should be here directing the retreat or conversing and planning with other officers. Where is Colonel Greer? Why isn't he taking charge?*

He had watched the Southern soldiers and warriors drifting away in the direction from which they had marched that morning. Some left in groups, even whole companies, most of whom had enlisted from the same county or town. Others walked or rode off alone. *Cowards!*

Taking a deep breath, he berated himself for criticizing them. He did not really hold them in disdain, for he knew how much they had suffered on the long march through the snowstorm.

While some lieutenants and captains tried in vain to halt the ill-conceived, disorganized retreat, others led their companies away with determination. He could only hope that some traveled to reassemble with the remains of Pike's command, though he knew for certain that many were headed for home, abandoning the cause, sure that they had lost the entire war because their generals were dead.

He knew that Colonel Armstrong was seeing to the proper burials of General McIntosh and General McCulloch. When a Christian minister came to him and asked where the dead generals were being interred, he merely pointed, for he could not escort the man, nor could he bring himself to look at General McCulloch's face. He did not think he could bear it.

At last, despite the pain in his chest, he mounted his horse and trotted it up the shallow hill where Colonel Greer maintained the Third Texas Cavalry. He was surprised to see Colonel Greer was halfway down the slope and on foot. He was attempting to put some order into the retreating men of Hebert's command. He listened while Greer directed soldiers in fierce, combative words to bolster their resolve, and ordered various youths to work as nurses to help the surgeons who were dealing with the wounded from the fray in Morgan's Woods.

Paul watched the colonel send couriers to ascertain which officers were still fit to serve. He was yelling orders as fast as he could think them up, pacing like a harried fox might when chased by hounds; more of a trot, back and forth. He would question a courier, then send him out again, grab a pencil and paper from an aide and dispatch another runner with the note. He was whirling and howling like a dervish.

His own regiment, save his aides, remained mounted in ragged lines in the forest beyond him.

"A moment, please, sir." Paul saluted.

Colonel Greer was wiping his wide brow of its sweat. His dark hair was matted. "Ah, yes. McCulloch's man. The scout."

"Yes, sir. Captain Paul McGavin. I was going to ask if you knew about the soldiers who are essentially dispersing to your right flank, some following General Pike, some just scattering and looking for food, others claiming they're going home."

Colonel Greer's let his head hang on his chest as if he was relinquishing the fight.

Paul waited. Nearby, the Third Texas Regiment's leather saddles creaked under their riders. Spurs and the metal aspects of reins, sabers, and guns clanked. Some of the men appeared ready to fall asleep in the saddle.

A barred owl hooted somewhere off toward the Union line. Night was settling fast. For the time being, the sound of battle had vanished, only hooves stamping, a man coughing. A pocket of silence pervaded the forest.

Finally, Greer spoke. "General McCulloch and General McIntosh are dead."

"Yes, sir."

"From all the reports, Colonels Hebert and Major Tunnard are captured. And the soldiers aren't goin' to follow General Pike. He has not the acumen, nor the standin'."

"I understand."

"I need orders, McGavin, from Van Dorn or Price. Should we create a redoubt here? Buckle down in a defensive position? Should we engender a new attack? What are we to do? I've heard nothin'."

"Yes." Paul wished the man was not so garrulous and was more decisive.

"You're a scout, correct?" Greer did not wait for an answer. "You know this whole area maybe bettah than any other. Take one more man with you, ride fast around the big mountain. Get to Van Dorn. Find out what his orders are."

"Yes, sir."

"Take Colonel Armstrong with you."

"Sir, I believe he is attending to the burial of our generals and the many needs of our wounded."

"Very well. Who then?"

Paul inadvertently winced at the pain in his chest. Greer took it to mean 'anyone' the colonel chose.

"Let me see." Greer put his gloved hand to his chin. "You there, Favor." He pointed at Joseph, in line with the rest of Company C.

Joseph rode up to the officers.

"You went on that surveillance mission with Cumby and Johnson in Springfield back in October, didn't you?"

"Yes, sir."

"Good! Therefore, you have experience on important night missions. Go with Captain McGavin here. Ride togethah with all haste around the Bentonville Detour. Find General Van Dorn and see what he wants us to do. Is your horse rested?"

"Yes, sir, but don't you think …."

"Question, Corporal Favor?" Greer's intense stare shut down Joseph's response.

Joseph pulled his kepi down on his brow, his sharp blue eyes ablaze, and saluted. "No, sir. I'm ready."

"Go quickly. And watch for the enemy. They are celebratin' being on Southern soil, and they are treacherous."

Joseph reluctantly followed behind Paul, who had headed his horse down the hill. He glanced at Ebie, who gave him a winsome smile and hoisted his saber high in a salute. Other friends in his company waved. The regiment, settling into a defensive position, had not charged down into the fields, gloriously arrayed, nor had they performed even any reconnaissance. They had been mere spectators of a rout of their army not by an overwhelming force, but by the frivolous and powerful *sister fates* twisting their choking threads of a new, unsuspected future for every man that no one had envisioned.

The night's gloom fell like a theatre curtain. Soldiers were starting scanty campfires like so many stage floor lamps, and officers strutted around on their muddy stage, ordering pickets to positions out into the field. Each actor of the drama taking their position. The cries of wounded and dying men echoed in sorrowful arias throughout the long line of white oaks and elms. A sort of chaotic opera had swollen up in the dark.

What final rations any of the soldiers had scraped together to share were soon gone. A few produced a handful of coffee grounds to make pale coffee.

"The Yanks won't have to fire a shot at us," Paul said over his shoulder to Joseph. "They'll just have to whistle at us, and we'll fall over."

Joseph said nothing. He had ambivalence snaking through him. He knew he could no longer fight as a rebel, but he was sorrowed by the Confederates' defeat of the day. Which side should he hope would win? Would he and his comrades be thrust into battle on the morrow and die ignominious deaths? Were his comrades' belief in the cause of state's rights of less importance than his own desire to free the slaves?

He had reached the point that his mind demanded that he ride away. Depart to any quiet place to sort things out. Disappear. Yet he continued accompanying this scout named Captain McGavin, leading the way along a dark road. His stomach was in knots.

For miles along the Ford Road and Bentonville Detour Road, Joseph and Paul passed elements of the Confederate army, both White man and Indian, the campfires sprinkled in the fields and among the trees.

Joseph's ambiguity expanded to thoughts of Cyntha, finally remembering her name, knowing much of their history together, pieces of their shared past struggling up into his memories. He could not help the thoughts, and he yearned to know her again as he once had, to rejoin her and then gather with the neighbor farm families back in Iowa. He knew his being raised in Tennessee had bequeathed him a Southern drawl, but he remembered, now, the expanse of his Iowa farm: the house, the barn, the chicken coop, the fields of grain, flowing in the wind, so golden in color that the fields rivaled the sun. His heart was *in* his farm and *for* his wife.

But what of Sara? Why were thoughts of her wedged tight in his mind, not like sore splinters in flesh, but veins of silver in a rich mine?. *Her smile is unequaled.* He could not control his thoughts of her slender waist and how it felt in his hands, her gentle blond curls, her indefatigable will that he so admired. *Where is she? Is she all right? I want to see her, to tell her I'm better now. Her strong will saved me.* His thinking on her almost caused him to ride his horse into a grove of tangled bushes and briars.

He stopped the horse in time and backed it up.

Paul halted and dismounted. "I hear a stream. The horses need some water and rest before we continue."

Together, Paul and Joseph found the stream a few feet from the road and let their steeds drink. They dismounted their horses and filled their own canteens. Neither had any food to offer the other, so the subject did not come up.

Standing in the dark, with the moon rising, looking like a blanched white lemon, Paul breathed slow breaths. *Is this the Corporal Favor that Sara is looking for? Should I tell him she is near? No, I won't.*

The thought callously crossed his mind that he could dispatch the corporal where he stood. One well-placed club just behind the ear with his revolver butt. Would one more battle death indicate anything criminal? Then he would be free to pursue the young woman whose image dwelt like a most welcome friend in his thoughts. He could not shake his feelings for her, nor his desire to be with her. If he could just brush his fingers across her hand. Maybe to have a few moments to look into her eyes.

Finally, Paul said, "Mount up, Corporal Favor. We've got more to go. Let's hope a sentry doesn't shoot us when we get close."

They rode for three hours, coming into view of Van Dorn's forces stretching from the valley below Elkhorn Tavern up to the top of the plateau. With mounted pickets holding torches while accompanying them, they rode up to where General Van Dorn sat gazing into a fire, his eyes reddened, his face pasty and streaked with gunpowder grime. He looked to be in a stupor and was shivering despite his nearness to the fire. Farther on, Elkhorn Tavern stood in shadows though all its windows blazed. Several soldiers hastened in and out of the wayside edifice.

Joseph noted the silhouettes of two women standing on the porch. Paul saw them as well and wondered who they might be. Women on a battlefield were rare.

Paul remembered riding up the same road to the tavern that dark evening a week previous, the night he escaped the Yankee cavalry patrol and the night he was sure his brother died. He thought for a moment to go to the house and inquire about Ben's grave, but his question would have to wait.

After Paul had introduced himself and Joseph to General Van Dorn and explained the purpose of their mission, the general laid out plans point-blank to order Colonel Greer to bring his regiment and all able soldiers with due diligence around the Bentonville Detour Road to join Price's Missouri Guards by morning. If he was able, General Pike was to follow, all to arrive before dawn.

For Paul, just raising his worrisome right leg over the saddle, coupled with his pained chest and back, he nearly lost his breath. Joseph looked with worry at his new companion, for Paul had lost all color in his face and appeared to swoon. Joseph grabbed his jacket sleeve and held him in place. In a moment, Paul made peace with the constant pain.

"Let's get moving," he said. "The quicker we get there, the quicker we get some rest."

Trotting away, Paul heard General Van Dorn ask someone, "Has anyone seen our ammunition wagons?"

Joseph and Paul rode north up the Telegraph Road toward the intersection with the Bentonville Detour Road. By the time the pickets left them, the moon had risen high and bathed the road and its environs with a bluish attribute.

Paul's body ached, and even the scratch on his forehead from his fall from the tree when General McCulloch was killed began to throb. Trying to distract himself, Paul said, "You don't talk much, Corporal Favor."

"Like as not. I generally talk more with the men, sir."

"I understand, but don't treat me as a typical officer. I'm nothing more than .... Be forthright, soldier. Tell me about yourself."

"Not much to tell, sir." Joseph knew he could not divulge his real story. "Just fighting with the Third Texas. Fought in the scrap at Bentonville. We almost caught old General Sigel." He hoped his downhome rattling sounded sincere.

"Ever met anyone that's lost his memory?"

Joseph was riding behind Paul in the dark and was glad he did not see him nearly drop the reins. He was unsure of how to answer. Most of the men in his regiment knew he had suffered from amnesia. He had not kept it a secret, though none of them, not even Ebie, knew of his recent revelations. Could this captain have heard of him? Finally, he said, "I took a good clubbing to my head at Wilson Creek, sir, but I'm better now."

Paul's suspicions were verified who this blond corporal was. Joseph did not need to say one more word. He was the one that Sara searched for even to the point of putting her own life at risk. His heartache now was deeper than any of the injuries he had received. He decided, for her sake, that he would not stand in the way of the two being rejoined and then married. For his part, though, he would do nothing to help that eventuality. No hints to Joseph. His secret would help him maintain his hope.

"Well, I hope you remember the way back," Paul said. "In case we get waylaid along this road, one of us needs to get to Colonel Greer. The army's counting on us."

"Yes, sir." Joseph had begun thinking hard about striking out alone when Paul had ridden far enough ahead of him. He allowed his mount to drift farther and farther behind the black-haired captain who seemed to ask too many questions. He was hatching a plan to escape north, away from the battle and to his old life. Re-joining the Iowa regiment was not in his plan.

His mind had been overrun with thoughts of Cyntha and Sara. He had strong recollections of Cyntha naked in his arms, the smooth feel of her body, the goose bumps rising on her skin when he brushed his hands lightly across her neck and breast, though her face was still hazy in his recollection. He remembered making love to her—soft love, kind love, but vigorous with both of them panting, then moaning in ecstasy, then collapsing in joy and welcome exhaustion.

Then Sara's face was on Cyntha's body, and he felt such confusion, he slapped his own face. He did not want to admit what he felt.

A mile up, where Telegraph Road and the Detour Road converged, B.F. Richards and his band had camped. Richards was awake, spinning the chamber of his revolver while he stared into the campfire. The two remaining marauders sat across from him. He spit in the fire.

SEVENTEEN

VILE CREATURES

MARCH 8, 1862, MIDNIGHT
BENTONVILLE DETOUR ROAD, NORTH OF BIG MOUNTAIN,
PEA RIDGE, ARKANSAS

The moon had risen above the treetops. Richards was perplexed. He sat, running his finger on the scar of his face, his revolver in the other hand, and staring at his dead horse. He had recently shot the horse after it stepped in a hole, snapping its leg.

Across the scant campfire from him sat the last two members of his marauder gang. One of the members had taken the nickname of Snake. Skinny as a post, he had a markedly narrow face, sunken cheeks, and a hawk nose. He had tied a snakeskin for his hatband, and he wore a rattlesnake's rattle on a leather necklace. His bushy mustache drooped three inches past his chin. He was holding his hands near the fire's flames. Richards pondered that if his skeletal companion got down and slithered along the ground that he might look like a snake.

The other marauder was as round as Snake was thin. His name was Bill Fleck, but called himself Buck. Richards laughed at his thought of a deer buck as fat as him would make for a long time of good eating. He breathed a harsh sigh. "Get up, Buck.

Snake. We've got to find me a horse, or I'll never get away from these damned armies."

The men rose lazily, stretched, and went to their horses, still saddled. Richards unbuttoned his trousers and peed on the fire. No sooner than Snake and Buck had risen in their saddles, all three men heard horses galloping.

"They's goin' pretty fast," Buck remarked. "Reckon one of them horses comin' is for you?"

Richards kicked dirt on the last of the flames and sparks. "Get off your horses. We'll take these riders from afoot." Gritting his teeth, he began growling, bear-like, and pushed his way through the underbrush to the edge of the road. With ample moonlight, he saw two riders, one behind the other and barely visible, coming fast up the Detour road. His companions took positions, prone in a ditch, revolvers ready.

When the first rider drew close, the three men scrambled into the road, revolvers aimed.

"Stop now!" Richards yelled. "Or I'll shoot you dead in your saddle!"

Paul McGavin drew his horse up as quick as he could. The horse reared and shrieked. He had reckoned on possibly running into some Yankees, but these crass individuals were cut from a different cloth. "Whoa!" he called, and the horse settled. He looked down at the three men holding positions around his horse, their guns drawn. The one with the dark beard and a white scar across the bridge of his nose and cheek stood nearest. The other marauders moved to his side and rear.

"Where's the other rider, damn it?" Richards glanced behind Paul's horse at the dark vacant road.

Joseph had slowed his mount in order to drift several yards behind Paul.

He snapped loose from his reverie when he heard the demanding calls of the marauders, many yards ahead of him. With dexterity, he eased his horse into the trees beside the thoroughfare like molasses flowing through a crack in a table, and immediately swept the reins into his teeth and pulled both revolvers from his belt. It was just like he had trained—ready for battle. He positioned the horse behind a thick oak and in shadow. The moon shed ample light on the event in the road. He watched the three men—varmints, Sara would have called them—surrounding Paul on his horse. He trained his eyes on them, evaluating each one. At a later time, he would be amazed at the speed of his reaction and the ferocity with which he would launch his attack.

For now, he listened.

"Snake," Richards demanded, "go down the road a piece. Find that other rider!"

The skinny man jogged down the road, hunched over, revolvers sweeping left and right, his eyes scanning both sides of the road. After a half a minute, he came back beside Paul's horse. "Ain't another 'un," he said.

"I'm afraid I can't help you much," Paul said, "if you're looking for money. I've got none."

"Shut your mouth!" Richards roared. "We're needin' horses, and yours will have to do."

Paul leaned over the saddle horn. "You from Arkansas?"

"What if I am?" Richards retorted. He pulled back the hammer of his revolver.

"Well, if you love Arkansas and the South, I'm bringing an important message for the generals, so the Confederates can win the battle going on back yonder."

"I ain't in love with the South or with Arkansas. Now raise your hands and ease off that saddle." With his free hand, Richards grabbed the horse's halter. "And hope I don't shoot you dead." His tone was maniacal.

All three of the thieves were standing now on the right side of the horse and nearest to where Joseph waited, hidden. He realized that the men meant to kill Paul. He had only just met the scout, but he knew he had to intervene.

His horse snorted and shifted a hoof in dry leaves. The three robbers turned toward the noise.

With whirlwind speed, the reins still in his teeth, one hand holding a Navy Colt revolver, and the horse's mane and the second gun in his other hand, Joseph punched spurs into the horse's side and galloped out from the trees onto the road. His revolvers blazed, and with marked accuracy, he shot Buck in the stomach with one gun and Snake in the arm with the other. Both men yelped, dropping their guns, and stumbled away into the trees.

When Richards turned to see his men falling, Paul had all the time he needed. He grabbed the reins, punched his spurs into his horse and rode down the marauder, knocking him to the ground. Richards' revolver sailed through the air and landed in the ditch. He sprang to his feet and followed his companions into the trees.

Paul and Joseph emptied their revolvers toward the trees where he disappeared.

Joseph rode up beside Paul. "Let's go!"

Neither was going to wait for the marauders to return with more weapons. They sped into the night on their exhausted horses.

When Paul and Joseph reached Colonel Greer at about two in the morning, the colonel unenthusiastically obeyed General Van Dorn's orders and set in motion his weary regiment and whatever elements of other regiments could be mustered to march around Big Mountain to join Van Dorn's and Price's troops. Some of the infantry who had united under General Pike led the trek, trudging in front of the cavalry. The men swayed in exhausted rhythm, jostling one another, stumbling along; and cursing their hunger, the icy cold, and their officers.

Through the rest of the frigid morning, the hundreds of Confederates made their way around the Bentonville Detour Road, turned south on the Telegraph Road and finally stopped, arriving just before dawn in the Tanyard ravine. The soldiers fell out in a wavery line from a half mile below Elkhorn Tavern to not far from the intersection of the Huntsville Road.

Colonel Greer, in the lead of the column, halted near the crossroads. He waved his gloved hand and muttered an order that really no one heard, but all understood, and the soldiers sank onto the cold ground like withered cornstalks blown over by a stout breeze. Some cavalrymen did not even bother to secure the horses to a tree, but slept on the ground where they landed, their horses' reins wrapped around their wrists.

Paul and Joseph had ridden near Colonel Lane, the Third Texas Cavalry bringing up the rear of the column and last to arrive where they could rest. Colonel Lane, usually as energetic as a man could be, dismounted like an ancient remnant of a man, removed the saddle and tied his horse to a sapling. He spread a blanket on the ground and collapsed on it.

After tying his horse to an elm, Paul settled near the colonel and sat awake for a while, leaning against the tree, rubbing his aching leg, then his chest.

Man and horse had reached their limits.

Paul watched the blond-headed soldier whom Sara loved, and who had saved his life. He felt gratitude toward him. In one day, his life had been saved twice by people he barely knew. Sara had saved it by the gift of a silver box, Joseph by his quick, brave action.

When Joseph muttered Sara's name in sweet tones in his dreams, Paul decided that it was obligatory for him to move on and let Joseph and Sara unite. He would not stand in their way. He leaned back against the elm, and fitful dreams of war overtook him.

EIGHTEEN

ॐ

THE DAY OF
RECKONING DAWNS

MARCH 8,1862, PRE-DAWN
ELKHORN TAVERN, ARKANSAS

Morning crept over the Confederate camp like a dark
beast, not bright with cordial sunshine, but gray-
haired and long-toothed. The temperature that had
dropped to freezing in the first part of the night was warming
rapidly. Water dripped from the eaves of the tavern like tinkling
bells—a pleasant prelude to the horrific symphony to come.

Anthony, Jeanette, Cyntha and Sara had worked through
the night assisting with the wounded. The Cox family had been
allocated a corner of an upstairs bedroom, where they huddled
in restless sleep. Reynolds slept near them, curled under a shabby
blanket, his bent arm as his pillow, his breathing laboring.

No one knew where Ben had gone.

Despite the arduous task of caring for the maimed soldiers,
Cyntha had reflected about Ben often, first pleasing thoughts,
then angry ones. She was entirely in two minds about him. The
surgeons kept her busy dictating notes to her to record in their
surgical journals.

With morning light glowing softly on the horizon, rifle fire increased, a constant pock, pock, pock. Some close, some far away.

Sara, woozy with fatigue, staggered to the door of the tavern and stared at the cold, starless sky. A fog had flooded the fields and forest. The moon's glow hazy behind the fog.

The tavern was warmed now by well-kept fires in both fireplaces. Outside, the cooler air took her breath. Lacking any shawl or coat, she shivered. She went back inside and put on the greatcoat a private had given her.

Most of the campfires had dwindled to mere dancing sparks and embers. She tried to discern where the generals had sat, but the fog was too impenetrable.

Sara watched the dim forms of the Rebels rousing from sleep. At first, slapping their arms about their bodies and stomping their feet in attempts to warm themselves; they then began rushing in all directions like chickens alerted to a fox in the coop. Officers yelled brash orders into the dense gray mist. Lanterns began to glow, and torches blazed up.

A sound like millions of pebbles clattering and jangling onto a cavern floor bled out from where the Union army was preparing for battle a mile away across the fields. The forest and the rocky granite escarpment on the south face of Big Mountain that extended out beyond the tavern echoed back the sound.

When Sara saw the extensive rows of dead soldiers of both armies laid out in the yard, tears trickled down her cheeks. "Don't be dead, Joseph," she whispered and sank down onto the porch step.

Cyntha came out beside Sara, then sat, her knees up to her chest, tucking her stained dress around her ankles. "The surgeons have quit. They've reached the limits of what is humanly possible and are trying to find sleep in any vacant corner." She put her arm around Sara. "You look like you need sleep, too."

Sara wiped her eyes with her sleeve and leaned against Cyntha's shoulder. "Thank you, Cyntha. I just don't know if I can bear this war anymore." She pointed to the long field beyond the tavern. "Somewhere out there, my fiancé, my heart, may be dead."

"It is a wonder how time pushes us along," Cyntha said. "No chance to pause, no moment to consider a different course. We are like a long thread steadily drawn across a patch of cloth stitching it to other patches, those other people who crowd into our lives that make up this disparate quilt. For some of these soldiers, their thread broke, no knot to repair the break. New soldiers will enlist, new threads to take their place, those to break, too."

Sara raised her head and looked at Cyntha's serene face. "The thread of my life crossed a brave soldier's, and our threads became entwined. Then the war yanked us apart like a seamstress ripping a hem."

Cyntha gave a small laugh. "I'm afraid we're both being too poetic. My late husband liked to write poetry. He claimed his poems were not any good, but I found them appealing."

"My fiancé and I once read poetry on a hillside. It seems like a long time ago." Her voice faded to a whisper. "Perhaps," said Sara, after a long pause, "I will find him, and you will find a new man to be your husband, someone new to love, not to fill your dead husband's place, but someone."

"If only that it were true." Cyntha bit her lip. "I may have found ...."

"Found what?"

"Nothing ... Actually. Hope. I may have found hope."

The clamor of the army preparing for the forthcoming conflict intensified.

"I guess," Sara said, rising, "I better get my mare before someone decides to take her into battle."

"You have a horse? Well, I guess that would make sense."

"That is how I reached this God-forsaken place. There was brutal fightin', and cruel savages scalpin' them soldiers on the far side of this mountain yesterday. I saw …. Oh, it doesn't matter what I saw. I just pray this war was over." She limped down the incline to where she had tied Esther. While taking care of the wounded, she had nearly forgotten about her own worrisome leg. Now the pain punched her calf like a hammer.

Reaching the grove of trees where she had tied Esther, enough light from torches indicated that all the horses were gone. The picket rope swung barren. Her horse and saddle were gone. "No! They've taken her." She spun around, calling for Esther.

After several minutes of screaming, hobbling up to every opaque, mounted rider, then crying when finding the rider sat atop his own steed, she sank to the ground. "Esther, oh, Esther." She sobbed awhile, then stood, fists tight. "I hate this war."

NINETEEN

RANCOR AND HOPE

MARCH 8, 1862, MORNING
ELKHORN TAVERN, ARKANSAS

The cannonading began before sunup, followed by all the concussion of battle. The fog melted. Paul and Joseph, and the rest of the Third Texas soldiers who had marched all night, their energy expended, rolled their weary bodies up into sitting positions. The regiment received no orders to join in or support the fight. They stayed idle.

In the late morning, a few hundred Rebels began barging through their bivouac. The first ones were marching away in orderly fashion. In ten minutes, the retreating men became like a flood, no longer organized. The Third Texas men secured their mounts to keep the panicked infantrymen from stealing them.

Many of the Missouri Guard ran in a chaotic fashion north down the Telegraph Road into the Tanyard valley where the Texans had bivouacked. The majority of Confederates withdrew east on the Huntsville Road. A sizable number scurried into the forest itself, finding a direction of their own making.

Paul led his horse through the melee toward the tavern, following Colonel Greer. Staggering with constant strikes of pain in his leg, chest and back, he observed General Van Dorn and Colonel Greer in a heated exchange of words. The officers sat on their nervous horses near the intersection of the Huntsville and Telegraph Roads. They were waving their arms and pointing in different directions. By the manner each was swaying and gesticulating, Paul thought they looked more like drunks ready to brawl than soldiers using proper military comportment.

When General Van Dorn dismounted his horse and walked to his ambulance, Colonel Greer saluted his general's back, his mouth open to ask a question which he never spoke.

The creaking ambulance jerked away onto the Huntsville Road. The wagon dipped down into a ravine and was soon lost from sight. Hundreds of soldiers, along with horses and mules pulling artillery and caissons, hastened after the ambulance.

The infantry who had been cobbled together by Colonel Greer hurried along last, grumbling. General Van Dorn had ordered the Third Texas cavalry to serve as the rear guard.

When Colonel Lane gave the order to prepare to cover the army's retreat, Paul barely moved. With strenuous effort, he mounted his exhausted horse.

The men of the Third Texas rose into saddle and rode a short distance to a wide mott of oaks and brush that straddled both roads to establish a defensive line—the rear guard. Paul was close enough to hear Colonel Greer complaining, "We were never ordered to fight! Now, our job is to cover their cowardly asses." He then announced to everyone within earshot, "Do you know what the general said? He said he had *not lost* the battle, only that his plans were not completely fulfilled! Had the army been better prepared, he would have won! Arrogant bastard!"

He took a huge breath, then barked orders for the regiment to move into defensive formation. Though they obeyed the order dutifully, the soldiers up and down the line muttered about their hunger and their ill feelings about the whole affair. The corporal next to Paul whimpered, "I ain't et in three days. I feel like my spine and my stomach have met and shook hands."

Paul nodded to him, but he was not worried about hunger. His body ached so much, he was tempted to beg some laudanum from Colonel Lane. *If I don't get some rest soon, I'll be of no use to any army.*

Joseph, weary beyond reckoning, had watched the encounter between General Van Dorn and Colonel Greer as well. He felt momentarily flummoxed watching the stream of worn-out Missouri Guard soldiers, most of them wearing filthy cotton uniforms. He watched the defeated men flowing out in wild fashion, channeling down the muddy roads or fanning out into the trees. Hollering, huffing, out of breath, trotting, then running, crowding together like sheep.

Officers shouted demands, vainly attempting to maintain a semblance of order. Then came some of the wounded who were able to walk, leaning on the arms of anxious comrades. It was as close to a rout as he could imagine.

He rose slowly, grabbed his revolvers from his horse's saddlebags. He was beginning to understand that, somehow, despite having greater numbers and the element of surprise, the Rebels had been defeated, which meant the Federal army would be storming through exactly where he stood in moments.

When Colonel Lane gave the orders to prepare for battle, Joseph began to devise his own plan. He backed slowly away. The strategy came to him almost in slow, dream-like visions, but fully realized, as if his current nightmare of existence was turning into a glorious life of ease. He would slip away and return to Sara. *No, wait! Return to my wife, Cyntha.*

He looked down at his shaking hands. The only woman he could think of was Sara. Could he find her and convince her to come with him north? But what of his wife? He wanted to find her, to embrace her, to return with her to their farm and the life they once had. The amnesia had not only stolen his memory. *My forgetting everything that mattered has taken away my common sense.*

After he had backed in amongst vine-woven bushes, he wondered what to do with his hands, for he did not want to be holding a weapon. He was unsure if he would have to shoot someone to keep from being killed. A forlorn-looking Rebel, his uniform muddy from collar to cuff, shuffled by him. Almost unaware of his own actions, Joseph offered his mare to the man, who took it joyfully and rode away.

Joseph faded farther into the shadows of abundant, skinny trees. He would wait until the Yankees arrived and then surrender to them and offer his story of amnesia to any officer who was hopefully willing to listen. He had inadvertently been a traitor to the United States army. Now, he was a traitor to the Confederate army. Would he be strung up as a turncoat by either side? His mind ran back and forth between hope and doubt.

Several yards away, Paul had dismounted and was peering out from behind a stout oak, his mount's reins held tight in one fist, his pistol aimed out toward where the Federals would surely be advancing. He caught sight of Joseph backing into the grove nearer to the tavern, and he wondered what the corporal was doing. After a moment of observing him, he realized that Joseph had decided to surrender. *What goes through a man's head and through his heart when he grows tired of fighting? Has Favor fought too much and too long? Is his will even to survive gone? If he surrenders, his fiancée will never find him.*

He pursed his lips, considering that his fortunes might have changed. *I can't get killed. That's what's most important now. Then we'll see what happens.*

He looked down at the short row of a dozen soldiers, their various rifles and shotguns shouldered, crouching in a ditch some twenty yards in front of the main line of the Third Texas. Those soldiers would feel the initial brunt of the Federal forces. Among those lying in the ditch and watching for the blue line to begin its assault was Ebie Dollander. He had a shotgun held tight against his shoulder. His saber lay at his side.

Joseph saw Ebie and wished to bid him farewell, but instead slunk farther into shadows.

Neither he, nor Paul, had any more time to ponder their futures, for the onslaught of blue swept out from Elkhorn Tavern, their yells strong and guttural, roaring like an avalanche.

The little line of Texans, Kansans, Arkansans, and one Englishman in the ditch opened fire first, dropping about a dozen Federals. The Federals faltered for a moment, then, raging even louder, they charged again. There was no time for the little advance group to fall back. Joseph watched Ebie rise and run from the mass of Yankees, waving his saber in the air. The immense wave of deep cobalt uniforms, not men—a total killing machine—washed over where Ebie had been. In the smothering smoke, he could see little of the struggle of blue against gray and could only hope that Ebie had survived. He figured that his friend had not.

Paul fired at the wall of blue until both revolvers were emptied, then he took his boot gun and emptied it. The rest of the Third Texas poured lead into the oncoming Yankees. The attacking line faltered, and the tide of blue receded.

The retreating Yankees continued to turn and shoot. Angry hornet bullets zipped past Paul's head. He ducked behind the trees and began reloading his revolvers.

After the Union soldiers had retreated as far as the tavern, Colonel Lane commanded in his Irish accent, "Fall back! Aye! We've held 'em for now, we have. A hundred yards further back, and we'll set a new line."

Paul gathered his horse's reins and mounted. He did not look back to see what happened to Joseph. He could no longer care. Ebie lay in a ditch, unconscious, with a gaping hole in his shoulder blade. He was not moving.

TWENTY

THE TEMPEST OF BATTLE

MARCH 8,1862, 11:00 A.M.
ELKHORN TAVERN, ARKANSAS

From the advent of the morning's conflict, Anthony and Jeanette had stayed in the upstairs of the tavern despite it shaking to its core with the concussive roar of cannons. The battle rolled across the fields and forest and stretched from the tavern yard to beyond the jumbled granite rocks below the escarpment of Big Mountain. With no wind, the smoke draped like a new fog everywhere.

When the Rebels began pulling back from their positions, Anthony and Jeanette slipped out cautiously onto the balcony of the tavern and stood behind a sturdy wooden parapet that the Confederates had constructed there from split timbers. Everyone else was inside with the wounded and the surgeons and nurses.

Both Anthony and his wife had developed a devil-may-care attitude toward the battle. No matter where they stood or hid, a bullet or canister from a cannon shell could have found them. One place was as good as another. They had become dulled to the peril.

As long as they ducked down behind the parapet, it protected them from errant gunfire and afforded them a view of a hundred or so Federal soldiers who had rushed well ahead of the main force into the yard and intermingled with handfuls of Rebel soldiers with minor wounds, but who could not flee. Those Rebels were surrendering, despite some pushing and scuffling and grappling for rifles. A few shots rang out. One Rebel, trying to run, was shot in the back and fell dead. The remaining thousands of fleeing Confederates seemed like party revelers exiting a barn dance, suddenly aware they had stayed past their curfew.

Anthony and Jeanette were appalled to see the entire area littered with dead or dying men and carcasses of mules and horses. The wounded soldiers called in anguish for water, or yelled prayers, or cursed, or lamented that they could not be with their mothers or sisters or brides.

The earlier deafening roar of battle had faded in leveled steps, from thunderous to loud, then to bothersome, then to the sounds of a few loud pops and neighs of horses, to a clatter of accoutrements and tromp of shoes, and finally to almost a vacuous whisper. The majority of General Curtis's attacking troops had halted just beyond the tavern yard in a long undulating line astride the Telegraph Road. Their guns aimed at the forest north of the tavern, they knelt or hunched over, hesitating, peering into the shadowy, almost leafless trees, waiting for Confederates to pour out of that gloom in a countercharge.

After several minutes, the officers ordered the troops forward, and the triumphant Yankees flooded into the tavern yard where once the Confederates had camped. They thronged together in groups, then broke away to join new groups, hugging, running and jumping, an azure sea, ebbing back and forth. Dead and wounded Confederates lay strewn in the yard, left behind by their comrades. A few Rebel nurses were attempting to aid them.

Federal officers danced their horses in the middle of the great throng, shouting orders to gather the wounded or tossing conflicting directions for where to take prisoners. The few hundred weary, captured Confederates seemed almost glad to be taken captive. Anthony and Jeanette heard several of them pleading for something to eat.

The entire Federal army burst into enthusiastic shouts and songs, surprised that they had won the battle. They tossed their caps and fired their rifles into the air. Their jubilant voices resounded like waves crashing against rocks.

After the celebration subsided, the officers formed the men into a battle line to pursue the retreating Confederates. The soldiers then charged at the trees below the tavern, only to be met with considerable gunfire. They halted and retreated to await new orders. In short order, they were celebrating again, despite the admonitions of their officers.

"The wounded will still need our help, dear husband," Jeanette shouted over the clamor.

"Yes, Jeanette."

They went inside where the Cox family huddled on the bedroom floor, the small ones whimpering. The beds had no sheets, coverlets, or mattresses. The doors of the armoires had been wrenched off by soldiers to be used as stretchers. The armoires stood empty, every piece of clothing taken and torn for binding wounds.

The little Cox boy said, "I want the shooting to stop." He batted his ears with his fists.

Mrs. Cox stroked his hair. "I think the battle is over ... at least for a while."

Downstairs, Cyntha and Sara had huddled together in the kitchen during the morning's fight. They rose and peered cautiously out the shattered window at the Yankees. Cyntha felt relief that the Union soldiers had turned the battle in their favor. Sara felt dismay and sorrow.

They turned from the window and surveyed the tavern's disarray, the walls riddled with holes. Throughout the morning, surgeons and nurses from both armies had worked side by side in the tavern and in the hospital tent. Chloroform and even whiskey had run out, so the soldiers' moans had increased to screams of agony.

A solitary Yankee fiddler stepped up on a chair on the porch and played "The Arkansas Traveler." It could barely be heard above the din of the celebrating soldiers.

Cyntha said to Sara, "It's so odd how soldiers labor so hard to kill each other, then men from both sides work together to help the wounded. And the ones still alive try to cover over the horror with a fiddle tune."

TWENTY-ONE

WAR AND RUMORS

MARCH 8, 1862, MID-AFTERNOON
WASHINGTON, DC

President Lincoln stood in the War Department second floor telegraph room. It was still being outfitted with desks and wiring, but a handful of telegraph keys were singing. He perused messages from Hampton Roads, shaking his head. "I'll take a walk." He set his stovepipe hat on his head and his shawl around his shoulders and ventured out onto the War Department building steps.

Taking a deep breath of chilly air, President Lincoln was acutely aware of the universal angst of the populace of Washington that had grown in recent days with rumors of the launch of the metal Confederate gunship. It was a monster clad with iron that made it impervious to cannon fire. This day, the ironclad had attacked and almost destroyed the Union's wooden blockade vessels at the James River.

The gunboat's title, "Virginia," was on most people's lips, for everyone knew its name. It was sure to be churning up Chesapeake Bay, then traversing the Potomac River unencumbered, and would soon be shelling Washington, DC without fear of retribution.

"Perhaps," President Lincoln mumbled, "that Secretary Stanton was right when he said he expected the Virginia to toss a cannonball through the walls of his department."

Word had spread like chaff in a blustery wind about the Confederate ironclad ram demolishing the Union fleet at Hampton Roads. The news flew first by courier, and then by telegraph keys, to newspaper offices as well as to the War Department. The newspapers were already setting type for headlines proclaiming terror and destruction.

On the steps, the president heard a soldier jawing with his cohorts. "No one is safe! That ship is indestructible and will destroy us all."

"We should be stretching a great chain across the river," another soldier railed, then seeing President Lincoln, said, "like they done in the Revolutionary War."

President Lincoln attempted a smile. The soldiers darted down the steps and blended into the crowd.

Leaning against a pillar, President Lincoln watched the flow of the brutal crowds in the street that stretched from the Executive Mansion to the War Department. Several individuals wove back and forth on the walkway, carrying placards denouncing the war. Their zeal for peace felt ironic to President Lincoln in the manner in which they hoisted the signs and violently shook their fists.

Many civilians had packed up belongings in barrows and were pushing the carts through the streets with the fervor of people with death on their tails.

President Lincoln occasionally spoke quips of his folksy humor to those civilians who recognized him and cared to listen. He waved and smiled at the pedestrians despite them frowning at him or even making untoward gestures with their arms. At last, his loyalty to the people had to make way for him to meet with his generals. He walked somberly to the Executive Mansion.

He, the presider of the faltering nation, had scheduled a meeting at four o'clock with all the Army of the Potomac lead officers to discuss the Urbanna Landing strategy that had been designed to assault Confederate General Joe Johnson's army, who remained in force a few miles outside Washington. He was concerned that General McClellan was too reticent and hoped to inspire him to march his army out to crush the rebellion.

When evening came around, the whole city seemed in anguish, as if the inhabitants had nothing else to concern them. The Virginia ironclad had sunk one ship, caused a second to burn, forced the grounding of a third, and chased off the remainder of the fleet that had been blockading the James River at Hampton Roads. When evening drew nigh, the Virginia had slunk back up the James River to be loaded with more cannonballs to return the next day and finish off any remaining wooden ships that dared confront her.

North of Washington by a mile, in Fort Massachusetts, an officious colonel had detained Lucas Reeder and Dred Workman, keeping them from entering the nation's capital.

Lucas and Workman listened to the scuttlebutt of the fort's garrison that ranged from despair to anger. The two friends sat on wooden boxes playing Quist while a guard lazed near them. Lucas knew they might pull off an escape, but the likelihood of a search party pursuing and catching them was not to his liking. Workman and he would have to wait to enter Washington.

TWENTY-TWO

To Punish the Innocent

MARCH 9, 1862, 3:00 P.M.
UNION CAMP, CROSS HOLLOWS, ARKANSAS

J oseph felt unsure of how his surrender to the Union forces
would be taken. He was being marched up to a lieutenant
seated at camp table in a cove of white oaks at Cross Hollows.
His hopes bore on the desire that every officer immediately take
his story to heart with beaming smiles and vigorous goodwill slaps
on the back and let him re-enlist. Like the other Confederates, he
looked wan and used up, like a vagabond in some land of dust,
for he had not eaten a meal in two days, nor slept more than a
few hours.

The lieutenant was scratching out orders on foolscap with pen
and ink. Joseph saw a long column of numbers, seemingly bereft
of meaning. Behind the lieutenant's station, a pack of long-eared
hunting dogs dozed together.

A sergeant whose dour expression was like that of a funeral
mourner pushed Joseph with violent jolts, keeping a revolver
trained on Joseph's ribs. "Move on, ingrate."

They stopped before the table.

The lieutenant looked up at the saluting sergeant. "What have
we here, Holcomb?"

Cuffing Joseph in the back of the head, the sergeant barked, "Lieutenant Peters, this one's got an odd story. He's been spoutin' it ever since we captured 'im. Got me vexed. He's talkin' a down south accent, and I'm havin' a hard time believin' 'im, but he's insistin' his story's true. Personally, I think he's endeavorin' to avoid imprisonment like all them other traitor curs." He thumbed over his shoulder to the hundreds of Confederate prisoners forty yards away.

Lieutenant Peters, who looked about the same age as Joseph, had a curl to his lip that gave him a permanent snarl. Joseph figured the portion of the man's lip had been sliced at some point in his life, leaving it misshapen. The officer's eyes were bloodshot, and his hair was greased with a pungent pomade, and he smelled like horse manure. Joseph glanced at the lieutenant's attire. Horse shit covered his boots.

The lieutenant pulled a half a cigar from a vest pocket. He lit it and blew the smoke into Joseph's face. He snickered when Joseph coughed. "What's your story, Secesh? I could use a good laugh."

Standing tall, Joseph said, "Yes, sir. Like I told Sergeant Holcomb. I'm really a First Iowa Volunteer. I'm Union. I enlisted and trained at Camp Keokuk. In July of sixty-one, I sailed with my regiment on the Leona Belle steamship down to St. Louis. We disembarked, and ..."

"I don't know why you're telling me this, Sesech."

"I'm not a Sesech. I support the northern cause."

The lieutenant blew more smoke in Joseph's face. "Continue, Sesech. If your story's good enough, maybe we won't hang you today."

Joseph cleared his throat. Before speaking, he thought, *Do they really mean to hang all the hundreds of us?* "Sir, I served in the First Iowa Volunteers. I fought in the battle of Wilson Creek."

"Our Union brothers lost that battle. Was that your fault?" The lieutenant stood, sneered, and chomped on his cigar. His face was inches from Joseph's.

"No, sir, what happened was..."

Peters blew smoke rings into the blue late afternoon sky, then winked at Joseph and sat again on his camp chair. The temperature had warmed from the previous day. Melting ice from the trees dripped in slow motion, tapping the trails of leaves. Joseph's heart pounded.

The sergeant swatted Joseph's back. "Continue."

"Sir." Joseph straightened. "In the battle, I was knocked unconscious. When I came to, I couldn't remember anything, not even my name."

"But you remember it now, huh? What's your name?"

"Joseph Favor. If you look on the original roles of the First Iowa, you'll see my name. Colonel Merritt was our regimental commander."

The lieutenant leaned forward over the clumsy table. "You could have made up that story by reading the letter of some poor dead Iowan soldier. You probably *did read* some man's letter to his beloved wife. Made it all up, like some tale from the Arabian Nights."

"No, sir. I've got a wife. I would never steal a man's private correspondence."

"And...?"

Joseph stammered; unsure what Peters wanted him to say. "Everyone who helped me recover from my head injury kept telling me I was a Confederate. One soldier I had known before my head injury told me my name and swore that I was a Rebel."

"How'd he know your name?"

"Well, that, sir, is why I remained so confused, until my memory started coming back in the last few days." He drew a deep breath. "The man who told me my name had been a soldier in the First Iowa, too, but he deserted and became a nurse for..."

Lieutenant Peters burst out laughing. "Now I've heard it all." Sergeant Holcomb and he both chortled for about a minute, the sergeant slapping his thigh with his free hand.

"So," the lieutenant continued, "the traitor fooled you into thinking you're a Rebel, and you believed him. You expect us to swallow that?"

"Sir," Joseph pleaded. "I had no memory at all. Not a stitch. It was a cruel trick he played, and I hope to get even with him."

"Take the liar away, Sergeant Holcomb." The sergeant began pulling Joseph's arm.

"Wait!" Joseph called. "I can tell you regimental information, officers names and ranks, their tactics, and...." He yanked his arm from the man's grasp, but the sergeant grabbed it again.

"And so can every other Southern traitor dog who killed our dear brothers in arms. And they'll do it for just a plate of beans. Goodbye, Sesech. I hope you rot in hell."

"Wait!" Joseph freed himself from the sergeant's grasp. "What if I become a spy. I have a southern accent. I know so much, I could easily infiltrate and ..."

"You know, if a spy gets caught, he gets hung." The lieutenant stubbed out the cigar on his boot.

The sergeant took a vice-like grip on Joseph's arm.

Lieutenant Peters beckoned a private who stood nearby. "Go tell Colonel Dodge some of this story and see if he wants, or even needs, a spy."

The private hurried away. Lieutenant Peters lifted his filthy boots onto the little desk and leaned back in his camp chair. He gathered up his papers and seemed content in perusing them. The sergeant kept his revolver shoved against Joseph's side.

Joseph had no idea why he had said he would be a spy. He abruptly lost feeling in his hands and feet and felt like he could swoon. Taking some deep breaths, he reminded himself that he had faced death when charging General Sigel's Union Cavalry, but this situation seemed more deadly.

Directly, a couple of Federals gathered up the ropes of the hunting dogs and trotted the gangly bunch of hounds, their floppy ears slapping on the ground, in amongst the Confederate captives. Each hound sniffed each prisoner. Joseph figured escape would be impossible. He got an impression in his mind's eye of the White soldiers being pursued by the dogs and armed men like the mobs that hunted down runaway slaves.

The lieutenant set his feet down and tossed his papers on the desk. "Do you know why I'm serving in this position, Sesech?"

Joseph raised his eyes. "I'm not a Sesech. I'm for the Union. I want the Negro to be freed."

The lieutenant rolled his eyes. "The Negras ain't nothing but contraband. Spoils of war. So, you might as well forget about that."

Joseph gulped, restraining himself from the error of commenting.

"The reason I'm sitting here," the lieutenant stated, "is because our captain got killed trying to preserve the Union. I've been promoted to fill his position. Promotion because of his death. And death like his is everywhere. Out yonder on that battlefield." He pointed north toward Elkhorn Tavern. "You can smell it this far away. The foul odor drifts on the air and sticks in your nostrils until you're ready to vomit. The captain and the other poor bastards did the best they could for the country they love. Some Sesech traitor's bullet killed them. Maybe you killed some."

Joseph found it hard to breathe, like the air in the cove of trees had been sucked away.

The private returned and saluted. "Colonel Dodge says he has no time for such foolishness. He's dealing with his own wounds, and he echoes what General Curtis demands—that all Rebs be treated as treacherous dogs."

In short order, Joseph was brought to a long line of seated Confederate prisoners. The sergeant tied his hands loosely with hemp robe and made him sit at the end of the line. A few Federal guards stood nearby, nervous and wary. The two hundred Rebel soldiers, mostly Missourians, all with their wrists tied haphazardly, looked as though they had lost not just a battle, but their best friends.

Joseph took a moment to study the faces of the men near him. Each man had dark circles under his eyes, each one's face was black with grime and gunpowder, even down in the wrinkles in their brows, the eyelids raw-looking; and their expressions all bore a sort of surprised dismay. Like Joseph, they would be tied together like common farm animals and forced to walk to some Northern prison in Rolla or St. Louis. Whether they would survive or not was a gamble.

A group sat in a circle like they were playing cards, talking in hushed tones, mostly griping about their hunger.

An almost toothless fellow gnawed on some hardtack, holding it with his bound hands.

"I could go for a plate of beans and some cornbread right now," a young fellow with his head wrapped in a bloody kerchief called out to the guards.

They ignored him.

A wizened codger with a long nose had an appearance akin to a gray marsh crane. He was standing with one leg raised and was looking down at the youth like he was searching a stream for a fish. "Some o' our boys, when they was marchin' yestaday, came upon a hog, killed it, butchered it, and ate it raw, chewin' on it while they marched. It's a shame them officers didn't see fit to feed us right."

Joseph turned his head and stared at the ground. Out of the corner of his eye, he noticed that the man next to him, who was twice Joseph's size, had managed to remove the bindings from his wrists. The soldier said, "You the one that told them Bluecoats that you was a Yank?"

Without thinking, Joseph blurted, "Yes, I should be fighting to preserve the Union."

The huge man said no word, but bear-pawed Joseph square in the face, flattening him. The man leapt astride Joseph and began pummeling his face. Joseph could barely thrust up his arms to fend off the attack. "Filthy Yank," the brute yelled with each iron-fisted blow.

Joseph was soon being kicked in his ribs and legs by the other men, who possessed enough latitude to move. They kept booting him as if he was their only chance to avenge their guilt and sorrow for losing the battle. Blackness enveloped his mind.

⚭

When Joseph awoke, he lay on a cot in a tent. He felt excruciating pain across his face and the top of his head. He lightly touched his cheeks with swollen fingers. It seemed to him like his head had puffed up to the size of a melon. A young man came forward, his apron bloody red, and daubed salve on Joseph's face. "Ah, you're awake," he said. "You still might die."

Joseph cringed. His head felt like it was on fire.

"Here, drink this." The nurse poured a sweet liquid down Joseph's throat.

Joseph began feeling fuzzy and tired, then sleep overtook him.

When he awoke again, he saw through filmy eyes a sincere-looking bearded colonel seated by his bed, his dark blue jacket hung open over a bare chest, revealing the wide dressings of a bullet wound in his side. His hand bore a bloody bandage as well. He smiled generously at Joseph. Behind him, a tall, gray-whiskered general stood, nose in the air. His bald pate gleamed in the lantern light.

"Is this the one?" the seated officer whispered to someone. Joseph glanced around to see that many soldiers, both in blue and gray, lay shoulder to shoulder in the crowded tent.

The officer took off his hat and moved his stool closer to Joseph's cot. "You took quite a beating, soldier."

Joseph had no spit in his mouth, his tongue engorged. He managed a nod and closed his swollen eyes.

"My name is Colonel Grenville Dodge. The officer behind me is General Samuel Curtis, commander."

Joseph glanced at the general and attempted a weak salute, then closed his eyes. General Curtis did not respond.

"Sergeant Holcomb," Colonel Dodge continued, "tells me you're a Union man from Iowa."

Joseph fully expected the man to burst into laughter, but he did not. When Joseph opened his eyes again, the colonel was still there. He said, "Sergeant Holcomb says you were beaten because you want to fight for the Union."

Joseph coughed and nodded.

"He said you want to be a spy for the Union."

With no means to utter even a syllable, Joseph wondered where the man was going with his remarks. Colonel Dodge patted Joseph's arm and turned to General Curtis. "He's told several officers he's fighting to free the slaves. Does he meet with your approval, sir?"

"I appreciate his sentiment to free the coloreds. I can't say that he does not meet with my approval. It is your decision, Dodge. And stop referring to yourself as a colonel. You've been promoted to brigadier general." General Curtis replaced his hat. "You've got other things to attend to than this confused reprobate." He departed in a huff.

∞

A week later, Joseph was dressed in a spanking new Union uniform, his ribs wrapped in tight bindings under his shirt and jacket, his face splotched with green and yellow bruises and one eye still partially swollen shut. He sat in front of Brigadier General Dodge, who was explaining how he had verified that Joseph had been in the First Iowa Volunteers, and that he was sending him north to speak with General Henry Halleck in St. Louis.

"You'll not be speaking directly with 'Old Brains,' for he is a military mastermind," General Dodge said, "but you're going to St. Louis where you will speak with one of his staff."

"Yes, sir. Thank you."

"Are you sure you want to serve as a spy for the Union?" The general peered over his glasses.

"Yes, I believe I can be of service. But, if I may, could I return to Iowa for a short time to visit my wife? If what you tell me in Colonel Merritt's report is that he listed me as dead, then she needs to know the truth. To see me alive."

"I'm afraid that is not possible. Matters now are urgent. Our armies east of the Mississippi in Tennessee are on the move. Since you are originally from that state, you may be of some assistance there. We have made efforts to contact your wife at the address you gave us."

"What efforts?"

"Considerable efforts." General Dodge gave a deep sigh and looked down at papers on his desk. "For now, you must trust me and do your duty. Prepare to travel. You will go with the Fourth Missouri in a wagon train to St. Louis."

"Yes, but…"

"Private Favor. We don't have time for further discourse. The Fourth Missouri leaves within the hour."

TWENTY-THREE

FIAT JUSTITIA, PEREAT COELUOS—LET JUSTICE BE DONE, THOUGH HEAVENS FALL
– JOHN ADAMS

MARCH 11,1862, 6:00 P.M.
MRS. CLEGG'S BOARDING HOUSE, FREDERICKTOWN, OHIO

John Coincoin was covered with sweat, his threadbare shirt clinging to his black skin. He had worked hard the entire day, cleaning the chimneys, then chopping firewood and stacking it by each of the fireplaces in the inn.

The owner of the inn, Mrs. Clegg, threatened to fire him twice for not performing a complex task quick enough. She was wont to repeat daily, "Slowest nigger I ever saw!"

John's son, James, was ill with a fever, so his daughters, who generally worked for free at the inn, stayed at home to care for their brother. Not having the extra unpaid help bothered Mrs. Clegg to no end. In her opinion, John's wife could not cook and serve the guests fast enough. Mrs. Clegg stayed in a tither the entire day.

John kept his thoughts to himself. *Sure. I been a runaway slave, but this is supposed to be a free state. Should be treated equal.*

After John made his rounds to douse the lamps, trim the candles, sweep the inn floor and porch, attend to travelers' horses, grease the owner's carriage's wheels, and a myriad other duties, he trod up the stairs at about eight in the evening to his little storage closet to clean up before going home to his family. When he opened the door, Maggie Fox stood with her back facing him.

She turned, her hands clasped behind her, and took on an almost violent demeanor. "How dare you enter without knocking!"

"I'm sorry, ma'am. This is my work closet. I store my tools, my axe, my things in here so as to be out of the way of guests."

"Well, don't let it happen again!" She stormed past John, her hands switched quickly in front of her, stumbling, and reeking of alcohol. She weaved her way to her room where her sisters were asleep.

After breakfast the next day, Mrs. Clegg went to the bank. When the boarding house guests departed, John helped the guests into their carriages, or saddled the horses for those who rode. He was glad to see the Fox sisters leave in a rented carriage with a hired driver.

Mrs. Clegg returned from the bank and placed several dollars in John's hands. "That's for you and your wife's good work. Now get busy cleaning the rooms."

"Yes 'm."

Later, John counted the money. It was two dollars short of the usual pay. "Can't say nothin'. I'm fortunate to have a job." He went upstairs to his tools closet. He bent down by a loose floorboard, lifted it and pulled out a cotton pouch to place the dollars in it. When he opened the pouch, he discovered it was empty. "Them sisters took my savings. My, Lord. Whatever shall I do?"

John was furious. He knew one of the Fox sisters, probably Maggie, had absconded with his life savings, and he was going to get it back. He punched a wall. Justice would be done.

They had not traveled by train; the younger sisters were too much afraid of riding on an iron horse. They were headed to Columbus to put on their show. He had heard Leah bragging about the expected "take" at the séance. If he rode his horse, the one given him by Paul McGavin, he might catch up with the carriage before it reached Columbus.

He was unsure how he would be able to wrest his funds from them, but he felt he had to try. He told his wife to explain to Mrs. Clegg that he had a fever, and that James, his son, would cover for him. Their house lay out of town, over half a mile from the inn, so he knew the owner would not come out that far to inspect his story.

"I don't know, John," Mrs. Coincoin said, "if'n they finds we lyin' to her, she likely to fetch a switch on us, or worse, fire us. Then where we be?"

"If we don't get that money back," John responded, "we be penniless anyway."

Mrs. Coincoin acquiesced.

The next morning, the stars still shining, he left their simple house. John knew they could lose everything, including the house. It all depended on his catching up to the carriage. He galloped his horse down the road to Columbus.

∞

A week later, John stared at a poster advertising the Fox Sisters forthcoming séance event. He saw the posters posted on a number of wooden fences advertising their séance for the crowds. Asking a kindly Negro woman where the sisters were staying, she told him. He located the hotel, went inside, and marched up to the check-in desk, holding an envelope he had sealed; and he declared to the clerk that he had to deliver the message personally. The clerk argued that he could not allow an unknown man up to their room, but John pleaded his story of life and death so well, the clerk relented and told him the room number.

John clambered up to the third floor, located the room, and knocked loudly on the door. No one answered. To his amazement, when he shoved on the door, it was unlocked. He inched inside. The ladies' trunks sat on the floor. Various garments lay on the beds. Frilly hats perched on the dressers like exotic birds. The room was outfitted with lace curtains, and the bedspreads and rugs were all of finest material. *Only the best for the rich!* John was livid at how they had so much wealth, and yet one of them still found it necessary to steal from him.

He carefully searched the room for his money. When he opened the armoire, filled with more dresses, scarves, and undergarments, he spied on the top shelf a metal box with a curved lid. He brought it down. A padlock held the latch shut. Shaking it, he heard the sound of coins banging. He unsheathed his hunting knife, but before he could pry the box open, he heard steps coming up the stairs.

He slid the box back in place, closed the armoire doors, and slipped out into the hall. He hid behind a tall urn that was festooned with flowing ferns. The Fox sisters arrived at the top of the stairs, chatting and laughing.

When Leah reached her key to the keyhole, she saw the door ajar. She burst into the room, followed by Maggie and Kate. "Maggie, did you not lock the door?" Leah screamed. "You were last out! You dimwitted idiot!"

Maggie shrank back from the shrill accusation of her sister. Leah rushed to the armoire, threw open the doors and checked the money box, pushing on it to feel its weight. Satisfied that it was still there and locked, she turned to her sister. "My dear sisters, we have much to lose. When we get to Cincinnati, I shall send our earnings to our bank in New York."

Maggie plopped on the bed. "I have a headache. I need a drink."

Her sisters ignored her while she groaned and laid her forearm across her forehead.

"I work the hardest, and all I get is grief from you, Leah," Maggie moaned.

Leah continued to pay no attention to her noisy sister. She did not notice that John had sneaked to their door and peered through the keyhole at them. He watched Leah pull wads of cash and handfuls of coins from her dress pockets. John wondered how she could walk with all that weight in her dress. He chuckled at the thought of Leah waddling along.

Leah turned in a rage. "Is someone at the door? Kate, check it!"

By the time Kate opened the door, John had disappeared down the stairs.

After seeing the Fox sisters' cash chest, John no longer desired just the return of the money they stole from him. He planned to even things out. The next day, he sent a message with a freeman who was traveling to Fredericktown to give to his wife. The note explained that she was to continue the false story of his illness to Mrs. Clegg, and make sure James and all their children were particularly solicitous to the owner. He added that she should explain that because of his being sick Mrs. Clegg could half his wages for the month when he returned.

If his plan to follow them to Cincinnati worked, it would not matter if the woman fired them.

TWENTY-FOUR

THE ADVENT OF THE STRATEGY FOR VENGEANCE AND PEACE

MARCH 12, 1862, 10:00 A.M.
WASHINGTON, DC

D red Workman, resplendent in the Union corporal's uniform he had stolen, drove the carriage bearing Major Lucas Reeder down the muddy nation's capital's avenues. Leaning against his knee was a special rifle, cased in a cloth pouch, that he had won in a card game with a drunken soldier. He felt proud to have it.

Considering what he saw in the city, he grimaced. Unaccustomed to the crowded nature of large cities, he felt that people in metropolises had generally lost their moorings on life.

He watched the citizens rushing along the boardwalks, the men in tall top hats, shiny coats and vests, with watch fobs slung from their pockets. The women wore frilly bonnets and blue or green or maroon dresses, spread wide with hoops. Their lace collars covered their necks, and their dresses were of finest fabric. Blue-coated soldiers paced rapidly along the boardwalks as if they had no other purpose in life but to hurry.

In contrast, huddled under store awnings and in alley shadows, listless negro families stood in pitiful, threadbare clothes. Their eyes stared blankly out of their dark faces. Workman reflected on their plight. *Most likely runaways. Came to this hellhole lookin' for freedom. City life is a poor excuse for living.*

The dichotomy of the races wore on him. "Some of the Yanks want to free the Negra," he muttered to himself, "but they ain't got no plan to deal with 'em. And I wonder what these rich and uppity sorts feel since they're spared from the real war. The poor farmers 'round Wilson Creek, Missouri knows what war is."

The carriage wrought its way along the mud-slogged street.

"What street we on?" he asked through his bushy mustache. He clucked at the pair of horses, struggling, lifting their mud-covered legs high out of the sludge of the road.

Lucas Reeder sat in the rear seat of the buggy. He held up his ear trumpet. "Say again."

"What street we on?" Workman stretched his long arm and pointed in a sweeping motion.

"The sign back there said Fifteenth Street. It heads down toward the canal by the Washington Mall. Why do you ask?" Lucas wore his major's dress uniform, no sword, but his broad-brimmed hat perched dapper-tilted on his head. He had shaved his face, all but his mustache and sideburns. Over his uniform, he wore a recently issued greatcoat that Workman had managed to steal.

Lucas's face was pinched, and he nervously glanced at any Union officer along the avenue. The outskirts' guards they had encountered coming into Washington from the north gave them no trouble. The pickets were fine with the document Lucas had forged. But the three-day delay at Fort Massachusetts had made him expressly worried. No matter how much he told them of his exploits in the battles of the War with Mexico, the officers who questioned them would not budge. *How much interrogation will we face, trying to even get close to Lincoln?* Ultimately, the fort's colonel allowed them to proceed into the city.

"I just was wonderin'," Workman said, pointing again at various edifices, "'bout all these scantily clad women, hangin' on the doorsteps of some of these houses. I think they'd feel cold in this frigid weather, but I'm thinkin' maybe they're sellin' somethin' they ought'n."

"Yes, I've noticed them, too. We've arrived at one of the working girls' creative arts section of town."

Lucas and Workman had heard plenty of stories in Fort Massachusetts that the red-lantern districts in the city and in its outskirts were flourishing. Workman nodded toward a soldier sneaking up the steps of one house where three women welcomed him overly much and ushered him inside. "The business goes on, despite the war."

He slowed the carriage to allow a squad of soldiers to march past. They were followed by a long line of Negro workers in crude attire, carrying shovels on their shoulders.

"So, all the Negro slaves who've escaped work on the plantations." Lucas's tone was bitter. "Are put to work shoveling the dirt and piling rocks for the rifle pits and foundations of all these forts. What freedom have they obtained?"

He had daily reprimanded himself for letting his former slave and best friend, Abram, go free. Was the old family servant and dear friend even alive?

After they had traveled a few more blocks, Workman announced, "What is that smell?" He covered his nose.

Lucas put a hand to his nose. "It's the canal. Today's newspaper has an article about it. Says an engineer has been hired to deal with the refuse problem. The article explains that it is disease-filled, and it may be the blame for the death of Lincoln's son, Willie. The headline calls it a blight on the city. It was originally supposed to bring commerce up from the Potomac. Now it's a garbage dump."

Workman drew up the carriage again to allow a peddler to push his cart slowly through the muddy street.

"Just a little farther, Dred," Lucas said. "I want to see the monument they're constructing to honor George Washington. It's up ahead." The partially completed monolith rose above the trees at the south end of the mall. "Then we'll find quarters and settle in." He lowered his voice to a whisper. "If we are to eliminate that foul Lincoln, we best have someplace quiet, yet close to the President's Mansion."

At length, Workman stopped at a spot near the sludgy canal, across from the Washington monument. Hundreds of cattle grazed on piles of hay strewn about the extensive mall lawn. Two herders stood nearby, and a handful of soldiers leaned on their rifles. Lucas got out and strode forward a few paces. In silence, he surveyed the monument for several minutes.

"I wish I'd met him," he called over his shoulder to Workman. "Washington was the best kind of dreamer. He saw a great nation could be crafted, and he had the wherewithal to see it through."

He stood with his hands clasped behind his back, silent for a long while.

Finally, he returned to the carriage and got inside. "We need to put this country back together."

Workman tapped at an advertisement in the Washington Post. "Found us an apartment, just off Pennsylvania Avenue. Hefty deposit, but says it desires only military or government people. I'm sure we can make up a good story'll satisfy 'em."

"Yes, the deposit will be fine. I doubt we'll have to pay a second month's rent. Hopefully, our task will be done within the month."

Workman turned the carriage around, and they headed back past the Capitol and then toward the President's Mansion. The capital's streets were crowded with throngs of people, all manner of wagons, carriages and carts. The going was slow.

When they arrived at the address of the apartment listed in the advertisement, Lucas was appalled at the perilous lean of the two-story structure. Despite that, a line of would-be renters was lined up off the porch, shivering in the chilly, early spring. "Well, I guess this might do for the short time we're here." Lucas stepped down from the carriage and took a place in line. Workman stayed in the carriage, poring over the newspaper.

Presently, a dowdy woman stepped out from the front door. She was short, pale, and gray-haired and had a scowl pasted on her face. Her dress was covered in grime, and, under her dress, her old breasts hung down toward her stomach. An olive-drab shawl draped across her shoulders. She cast her eyes on each man in the line, looking them up and down. Three of the men were well-dressed, a fourth wore overalls, and the one in front of Lucas wore a lieutenant's uniform.

She swirled around and pointed at the man in overalls.

"You, leave."

He plodded off the porch, his head down.

She dispatched the remaining civilians in similar fashion. One portly fellow tried to speak, then threw up his hands. Leaving, he displayed an offensive arm gesture at her, turned, and slogged down the muddy avenue. She yelled after him, "You'd eat too much. Get ya gone."

She came to the lieutenant. "What's your story?"

"Yes, ma'am. I have the deposit. I want to rent the apartment for myself and my new bride. I've been given a one-month furlough, and..."

"Lord o' mercy. I'd never get any sleep. With the wailin' and the moanin' and the rockin' of the bed all night long from newlyweds, then the fights which always come along. Get ya gone." Turning her back on him, she thumbed over her shoulder, and the lieutenant hurried away.

She moseyed up to Lucas.

"Hello, ma'am. My name is Major Lucas Reeder. My aide is Corporal Dred Workman. We wish to rent the room." He held his trumpet to his ear to hear her response above the clatter of the street noise.

"Just one bed. You mind sharin' it? There is a divan though."

"Don't mind. We'll make arrangements."

"Now, answer my big question. Why ain't you out in the camps, directin' the war?"

"My companion and I work for the War Department." Lucas was not sure of where he would be working, but he did not see a reason to let the woman know much of anything about them.

"War Department, huh. What do ya do there?"

"It's confidential, ma'am."

The old woman crossed her arms, then twirled her fingers on her lips, making a burring sound. "All right, then. Pay the deposit and first month's rent. Here's the rules. I provide one meal in the morning. It's at seven o'clock. If you ain't there, I ain't cookin' any more after that. What else you eat is up to you, but no cookin' in the room. No racket. Lights out by nine o'clock or you're out on your rears. Questions?"

"Your name, please."

"Cora Switcher. Get your things and park your buggy."

Workman secured the horses to a hitching post, slung the cased rifle on his shoulder, and Lucas and he carried their carpetbags and Lucas's trunk up the stairs of the boarding house.

Miss Switcher opened the door to the room. It had an iron-railed bed, a small desk and chair, a washbasin on a stand and a sofa. The room smelled dank, and a window was open, a pale curtain flipping in the breeze. Ice was lumped up on the window ledge. "I forgot to tell ya. The last tenant died o' yellow fever last summer. That's why I didn't let it out for a few months. I think it's safe to live in now. But I'd advise ya to wash the sheets."

Lucas walked into the shabby dwelling, its wallpaper peeled, and numerous cracks in the floor. Rat droppings along the baseboards. One small woven rug sat under the desk. He was about to turn down the room when he looked out the window. Despite a powdery fog of smoke, he could make out the War Department building, and, beyond it, the President's Palace. "This will do fine." He handed the landlady the cash, which she promptly counted before giving him the keys.

After she departed, Lucas whispered, "Tomorrow we begin our hunt. Abe Lincoln is our quarry."

Workman nodded, a sly grin on his face. He opened his rifle case, revealing the scoped Whitworth sharpshooter's weapon. He clucked his tongue and opened a box of bullets.

TWENTY-FIVE

FAMILY REUNION

MARCH 12, 1862, 10:00 A.M.
RAILROAD DEPOT, CAIRO, ILLINOIS

Cairo, Illinois was a muddy, stinking hell. Julia Dent Grant held her gloved hand to her nose while she stood on the train's one passenger car's steps and waited for the train to ease to a complete halt. When it had ceased to move, the condensation drips from the engine's steam pinging on the hot iron, she stepped down from the huffing and spewing locomotive. She was wearing her best travel dress, burgundy with a lace collar and sleeves.

She was careful not to catch the toe of her shoe in a hoop when she stepped from the railcar. Three of her four children waited on the steps behind her. The train station boardwalk was slippery with mud.

Immediately, the heavy doors of the railcars slid open like a dozen treasure boxes, and hundreds of Union soldiers, blue uniforms, followed by blue, and then more blue, exited. The soldiers were like priceless sapphires to Julia, for they were soldiers for her husband's army. Pride welled up in her.

General Ulysses Grant, her husband, stood at the end of the platform, balancing on a cart filled with sacks of coffee and beans.

It was top-heavy, and he doddered on it, trying to maintain his balance while attempting to garner his family's attention.

"There's Papa!" Frederick, at eleven years and oldest of their children, saw his father first and stepped down beside his mother.

Julia looked in the direction Frederick pointed and saw her husband, his jacket hung open, his hat rakish on his head, his beard black and full, and she could see his broad smile even at the distance. She wished to go to him, but the onrush of soldiers, hurried by officers, and packed tight together, their rifles and accoutrements rattling, flooded by her and her children. Those on the edge of the throng, that noticed her, tipped their forage caps and said, "Ma'am," politely.

"Papa looks like he's riding a new wild horse, bucking away," Nellie Grant giggled taking her mother's hand. She was six, going on a dozen years.

"Don't you be saying silly stuff like little Jesse, Nellie. I don't need two jokesters in the family."

"Yes, ma'am."

"Where is Jesse anyway?" Julia looked around her.

"He be holdin' onto Abram on the top step there," Jule, the personal slave of Julia, said matter-of-factly. "Don't you worry none. Abram holdin' him good and tight." Jule, the same age as Julia, a birthday gift when Julia was born, had stayed inseparable from her mistress their whole lives. She wore a delicate, light blue dress with filigree along the hem and rows of six buttons along the sleeves. She wore a new wool cape, all gifts from Julia. She had tied a yellow scarf on her head.

The women turned to see Abram on the upper step, holding the three-year-old in his arms, along with Julia's parasol. "Does you need your parasol, Miss Julia?" Abram asked.

"Not now, Abram, thank you." She reached up and took Jesse into her arms. When the last of the soldiers had hiked off the platform and down the sloppy road through the town toward the camps, Julia rushed to her husband. He jumped from his perch and sprinted to her. When they met, they embraced, but did not kiss. He attempted to caress her, but she placed her gloved hand to his lips, smiling. "Not in front of the children, dear."

General Grant, instead, kissed her hand. Then he lifted Jesse into his arms and kissed the child's pudgy cheeks.

Jule came up, carrying two heavy carpetbags, Frederick and Nellie on her heels, each carrying a small bag.

"Good morning, Miss Jule," General Grant said. "How are you this fine day?" He felt genuinely happy to see his wife's bosom pal since childhood. He turned to Frederick and Nellie. "How good to see you children. My day is complete."

A porter rolled up a large cart filled with trunks beside the family. Last came Abram. He had opened the parasol and held it over his head, twirling it.

General Grant and his family gawped at Abram, then broke into laughs. Abram smiled and twirled the parasol faster. When they finished laughing, Julia said, "Ulysses, I want you to meet Abram, a freeman and our new employee. He has been a world of help here on our journey, doing a marvelous job keeping the children entertained. He was a slave until recently for Emily and Lucas Reeder. Lucas granted him his freedom, and here he is now."

"Pleased to meet you, Abram." General Grant gave a slight bow.

"I am honored to meet such a fine officer as you, sir." Abram bowed in return. "I have enjoyed reading about your victories at Forts Henry and Donnelson."

"Yes, I have a new nickname because of it. Not sure I care for it."

"Every newspaper story I read," Julia commented, "calls you Unconditional Surrender Grant. It gets tiresome, but I'm still proud."

"At least, they don't call me 'Useless' like my papa did." General Grant smiled. "Or my given name, Hiram." His smile broadened.

Frederick and Nellie, bouncing on their toes and unable to wait any longer, rushed to their father, hugged him and kissed his cheeks. "I'm so glad you are finally here," he said. Tears clung to his eyelids. "You'll have to tell me about your journey while we make our way back to camp. There always seems to be something to do there." He tickled Jesse. "And something fun for little boys to do."

Jesse giggled and squirmed.

"Father." Julia referred to him by that name often in front of the children. "What is that awful smell? Please tell me it's dead Confederates."

"No, Julia...Mother." General Grant bent down and lifted Nellie into his other arm, a child in each. "That is the hog pen and the hog rendering plant. It's near the tracks, that way we don't have to drive the hogs through the town. Keeps the smell out here."

"That's smart," Frederick said, hanging close to his father while they walked along.

"That there smell is the smell of commerce," Abram said. "And it's keepin' these boys fed, so they be fightin' better."

General Grant and Julia stopped and looked at Abram, amazed.

He twirled the parasol and smiled.

"I'll take the parasol now, Abram. You look foolish with it." Julia smirked.

He handed her the parasol, and the group continued to two carriages that General Grant had procured. General Grant helped each member of his family into the lead carriage, where a sergeant, the driver, waited. He assisted Julia last. "I'm afraid your stay will be short, darling Julia. We will travel by boat to Paducah. There you must disembark and go to your family in Covington. There..." He lowered his voice to a whisper. "Is going to be a major push down the Tennessee River. General

Halleck has ordered the armies to head to Corinth and take it. It's a major rail crossroads for the Rebels."

Julia did her best not to look disappointed at the news that she would have to depart so soon.

General Grant climbed onto a tall stallion that he had tied to a post. He tapped the horse's sides just enough to make the animal rear and flail its legs in the air.

"Showing off," Julia proclaimed. "You may be an excellent horseman, dear husband, but it wouldn't do for you to tumble and bust your tailbone. The army needs you."

General Grant laughed and galloped ahead.

Jule and Abram rode in the second carriage, the luggage piled in the back. Jule turned to Abram, who was singing the song, "The Blackest Crow."

"Don't be gettin' all melancholy," she said. "And whatever you do, don't get uppity. Dey may be Union round heah, but dey still are White folk dat thinks dey are de best folks. Us colored do best when we keep to ourselves, keep our mouths shut."

Abram stopped singing, but whistled the tune. He had heard a little of what the general had whispered to Julia. He wondered if he would be required to accompany General Grant in the army's offensive into Tennessee.

TWENTY-SIX

THE PRIVATIONS OF WAR

MARCH 13, 1862, 10:00 A.M.
ELKHORN TAVERN, ARKANSAS

F ederal soldiers, enough to fill a dozen Sibley tents, still camped in the yard of Elkhorn Tavern.

Cyntha and Sara sat on ladderback chairs on the front porch of Elkhorn Tavern watching the bluecoats gamble at card games of Quist, Faro, and Poker, or sometimes fall down in a wrestling match, or join in fisticuffs, or unload the wagons that arrived from St. Louis twice daily, which were always accompanied by a large cavalry unit.

Sara and Cyntha wore dresses given to them by a lady who had come up from Leetown along with townsfolk and neighbor farmers to help with the wounded. When the cheery woman with ample dimensions saw the despoiled dresses they were wearing, each covered from collar to hem with blood, she hurried back to her home and brought them the garments she had grown too large to wear. "Take these," she said, "with my blessings. Surely, you have done the Lord's work helping the poor souls in this travesty. Amen, if this is how we treat our fellow man, the end-times are coming soon." She then gave three jars of canned plums to Polly Cox.

Sara's and Cyntha's hand-me-down dresses were simple cotton fabric; Sara's a faded blue print with tiny beige flowers lined up in crisscross fashion; Cyntha's, a blousy, light coffee-toned thing was big bosomed in its cut. "Wearing this," she bemoaned, "the same shade as the Southern army uniform, makes me look like a Rebel."

"And what's wrong with that?" Sara asked flatly.

Cyntha did not respond.

Though the yard had been cleared of all dead and wounded, corpses were still being found in amongst the ravines and hollows. The soldiers tasked with burying the bodies kept cloths over their mouths and gloves on their hands. They hoisted the swollen bodies into pushcarts and passed the tavern often.

Sara saw one particular corpse, his teeth smashed in by a bullet, his lips peeled back, his face as swollen and orange as a pumpkin. That image haunted her thoughts.

The graves were generally dug down in the Tanyard ravine, but the clink and clank of the pickaxes and shovels sounded day after day.

The tavern was occupied now only by the Cox family, the Atkinson family, Reynolds, Cyntha and Sara. The group had eaten sparse remnants of food thrown aside by the Union army since the battle. All of the house's food stores had been removed by the two armies.

Anthony came out on the porch and leaned against a post. "I feel as if I've become one of those wretches who live on the streets in the big cities, my hand holding a tin cup, begging for alms." He watched his daughter, Clara, playing a game of tag in the yard with the young Cox boys. They ran listlessly as if they were trying to make joy where none could be found. "If only I could try to forget the last several days like these children seem to have done. And I am fearful for Jeanette's mind. When the last wounded man was taken from the tavern, she went upstairs and sat in the corner and won't speak, nor eat."

"Ain't none of us eatin' much anyway," Sara said.

"Give her time, dear brother," Cyntha said. "For the life of me, I don't know why I am not behaving the exact same way. I have to force myself not to think on it."

Sara abruptly stood. "I am ready to depart this place of evil. If some devil hadn't stolen my mare, I'd be gone now." With Esther gone, and the Yankees camped in all directions, she ached about her predicament. She stomped into the house, then into the kitchen, and began washing pots and pans.

Cyntha rose. "I'll help her." Upon entering the darkened parlor, she saw Reynolds asleep in a blood-stained chair, his legs outstretched, his chin on his breast. His breathing was labored, and his cheeks were sunken. He was markedly thinner than he had been when she first insisted that he accompany her to Arkansas and Missouri to find the grave of Joseph.

Blood that he had coughed up from his frayed lungs stained his beard and the handkerchief he clutched in his hand. She wished to wake him, and, somehow, by force of her will, make him well again. The consumption was killing him faster than she had originally noticed. In this slow assassination, he had never complained, and she had been too wrapped up in her own sorrow to notice his troubles. The tears flooded down her cheeks.

Then her selfish thoughts overtook her. If he died, and with Joseph deceased, she would be truly alone. During the course of the battle, she had not thought to secure her money, the abundant silver coins stored in leather pouches that she had hidden in a secret compartment in her clothes trunk. When the Federal soldiers raided the trunk for clothes to tear into bandages, a soldier, a shadowy outlaw in her imagination, found the hidden pouches and absconded with her entire funds. With scant money in the bank in Iowa, she would not be able to pay the yearly mortgage fee for the farm. Without Reynolds, she would be destitute, for she could not work the land by herself.

Her world had crashed in upon itself. She could not ask to stay indefinitely with the Cox family, for they had enough problems of their own, with their home and business wrecked. Her brother, Anthony, with his wife and child, had too much to handle to take on an impoverished sister, a widowed spinster. The letter that Colonel Merritt had written, telling her of Joseph's death and of his bravery reported by other soldiers, was now lost. The letters he had written her before the Wilson Creek battle were spoiled with blood.

Ben was gone as well, and she missed him more than she ever had thought possible.

Wiping her cheeks on her sleeve, she prayed, more of a lamentation, a complete surrender to the devastation of the life she faced. She stumbled to the kitchen, grabbing the tops of chairs to keep from falling, and joined Sara at the washtub. Sara washed the dishes listlessly and placed them on the counter. Cyntha picked up a cloth to dry, and she observed the tears streaming down Sara's cheeks.

Neither woman spoke. Both women quietly wept.

When Sara set the last cup on the counter, she said, "The tub needs to be poured out." She stared at the wall, peppered with bullet holes, dozens of specks of light glancing through each gap.

"Let me do it." Cyntha lifted the tub of sudsy water and carried it into the back yard.

Sara remained. In a moment, she heard Cyntha call, "Sara, come quick!"

She ran outside.

Emerging from the deep ravine, his face wrenched in agony, Ben McGavin hopped and stumbled slowly forward. He led a pretty roan mare with a white blaze down its nose.

"Esther!" Sara yelled.

"Ben!" Cyntha outpaced Sara, both running full out toward Ben and the horse.

Ben crumpled onto the ground.

When the women reached him, he choked out, "I've destroyed my ankle. I tried to ride away, to escape…"

"Oh, Ben," Cyntha said soothingly. "Not all the Federals have left yet. We'll get you a doctor."

Sara knelt and lifted his torn trouser leg to peer at the bent ankle, purple and black bruises spilling across the entire swollen lower leg and foot. She looked at Cyntha and shook her head. "Who is this soldier, Cyntha? He's sure to lose this mangled foot."

Ben clenched his eyes shut and moaned, "Please, Cyntha, don't let 'em take my leg. I'd rather die." Pain racked him, and he collapsed.

Esther clopped up to Sara, bent her head and nuzzled Sara's hair with her velvet nose, blowing soft breaths. Sara stroked the horse's head. Then she rose and clutched the horse by the neck and hugged her. She released her hold on the horse and turned to Cyntha. "So, this is the one that filched my Esther. Damn him."

"He brought your horse back, Sara," Cyntha said.

"Only because he maimed his own leg." Her tone was brutal.

"Not everything in this world is about your cares and wants! You don't know his story. You don't know him." She cradled Ben's head in her lap.

Federal soldiers arrived providentially with a stretcher and bore him inside and laid him on a mat in the parlor. "Looks like," one of them said, "old sawbones gets to cut another leg for the heap."

TWENTY-SEVEN

PITY BARELY GIVEN, ANGER UNBRIDLED

MARCH 13, 1862 8:00 P.M.
ELKHORN TAVERN, ARKANSAS

That evening, a Union surgeon with pale eyes below bushy, white eyebrows told Ben, "It's not a good idea to let that torn ankle fester. It should come off. You may lose your life, instead of just your leg."

"I'll take that chance, Doc," Ben said, then groaned.

The surgeon doused the area of the break with liniment and gave Cyntha some paper packets of soluble laudanum, with instruction to administer the doses in water and to do so frugally. "Keep the wound covered with cold rags, cold as possible. Change them regularly. Try to keep the swelling down." He handed her a brown bottle. "Give him a teaspoon of this willow powder every hour to fend off the fever." He thrust his medical instruments into his bag and rose to leave.

"Thank you, sir," Ben said, "for your pity."

Cyntha followed the surgeon outside. He turned to her. "I can't fathom why you care so much about a fool Rebel. Not one of them is worth the milk their bitch mother's fed 'em."

Cyntha overcame her initial shock at his comment, then slowly chewed the words of her response, pronouncing each syllable like a clock tolling its chime. "You don't know him. He was here in this tavern trying to save Union soldier's lives, just like the rest of us."

The surgeon said nothing, donned his hat, and walked away to an ambulance wagon.

∞

In the morning, Sara was helping Polly Cox hoe a garden behind the house for spring planting. The labor helped her deal with the injustice she felt in the defeat of the Southern army. She had hoped that the Confederates would have swept the Yankees away from Arkansas and Missouri. *Why won't they leave? This is not their home.*

She hammered the clods of dirt with her hoe with such force that the handle shuddered in her grip.

"Be easy on my tools, please," Polly Cox said. "They're the only ones I've got. The Yankees took every bit of food and our clothes; and both armies... destroyed my home." She began sobbing, pulled up her long apron to cover her tears, and ran into the house.

Sara straightened and leaned on the hoe. She felt sorry for Polly Cox and for everyone she knew, but most particularly sorry for herself. *I have no idea if Joseph is alive or dead. I have nowhere to go except back to Springfield to Miss Dindle's Boarding House. What help am I to the cause of Southern rights working in a café? My father would have fought for General McCulloch if his hearing had not limited him so. I am Lucas Reeder's daughter. Even if I should die, I must do my part to rid these Yankee beasts who despoil our homes and ravage our land.*

She brought her hand to her nose because a new northern breeze blew a vile stench toward her. She looked around for its source—near the forest. Both Confederate and Union uniforms of those who had been wounded and some of those killed were piled in a heap of cobalt, tan, mustard brown, gray and spoiled cream-colored. The five-foot-high, soggy mound of uniforms steamed in the spring sun. Vermin of all sizes roamed over it, in and out of the creases and pockets; and mounds of white maggots fed on the blood. Sara wondered why not one of the Yankees had considered ridding the place of the putrid mess.

Her revulsion and anger swelled.

She was about to turn away when she spied a pair of trousers hanging on a tree limb near the rotten pile. She guessed the pants had been tossed toward the pile but were slung too high and got caught on the limb. She strode rapidly to the tree. The butterscotch-toned pants, though dirty, were not torn, and the suspenders still attached. On the ground lay an untarnished gray jacket. A Confederate private's uniform, less the shirt and brogans. The pants and jacket were sized for a small man. *Or for a woman!*

An idea formed instantly—a solution—a chance to find her Joseph—and a chance to serve the Southern States Rights cause. Her anger, which had spun almost out of control at what the Federal soldiers had wrought, subsided now that she had formulated a plan. She resolved, *Yes, I'll do it. I'll wait three days to allow Esther to recuperate, then I'll be a diligent, hard-fightin' soldier. And I will kill every bluecoat I see.*

Moving quickly, she gathered the jacket and pants, searched them for bugs or worms, and, finding none, stealthily removed her apron and wadded the uniform up in it.

She turned and ran to where Esther was standing in the shade. She had tethered her to a tree near the back door, tying the rope in a complex knot. The rope itself was festooned with various bells and tin cans. If any soldier attempted to loosen the knot and steal her horse, she would know immediately, and she would shoot anyone who tried.

That evening, standing before a cracked mirror, she asked Cyntha to cut her long blond hair off to her ears. "I can't stand that my hair was so covered with blood. Even though I wash it, my hair still feels the blood." That was her excuse.

Cyntha cut the hair in a ragged bowl-cut, the tresses falling to the blood-stained floor.

TWENTY-EIGHT

∞

EVEN IN WAR, ONE SHOULD DANCE

MARCH 14, 1862, 10:00 A.M.
ELKHORN TAVERN, ARKANSAS

A clock ticked obtrusively on a wall shelf. Cyntha sat on a handmade stool with one leg shorter than the other three, so it wobbled with her slightest movement. She tried to hold still, but still it rocked. She was watching Ben sleeping, not on a bed, but on a mat on the floor; his injured leg with a moist rag atop it was raised on a pillow. The Rebels had taken the wooden bedframes to fuel their fires the first night of the battle. His sleep was restless, despite the morphine the doctor had given him. Reynolds sat beside her on a stool.

Cyntha turned to him. "Does he look like anyone you know?"

Reynolds eyed the slumbering Rebel scout, then whispered. "Can't say."

"No one?"

Reynolds shook his head.

Cyntha knew that Reynolds was avoiding the truth, either to be polite, or to test her. She knew this brash, ill-bred young man looked slightly similar in appearance to her deceased husband. Both were blond and about the same height and build. What was

God's purpose in bringing this man into her life? She sighed. *Yes, I am attracted to him, as unlikely as that seems.* Not because he looked somewhat like Joseph, but because of the wildness in him, his whole take-on-the-world attitude. She saw him not as devil-may-care, but intense in his strivings, like every action he took had the urgency of life or death. That is what she admired. She considered what it would be like to be courted by him, and she laughed.

"Somethin' funny?" Reynolds asked.

"No, no, dear Josiah. I'm just trying to deal with all that has happened."

Reynolds began coughing, and he seemed unable to catch his breath.

"Josiah, go lie down right now. Ben is not so hurt that he needs you watching after him."

Reynolds ambled to the corner and lay on a paltry blanket. He lay his head on the only other pillow in the house.

Ben awakened, bleary. "What's going on? We under attack?" He struggled with the blankets, unable to untangle himself in a fury of wild movements. He stopped and gritted his teeth when he accidentally swerved his foot off the pillow.

Cyntha rose quickly and took a gentle hold of his arms. "It is all right, Ben. Relax. No battle. Just us."

"What's that clock say?" Ben pointed.

"Ten o'clock."

"How long I been asleep?"

"Well, the doctor left about nine last night. So, thirteen hours. How's your ankle feel?"

"Hurts like hell." Ben twisted his foot slightly and could just hear the sound of bone rubbing on bone. He lifted the wet cloth and looked at his swollen ankle.

"You want me to get another cold cloth?" Reynolds called, raising himself on his elbow.

"No," Cyntha answered. "You and Ben are both fine. Just lie still."

Reynolds lay back and was instantly asleep.

"What's wrong with Reynolds?" Ben asked.

Cyntha looked up to stop any tears. "He's consumptive. He's dying."

"Dyin'?" Ben pointed at the sleeping freeman. "That old nigger's my friend! He's dyin' you say? And he was gonna go get a cloth for my leg?" He turned his head toward the wall. "I don't want him to die. Lord, let me die instead."

Cyntha gasped. She stood, gazing back and forth at the two people she cared for the most. One was surely dying and the other wished to die.

Ben finally turned away from the wall. "My leg sure hurts."

"Would you like some of the medicine the doctor left?"

"Naw, I imagine if Reynolds can suffer with his lungs falling apart, I can offer up my suffering for...my sins."

Cyntha sat again on the stool and pulled up close to Ben. She looked down into the brightest blue eyes she had ever known. "Why did you say that, Ben?"

"When I was a little 'un, my parents died, and Paul and me, we was raised by our older brother, Asa. I may have told you about him. He died in quicksand on the Red River."

"Yes, you told me once. But I didn't know he had raised you."

"Well, I'm sure it wasn't easy for him. I'm not that pleasant to get along with." He attempted a smirk, and when he saw Cyntha's surprised expression, his smile broadened. "He raised us best he could, but I was hard-headed. There was a family that lived across the road from us. They had slaves, and all they ever did was complain about 'em. How lazy they were, how dishonest. Like they weren't even human. You understand?"

"Yes, I believe I do."

"Well, that and other things I heard some White folks say was all I ever knew about the niggers. I thought they were a waste of time and money."

"They're humans, equal to us in form and spirit; most with good hearts. We're all made in God's image."

"And some of 'em maybe even *more* human than me, like old Reynolds there."

"All men should have equal rights under the law, and…" Cyntha halted the assertion she had rehearsed a hundred times in her mind when she noticed Ben grimacing

He shifted on the mat, the pain causing him to double over. "Ow! Dang, that hurts!"

"Be careful, Ben." Cyntha bent and placed the wet cloth back on his ankle. Then she felt his forehead. "No fever yet."

"Nah. That's one thing my older brother taught me. To be tough. Life is tough."

"Yes, it is."

Polly Cox and her family, along with other joyous voices swept up from downstairs. A party with friends. Soon, a fiddler began a lively tune, and Cyntha and Ben heard the clump of children's feet in a dance step.

After they had listened awhile to the music, Ben took Cyntha's hand. "I should like to dance with you some day."

Cyntha's first reaction was to draw her hand away and act as though she was appalled, but she left her hand in his. Ben used his other hand to stroke her palm gently, then lightly touch the tips of each finger. He then enfolded her hand in both of his and gazed down at her wrist that showed just below the end of the sleeve and observed her lustrous, soft skin. He looked up at her face.

Her cheeks were blushing.

Ben released her hand. "Asa used to read the Bible to us most nights, primarily to get Paul and me to settle down. We listened to the old-time stories. I especially liked the ones about the Israel slaves escaping the Egyptians, and they were white slaves, or brown, or whatever color they are over there in the Holy Land."

"Yes, slavery's been around a long time...unfortunately. It's time for it to end."

"Ain't never gonna end. There'll always be some kind of slavery in the world. A hundred years from now, there'll be slaves."

"I hope not. And..." Cyntha stopped herself with a sudden deep realization that Ben was probably right. She knew of the peasants in Russia and the manner in which the Chinese emperors treated their subjects.

"You know, Asa told us a story that wasn't in the Bible. Our pap died before I was old enough to know him, but he had been a Marine back in the early days of America. Spent his time on warships. Turns out, some black Africans, pirates they was, kept taking white slaves off o' ships in the ocean by a place named Tripoli. Them pirates took 'em off European ships and, worse, they took American ones."

"The Mediterranean Sea."

"The what?"

"The Mediterranean. That's the name of the sea by Tripoli, Africa."

Ben shrugged. "Oh. So, my pap was a Marine with Lieutenant O'Bannon that sailed to that sea. Him and the other Marines slipped ashore, trooped five hundred miles from Egypt, and sneaked up behind the Africans, took their city, and stopped 'em from takin' any more slaves. He was wounded in the attack and got sent home. That war didn't last long, but the Americans won. When pap got home, he got married, and ma had us boys."

He quit speaking and licked his dry lips, and pulled the blanket up to his chin. "I'm kinda tired."

Cyntha reached over and took Ben's hand. "I would be honored to dance with you."

It was Ben's turn to blush.

"When your leg is better. In the morning, I want to tell you of a proposition," Cyntha whispered. "If you continue to recover, it may be something you would want to do."

Ben said nothing, but clasped her hand until he was breathing in measured breaths, asleep.

TWENTY-NINE

ILL-TEMPERED ADVISORS, CONSUMMATE FRIENDS

MARCH 14, 1862, 11:30 A.M.
THE PRESIDENT'S MANSION, WASHINGTON, DC

President Lincoln sat in his desk chair of his large office, an extension of the upstairs reception hall in the East Wing. He was troubled beyond his reckoning. With his gold-rimmed spectacles pulled low on his nose, he listened to the admonitions of his cabinet members who sat or stood around a long walnut table that was covered with maps, photographs, and newspaper clippings. Some clutched folded newspapers in their fists and occasionally slapped the papers against their palms to add emphasis to their contention.

At a small desk in one corner, presidential aide William Stoddard wrote the meeting minutes.

The vice president, Hannibal Hamlin, lounged off to the side on a pale, green, horsehair sofa, avoiding interaction with the rest of the vociferous men. Each man shared his anxiety or anger about the Army of the Potomac which was still sitting behind earthworks and forts around Washington, DC while Virginian Confederate cavalry played havoc only a few miles from the capital. The six men complained of being hard-pressed by constituents that the army should *actually do something*.

"General McClellan is an embarrassment." Salmon Chase was perched on the edge of his seat, his face flushed. "He swore the Rebels were entrenched at Centreville. When the army finally moved there, they found nothing but blackened tree trunks. Quaker guns."

"And that Reb snake, Mosby," Secretary of the Navy Gideon Welles proclaimed, waving his arms about, "is making a mockery of our armies. He goes where he wishes, wreaks havoc, and vanishes like a ghost. And General Jackson in the Shenandoah Valley. He's a curse!"

The president leaned forward, his elbows on his knees, his chin on his fists, his eyes trained on Welles, then on each man who raised a concern or brought up an old point for another round.

Bright midday sunshine slammed through the windows past heavy, olive-toned drapes that were drawn back with rope ties, the light shimmering off the polished tabletop. Lincoln's drab desk was in need of a polishing, but was covered with telegrams and correspondence from families pleading for information on the whereabouts of the graves of their sons or fathers or brothers. A thick book on the Napoleonic wars was open atop the papers.

Secretary of State, William Seward, shaded his eyes from the sun's glare, and barked, "Can't something be done about the glare?"

Lincoln pulled the bell cord by his desk, and, immediately, a Negro servant entered. He wore a short, blue waistcoat with a double row of brass buttons and brocaded sleeves, his hands adorned with white gloves. Lincoln pointed at the windows, and the servant, sporting a bright smile, moved quickly to draw the drapes.

Recently installed gas lamps on the walls lit the room, sputtering; and President Lincoln sniffed the gas odor that issued from one of the lamps. He was unsure which one leaked, though the smell seemed to have worsened in recent days. He pulled a handkerchief from his pocket and briefly held it to his nose. *Think I'd rather do without the lamps.*

In that extent of time when none of the men spoke, but watched the servant at his task, the rattle of wagons and marching soldiers sounded louder along Pennsylvania Avenue.

Church bells pealed twelve o'clock.

When the servant exited, Welles stood and thumped the front page of a Philadelphia newspaper, the headline of which read *Soldiers Losing Will to Fight the Longer the Generals Wait.* His voice rang with rancor, and he blamed any general and officer he could think of and rained his heaviest insults on General McClellan. "That little twit who thinks himself Napoleon is nothing, I say, *nothing* but a coward. Must we be forced to win the war on the rivers and the seas alone?"

Each cabinet member shouted their interpretation of Welles' statement.

When the men's angry bellows had become loud enough to shake the windows, the double doors of the office burst open, clattering against the walls. Mary Todd Lincoln stood in the doorway slapping at the hands of a tall sergeant who was stationed at the door and was attempting mildly to restrain her. Freeing herself from the officious guard, she fluttered into the room, tacking from side to side as if she were drunk. She almost bumped into Secretary of War Stanton. Her face was crimson, a deep set of frown wrinkles on her brow. She clenched her dress with both hands, lifting it so the petticoats showed, and marched up to her husband, who had stood when she entered. He bowed to her and took her hand.

"What is the meaning of this woman interrupting this conference?" Secretary Welles declared. "This is no place for a woman, despite the fact she is your wife, Abraham."

The other secretaries mumbled similar sentiments, but Mary Lincoln paid them no heed. She flicked her hand at them like they were a pesky swarm of insects.

Drawing closer to her husband, she smiled glowingly up at him and clutched one arm by the biceps in both her hands. The secretaries quieted, wagging their heads in disgust.

"What is it you wish, my dear?" President Lincoln said. "We are deeply involved in a strategic planning for the..."

"Oh, I shan't bother your meeting with these stodgy old men," Mary responded. "But I have two items to relay to you which are of utmost importance and cannot wait."

The president patted her hands. "And what might that be?" His smile, though cordial, was brief, and his eyes showed embarrassment. He glanced around at the secretaries, most of whom stood with their arms about their chests, and he could see they looked close to exploding.

"Yes, well," Mary began. "First, you must insist that any soldier, indeed anyone, who is stationed at a door to your meetings is not to ever stop me from entering." She turned and eyed the door, now closed.

"We'll talk about that in our afternoon carriage ride." President Lincoln nodded.

"Second." She stood on tiptoes to her husband's ear as if to whisper, though every word she said was particularly loud. "Our dear mulatto maid and marvelous seamstress, Elizabeth Keckley, has informed me that we may be able to obtain the services of a medium, a Charles Colchester, who can speak to our dear son, Willie, who even now..." She paused, took a handkerchief from her sleeve, and dabbed her eyes. "Elizabeth says that she knows Willie wishes to speak to us, and a new medium can make that possible in a séance. Our dear friend and spiritualist, Nettie Colburn Maynard, has fallen ill and requests she be relieved temporarily from her duties as our medium. She did emphasize 'temporarily.'"

President Lincoln waggled his head and tightened his lips. He patted her hands again. "We will speak of this later today, Mary. Let us not speak of our dear departed son in front of..." He paused to raise his head to hold back tears. "In front of our friends, these hard-working gentlemen who are desirous of saving our union. Let us discuss the matter this evening."

Mary Lincoln searched her husband's eyes for a few seconds, then nodded her head. "It is..." she began. "It is of paramount importance. This war will go on whether your cabinet or a gaggle of congressmen argue about it or not." She turned to the secretaries. "Gentlemen, by your leave." She hurried from the room.

The secretaries and Vice President Hamlin made polite bows, then turned to the president to continue their harangue.

After another hour of fierce discussion, President Lincoln called an end to the meeting, mentioning it was well past noonday mealtime and begging forgiveness in that he had a foreign dignitary to entertain. The men headed for the door. When Secretary Stanton opened it, there stood Ward Hill Lamon, revolvers in shouldered holsters, and the handles showing under his open jacket. He held a banjo by the neck in his left hand. Smiling, he shook the hand of each secretary.

"Marshall Lamon," each man said, though with no particular respect in tone. After Secretary Chase exited last, Lamon pretended to shove his boot at the man's buttocks in a mock kick. He then shut the doors and smiled sheepishly at President Lincoln. Stoddard finished the minutes, stacked the pages, and laid them on the desk for President Lincoln to read later. He rushed down the back exit.

"Ol' Stoddard wants to avoid the cabinet riff-raff, too," Lamon chuckled. He raised the banjo and plunked out the melody to "Old Dan Tucker."

President Lincoln slumped down on the couch, crossed one leg over the other and patted it in time with the song. While Lamon crooned the fanciful words, President Lincoln stared blankly at the painting of Andrew Jackson that hung above the fireplace.

"Hill. Stop a moment. I've got to do some thinking about McClellan." Lincoln stood, buttoned his jacket. "I'm going for a ride."

"Then I shall be your silent partner while you ride and think."

The president nodded assent.

"I won't even play the banjo."

"Nor sing, nor hum, nor roll the bullet chambers in your guns, nor tap a rhythm on your saddle pummel." He grinned at his boon friend and body guard.

"No, siree." Lamon leaned his banjo against the couch.

The good friends strolled to one of the tall windows facing east. Thrusting back the curtains, President Lincoln and Lamon looked out. They watched the activity of stable hands and grooms at the mansion's stables. Most of the men appeared busy at some task, but one fellow lounged on a hay bale. The man lit a cigarette and tossed the match on the ground. The flame went out. President Lincoln grimaced. "I wish the man would not smoke near the horses."

"Indeed." Lamon agreed.

President Lincoln sighed. "I have greater concerns than a man smoking where he shouldn't be."

His hands clutched behind his back, he strolled to a south-faced window. Lamon followed, twirling his fingers for an imaginary banjo tune. They scanned the partially completed Washington monument at the far end of the grassy mall.

"'Tis a shame, your excellency, President Washington," Lincoln said, knowing he was speaking to the ethereal. "Thousands of men and women labored heartily to build up a nation with their bare hands, and then with anguished souls, they fought to set it free. But, lately, some recalcitrant slaveholders are trying to tear it down whilst it's still being built. I'm glad, President Washington, you're not here to see it."

Work had ceased on the half-finished Washington monolith during the cold, wet winter. The heavy cranes and machinery sat atop it, like black praying mantises.

President Lincoln lowered his gaze to a bevy of citizens beyond the fence that circled the Executive Mansion compound. The ragtag bunch were gawking at the structure and pointing. A fellow with a camera had set up a tripod. Tourists.

Armed soldiers stood beside the gate. Mounted cavalrymen were alert within the fence.

Lincoln noticed a tall soldier with a gangly frame not unlike a scarecrow who kept turning in slow circles, first toward Philadelphia Avenue and then back to the mansion. Lincoln retrieved a pair of binoculars from a desk drawer, then returned to the window.

He watched the man's peculiar behavior. At one point, the man bent down and pretended to tie his shoes, staring through the fence rails. He seemed to be smirking. President Lincoln thought that the man looked somewhat like himself when he was younger. He rubbed his bearded chin and imagined what his face would look like with only a mustache like the one decorating the upper lip of the strange soldier.

"Do you see the tall man beyond the fence?" President Lincoln said.

"Yes, I've had my eyes on him this whole time. Looks like a trouble-maker."

"Yes."

"Shall I arrest him?"

"No, Hill, I don't think he means any harm. We cannot arrest a man who looks like a trouble-maker. Our constitution forbids it. Perhaps he's lost."

After a while, the skinny tourist walked away.

The president took his wool wrap from his chair, swept his stovepipe hat from a hook and donned it, and departed the room with Lamon on his heels, both men sneaking down a covert stairs, then through the basement, allowing them to avoid anyone seeking the president's attention. They strolled to the compound's stables.

Four stable hands, stripped to their white blousy shirts with the sleeves rolled up, their blue trousers soiled, were busy cleaning stalls. A third coachman hotwalked a lathered stud which had finished a workout run. He stopped by a rail and spread a horse blanket over the animal's back. When he saw President Lincoln, he hollered. "Out for a ride today, sir?"

President Lincoln strolled up to the stallion and stroked its nose. "Yes, Mr. McGee, I shall visit my son's final resting place at Oak Hill. I believe his soul is comforted by my presence." He paused and looked directly at the trim soldier with rosy cheeks and a willing smile. "At least, my visit will comfort me. Can you prepare the gray gelding for me?"

"Yes, sir, and a horse for your body guard, as well."

"Yes. I think Marshall Lamon will not allow me to go it alone today."

When the coachman brought the long-legged, high-headed, gray horse out, the stirrups of the saddle extended to the lowest hole, President Lincoln mounted the steed, his knees bent. He seemed at ease in the saddle. Lamon rose up on a black mare. Before they trotted away, the president said, "I'm heading to Oak Hill. Should anyone ask, Mr. McGee." He looked around. "Do you have enough help here?"

"Actually, Mr. President, we could use another pair of hands."

"I'll see to it." With Lamon riding at his side, he trotted the horse toward Willie's resting place.

The president did not see McGee sneer at him. "And pay me a decent wage."

THIRTY

THEFT, SCRABBLING, INVENTION, JOURNEY

MARCH 16, 1862, 2:00 P.M.
ELKHORN TAVERN, ARKANSAS

Sara, Cyntha and Ben, and the families who were abiding in the tavern, were starving. Cyntha and Sara had watched Anthony sally forth into the Federal camp and attempt to barter for food. He gave up his hat, his vest, and his walking cane for small amounts of biscuits, hardtack, dried beef, and beans.

One afternoon, after giving up his watchchain and returning with pickles, a small sack of flour, and some beef tripe, Anthony told the women, "I'll give up the chain, but not the watch."

"I wish I had something to barter with," Polly said, "but I've got nothing. Nothing at all."

Sara looked out the window at a gray morning, the sun slipping here and there through the pale clouds in dazzling streams; and the dew-moistened grass gleaming. She set down the cup of burnt rye she had been sipping, a foul black fluid that was supposed to pass for coffee, and pushed back from the table.

She gathered a pair of wooden buckets, marched up to Polly Cox's sons, and took them by the sleeves. "You're coming with me. These Yanks are full to the brim. Let's see what they wasted."

With marked bravado, she directed the Cox boys to gather up the hog offal piled in heaps on cutting tables of the Yankee camp cooks. They gathered the leavings into the buckets with their bare hands. When the boys trudged back to the tavern with the buckets of hog renderings, Sara swiped a half sack of buckwheat flour.

They brought the flour, the hog's head, heart, liver and other leavings into the tavern to Polly Cox. She and Cyntha boiled the hog's head and innards on the kitchen hearth. After it cooled, they set about extracting the leavings into a bowl, then mixed some of the broth with what little cornmeal they still possessed and some of the buckwheat that Sara had pilfered, stirring it until it formed a mush. After they had done this, they added back to the mush the finely chopped meat, along with sage, thyme and black pepper, and pressed the concoction into three loaves and set them in the larder.

The next morning, Polly and Cyntha took the formed *scrapple*, cut it into slices and fried them up in lard. Then they made buckwheat pancakes. Sara went down in the cellar and gathered the last jar of apple jam to spread on top of the repast.

The Coxes, the Atkinsons, Cyntha and Sara, and even Reynolds, though he did not eat much, had their first full meal in days. Cyntha brought a plate up to Ben. She noticed he had good color and seemed to be mending fast.

After the breakfast, Sara set about stealing whatever else she could from the bluecoats while they were preparing to march to join their army at Cross Hollows. The soldiers were used to seeing her and tried to flirt with her whenever she asked for any scrap of food. Some gave her a few biscuits or hardtack, others smirked at her.

Although she had no intention of consorting with them, she saw it as a task to endure, and she tried to gather information she could later share with Confederates. The soldiers and even the officers, however, knew little about anything going on and were more intent on flirting. One leering private took the opportunity once to pinch her on her buttocks. He spoke German and she knew not what he said. She slapped his face, all to the guffaws of his companions.

The only news she found helpful from any of them was that Van Dorn's Confederate army had fallen back in its entirety to Frog Bayou on the White River.

Later in the morning, while the soldiers were busy striking their tents, Sara absconded with several cans of fruit, another half-full sack of flour, and a Colt revolver and bullets. She gave the flour to Polly and the revolver and bullets to Anthony. She kept the cans of fruit for herself as part of her plan to search for Joseph and help the Rebel cause.

At noon, she went outside and began grooming her mare's coat until it gleamed. Esther's ears perked at the tapping rhythm of the drummer marking time while the last of the Union troops filed away from Elkhorn Tavern. They left behind a pile of rubbish—empty tins, buzzing flies, soggy newspapers, worn-out clothes, dilapidated shoes and piles of charcoal black wood of smoldering campfires. Sara sought the charcoal.

She also wanted secrecy so that she could put her design into action.

She planned to slip through the Union lines now formed miles from the tavern, all the time acting like a farmgirl returning home from a visit to relatives. She would bribe any overly officious guard with the cans of fruit and some dried meat she had purloined earlier. She had prepared a burlap sack filled with the stolen cans of fruit and the dried beef to take with her.

The cans and meat were stored in the cellar. No one in the Cox family went down there anymore. Their remembrance of the blood leaking through the floorboards onto their clothes and skin had left that part of the home off-limits for the time-being, a quarantine of a ghastly, tragic memory. The blood staining the floors and furniture was the legacy left the tavern.

Brushing Esther's roan coat, she smiled, cheered about her plans to leave. Head south. Join in the fight for the cause. *I'll be dogged. I won't quit.*

She saddled her horse and ventured out to the vacant campsite and found a chunk of charcoal that she could use to blacken her jaw and upper lip, hoping her face would appear more manly. She returned to her mare and tucked the wood inside the bedroll she had strapped to the saddle. In the saddlebags, she had stuffed the uniform she had found, a clean shirt, socks, and some cavalry boots near her foot size.

She figured that, once past the Yankees, she would bind her bosom tight, don the soldier's clothes, stick her revolver in her belt, pull a slouch hat down low on her brow, blacken her cheeks with the charcoal, and lower her voice. *I will no longer stand idle while the invaders wreak havoc on my homeland.* She had almost killed one marauder when he set fire to the barn where she and the Cherokees were hiding. Grazed his head with a bullet. She could have killed B. F. Richards after she pulled the gun on him when he tried to rape her. Still angry that she should have slain him, from this time forth, she would shoot to kill.

Tightening the cinch strap of the saddle, she patted the big mare's forelock. "Esther, I'll escape when everyone goes down for a nap. I can't be travelin' by night any more. That got me into enough trouble with those moonshiners. I can't trust no one. Besides, the Yank guards ain't gonna worry as much if they see me travelin' during the day."

A few rainclouds were gathering, silver gray, and the wind picked up. "And this is the last time I'm gonna try to find Joseph. If he's alive, I'll make him marry me if I have to tie him up." She chuckled, then frowned. "If he's...dead, I gotta see what I can do to help the South win this woeful struggle. I wish my papa was here. After I strike a few blows for the South, I'll make my way to Richmond and hopefully find him."

From an upstairs tavern window, Anthony watched Sara, and he knew what she was planning. When she came upstairs to secure her pistol from where she had hidden it behind a wallboard, Anthony pulled her into the empty bedroom. Ben was in a deep sleep. The Coxes were sitting on the porch enjoying the bright day and watching the slow storm approach.

"Sara, you don't know me that well," Anthony said, "but I hope that I can caution you on what you're about to do."

Sara stared at the floor, a bothered look on her face. "What do you think I'm about to do? With the Yanks finally gone, I'm only gonna take Esther for a short ride."

"With your gun?"

"I take this revolver in case I'm attacked by a marauder. They're everywhere, you know."

"Yes, that's true. And I'm grateful you gave me the gun and the bullets you stole, because I fear our largest threat now will be from marauding gangs. I've heard enough stories of their crimes."

"So?" She turned her head to stare at him.

"Sara, I know you're not coming back. I know you have stowed a basket of food in the cellar, and packed a Confederate uniform in your saddle bags along with boots."

"How'd you know? I was so careful."

"It's the being careful that made you obvious. But I think I'm the only one who knows."

Sara wheeled to go. "I have to leave."

Anthony intervened at the stairwell opening. "You have friends downstairs. You owe it to them to say goodbye."

"That's what I don't want to do. I've had enough sad goodbyes in my life, too many good people dyin', my papa gone to Richmond, and I may never see him again. My fiancé left me to fight this horrid war, and I can't find him no matter how hard I try. I had a nice captain help me in the snowstorm back before the battle. I had to say goodbye to him. My papa's good friend,

General McCulloch, is dead. Had a fine man of the cloth and some kind-hearted Indians that I had to say goodbye to. I had a lovely French Cajun man got himself captured by them damn bluecoats. There's more. You wanna hear 'em?"

Anthony lightly held her shoulders. "I understand and wish you well."

"I figure, Anthony, that if I just leave and don't say goodbye to them, they will always be with me, like I've never left. I've got to figure things out. Either find Joseph or die tryin'."

"Joseph? Is that your fiancé's name? That was the name of Cyntha's husband that died in battle."

"What of it? It's a common enough name. I gotta leave. I got to make a difference in this fight."

Anthony had a sudden realization. "Sara, you mean to use that uniform to disguise yourself as a soldier." He paused while his own words sank into his own understanding. "Sara, you could be killed, or raped by the very men you hope to be fighting alongside."

"Well, that's what I'm gonna do, and you can't stop me."

"Sara, you're too petite and too feminine. No one will believe you."

Sara tried to push past him. "I gotta go! I have to stop these vile invaders from destroying my homeland!"

Anthony grabbed her wrists firmly. She had tears in her eyes, but she stopped her struggle when she saw tears falling down his cheeks.

Anthony spoke almost in a whisper. "Sara. I lived up north. I know these Yanks. Calm mostly, but get them riled up, and there's no stopping them. For every Rebel fighting, there's up to five Yanks. Do you even know why the Rebs are fighting this war?"

Sara blinked and shrugged her shoulders.

"At first, I thought our southern states just wanted their own say, not to be dictated to by an all-powerful central government, and that they were refuting the high tariffs placed upon them by Northern legislators. They wanted more freedom to run their own affairs, actually live under the constitution as it was written...."

"I've got to go."

"Hold on, Sara. But of late, I found out why the southern states seceded was not because of people like you and me who want to run our own lives, but because every southern legislature was filled with rich plantation owners who owned slaves. The huge majority of folks who don't own slaves didn't have a say. Most of them wanted to work things out."

Sara stepped back, fully listening to Anthony's words.

"But a handful of hellbent, condescending slavers," Anthony continued, "full of bravado and callous disregard for all humans, especially if there's wealth attached to owning them—they're the ones who voted to secede. They don't care a bit if young men like your fiancé die, as long as they keep their cotton wealth and their slaves."

"I ain't fightin' to keep no slaves. I wish they were all free."

"That handful of boasting, brutish fools," Anthony choked out the words. "The slave-holders have brought ruin to the South. No matter what the armies do, nor what I do, nor what General McCulloch could have done, nor what you could ever do, will help the South win this war. The South has no way to manufacture rifles, they have no ships, and no shipyards in which to build them; they are outnumbered heavily; and, if I know anything for sure, *arrogant boasts* have never won a war. The South will lose horribly, and there will be hell to pay for generations."

Sara sighed and shook her head no. "Thank you for your concern, but I feel you are *wrong*. We *will win* our independence. Those brave men whose bodies were thrown into the mass graves yonder in the vale *will not have died in vain*!" She broke away from his grip and swept past him down the stairs, out the back door, then mounted Esther, and, in a moment, had galloped into the trees, out of sight.

Cyntha, on the porch, heard her speed down the stairs. She strode to the back of the house and watched her ride away.

THIRTY-ONE

LOVE AND PAIN BE KINFOLK TWAIN

– SIDNEY LANIER

MARCH 17, 1862, LATE AFTERNOON
ELKHORN TAVERN, ARKANSAS

Ben was standing on one foot beside the mat he had lain upon, grinning from ear to ear. He raised his right leg up and down, lightly touching his foot to the floor, though putting no pressure on it.

Cyntha stood in the doorway smiling at him. "You're supposed to be suffering with that damaged foot, yet there you are standing."

Ben winced. "Hurts like hell, but I can't stay here. I need to..." His eyes showed some thought had cowed him, then his whole demeanor showed genuine fright. He began to shudder.

Cyntha rushed to him and helped him settle into the short-legged chair. "What is wrong, Ben?"

"I'm scared plumb silly." He took a long breath. "It's finally come to me like a hammer blow. I've been shoved into a corner of life. If I can't ride, what will I do? That's been my whole life." He flinched at his realization, almost crouching, like a huge bully stood over him. "My future's comin' at me like a mad bear, and it's clawing me down."

Standing behind him, Cyntha could tell that he was sensing a dark presence. How could a cowboy who could no longer ride build a future? She rubbed his shoulders. "Oh, Ben. You're being silly. You don't have to ride a horse to have a good life. You can..."

"I can what?"

Cyntha hesitated. "You can come with me. I'm heading east to Ohio, then to New York. I have a farm I'm willing to sell... since my husband is dead. You see, Reynolds is dying, and he knows it, and he has family in Cincinnati. I plan to take him there, and I believe you could help me start a mercantile of some sort. We'd be away from this war. A business in a nice town." She stopped when she saw Ben's look of incredulity.

"You want me to come with you and be your servant."

"No, I would be honored if you would be my partner, a business partner. I would put up the cash from the sale of my farm, and you would be the proprietor. If you're running a business, maybe a dry goods store, you would not have to use your leg that much, and you can ride in a carriage."

"Go away!"

Cyntha stepped back, dismayed.

"I said go away!"

Cyntha rushed from the room, slamming the door. Downstairs she berated herself. "How could I ever expect that sordid scoundrel to care a whit about me? He's a bas..." She stopped herself. "No, I will not lose my dignity because of him." She sprinted out into the forest and down the Huntsville Road. Stopping, she leaned against a tree and wept, then slowly slumped onto the ground. She stayed there for over an hour, feeling like she was a mendicant, begging for a handout. Like Ben had said, she felt no hope for her future.

A rifle shot echoed out in the woods. She ignored it for several minutes, then, fearing that marauders may already be in the area, she considered her peril and fled back to the tavern.

Seeing her running toward them, Jeanette and Polly came out to comfort her. The friends hugged, then Polly said, "I think you need to go see Ben."

"Yes," enjoined Jeanette. "Ben has something to say to you."

"What?" Cyntha replied. "I've lost my husband. I've lost what money I had. Reynolds is dying. What does that unkind man want? Is he going to deride me and add to my misery?"

"Not at all," Jeanette said. "Just the opposite."

Cyntha paused a moment, and then strode cautiously into the tavern. She saw the Cox boys playing with their metal toy soldiers in the parlor. Lucinda was knitting while her husband, Joe, held the yarn stretched between his hands. Cyntha went upstairs. Ben was not there.

Coming down the stairs, she caught sight of Ben sitting on the back-porch steps. The Coxs' rifle leaned against the wall. When she drew closer, she saw that he was gutting a freshly killed deer. He looked up, wiped his hunting knife on a cloth, and stood carefully, being prudent of his injured ankle. "Hello, Cyntha." He swept off his hat and made a clumsy bow. "I'm afraid I have acted in an... ungentlemanly fashion toward you. I ain't good at apologies, but here it is. Of late, I find myself needin' to say I'm sorry a great deal. I had no right to speak to you like I did."

Cyntha smiled, relief pouring through her. "I forgive you. I..."

"Let me finish, dear lady. You and Reynolds both have been so generous to me. I ain't sayin' I'm worth all the trouble you've been through on my behalf, but I owe you my life." He cleared his throat, shifted his weight, stuck the hunting knife in its scabbard. "I ain't sayin' yet that I'd ever want to be a shopkeep. I gotta think on that awhile. I guess there's more onerous jobs in the world. But old Reynolds can't escort you by himself to Ohio or wherever you're going. He deserves to be with his family. He's my...friend. There, I said it."

"Oh, thank you, Ben." She hugged him.

Ben hugged her back, then he held her away and looked at her face. "You've been cryin' 'cause o' me. I don't ever want to be the cause of your pretty eyes cryin' again."

Cyntha wiped her face with her apron.

"First thing, then, I got to finish dressin' and cleanin' this deer that wandered into the yard. We're gonna have venison tonight. Last thing I got to ask you is how we gonna go to Ohio if we don't have no carriage? I can't ride no more, and I don't see no horses 'round here neither."

"Let me worry about that. My brother Anthony has been walking about some goodly distances in the last few days, even with his wooden leg. He's quite strong. He found a carriage near Leetown that a man's willing to part with."

While Cyntha watched over his shoulder, Ben begun cutting the head and hooves from the deer. When he began stripping the hide from the carcass, he said, "You can go, Cyntha. I'm fine."

Cyntha went inside and looked in on Reynolds upstairs, sleeping. Back downstairs, she asked Anthony to procure the carriage, and he assured her that he would have it the next day, and with a team of horses.

When Ben finished dressing the deer, he lifted it inside for Joe and Polly to carve up. He was weary. That night, he had troubled dreams of battle and death.

THIRTY-TWO

MISFORTUNE ABOUNDING, UNEXPECTED BENEVOLENCE FLOWING

MARCH 17, 1862, LATE AFTERNOON
EASTERN ARKANSAS BACK COUNTRY

Constance Felder pulled the blanket around her tighter, and then clinched Edward Felder's biceps, narrow as it was, with both hands. They wore no rings, but were husband and wife. Had been married for two days.

The bright blue day was fading down to gray and purple, spears of the late afternoon sun flashing through the trees along the narrow, wild east Arkansas road where the tree limbs leaned across the road to form a sort of tunnel. Constance felt that surely no danger would ever confront them again.

They rode in a buckboard wagon given to them by Reverend Martin. After the wedding, the retired pastor and his wife gave as a gift the wagon, a wooden chair, a bundle of fresh clothes, and bags of corn and turnips and some cooked hams, swathed in cloth. Last of all, the pastor added a wide tarp to cover it all.

Along their journey through the swampy country, Constance had increased their bounty by setting rabbit traps and digging up wild onions along creek beds. She wore a starched flower-pattern dress given her by Mrs. Martin, though it was wider than her frame and blousy in the bosom. Except for when she knelt in the dirt to set the rabbit traps and dig up the onions, she had managed to keep the dress relatively clean. It smelled of starch and sunshine.

"Do you think God will lean on me for all my errant ways before I met you?" she said.

"Lean on you? I think not. God bears a great many of our missteps, my dearest Mrs. Felder," Edward said. "Why, the Israelites made a golden calf and worshiped it like it was a god, and the Lord forgave them. Despite yours and my tawdry beginnings and many transgressions against His word, Reverend Martin married us; so our souls may range freer, and he blessed our union further with this wagon. Our horses pull it fine." He leaned back on the reins while the horses negotiated a steep slope.

"Mrs. Edward Felder!" Constance said. "I can cotton to the sound o' that." She smiled and began humming "The Blackest Crow."

"Do you know the words, Constance?"

"Nah. My pap used to sing it when I was a little scrapper. It's supposed to be about a river. I think the tune sounds like a river flowin'."

"It does a bit."

Though the weather was still sharp cold when they left the burned-out Reeder home, riding their horses and with nothing more to eat than the remains of the wild turkey that Constance had shot, they had traveled to just outside of Pocahontas, Arkansas and found the home of the retired reverend and his wife, who took them in. Reverend Martin performed the marriage ceremony for the lovers the next day and allowed them to recuperate for another day in a spare room.

Constance, her black hair gleaming in the vanishing sunlight, focused her vision through the tiny five-inch space between her horse's perked black ears, trying for the fun of it to concentrate on just that line of road which lay before them. She knew the animal had almost 360 degrees of eyesight and could see things in front of it, to the sides of it, and even much behind it simultaneously. She figured her swarthy horse as being content to watch just the road ahead and pull.

At the bottom of the slope, a narrow creek flowed. Constance pointed at a big catfish wallowing in the muddy ebb. When the wagon's shadow fell across the creek, the fish swished away. "Damn, it got away before I could drop a line. Oh, I mean dang! I'm sorry for swearin', Eddie. I'm tryin'."

Eddie nodded, clucked his tongue, and flicked the reins, encouraging the horses to draw the wagon through the shallow water. "I have a feeling that *you* will make sure we are always well-fed."

Constance smiled.

"But we must always put the Lord first, and the well-being of my congregation before our own wants. If someone is hungry, it is better for us to go without, than they." His face took on a sternness, with elements of the melancholy.

Constance looked hard at him. "Is that what the Lord always wants?"

"Generally, yes. It's always good to ask Him." He sounded firm, like each decision must be one that the Lord decided. Constance figured she would have a lot of getting used to.

She patted the stiff dress fabric. "This is only the fourth dress I've ever owned." Seeing Edward's surprise, she added, "That's right. Our family was poor. Tragically poor sometimes. I had one dress when I was a little girl. I had one that Sara Reeder gave me afore I left to be a laundress for the army, then Mrs. Schmidt, the proprietor at the boarding house, gi' me a black one to wear that I didn't care a twit for, so I tossed it when we escaped from Springfield."

Edward's surprised look turned to concern and a sort of wondering admiration.

"So, until this one, most times I wore pants and a shirt like my pap. Seemed logical."

Almost in unison, the pair burst into laughing.

"Well, you are my fine wife now. All woman."

With the afternoon waning, they began looking for a place to camp. Near a swale of the road, a shabby, unpainted house with a high-pitched roof, its walls with a definitive lean to the south, its windows shuttered, came into view. A ladder leaned against the side, its top near a small door in the attic. In front of the house, the remains of a fire burned in a black circle. Edward slowed the wagon in front of the house, and they looked around for anyone. Edward shouted hello a few times.

Constance heard a sort of burring sound like would be made by a small rattling steam engine. It was coming from under the house. A murder of crows sat on the porch roof, and they seemed to be heckling something, cawing and swooping up and down and then alighting again.

After a few minutes, when no one showed, Edward jiggled the reins.

The moment the horses started, a huge black dog charged from under the porch in a stumbling manner like its legs were not working together, but still straight at Edward's gelding. Constance saw the foam around the dog's jaws just before it clamped its teeth into the horse's haunch and began tearing. The horse, its ears pinned back, its eyes rolled back almost full white, squealed like a rasp raked across iron and kicked and leaped in its harness, forcing the wagon to shimmy off the road. When the horse reared, the wagon tilted on two wheels, ready to tip over.

The dog fell loose, then went in for another bite. A man in a filthy shirt, his suspenders down, ran out of the door of the house, jerked out a pistol from his pants pocket and shot the dog. It yelped and fell dead, the bullet through its head.

The horse continued to leap, and it took Constance jumping from the wagon, grabbing the reins and wrestling the terrified horse to stand still. In doing so, she jerked her arm briefly out of socket, and she fell dangerously close to the dead dog.

"I wouldn't get too near that creature from hell," the suspendered man said. "Rabies."

Constance rolled away.

"I been holed up in my cabin a day and a half," the man stated, frank as a lawyer in court, "waitin' for the damn thing to come out from under the porch. I threw some burning logs from my hearth out into the yards hopin' to scare it away, but it didn't budge." The man stepped down from his porch and walked toward the wagon. He had blotchy skin and hollow cheeks; his bearing was skinny in the chest and bulbous at the belly. His left arm ended just past his elbow. He approached the dog and nudged it with his boot. Satisfied that it was dead, he stepped back.

Edward had climbed down and was attending to Constance who was breathing hard from the pain, and her brow was sweating like a rainstorm. Finally, she said, "I'm fine now, Eddie." She drew a deep breath several times, and he helped her to her feet. She rubbed her tender shoulder.

The gelding, eyes still wide, ears swept back, was bleeding profusely, the blood trickling down its legs and making a little stream flowing to where Edward and Constance stood.

"You best step away from that blood," the man said. "It's as dangerous as a bite from that dog. And you don't want to get the hydrophobia."

Edward and Constance moved away, and Edward took hold of the bridle of Constance's brown horse to hold it steady.

"We're gonna have to kill that horse." The man eyed the wounds. "Wash the other one good."

"What do you mean?" Edward exclaimed. "We need that horse to finish our journey."

The man gawped at Edward. "Nah, you don't. That animal is as good as dead now. Later, it'll bite your good horse or bite you, and you're done for. Name's Coburn. Walter Coburn. And what might yours be?"

"I'm Reverend Edward Felder. This is my new bride, Mrs. Constance Felder."

"A reverend? I'll be." Coburn set his revolver back in his belt, then carefully removed the harness and straps to Edward's gelding. He took hold of the bridle near the horse's jaw and coaxed the jittery horse to the side of the house, stepping abroad of the animal's bloody leg. He led the horse out of sight farther down into the swale. In perhaps five minutes, Constance and Edward heard the gunshot.

A minute later, Coburn plodded back, holding the bridle. "We'll have to burn the body, so no other varmint takes a bite of it." He set down his gun, went to the unpainted barn behind the house. He returned with a pitchfork, and in short order, pierced the dead dog with the tines and carried it out to where the dead horse lay. On his return, he began gathering logs from his woodpile. "I'd be obliged if you'd help me carry some of this tinder."

Edward insisted Constance sit on the porch, and he took up several logs and followed Coburn. The blaze lit up the dismal sky, black vile-smelling smoke rising into the darkening night. When the men came back to the porch, Coburn said, "The ground's too marshy for anything else to catch fire. You're welcome to stay the night. Put your horse up in the barn after we slosh some water on it to rid the blood. You best sleep inside. If the snakes don't get ya, the wolves will."

After Constance's gelding was secured in the barn alongside the man's swaybacked mare, the three went inside. The man pushed open the shutters and let the last vestiges of evening light into the darkened room. He lit several oil lamps. In a far corner, almost in shadow, an old woman sat in a rocker. She was palest white, the blue veins showing along her boney arms, and white hairs curled from her chin and above her lip. She gave them a toothless grin, and her eyes sparkled blue and gray. "Be good," she said. "Always be good." She rocked and hummed "The Water is Wide." She was surprisingly on pitch, and her tone was lilting.

"You sing right well," Constance said to the woman.

The woman nodded.

"I'm Constance Felder. This is my husband, Edward."

"Name's Edna Leigh Coburn." She commenced to humming and rocking again.

"That's my ma," Coburn said. "Only relative I got left. Wife's dead. Young'uns dead."

"I'm sorry for your loss," Edward said. "How did they die, if I be that bold to ask?"

"All of 'em drowned," Coburn said. "The wife was a carefree sort. Didn't always think things through. She thought she'd take the boys on a picnic by the creek. Well, none of 'em could swim. When the little 'un fell in, the older one tried to save 'im and jumped in, so they both was drownin', then my wife followed and drowned herself, too." He gave a deep sigh. "Found their bodies later a mile down river."

"My condolences, Walter," Edward said.

"I'm sorry, too." Constance sat on a ladderback chair. Her shoulder was feeling better, and she assayed the one room house. Not a picture on the wall or the mantel. No books on a shelf. A large wardrobe stood against one wall, four wooden chairs. Lamps sat on small tables and stools. A stove and larder behind where the old woman rocked. Two beds, one wide, one narrow, sat on opposite sides of the room. A flimsy sheet hung on a line around the narrow one. Constance figured that was the bed for the mother and that the children must have slept in the attic.

On the hearth, a few pans were stacked, all filthy-ringed, caked with old, burned food. Several jugs leaned on the hearthstones, some stoppered, some not. Though the floor was level, the walls of the house bore an obvious lean, and they wavered and creaked with the breeze, so if Constance looked too long at the walls, it made her stomach a bit queasy.

"Ain't nothin' to eat," Coburn said. "I ain't felt much like huntin' or tendin' garden since they died. House needs repairin'. And..." He sank on a chair and set his revolver on the hearth.

Constance felt unsettled. She sensed there was more to the story.

Coburn sat with his elbows on his knees, head down, just eyeing the floor like he expected something to come up through one of the cracks.

A brisk wind blew, and the walls tilted several inches, the whole house sounding like it was ripping apart. Constance eyed Edward nervously.

"Where you headed?" Coburn said at last, never looking up.

"Tennessee," Edward said, trying to sound optimistic. "I'm going to help pastor a flock in a little church. It's a new start for us."

Coburn mumbled something.

"Excuse me," Edward said. "I didn't hear you."

"I said," Coburn replied, "You don't fool me none. Sayin' yor a minister and yor married to that woman and neither of you wearin' weddin' rings." He twisted the band on his finger. "What kind of idiot do you take me for, and what kind of liar are you?" His face began to turn red.

Edward stepped back. "Sir, I assure you I am a man of the cloth, and Constance is indeed my wife." He pulled his worn Bible from his jacket pocket and held it out.

"That be right," Constance said. "We both lost everything. The Yanks burned his church and ran him out of town. The marauding gangs burned my house and barn, and that's the honest truth." She stood and strode to the man, her eyes flashing. "We ain't got nothin' 'cept what was given us by the good Reverend Martin and his wife. We're poorer than you."

"So, you ain't some kinda whore and her dandy?" Coburn said. "Because I'll not have that kind in my home. This is a Christian home."

"Well then," Edward said. "Since you saw fit to question my honesty, where is your Bible?"

Coburn stood and walked shakily to a place on the mantel and pointed at a rectangle where the dust was not evident. "It used to be there. When my family died, I threw it into the river. I almost lost my faith." The sobs from him came heavy, and his body quaked.

His old mother stood and with stuttering steps came up behind him and put her frail hands on his shoulders. "Be good."

Coburn finally turned and brushed his eyes with his dirty palms. "You newlyweds can sleep in my bed. A man should have his wife in his bed. That's all. I'll catch enough sleep in a chair."

True to his word, Coburn had not a thing to eat, not a turnip, nor onion, nor even strips of dried meat. It was too late to search the pitiful garden for some root or berry, so Edward offered to share their ham. Coburn managed to find some clean tin plates and mugs, and the four dined moderately on the meat alone.

Before he assisted his poor mother to disrobe, helped her put on a gown, and helped her lie on her mattress, he sent the newlyweds to bed. Constance admired the gentle nature that the man with only one hand and the stub of an arm used to help the aged woman.

When finished, Coburn drew the threadbare sheet across the line, so the woman had a measure of privacy. Then he rifled through an old chest, pulled forth two large iron traps. He set to filing down the teeth with a rasp, then dug some lard from the tub by the stove and swabbed the grease over the springs. When finished he carried the traps and ham bones outside. Constance and Edward listened to his steps walking about the yard, then the clang of him setting the traps and pinning the chain anchor down with a spike.

THIRTY-THREE

DEATH COMES BY A MYRIAD WAYS

MARCH 18, 1862, 9:00 P.M.
COBURN'S HOUSE, EASTERN ARKANSAS

That night, Constance and Edward lay under a sheet and blanket, whispering sweet comments to each other. Constance ran her fingers through his long, sleek hair. He held her shoulders and stroked her brown, sinewy arms, then he took her hands and caressed her fingertips. He had never felt such an abundance of joy and satisfaction as he felt lying in the arms of this confounding, tough, and yet gentle half-Cherokee. When the fire fell to coals, they slept.

Later in the pitch-black night, Constance was awakened by the sharp, piercing howls of wolves. When at last the pack quit their lament at the moon, she cuddled closer to Edward, and sleep again overtook her.

Later still, both were awakened when something heavy bumped their bed. Blinking awake, they perceived the shadowy form of Coburn leaning over them, whiskey jug in the crook of his short arm, a large knife gleaming in his hand. A lamp glowed on a table behind him. His form looked dark and menacing. They could not see his face, save his eyes glaring.

Sitting up, Edward pulled Constance behind him, ready to take the plunge of the knife.

For what seemed like an eternity, Coburn stood flush up against the bed, glaring at them. Finally, he let the knife loose, and it clattered to the floor. Drawing a deep breath. "Yor a minister. You need to know the truth, and I have a proposition for you."

"Yes, by all means." Edward struggled up from the bed, standing before him, wearing nothing but his long underwear. Constance pulled the blanket up to her chin and backed against the wall.

Coburn belched an alcohol-laden breath, potent and sour. "My family didn't drown. I shot 'em."

Edward could not help letting out a gasp. Constance, quick as a rabbit, reached for the knife on the floor, gathered it up, and held it under the blanket.

Coburn drew himself up to his full height, looking like a geyser in him was about to burst. "I had to shoot 'em. That hydrophobic dog bit all three. They were all gonna die a vile death. So, I shot each one in the heart. My wife pleaded with me at first not to, then she pleaded that I would. You see... I had to. It was not a while ago like I tried to put on. It was yesterday. And I threw the Bible in the river weeks ago when my wife's baby died in birth."

"I understand. You had no choice." Edward eased the jug from the man, set it on the floor, then hugged him. "Your Father in Heaven understands. He will forgive you." He released the hug and, despite his fear, tried to show compassion in his face.

"But how can I forgive myself?"

"Time." Constance said. "I learned that. Time heals. I had to let my first husband go off to war, knowing he would probably die, bound to be dead, and that I might not ever be married again or have a chance to have a child."

Coburn looked at her and wept. "Time. I see." Choking, he said, "Here's my proposition. You hep me bury my family, say your reverend words, read the scripture. And let me and my ma ride in yor wagon as far as the Arkansas side of Memphis. Got family there. My old horse can hep pull your wagon. Ain't really anything much we need to take, 'cept Ma's rockin' chair."

Edward looked at Constance, and she nodded. "Very well," he said. "We'll help you bury your family, and we'll all go together to Memphis. That's where we cross into Tennessee. It will work."

"Fine. I'll wake you at first light." He picked up his jug and threw it against the hearth, smashing it. Then he turned to Constance, his words harsh. "Gi' me my knife now."

Constance slowly brought the knife from under the blanket and handed it him. He went and blew out the lamp and curled into a ball on the floor. Soon he was snoring. Edward stayed awake, his eyes ever on the man.

Coburn woke Constance and Edward before the sun was up, and he had biscuits baking in a pot set on coals outside in the ground. "I took the last of our flour and leavenin' and made these a'fore sunup," he said. "Nothin' left after that. No animal stepped in my traps. Likely, we'll starve."

After they ate, he showed them the gray, stiff, and swollen bodies of his wife and children laid under a tarp in a tool shed. Flies buzzed and crawled atop the tarp. After the two men dug the holes for the bodies, Edward was dissatisfied with the simple wood crosses that Coburn had fashioned. He took the better half of the day, using old board scraps on which he carved the dead's names, then whitewashed each board. He nailed the crosspieces securely, creating what he considered to be more suitable adornments for the graves.

He and Coburn hammered the new crosses into the soil at the head of each mound. Edward read from the Bible, and they knelt and said multiple prayers. He gave Constance the Bible to read the twenty-third psalm. Coburn remained mute throughout, often weeping.

When Edward completed the ceremony, Coburn said, "I can't stay here no longer, but I ain't goin' with ya. Just take my ma."

In mid-afternoon, Coburn lifted his frail mother onto her corncob mattress he had placed in the rear of the Felders' wagon. Then he added her rocker. He helped Constance harness up her horse and his old swayback horse to the wagon. The Felders said their goodbyes to Coburn and departed.

Soon after they left, while traveling the winding road, it veered once quite close to a narrowing in the White river. Edward's mouth fell open. He jerked the wagon to a halt and pointed. Constance and he watched Coburn wading across to the other side of the river. Then he disappeared into the brush. His old mama called after him, "Be good!"

THIRTY-FOUR

SNATCHED AWAY, LEST WICKEDNESS PERVERT

– WISDOM 4:11

MARCH 18, 1862
CENTRAL ARKANSAS

After leaving Elkhorn, Sara rode slowly for two days and had no problems passing through the Union camps. She had to bribe only one sentry, relinquishing to him a can of fruit and the dried meat.

Traveling the Telegraph Road through the camp, she saw copious numbers of runaway slaves, all vying for attention from any officer they could find. The slaves carried their clothes and sundry items bound up in white sheets. Black men with white bundles, black women carrying white flour sacks on their backs and a few carrying babies tied up in white cloth slings dangling from their necks. Sara watched a small Negro girl, holding a tattered cloth doll in one hand, toddle along in the center of one group. Her heart went out to them all, but particularly to the tiny child. She felt an anguish she had not felt before about the Negroes, and she recognized the feeling as guilt. White and black, over and over, the castoffs of a broken, guilty land.

Sara had always considered Negroes as "regular folks," not dissimilar to Abram, no different than her brothers, or her father, or herself.

While she watched them, a Negro man with a bass voice initiated a spiritual song. The others joined in. *Go Down, Moses* in perfect harmony.

In her earlier life, Sara had given little thought to whether any Negro was slave or free, though she figured they preferred some freedom. She remembered what the slave, Billie Sue, had told her about all persons being indebted to someone or in some way enslaved to a person. *All of us on a journey to freedom.*

Sara was troubled more by the presence of Yankees in what she considered to be *her* land and could not fathom why the Coloreds were falling in with such a horde. Her heart burned against the Yankees.

When she saw one Union ruffian manhandling a small Negro boy, she rode up and kicked the soldier in the back, knocking him flat. "Be gone, Satan!" she yelled. While she trotted Esther away, the young black male eluded his tormentor.

She rode through the long Federal camp. Outside of the camp by half a mile, she changed into her soldier garb, then rubbed the charcoal on her cheeks and upper lip. Pushing a floppy-brimmed hat low on her brow, she said, "That's as good as I can get it."

Following the trail of abandoned Rebel camps with rows of black fire circles for two more days, she arrived at Frog Bayou near nightfall. She came to the edge of a line of tents, each lit with campfires. Dismounting, she acted her best to walk like a bow-legged cowhand. She lowered her voice as deep as possible, adding a gravelly yowl to her words. Coming upon a young soldier, she asked him where to find the Third Texas Cavalry.

Despite his apparent youth, the soldier said, "Over yonder, young 'un." He pointed into the dark patches of trees where the tree frogs croaked in a back and forth cadence. "You sound like you got one of them frogs in your throat. If it don't get better, you best see the doctor."

"Thank you kindly," Sara growled. "Yeah, took a hit to my throat from a Yank's gunstock. Pains me some."

The soldier nodded as if he understood.

Sara led Esther through the woods, looking for the telltale flag of the cavalry regiment. She found a string of horses, then spotted the regimental Third Texas flag on a pole by a large tent. "Must be Colonel Greer's headquarters," she whispered.

Beyond the colonel's tent, she could make out a group of men sitting and standing around a roaring, hissing campfire.

The darkness or the deprivations of war had not dampened the spirits of these Third Texas men. Someone had found a keg of moonshine, and the mugs and cups of every soldier were filled. One soldier began thumping on a banjo, another stroked a fiddle, and the boisterous group, with twangs and drawls, burst into singing "The Girl I Left Behind Me." One fellow beat on a hollow log, another grabbed a mouth-harp, and though the entire group never approached singing on the same pitch, they, in Sara's estimation, bellowed like stuck hogs trying to out-squeal each other.

The firelight flickered back and forth over each man's countenance, each one appearing as happy as any man might be. They smelled like wet wool, unwashed bodies, mud and sour mash liquor.

When the song ended, Sara ambled up to the edge of the campfire light, but before she could speak, one of the soldiers with a burly beard and a round belly, his suspenders hanging down, pointed at her and called out. "Look! It's one of them new recruits. Already got 'im a uneeform. How come you gets a uneeform before I gets one?" He wagged a finger at her.

The other men around the fire were quiet. Sara wanted to back away. Then the cavalrymen erupted into wide chortles. Sara smiled, relieved.

"I was just joshin' you, son," the bearded soldier said, "but I'm glad you have that dandy uneeform. My name's Franklin Bell. What's your name, Private?"

Sara had not considered adopting a man's name. "Un, Lucas Reeder."

"Well, hello, Private Reeder. Welcome to the Third Texas. You just get here?"

"Naw," she drawled. "Joined yesterday. Went back for the uniform."

"You ain't tol' me where you got them duds."

Sara deliberated a moment, then replied. "They belonged to my brother what was killed by a Yank. Our cousin sent the uniform home to ma, and I swore I'd take my brother's place. That's all."

"Oh." Bell softened his tone. "May he rest in peace."

The rest of the men echoed similar sentiments.

"Why don't you tie up your pony and join us?" Bell said.

Sara tied Esther to the rope picket and secured the reins, then returned to the circle.

"Ain't ya gonna take the saddle off your mount?" another soldier called.

Sara looked back. "In a bit." She was considering bolting, but she steeled herself to continue her attempt at soldiering.

One of the men offered her a pull on a crock jug.

"No thanks, never touch it," Sara said in her gravelly voice.

"That so?" Bell said. "So how old you be, Private Reeder?"

"Um, eighteen this month."

"Ya don't look even fourteen. I mean it's all good you goin' to take the place of your brother, but they's some hard fightin' ahead. Ain't nothin' simple about it."

"I know."

"Well, sit ya down, and hear what these Texians have to say. Ya might learn somethin."

Sara sat on a tree stump beside a man who smelled of rancid pork, and his nose whistled when he breathed out. She listened to the campfire jabbering of the men for what seemed like an eternity. They were loose with their cursing and risqué jokes.

In a break in the talk, unable to restrain herself, she blurted, "Any of you know where I could find Corporal Joseph Favor?"

Some of the men ceased their conversation and turned toward her.

"How do you know Corporal Favor?" A man who had been standing on the periphery of the circle spoke with a decidedly British accent.

Sara looked up at him.

"Hello, young lad," the Englishman said. "I'm Sergeant Ebenezer Dollander, but you can call me Ebie. I got wounded in the recent fray at Elkhorn, so they promoted me." He pointed at the chevron on his sleeves, one sleeve with a ragged re-stitching over a large tear. "Got these stripes today. Means I can give orders to these yahoos, and they can ignore me as fast as I give them."

The company guffawed.

One soldier said, "Damn right."

"I got these stripes because I got shot in the shoulder. I figure that if I get shot in the leg, they'll make me a captain, and if I get shot in the ass, they'll probably make me a general."

The cavalrymen tilted from their seats, laughing, almost falling over.

"You tell 'em, Ebie," another soldier hollered.

"How do you know Corporal Favor?" Ebie asked again. He leaned closer to her, cocking his head and closing one eye, like he was checking if a possum was truly dead or just pretending.

"I knew of him, 'cause he knew my brother."

"What's your brother's name? Maybe I know him."

"Like as not," Sara lowered her head as Ebie drew closer. She spoke the story she had rehearsed in her mind. "He'd just joined the Third Texas the day before the Wilson Creek battle. Died the next day. Probably wasn't on any roster. But he wrote a letter to Ma that day before he died, and he spoke highly of Corporal Favor. That's all."

Ebie straightened and walked a few paces away. Turning, he said, "Corporal Favor isn't with us anymore. Either he got killed or captured at Elkhorn. Probably killed. Snatched away from the war, lest its wickedness pervert him."

Sara had prepared herself as best she could for just this sort of devastating news, but hearing it said aloud tore at her heart. She choked, "That is sad news. I will have to tell my ma this further sorry tale of woe."

"You still ain't tol' us," Bell interjected, "the name of your brother that signed up the day before the battle. I've been with the Third since its beginnin'.

"Oh, apologies, fellas. His name was, um, Paul McGavin." She had not expected the interrogation, and her thoughts flew to the one name. "He…uh, was my brother from a different father who died a long time ago. My ma married again, married Pa Reeder, after her first husband died."

"Well, ain't that a fine thing," Bell said. "There's a Captain Paul McGavin in this division. Was a scout for McCulloch mostly before the general was killed, but McGavin scouts for General Van Dorn now. He, for sure, ain't dead. No telling where he's at, though. Probably ranging all over, watching for them Yanks. But if he's related, I'm sure he'd be glad to see you."

Sara was backpedaling. "Un, what's he look like?"

"Dark hair, wears specs, limps on his right leg. Quiet type."

"Well," Sara said, "that's not what my brother looked like. He was sort of heavy set and balding. But he might be a distant relative. How about another song?"

The men, half them lying couchant like a pride of lions, and drunken enough to be easily distracted, returned to their revelry and started a new song.

When no one troubled her further with questions, she picked up a stick and drew aimlessly in the dirt. If Joseph was captured, he might as well be dead. She thought, *Somewhere in a northern prison in the cold, and dyin' slow.*

She rose and brushed past Ebie, who was lighting a long-stemmed pipe, then she turned. "Where would I find this Captain McGavin?" She needed to talk to someone she knew, to lessen her sorrow. She trusted him. "Maybe he's related."

"No idea." Ebie came close to her and whispered in her ear. "I don't know where he is, little lady."

Sara's eyes widened with surprise and disappointment. Her ruse had failed utterly.

"And you'll do more for this army by being a laundress or carrying mail or stitching socks or anything else. Glory be! I wouldn't stay around here. Some of these men, just a few, if they find out you're a woman ..."

"I understand. Please keep your knowin' to yourself."

"I intend to. And Joseph Favor was a good friend of mine, too. My best friend. I believe God snatched him up, so he wouldn't have to be in this wicked war any more. He was a good man. No wonder your brother spoke highly of him. I will miss him. Sometimes, I feel his ghost coming around to see if I'm doing all right."

Sara's emotions could not be contained. The tears streaked down her face, leaving wet trails in the smeared charcoal. Ebie, puffing on his overlong pipe clenched tight in his teeth, patted her shoulders. "Get gone now. Find another way to help."

Sara turned, untied Esther, and climbed into the saddle. She galloped along the moonlit road for miles.

Finally, she pulled Esther to a halt and stroked the mare's neck. "That a girl. Let's find you some water."

It was not long before she found a stream running near the road. She got down from Esther and led the horse to the water. She bent to the stream and cupped her hands, drinking noisily, and then bathed her face of the charcoal grime. After her horse had drunk, she led her horse into a grassy cove and set up a camp. She made a small campfire, opened one of the cans of fruit, punching ragged holes in the lid with her knife, and ate the contents, then slurped the liquid. She laid out her bedroll and sat on it. "Find another way to help, he said. I will do just that."

She prayed for Joseph's soul, because she knew in her heart that he was dead.

With her great desire to share her pain of loss and share her conviction to help the Southern army, she realized she firmly trusted Paul McGavin, and quickly determined to sneak back to General Van Dorn's army's camp and find Paul.

THIRTY-FIVE

❧

Schemes and Contrivances

March 20, 1862, 8:00 a.m.
Washington, DC

Lucas Reeder pored over a tattered manual of Federal Army telegraph operations. The next day, he was applying for a job as a telegraph operator for the War Department. He hoped his acquaintance, Captain Thomas Eckert, would support his obtaining a job. He had already watched President Lincoln trek the block and a half several times from the President's Mansion to the War Department building. His hope was that he could find an opportune moment to dispatch the President, thus hastening an end to the war and, thereby, bring the nation back together. He pondered, *With Lincoln gone, the Southern states would surely rush back to the Union.*

Several times a day he reminded himself of what he had discerned—that Lincoln's very presence was the cause of the war. His demise would bring about its end and reunite the country. So certain was he, his imagination perceived a newspaper headline heralding him a hero for saving the nation.

The manual was boring him. He lifted his right boot to stare at its flimsy sole, as thin as tissue paper, the front end loose and curled. His old uniform jacket, hanging on the door, was no longer regulation, and he remained amazed that no one had called him on it. It had stayed markedly cold into late March, so he had seldom gone out without his greatcoat.

Pausing, he looked out the dusty window to watch a long sleigh with oak runners being pulled slowly by shaggy-maned draft horses with immense hooves along the muddy slop of Philadelphia Avenue. Several dandies sat in the sled, dressed in as foppish a fashion as he could imagine. The men wore all manner of broad hats decorated with ribbons and greenery. Each man sported a coat of outlandish design; purple, or spotted like a leopard, or striped. Reeling while the sled lurched along, each one hoisted great brass tankards, sloshing the contents. A placard on the back of the sled announced, "New Recruits for the Grand Army of the Potomac." A single, uniformed sergeant in the sleigh held the reins of the team of horses. Three armed sentries slogged along behind the sleigh.

The group bellowed a song that he had heard before only once. He recognized the tune of "John Brown's Body," but the words were new and fraught with calls for God to bring calamitous defeat to enemies. He caught a few of the slurred words. *Trampling out the vintage where the grapes of wrath are stored.*

"Perhaps," he whispered, "I needn't worry about the war ending if those men are the best the North has to offer."

He glanced over at Workman. His companion had an interview today for a position of groom at the President's Mansion stables. Workman had learned of the position from a talkative army private in a bar, and since Workman had grown up in Kentucky working on the farms of the great thoroughbreds, he had good cause to think he would be hired. He only needed to be a soldier. Citizens need not apply.

∽

MARCH 20, 1862, 9:00 A.M.
TENNESSEE RIVER, BELOW SAVANNAH, TENNESSEE

Bluish gray clouds were gathering rapidly from the west, rolling and hurling rain with a fierce, howling wind. Joseph watched the storm approaching while riding in the stern of a small rowboat with a man who had the ruddy complexion of a salty seaman and was attired in ragged clothes. The old seadog rowed the dinghy up to the paddle-wheeler, Tigress, anchored along the east shore of the Tennessee River, adjacent to Savannah. Joseph remembered playing in his youth alongside the Mississippi often when Memphis was his home. However, he seldom had ventured out on the great river in any sort of vessel. The waves of the rapid Tennessee River, driven by the harsh wind, sloshed threateningly against the gunwales of the little boat. Coming alongside the sidewheeler, near a ramp that extended down to the waterline, a sailor reached out a hand and helped Joseph to gain a foothold on the ramp. The seadog in the dinghy never said a word, but rowed back to the opposite shore.

The sailor escorted Joseph to the deck and then bade him to wait. Joseph put a hand on the railing, for the ship rocked considerably.

An ensign with a scabbarded sword and an old flintlock pistol in his belt approached Joseph, but stopped and took an eased stance, one hand behind his back. He spoke no word. When Joseph took a step forward, the ensign quickly held out a gloved hand toward Joseph, who halted.

Joseph and the ensign stood there the better part of a half an hour. The rocking of the boat continued, and the wind buffeted Joseph and made his eyes water. Several raindrops plopped onto the deck, onto the bill of the ensign's cap and onto Joseph's kepi and face.

A pink-faced sailor rushed up to the ensign and whispered in his ear. The ensign nodded and beckoned Joseph, motioning with his hand to follow him. Joseph was led through an interior cabin with chairs and tables where numerous marines sat playing cards.

Joseph and the ensign climbed a stair into a small upper office, more like a storage compartment, with space for only a desk and chair and a few inches in which to stand. A bearded officer in his early thirties sat behind the desk, writing fervently. After he had finished the document, he slapped it into a file box and looked up.

Joseph snapped to attention and saluted, and the officer returned the salute.

"The spy, sir," the ensign said.

The officer rose and dismissed the ensign. He extended his hand to Joseph. "Welcome, Private Favor, I am Captain Rawlins. I would offer you a seat, but as you can see, there's no room. I'm a little informal, at least, compared to some officers. You are to wait here until General Grant has a free moment to speak to you. Can you stand there while I complete some paperwork?"

"Yes, sir." Joseph stood at ease. Captain Rawlins began toiling his way through a pile of papers.

The storm that had been brewing attacked the boat, sending it into a starboard lean, then flouncing back, swaying wildly at its anchor. Joseph's stomach immediately began to feel queasy. He had difficulty keeping his footing. His nausea grew worse.

Joseph jumped when he heard what sounded like a lion's roar. "John, send the spy in." The voice came from behind the wall where Captain Rawlins sat. The officer rose, opened the narrow door behind him, and, immediately, volumes of cigar smoke poured into the small office.

"This way," Captain Rawlins said.

Joseph, stumbling with the undulating movement of the ship, followed the captain into a narrow hallway.

Captain Rawlins opened another door. Joseph entered a larger room, outfitted with a built-in bed, windows, and a desk and several chairs. Each chair slid a little with each dip of the boat. Seated behind the desk, General Ulysses S. Grant puffed on a fat cigar. A cloud of smoke floated about eye level. On the desk sat a single telegram and a pencil. The general rose when Joseph and Captain Rawlins entered.

"Is this the spy, John?" General Grant said.

Captain Rawlins saluted, "Yes, Sam. This is Private Joseph Favor. Late of Tennessee, then Iowa, then the First Iowa Volunteers, knocked out and let loose of his faculties and memories at Wilson Creek, fought a while for the Reb Third Texian Cavs. And from what General Halleck's correspondence says, he's seen the elephant. Got his memory back, and here he is to help save the Union. At least, General Halleck sent him to us."

During this introduction, Joseph was holding a weak salute and trying not to vomit.

"Settle down, son," General Grant said to Joseph, then to Captain Rawlins, "Thank you, John, go ahead and get back to all your paperwork."

Captain Rawlins departed, closing the door.

"Sit, Private." General Grant indicated a chair. "You look green. I'm going to have to ask you not to toss up your breakfast in my office."

"I'll do my best, sir," Joseph sat, and then caught some acrid fluid in his mouth and forced himself to swallow it. He closed his eyes and concentrated. The rain thumped at the window.

"I'm sorry about the smoke. I had the window open, but had to close it when the storm hit. Rain was coming in."

Joseph was nonplussed.

"I take it you're not used to the ebb and flow of a riverboat."

"No, sir, at least, not in a storm." He began to sweat. The cigar smoke was tearing at his nose, making him feel the urge to vomit.

Grant stubbed out his cigar in an ashtray, rose, and opened the window a small amount, letting in a fresh breeze and a little rain. He sat again and stared at Joseph a while. "Why're you fighting this war, Private Favor?"

"I am fighting to free the Negro from bondage, sir."

"I'm inclined to agree with your sentiments. My father is a staunch abolitionist, and I would be, too, except that my wife's family owns slaves back in Missouri."

Joseph was startled. "I beg pardon."

"Son, I do not like to repeat myself. I am inclined to agree with you, but ending slavery, at least for the time being, is not why we're fighting this war. The reason we are fighting is to put down the rebellion. We must continue this great experiment, this miracle, called a democratic republic. For that, we need all the states. Not just some of them. And, hopefully, if things work out, we'll free the slaves, too." He drew a cigar from his jacket pocket, struck a match, and nearly lit the cigar, but stopped when he saw Joseph grimacing.

He blew out the match, but still held the cigar between his fingers. "What do you hope to accomplish as a spy, son? But before you begin, I've read the whole litany of your sordid story, so I hold some doubts as to the veracity of your interest. You could just as easily be a spy for the Rebs."

"I've considered that notion myself, General Grant. I assure you I am sincere. I am fervent in my desire that we win this war, teach the rebels a lesson, and make them pay for placing good people in bondage."

"So, you don't want to just free the slaves. You want to punish the Southern White folks?"

"Since you put it that way, I guess not. I'm just angry that some people would make slaves of others."

"Favor, there's been slaves since before Biblical times. There's slaves presently in China. For centuries, India society has employed and continues to utilize what's called a caste system where most of their population might as well be slaves. In fact, they're probably not treated as well as slaves. And where did you think those white slavers got the black slaves?"

"I believe they went in the jungle, hunted them down, and netted them, and then drug them on board slave ships."

"Maybe a few. But most of those black slaves were already slaves of African warlords who sold them to the Whites for gold or for our weapons. It was African warriors who hunted down less fortunate Africans, and bound them, and made them march to the beaches where the White men traded for them."

"You're saying the Africans were already slaves to other Africans?"

"Yes, sadly. But America's supposed to be of nobler fiber. This country can do just fine without slaves. Work hard and pay your taxes, and the dream is yours to grab. And any man can become the president, even a rail-splitter like President Lincoln."

"Yes." Joseph paused, dumbfounded about the knowledge of how the slaves were captured. Finally, he said, "Anyway, I want to help, and I think my knowledge of Southern thinking and Southern attitudes will make me good at this. My family's farm was just thirty miles east of Memphis. My pa and me used to drive our carts of corn along the road that runs alongside the Memphis and Atlanta railroad. We used to wave at the trains when they passed by. I can infiltrate. And... if you're worried that I'll abscond with information and plans and pass them to the Rebels, then assign someone to go with me and keep an eye on me."

"That's an intriguing idea." General Grant twirled the cigar in his fingers. "Your family for the North or for the South?"

"My parents and brother are dead. They died of Yellow Fever years ago. I sold the farm."

"No relatives?"

"Cousins in Baltimore. And my wife, whom I've not seen since July of sixty-one. I'd like to send her a letter, but no one will let me."

"I'll send it. Do you have the letter?"

"Yes, it's addressed and ready to send."

"Give it to me."

Joseph handed the general the letter. He looked briefly at the name and address, and then stuck it in his jacket pocket. "I'll make sure it gets mailed." He clasped his hands together and looked a long time at Joseph. "Private, I can't say I need a spy at this time. I've got plenty of scouts who give ample reports on the enemy, almost hourly sometimes. And General Sherman says he already has enough spies."

"Enough spies?"

"Yes, the newspaper reporters that hound him day in and day out. They do more spying than a whole host of hired spies. Then they print our plans in the papers. So, I can't see that you'd do me any good. I'd have to be worrying that you would get caught and accidentally reveal something."

Joseph's eyes fell. "But, sir."

"Now, don't get upset. I'm sending you to Washington. I know they have enough intrigue and subterfuge going on there that you might be pretty handy. Maybe they'll send you Richmond to spy on President Davis. I'll give you a personal note to give to General McClellan. He relies a great deal on spies fetching information for him. Has a whole spy department run by a Scotsman named Pinkerton."

Joseph opened his mouth to object, for he knew nothing of Washington, and going there took him even further away from Iowa, where he thought Cyntha still abided. He had a vision of her sitting in a mourning dress, poring over one of his letters, tears runneling down her cheeks.

General Grant waved his hand dismissively. "Now, that's my order. I'm promoting you to sergeant. No self-respecting spy should be of any lower rank. As soon as this storm passes, this ship's sailing to the other side of the river to Pittsburg Landing. I need to review the situation there with General Sherman. Our superior General Halleck has made it explicit that we are not in any way to engage the Rebs. I intend to honor that. I'm sorry I can't use you right now. Maybe General McClellan can."

"Yes, sir."

"When the weather clears, I'm sending you with Captain Rawlins ashore to my headquarters at the Cherry family mansion. They're good Unionists, like most of the residents of this part of Tennessee. They don't like the Secessionists one bit. You go with him. He'll issue you your sergeant bars, and get you the necessary papers to take with you to Washington."

"I understand. It's not what I'd hoped for, but I'm glad to do my duty, and thankful I'm fighting for the right side."

"Good man, Favor." General Grant stood, struck a match, and lit his cigar, puffing the smoke toward the window. "Looks like the storm's passing."

Blue sky was evident out the window, and the rocking of the boat had subsided considerably.

Joseph saluted.

"Here." General Grant withdrew a bottle of whiskey from a desk drawer and handed it to Joseph. "A friend secreted this liquor to me so that I might drink it if I got bored, but I swore to Captain Rawlins never to let liquor cross my lips, and I mean to keep my promise. Give it to him."

"Yes, sir."

"Favor, before I send you ashore. Are you an admirer of music?"

"Why, yes I am."

"Good. I can't stand it myself. Just racket that breaks my thinking. I can't carry pitch, and I like only two songs—one is Yankee Doodle, and the other one isn't." He chuckled.

"Yes, sir. I like good music."

"Fine. When you get to the Cherry family home, my wife left an old Negro servant with me, supposedly to keep me entertained. He's too old to travel all the time with her, and my kids wear him out, so he likes to play his *banja* for anyone'd listen. So, you be sure to let him play for you when you get there and stay awhile, so he doesn't feel like he has to perform for me."

"Yes, sir." Joseph saluted and turned to go. He was feeling a bit less nauseous, and was anxious to quit the smoky room.

"His name's Abram," General Grant mentioned while Joseph exited.

"Yes, sir. Abram."

Right after Joseph closed the door, he heard General Grant call clearly, "Abram Reeder."

THIRTY-SIX

OLD ACQUAINTANCES MET, AN ALARMING REALIZATION

MARCH 20, 1862, 11:00 A.M.
TENNESSEE RIVER, BELOW SAVANNAH, TENNESSEE

Joseph stutter-stepped and considered opening the door to ask General Grant to verify the name he heard. *Surely*, he thought, *it can't be the Abram of Wilson Creek. He knows about me and Sara.* He walked slowly down the narrow hall, but waited before opening the door to Captain Rawlins's office.

He gathered his breath and thought about what he had known since his younger days of prowess and being highly attracted to certain girls. He knew it was evident that he was attracted to Sara.

He was cognizant of the fact that when two vibrant youths of the opposite sex in their prime met in proximity, away from any crowd, that nature would gain governance over their emotions and common sense; and forsaking all vows, nature would ply its way into their actions. In secret, he had watched his older brother in a secluded spot some distance from a barn dance bring a maiden to ruin, though she was no unwilling partner. Later, the maiden had been sent to stay with relatives. Most folks living in the vicinity presumed she was with child.

Joseph had been wont to scold his older brother, but, to Joseph's astonishment, the brother, either at the behest of their parents or of his own accord, fetched up the maiden and made her his wife.

They moved to Memphis, and it was there where his brother, wife, and their child contracted Yellow Fever and died; and there, in the hot, humid, dismal days of summer that his parents went to the aid of their son and daughter-in-law and grandson, and they, too, contracted the malady as well, and directly died.

Joseph was left alone with the farm. Not old enough to ferret the technicalities of running a thriving farm, he opted to sell the land to a farmer living adjacent. With those funds, he moved to Memphis, and found employment at a livery stable and at the Memphis Tribune newspaper, setting type. In the summers, he hired himself out, harvesting crops on the farm he had sold.

Despite his industrious use of his time, he happened to meet one Cyntha Anne Atkinson, the daughter of a successful Memphis merchant family. He fell wildly in love with her, and began performing all types of hijinks to get her attention. She soon succumbed to his entreaties and returned her love for him. They were married a month later.

Cyntha had always dreamed of leaving Memphis, feigning to her parents a desire for freedom to experience the world, but secretly despising the wanton support of slavery rampant in the city. Joseph wanted to return to farming. Cyntha's brother, Anthony Atkinson, owned a substantial tract of farmland in Iowa. At a loss to himself, he set up mortgage payments at the bank for them. They moved to the farm within a month of marrying.

Just before departing, she convinced Joseph to purchase the slave, Josiah Reynolds, from a neighbor who needed the money to settle some gambling debts. When the three reached their new farm in Iowa, Joseph and Cyntha Favor granted Reynolds his freedom. He opted to stay on to help them farm the land, and they allotted him a comfortable wage.

Joseph longed to see Cyntha again and hoped Reynolds was taking good care of her.

Standing in the ship corridor, he recalled Cyntha's tender kisses. Then he remembered the smell of her perfume; a hint of lilac was as enticing a call to lovemaking as he could ever imagine. And the admiration she showed him in her eyes when he looked at her exquisite face, he wondered if she actually loved him more than he loved her. He knew for sure that he yearned to rejoin her. He simply *could not* return to Sara. He whispered emphatically, "I'm sure, sure, sure. I'm sure."

He knocked on Captain Rawlins's door. The captain opened it and encouraged him to go out on the lower deck. He gained the deck where the air after the rain smelled fresh.

By the time Joseph began ascending the steep bank from the sidewheeler's gangplank on his way to the Cherry mansion, the storm had settled into a mizzling drizzle. While Captain Rawlins went ahead, Joseph struggled up the muddy trail. He was a sergeant now, and would get his stripes soon. But in the deep gray fog that had lodged along the shore, he felt out of place in the entire world, as if he was merely a faint image of someone who used to be alive, but now was shoved into barely remembered memories. Could he actually measure up as a spy?

Nearing the top of the hill, he heard a banjo, then heard the raspy voice he distinctly remembered. He turned the corner of the house. There sat Abram Reeder on a bench on a broad porch, staring out at the broad river, and lightly plucking a new banjo and humming.

When he saw Joseph, he stopped his song, and his eyebrows raised. Then his lips broke into a broad smile. He laughed and began slapping his knee. "Have you given up your Southern cause for the Northern one, Joseph?"

"Hello, Abram, dear friend." Joseph walked up and shook the old Negro's hand. He took a moment to study the wrinkled, freckled face which now bore a long white beard. "You look well."

"Yes, I am well in so many ways. A Freeman, well-fed and treated by the Cherry family like a fine musician performer. I woulda never thought it."

"How'd you get here, all the way from Missouri?"

Abram set down his banjo and motioned for Joseph to sit beside him on the bench. When Joseph sat, he said, "Times are changin', Joseph. It's a new world a'comin'. Free colored men and women everywhere. Us colored folks won't be slaves no more, regardless of how this war turns out."

"Oh?"

"All I hear is that the Coloreds are traipsin' off the plantations in droves, comin' to be with the bluecoats. Some of 'em want to fight with the army, so they can go free the rest of their family and friends."

"Do you really think the Negro will be free? That would be such a victory."

"Yes, I do. But the Yank army don't know what to do with 'em all. They put most of 'em in what they call contraband camps, feed 'em some, put some of 'em to work. The army doesn't know about takin' care of no runaways, and the Coloreds are just as lost as they are. They's all standin' around with empty hands and empty looks in their eyes, like it's the biggest folly that ever descended upon man."

"But, I..." Joseph's thoughts were jumbled. In his vision of the future of the freed slaves, all them moved into upstanding jobs, working alongside their White counterparts. He fumbled for words. "Abram, I want you to know that I was originally in the Union army, the First Iowa Volunteers, fighting this war to free the Negro from bondage, and when I was hit on the head, all my memories were lost. It's Dred's fault. He misled me into thinking I was a Confederate. Threw my life away. That's what he did."

"So, you been fightin' a while for the Rebels. Good for you."

"What?"

"Nothin' worthwhile was ever easy to accomplish. Surely, you know that."

"Of course, that's why I signed up to fight. To free the slaves."

"Yes. But you must surely know that in England and all the civilized nations, slave holdin' has been swept away. Not by war, but by law and public opinion. If the Yankees hadn't been so fired up about fightin' to save the Union, and let things alone,… in a while, maybe not in my lifetime, but certainly in yours, the plantation owners would see they can make more profit if they pay workers a livin' wage."

"You're saying slavery should stay."

"Absolutely not. It's just us humans think that if we *force* somethin', it'll happen all easy like. T'ain't so. Come here. I wanna show you somethin'." Abram rose slowly. Joseph remembered Abram had arthritis. He followed behind the old man, who shuffled around the side of the house.

On the other side of the plantation home stretched a hodgepodge of shacks, lean-tos, tents made of sheets and of towels, and even from women's dresses; a few wagons, and a vast sea of black people. They gathered around meager fires, and clustered under tent flaps. A few Union soldiers stood around, some talking with the Negroes, others staring, bored.

Joseph gasped.

"That's just one of the contraband camps," Abram said, pointing. "This part of Tennessee is generally for the Union. But no one knows what to do with the runaways. They're all lost, with no idea what the future will allow."

"But, at least, they're free."

"Well, General Grant won't hear of 'em bein' returned to their former owners. There's just no plan. More of 'em comin' every day."

"I can only pray this is the beginning. Things will get better."

"Yes, they will, Joseph. But not for a while. C'mon. I'll play you a song—'Billy Boy.'"

"That would be a welcome relief to this day, Abram."

"How long you here?"

"I'm only here for a day, then I go to Washington to do some undercover spying."

"What 'bout Miss Sara? She was fond of you and you of her."

"I'm married, Abram. I hope to rejoin my wife in Iowa. I care for Sara, but…"

Abram raised his eyebrows and nodded. He retrieved his banjo and set to strumming and singing.

That evening, Joseph sat at a small desk in the Cherry mansion and penned a new letter to Cyntha, who he hoped was still in Iowa. The official correspondence he carried from General Halleck via General Grant to Secretary of War Stanton was specific. Joseph was to serve as an undercover spy, but he wondered whether the war secretary would put him to work gathering information as a spy, or, instead, send him to the front, or maybe allow him to go home to Iowa and Cyntha.

THIRTY-SEVEN

RATHER BE A SERF, THAN A KING OF THE DEAD AND DESTROYED

– THE ODYSSEY BY HOMER

MARCH 21, 1862, 9:00 A.M.
WASHINGTON, DC

Lucas stood at the bottom of the steps to the War Department building. Holding his hearing trumpet in his right hand, he worried with the collar of his outdated uniform with his left. His stomach was broader than when he had worn the uniform in the 1840's, his neck thicker, and the collar chafed his skin. He could still button the pants and the jacket, but they were tight.

Despite his limited hearing, he heard the clattering and banging of a multitude of carpenters and bricklayers striving along the scaffolds, adding another level to the once two-story building. He wondered how people could get any work done inside the building with the clamorous noise abounding.

Shabbily-clothed children played tag, and tawdry-looking women bent to show their cleavage in their low-cut blouses and waved at any soldier or civilian man passing.

A line of civilian men and women stood outside the large doors. Lucas knew that they brought their complaints and pleas to set before the Secretary of War. They hoped he would have answers for them.

A couple of nefarious scoundrels moved stealthily from person to unsuspecting person, attempting to encourage individuals to part with their money in order to gain special treatment inside. A few relinquished a few dollars for a printed flier.

When Secretary Edwin Stanton arrived and marched through the front doors, the long line of job seekers or special consideration seekers followed. When Lucas entered, he immediately met with his old friend Captain Thomas Eckert. After stepping to a quiet office, they shared old stories of their time together in uniform, and Lucas told him of his desire to work as a telegraph operator.

"I can tell you this, Lucas," Captain Eckert said, "with your hearing issue, Stanton may not wish to hire you, but I believe he will listen to my endorsement."

"I'm here to help. I guess you could say I'm all ears."

They chuckled at Lucas's self-deprecation and went to wait in line outside the secretary's door.

After the last of the line of persons had filed from the room, having received either an assent or refusal from Stanton, Captain Eckert approached him and introduced Lucas. After much hemming and hawing by Stanton, and fervent arguments from Eckert and Lucas, Stanton coughed and took off his glasses. "See here, Major Reeder. I have no time, nor inclination, to waste words at a man who cannot hear. Go home and be about recalling your sterling military service. Write a memoir. Those are popular now."

"I cannot, sir," Lucas said, for with Stanton's booming voice he had no trouble understanding his comments. "I *will* work here. Put me on standby, should one of your regular telegraph operators falls ill, or…"

"Goodbye, Major Reeder."

Lucas lowered his eyes. His hopes dashed, he barely could keep from yelling at the man. But he made no effort to leave.

Then Stanton's voice thundered. "You are an insistent man, Major Reeder!"

Lucas held his trumpet to his ear.

"And I say that with all respect. I am not a man to compromise, and… Oh, never mind. I give you the job to be on standby, but you are only to be paid for the time you actually work. You may sit out of the way, and be ready if called upon. There may be some days soon with General McClellan finally moving the army that it gets busier here. I foresee it. Will that suit you?"

"I am indebted, Mr. Stanton." Lucas's face glowed.

"You may be military, but here, we run this as a civilian service of the government, so don't be thinking you can give orders to anyone." He hmphed.

"Understood." Lucas saluted.

"And, for God's sake, never salute me. Salute the president if you ever see him. Captain Eckert, take your friend to Bates to see if he is as good as he claims."

"Yes, sir." Eckert led Lucas quickly away and out of earshot. "That went much better than I thought it would. Congratulations, old friend."

Lucas's heart raced. Now, he would be in the building only a few strides from the executive mansion.

When he took a brief test on the telegraph key, both to receive and send messages, he did not do as well as he would have liked. David Bates, a young fellow with golden hair and a fresh, freckled face, frowned, but said, "You'll do." He handed him a piece of paper with a few scribbles on it. "Take this to the bursar, so you can be paid when you do work. The bursar knows how to handle it."

Lucas bade farewell to Captain Eckert and strolled down G Street that ran behind the Executive Mansion and the State Department Building. Feeling great satisfaction, he decided to take in the air. He turned up New York Avenue. For a few steps, he set to twirling his ear trumpet like a baton. He whistled the new tune, "The Battle Hymn of the Republic."

He quit the song when a dozen women dressed in black, veils over their faces, walked slowly down the steps out from the New York Avenue Presbyterian Church. Without his ear trumpet, he could still hear some of them wailing. A white-frocked pastor stood on the steps outside the door, grasping each woman's hand and speaking to each one. Six pallbearers wearing black jackets, pants, and hats, and white gloves, emerged from the church bearing a metal coffin down the steps and placed it slowly onto a hearse. Each man doffed his tall hat, then they, in unison, placed their hats back on their heads. With a single drummer beating a dirge rhythm, the entourage walked in a stilted cadence, following the black-draped hearse, drawn by four black horses. Each horse sported purple plumes attached to their headgear that jutted above their heads. The somber women trailed on foot behind the pallbearers.

The women were now queens of sorrow, monarchs of lost lives.

Workman appeared beside Lucas, giving him a start.

"I'm sorry, Lucas," Workman said. "At least some of 'em what's died get a real funeral."

They watched the funeral procession until it turned a corner.

"I heard one of the ladies say," Workman stated, "that everyone of 'em's lost a loved one, every soldier dead from dysentery or smallpox just in the last few weeks. Not a one died in battle."

"It is a sad disintegration of the nation because of that dissembling vulture in the Presidential Palace." Lucas sighed, and the two stood quietly, watching the pastor of the church trudge up the steps and close the great doors. Lucas said, "But the good news is I got the job."

"I figured you would."

"I'm going into the church. This nation needs prayers." He started up the steps, then turned to Workman. "You coming?"

"Naw, I got a hankerin' for a different religion. I'm gonna visit the bars down by the National Hotel. I know I'll feel better about the nation in a real short while, and I know I'll hear a whole lot of confessin' of sins goin' on. Like as not. I can tell ya now, I'm thinkin' this city is a hotbed of secessionists, lyin' low. We may not get a chance to carry out our plan. Somebody else might beat us to it."

Lucas shrugged his shoulders and continued into the church. He was content to be merely a serf in this kingdom of degradation, but he began worrying that some hothead slave owner, in a drunken display, would take a swing at Lincoln, and thus the president's guards would increase in number, making killing him much harder. He was glad that the president seldom had a guard with him on his jaunts to and from the President's Mansion. He made himself comfortable in a back pew, but he wondered what exactly he should pray for.

THIRTY-EIGHT

THE SNAKE AND THE PURVEYOR OF LIES

MARCH 21, 1862, EVENING
WASHINGTON, DC

Workman jogged past the President's Mansion and planted his gangly legs onto Philadelphia Avenue, pacing as fast as he could through the crowds of soldiers, civilians and cart merchants plying their wares. Walking in the muddy streets was entirely too daunting. He wished to look and smell fresh if he should meet a comely barmaid in one of the taverns that were posted just past the National Hotel.

At length, he came upon a string of bars lined up like headstones in a graveyard. He was standing by a lamppost, deciding which bar to select, when two well-dressed gentlemen, who were engaging in imaginary fisticuffs, bumped into him.

"Quite sorry, old chap," the tall, broad one, dressed in coat, vest and ascot stated, sweeping off his stovepipe hat in a false bow. "It was entirely my fault." His accent was obviously British. He was square-shouldered, had a ruddy face, deep blue eyes, and a fluffy moustache that, at the moment, was sprinkled with the froth of beer.

The shorter man, built like a tight-muscled circus acrobat, wore a wide-brimmed straw hat and no jacket, and only a silk vest over his shirt. He had long black hair and a well-trimmed moustache. He looked uncomfortable, his high shirt collar chafing his neck. His cheeks were raw red, like they had been scrubbed far too often. "Beg pahdon," he said with a decidedly Southern drawl.

"No pardon required," Workman said, "I've been known to bump into a few folks myself. But, say, could either of you gents tell me which of these bars are most likely to slake my thirst without emptying my pockets?"

"Of course," said the tall one, smiling broadly. "This is indeed fortunate." He slapped his hand against the lamppost. "The spirits frolicking here about do insist it is time for a libation. You look like an amiable chap. Why don't you accompany us into yonder establishment, 'The Cordial Tap.' In there, I can impress my friend here by telling you your fortune."

"You're welcome to come along," the shorter one said, though he did not smile.

"I might as well. I'm new in the city," Workman said.

"I knew as much immediately," the tall stranger said, "I am Lord Charles Colchester. Son of an English duke." He extended his hand.

"But an illegitimate one," the shorter man said.

Workman shook Colchester's hand. "A lord! I must be in fancy company."

"Yes, indeed you are. In fact, you are in the company of the illustrious actor, who is much-sought-after across the nation and in Europe, the esteemed bard of great renown, Mr. John Wilkes Booth."

Booth swept off his hat and bowed low. Rising, he said, "Count Colchester is one of mah adorin' fans. But I must say I am one of his as well."

"How do. My name is Dred Workman." Workman shook hands with Booth.

The three entered the dark establishment, brick-walled on the inside, dim lamps swinging from rafters. The bar was packed with soldiers and civilians, but the three approached the bar and muscled away a small meek, bookish man who gave them no backtalk. They sat on tall stools.

"Three whiskeys," Colchester called out to the barmaid when they were seated.

Workman immediately took notice of a barmaid with her back to them, possessing an hourglass figure, the curve of her hips and the shadow of the indention in her buttocks showing through the flimsy skirt. She turned to face the three. She wore a revealing blouse displaying ample cleavage. Workman's initial interest waned when she drew closer into the light of the lamp suspended from a rafter above the bar. She stood before them with her hands on her hips, and her mouth turned down in boredom. Her face, bosom, and arms were covered with scaly sores.

"Syphilis," Workman whispered while ducking his head.

"What'd you say?" Booth asked.

"Later."

"What'll it be?" the barmaid said. She pointed at Colchester. "And, you, your Lordship, you better have coin to pay this time."

"Not to worry, my bonny lass." Colchester began fingering pockets in his vest, then his jacket and pants pockets, at last removing a shoe, and finding a dime, he placed it on the counter. "There you are. Coin of the realm."

"Whiskey's fifteen cents," the barmaid turned to leave.

Booth slapped three quarters on the bar. "That's enough for two rounds a piece."

"Close enough." The barmaid picked up the coins, grabbed a bottle from the shelf, and poured whiskey into three smudged glasses.

"Thank you, Mr. Booth." Workman downed his shot, then said, "Ahhh."

"Yes, Mr. Booth," Colchester said, slurping his whiskey, "always comes through in a pinch. But then I have been helpful to his brother, Edwin, and him in contacting poor, bereaved Edwin's deceased wife."

Workman looked at Booth, who was sipping his drink. He nodded.

"So, you speak to haunts, but what does it mean about what you said on the street that you can tell my fortune?" Workman asked, motioning for the barmaid to pour him another shot. "If you can tell my fortune, I'll buy the next round."

The barmaid poured a shot for him and Colchester. Booth, staring forward, still sipped his first drink. Workman took notice of Booth's eyes, like the slit eyes of a viper, constantly glancing around the room. They bore a furtiveness, like one beset by a predator or by demons. On the other hand, perhaps this man was more the predator. He determined to keep a close handle on his wallet around these new acquaintances.

Colchester emptied the second shot down his throat, smacked his lips, then popped his knuckles. He bent close to Workman, and burped the sour mash into Workman's face. "Tell me one thing. Why you're here in the nation's capital. Then I will tell your fortune."

"Why I'm here is my business." Workman turned to face Colchester, his back to Booth, who leaned on the greasy bar. Workman made a point to close his left arm tight to his chest where his wallet sat in his inside jacket pocket.

Colchester tilted back a little on his stool, laid his hat on the bar and wiggled his fingers for a long moment. Then looking up at the ceiling, he began warbling like a bird, then whistling. His eyes rolled back.

Workman nudged Booth. "What's he doing?"

"He can't tell your future by himself. He has to ask a spirit to assist him. Then he relays what he heahs from them. Sometimes there's a spirit, sometimes none show up. It depends. But I've seen him speak to the dead. It's as sure a thing as the nose on your face, to sound cliché. I actually hate clichés. If only the world spoke more Latin."

"That is a thought." Workman tried to be noncommittal.

"What did you say under your breath a while ago, Dred?"

Workman lowered his voice. "The barmaid has syphilis. It's as plain as the nose on her face, and her nose skin is peeling."

"Can't she take some cure? I hear the mercury infusions work."

"Mercury never cured anything. The doctors hand it out like it was gift from the gods, and I've yet to see anyone cured. We had an epidemic back where I was servin' at a fort in Texas. The men took the mercury. Most of them suffered with the calamity for years. I never saw one of 'em get any better. The fact is medical science ain't discovered a cure."

Booth pointed at the barmaid flirting with an all-too-interested rosy-cheeked soldier. "He better watch where he puts his hat hanger."

Workman smirked. "Yeah, he's twistin' that ring on his finger. Hope he uses some proper judgment."

"Too late."

The barmaid took the arm of the young man in the blue uniform, his face blushing, and she led him through a rear door. His companions hooted and hollered after him.

Booth and Workman turned to watch Colchester.

The spirit medium sat stiff on his stool, looking like he was in a stupor.

After watching him for a couple of minutes, Workman asked Booth, "So, you're an actor?"

Booth finished his glass and beckoned a second barmaid. She came and poured him his drink.

Booth straightened to his full height. "I am a thespian, an artiste. Here in Washington and elsewhere. I am in extremely high demand. I am currently rehearsin' for a rendition of Shakespeare's 'King John.' It is a challengin' part, but should win me some laurels."

"I'll have to come watch the play. Is it a comedy?"

"Hardly. It's one of Shakespeare's great tragedies. It's about a nefarious king who destroys his own kingdom. A lot like the president we have now." He tossed back the whiskey and growled, "I could slay the man right now." He turned a wolf's glare at Workman.

Workman was surprised. "Now, there's a statement."

"Then you agree with me he should be dead. The nation, and indeed, the whole world, would be a better place." Booth's dark eyes held flame.

"Can't say that I disagree with you at all." Workman turned toward the bar and raised his voice. "In fact, I'll buy the next round in honor of the speedy demise of President Lincoln, even if Colchester ain't tol' me my future yet."

"Shhhh," Booth commanded, nudging Workman. "Don't be so loud. Most of the folks livin' in this city hate the cur. Only the army's for him. You have to look out for Pinkerton's men, his spies. They're lurkin' all around. So, you have to keep your opinion on the down low. Understand?"

"I get it." Workman turned to see Colchester, who had laid his head on the bar and appeared to be sleeping. "What's he doin'?"

"He's still summonin' the spirits."

"Well, while I'm a waitin', I'll have another drink. Miss, another round for all of us!"

Colchester bolted up. "I have made contact with a spirit." He turned red-rimmed eyes toward Workman. "Ah," he said while the barmaid poured his third whiskey. "Another libation. Queen Victoria will be thrilled when I return to England and tell her of the generous nature of the American people." He downed the drink with a flourish.

Workman paid the forty-five cents and swallowed his drink.

Booth finished his second whiskey.

"Now, Dred," Colchester put his hand on Workman's shoulder. "The spirit has told me that you have had a rough life with mixed results and conflicting allegiances. Is that true?"

"Yeah, I'd say as much."

"You've lost your parents, and you've been a military man, but you're not now."

"Yeah again."

"And you care not for the current president."

"I said that just a moment ago."

"I did not hear you. I was in a trance."

"What about my future? You ain't said a thing about that. Just the past."

"I'm getting to that. The spirit, the Seminole Chief Gold Eagle, speaks to me from the golden lands and tells me that you are to come into a sizable amount of money."

"Oh? Who's Chief Gold Eagle?"

Colchester harrumphed. "But don't get your hopes up. It's later, not sooner. And... you have a friend who is disabled and will soon be in danger."

"What? What kind of danger?"

A piano player struck up a jaunty tune in the back of the bar, and the soldiers and civilians joined in singing the words in slurred, disjointed, louder and louder cacophony.

"Damn!" Colchester screamed at the room. "You have chased away my spirit contact. I cannot work under these conditions. These ruffians! These scoundrels!"

"What about my friend and the danger?"

"I am sorry, Dred." Colchester again put his hand on Dred's shoulder. "The noise in here is not conducive to communing with the spirit world. You'll have to come to one of my séances. I can help you speak to your dead relatives. Here's my contact information. I'm staying here at the National Hotel. John Wilkes resides there as well." He handed Workman a printed card.

Booth stood to leave. "I don't want the last drink. Charles, you can have mine." He rose to leave.

Workman said, "Why're you leavin'?"

"I've got to study my part for the play. And..." Booth paused, then whispered in Workman's ear, "Find a way to either kidnap or kill the president." He sauntered off into the gray, dying day.

THIRTY-NINE

PARTING AND HOPE

MARCH 22, 1862, 8:00 A.M.
ELKHORN TAVERN, ARKANSAS

Anthony stood holding onto a support porch on the tavern porch without his prosthetic leg attached. His oak leg had lost its brass endcap in the commotion of the battle, and the stump had cracked. Skinny, yet muscled, Joe Cox, Mrs. Cox's oldest son, was seated on a stool by his wife in the kitchen, securing an iron ring around the stump, having sealed the crack with a thick glue made of horse hoof, then shellacking the whole artificial leg with tree resin.

Anthony hoped the young, quiet fellow knew what he was doing.

The Cox family, with the aid of Ben McGavin shooting deer and rabbits, then drying the meat in the badly battle-mangled smokehouse, finally had real food for the family. The garden showed small sprigs of life. One of the supply wagons passing through for Curtis's troops had a kind driver who gave the family a month's provision of dried beans, leavening, and sacks of flour from his supply. "Ain't nothin'," the driver said. "This outfit's got enough food for three armies." The privations caused by the battle had been ameliorated.

Two days previously, Anthony had walked all the way to Leetown and bartered for a small carriage from Mr. Foster and for an ancient muley cow that daily rendered a modicum of milk, purchasing the animal and the carriage with money he had been saving to buy land and a new home in Texas for himself and for his wife and child. He had resolved to stay at Elkhorn long enough to help Polly's family get back on their feet. Her husband had not yet returned from selling cattle to the Union army.

Anthony watched his daughter playing with cornhusk dolls on the porch while the Cox boys shot marbles in a ring in the grassless yard. Polly Cox and her daughter-in-law were busy in the parlor sewing a new dress with a measure of cloth given them by a neighbor whose home had not been ravaged by battle.

Reynolds, his gray hair sticking out in tufts on the sides of his balding head, sat on the porch, breathing in spasmodic pants. Anthony knew the tuberculosis was rapidly carving out the old freeman's lungs. Cyntha had said they must leave soon if they were to get Reynolds to his family in Cincinnati before he succumbed to the illness.

The morning sky was clear, and Cyntha was packing the cabriolet carriage that Anthony had purchased. She laid a sack of clothes in the driver's bench. Her empty, heavy trunk was left behind with the Coxes. Ben, limping, hitched a stout, bay gelding to the front of the carriage. A second black gelding was tied in the rear of the cabriolet. Both horses were strong-muscled with smooth, shiny coats. Not draft horses, but artillery horses. A forty-pound sack of grain for the steeds that Anthony had obtained sat in a latched, wooden box on the tailboard.

Cyntha loaded a small basket of biscuits and dried venison in the seat, and then paced with deliberate steps to Anthony, her face solemn. She stopped a foot from him, unable to look at his face. Without raising her eyes, she said, "I cannot thank you enough, dear brother, for spending the last of your money buying this carriage for me and Reynolds... and for Ben. You are the most wonderful man."

"I do what I can. Besides, your need is greater. You must set your husband's soul to rest, and Josiah deserves to be with his family. He has paid his dues to this world, always serving others, even at the expense of his own well-being."

"In that way, you and Josiah are a lot alike. If only..." She hesitated. She knew that Anthony had purchased the carriage and that he had stolen the horses from the Federal army. She did not want to know how he stole them, but she was grateful he had. She remembered guiltily how she had remonstrated him weeks before for not telling her whether or not he had stolen money from his bank. He certainly was near penniless now.

Cyntha considered the irony that, in her high and mighty attitude, she had been so quick to judge him; but she now possessed nothing except erstwhile gratitude for him securing the means for her to head east to her destinations—to Cincinnati for Reynolds, and to New York and the Fox sisters for a séance to free Joseph's soul.

"Oh," Anthony said. He picked up her hand and placed a pouch of silver coins in her palm and then squeezed her hand shut. "That's enough to get you on a riverboat at St. Louis to Cincinnati. Should be enough for all three of you." He did not want to discuss his sacrifice any further, so switched the subject. "With the Northern forces firmly in control of the roadways through Missouri now, it should be a less worrisome trip than previous ones."

Cyntha gasped. "Have you nothing left for your family?"

Anthony shrugged, and pointed to the sky. "A flock of geese. See them?"

Cyntha did not turn to look, but tears wet her cheeks. "Thank you, Anthony. I love you."

"I love you, too, dear sister. Write as much as you can. You know where we're living." He gave a slight smile, wobbling a little, supporting himself on his one full leg.

With that, Cyntha went around and gave generous hugs and well-wishes to all the Coxes. She found Jeanette Atkinson upstairs, reading the Bible with Clara. She cried again upon saying her farewells.

When she returned downstairs, Ben had already assisted Reynolds into the carriage seat, and he sat with the reins in his hands. When he saw Cyntha, he hollered, "Time to go. New York's a long way away, and I could still change my mind any time."

FORTY

∞

WITH MALICE TOWARD NONE
– ABRAHAM LINCOLN

MARCH 22, 1862, MORNING
WASHINGTON, DC

Lucas sat on a bench in the stuffy, second story cavern of the War Department telegraph office, his trumpet to his ear, listening to the abundant rat-a-tat of the telegraph keys. The high walls and the tall windows gave him a sense of being in a medieval cathedral, less the trappings of religion. Messages were coming in from several sources in a steady stream. Only twice had there been a break in the flow. The telegraph operators and decipherers copied the clicking messages, then opened their decipher books and ran their fingers up and down the pages, then wrote the decoded texts on paper tablets.

Though the high windows let in ample light, Lucas was straining to remain awake and caught himself nodding. In his anticipation of the new job, he had not slept the night before. When the office manager, David Bates, walked up and nudged Lucas's shoulder, he had not realized he was napping. He looked up, bleary-eyed. "I apologize, sir."

"Major Reeder, Albert Chandler needs to avail himself of the john. Something he ate last night, I presume. You may sit in his stead for a few moments. Study the decipher book."

"Yes, sir."

"Please, Major, no need to *sir* me."

Lucas, being careful not to step on the myriad of wires snaking across the floor, walked to a plain desk with several drawers. Atop it was a single telegraph key, pads of paper, pens, and pencils. He took the seat where Al Chandler usually sat. The key was still. He stared at it a while, poised for it to begin clicking. Tiring of watching it, he began studying one of the decode books. "I wish we had had this communication available in the Mexican War."

Bates turned. "I think it could have made a great difference in saving lives."

Just as quickly as they had begun, the other keys in the room stopped tapping. Charles Tinker and Bates began thumbing through the messages that they had copied and inserting them into narrow, built-in pigeonholes in the shelving sitting atop the desk. Bates came to where Lucas sat and picked up the one-inch stack of notes, placing each into unmarked nooks. He took three of the notes with him and slid them into a top drawer of his own desk.

The key on Lucas' desk began a short alert tap.

"Answer it, Major." Bates said.

Lucas sent the standard reply message.

In a moment, the key clacked ardently. Lucas grabbed a pencil and pad and began deciphering the dots and dashes. Certain words seemed to make no sense, but he wrote them as he interpreted them. Then the clicking stopped, followed by a brief farewell set of clicks. He held up the confusing set of sentences and phrases.

Bates walked over, and Lucas handed the page to him. Bates lowered his spectacles from atop his head to his nose, looked at the page, gave a broad smile and nodded. "Well done."

Chandler returned, looking relieved, and Lucas gave him back his chair.

Lucas decided to walk around the room which had been a library years before. Massive shelves were festooned with fascinating books and old ledgers. At one point, while he was perusing an atlas of maps of the Crimean War between the British and the Turks decades before, he looked up and noticed in the high corners of the room several elaborate spiderwebs with an abundance of spiders spinning and crawling. *I've always been amazed at their industriousness.* He watched the spiders until his neck became sore, then picked up a book of paintings by Audubon and sat on the bench to look at it.

For an hour, no messages came, and the telegraph operators sent no messages. Admiring the intricate paintings of Audubon's book, Lucas did not notice when President Lincoln entered the room. Glancing up, his surprise showed. He knew that the president often frequented the War Department building, but he had figured that the tall, rangy president was always meeting with Secretary Stanton in the next office.

President Lincoln was skimming through a small stack of deciphered messages. "Ah," he said, "McClellan seems to be making do with his landing on the peninsula. He reports all is going to plan. Good. Good. Finally, some movement." He sensed that he was being watched, for he put down his page, then looked at Lucas and lowered his spectacles to peer more carefully. "Major." He nodded.

Lucas nodded in return. He felt like a voyeur sneaking a glance at a demon from hell. He hated President Lincoln with inordinate rage, and he found it difficult not to bolt from his seat and strangle the man. *No man has caused more malice in the world and created more sorrow than that imbecile there.*

Lucas recalled the piles of dead bodies on the battlefield of Wilson Creek, some burned black by cannon shot, some rotting in the heat, their bowels plucked out by vultures. He had read the papers of so many more deaths in other battles. He had seen the slashed and charred warriors with maimed limbs wandering the capital's street, flinching at any noise or staring stone-faced into nothingness. All this was the fault of President Lincoln. *Why can't he negotiate with the Southerners for peace? Let things abide for a while.* Lucas's nostrils flared, and he sensed he could smell the burned ground of Hades.

He reflected that, in Christian charity, if he could catch the charlatan alone, he would endeavor to convince him to abdicate the presidency for the good of the country. *I would be erstwhile in my recommendations, for I want no man to die, even one as guilty as he.* Lucas did not want the continuation of the Confederacy, a separate nation. He wanted the whole nation rejoined, and the removal of the demon in the Executive Mansion was the catalyst to bring about reunion.

President Lincoln removed his jacket and, lifting his feet onto the table, leaned back in his chair and began reading a pamphlet of sorts. In a moment, he was chuckling. "I believe that the author of these Nasby Papers is a genius. If I ever meet the man, and if he would teach me his skill for sarcasm about the Confederates and Copperheads, I would offer to trade jobs with him."

The telegraph operators and decipherer agents laughed. They seemed to know of the sarcastic sentiments of the pages which the president mentioned. They snickered acknowledgements. After the laughing subsided, each man gathered a magazine or book and began reading.

The tomblike quiet was almost too much for Lucas to bear. He rose. "I think I'll take a walk."

"Yes," Bates said. "Tell us what the outside world is doing. In this catacomb, this old musty library, we have all this communication coming and going, but the real world is doing its own conversing and sharing. Come tell us what you see and hear."

"Much more human outside, don't you think?" Lucas said.

President Lincoln lowered his legs and turned toward Lucas, who was putting on his hat. "Hear, hear, sir! I think that in a while I shall go out amongst the throngs of humanity. Get a feel for what they're thinking." He set his feet back on the table and continued reading.

Lucas did not respond, but exited the room, shoving his hat down on his head. He returned once and retrieved his ear trumpet.

FORTY-ONE

DETAILS AND APPREHENSION

General Albert Sidney Johnston, standing in a sizable farmhouse parlor, stroked his chin, looking at maps. He felt tired and old. In the last month since Forts Henry and Donnelson were lost to Grant's northern army, he had shriveled in weight, and his jacket sagged loose on his once robust frame. More exhausted than at any time he could remember, he swayed like a reed in a fat breeze, his eyes watering.

With his aide at his shoulder, he perused slips of paper that had been handed to him by scouts. The scouts with scroungy beards, teeth blackened by tobacco, and a devil-may-care aloofness stood at ease by the door. They had a considerable amount of mud caked over their boots and lower pants, and mud splattered on their jackets and faces.

He crumpled the pages into a ball. "This rain is enough to drive me to distraction." He pointed out the window of the farmhouse at the downpour. Sheets of water smacked the farmhouse, the barn, and grounds; and a ferocious wind beat against the trees. He leaned to his left, putting his weight on his left foot, for his right leg pained him, like it generally did. Two days of hard riding while pressing the last of his troops that he had pulled from Kentucky to hurry to Corinth, Mississippi, bore harshly on him.

Though he appreciated the unequivocal support of his bosom friend, President Jefferson Davis, after the disastrous loss of the forts, he felt impotent for being out-maneuvered. The Confederate defensive line that had extended from eastern Kentucky through the top of Tennessee into Missouri, though impressive on paper, was untenable. He knew long before Donnelson fell or before the papers printed a single headline. But there it was. His defense had melted in a week's time. He had to order a retreat. *The newspapers be damned. They do not understand the strategic consequences of losing the valuable railroad link across northern Mississippi and Tennessee.* If Corinth fell, getting any of the wealth of cattle, corn and cotton from west of the great river would be incredibly difficult.

"At least," his aide, Colonel William Preston, said, "the Feds are bogged down in the rain, too. The Tennessee River is flooding, highest that anyone remembers." He paused to watch General Johnston's reaction, but his brother-in-law seemed oblivious to his comment. "They can't move any further up the river to have their troops disembark."

General Johnston turned to the scouts. "Good work, gentlemen. Let your horses rest a day. I think the good woman of the house may afford you some real coffee." He smiled at the sopping wet, brown and gray-uniformed soldiers. "Yes, it's *real* coffee. Go in the kitchen and get you a cup."

The scouts saluted and slouched into the kitchen, scuffing mud across the carpet.

"William," General Johnston said in whisper, once the scouts had left the room. "We shall be in Corinth tomorrow. Hardee's troops are there. More arriving daily. Beauregard, if he's not too ill, should have already obtained generous means to keep them all fed and in tents. But I'm deeply worried."

"Elaborate, please, brother-in-law?"

"Are we too few? Is the Union army too vast? Most of the weapons our ebullient band of patriot soldiers carry are old flintlocks, muskets, and shotguns they brought from home."

"But ten thousand of them have been recently outfitted with Enfield rifles. That's an improvement. And their spirits are high. You've said so yourself." Colonel Preston attempted a smile.

"Still. I am afraid we don't have the firepower to launch a successful attack against the Yankees. They have riverboats with huge guns. They've got Grant in charge now that C. F. Smith has tetanus and can no longer lead. Grant's already captured Forts Henry and Donnelson without so much as a struggle.... He's tasted victory, and he wants more." Johnston stared out the window at the storm buffeting the house. "The vast majority of our volunteers have never been in a campaign, much less a battle."

"We have General Ruggles' troops up from the coast and in Corinth now. We've pulled the army from New Orleans. General Bragg's Corps, too." Colonel Preston's demeanor took on almost a pleading appearance. "Surely, that's a large enough force to repel the invaders."

"Yes, I know. Bragg is quite the task master, and he is generally cordial enough... except when he's not." He strode toward the window. In the farm's fields, the remnants of General George Crittenden's Division sat in mud and rain-drenched tents that stretched into the forest. He could not see a soul stirring in the camp. "If some Union cavalry rushed this camp, they'd have little trouble destroying any semblance of order that we have." He stopped to listen to Mrs. Medina, the lady of the house, chatting with the scouts and other members of his staff in the kitchen. He wondered if any of the soldiers ever sustained a thought to the gravity of the Southern army's precarious position. "I know

General Beauregard has already ordered General Van Dorn to come to our aid, but remind me to reiterate the order to cross the Mississippi at Memphis and join us with all haste. He has twenty thousand troops, and that many soldiers may give us an equivalence to the Federals."

Colonel Preston jotted a note to himself, then looked up. "What did the scout's messages say?"

General Johnston straightened to his full, imposing, six-foot height, swept back his short-cropped, graying hair, and looked again at the crumpled pages. "These are from one of our spies who tapped into a telegraph line running across Kentucky. The date was March sixteenth. Who knows who this individual is? Both messages, essentially identical, were then transferred several times into different hands, and finally into the saddlebags of those stalwart scouts, who forded swollen rivers and dodged Yankee patrols to get the word to me."

"And…"

"This is why we must act within days. The messages contain knowledge that General Halleck has ordered General Don Carlos Buell to leave central Tennessee and join with Generals Sherman and Grant to bolster that army so as to become an unstoppable force. That's the gist."

"General Beauregard had guessed as much. He's already been devising a plan to surprise Grant before he receives any more reinforcements."

"I imagine he is. Beauregard is a genius. Oversaw the bombing of Fort Sumter, then whipped the Yanks decisively at Manassas. And he brought our soldiers safely back from Columbus, Kentucky. He's salt of the earth. However, his genius does none of us any good if he remains constantly in bed with a fever. His complaining about his illness is worse than his constant coughing."

"Well, he did have surgery on his throat, Sidney."

General Johnston glowered at his brother-in-law, his expression so fierce that Colonel Preston took a step back.

The general sighed. "My dear relative. My anger is not directed at you. We have no room for excuses, be they illness or a shortage of arms. Tomorrow, in Corinth, we will meet with the commanders and plan for battle—our victory. We must drive the enemy away. We must conquer or perish."

General Johnston walked again to the window to stare at the dark clouds, and watched the lightning lace its fingers through the sky, then listened for thunder to rumble seconds later. His brother-in-law came up and placed his hand on his shoulder.

In an almost inaudible whisper, the general said, "Conquer or perish."

FORTY-TWO

THE BEST LAID PLANS OFTEN GO AWRY

– ROBERT BURNS

MARCH 24, 1862
SOUTHERN OHIO

John Coincoin had managed to arrive in Cincinnati, sometimes trotting alongside wagons of friendly farmers. Once, he found himself riding beside a pretty, white teenage girl on a donkey. It did not take him long to determine from her animated talk and forward attitude that she was being a little too coy, and she wanted something from him in return for her company, something that he was unwilling to give. He turned off the road and allowed her to trot on ahead.

The next day, a young Negro freeman, nicely dressed in a ditto suit, riding in a wagon, led him along the various twisting roads the last portion of the trip into the outskirts of Cincinnati. His smooth, black-as-tar complexion shone in the noon sun. John could not help but notice the ragged, puffy, purple scar on the man's forehead.

"How'd you get the cut?" John asked.

"The Butternuts gave it to me. Mean White men that don't care none for the Freemen whupped me good. And it ain't the first time neither."

"Butternuts? Who are they?"

The youth clucked his tongue. "The Butternuts is White folks what think any Negro that's livin' in Ohio is contrivin' to take theys jobs. I'm headin' back to Cincinnati to get the last of my kit, and a few pieces of furniture. Me and my family be movin' outta that town. Ain't no place for a colored man. No, suh."

"But Ohio ain't a slave state."

"No, it ain't. But the southern parcel of Ohio has a heap of White folks roun' about who is afraid of the Coloreds. They take a gander across the river into Kentucky and see all dem slaves there. They think if the North wins this war, all of dem coloreds gonna flock up here like geese and settle here and work for less and take theys livelihoods."

"Well, I guess I understand. My life ain't been a bed of roses with some of the White folks. But I must say most have been downright kind to me and my family. Welcomes us to their church. Says hello on the streets."

"You must be from upstate. And don't get me wrong. They's lots of friendly Whites. Just too many Butternuts."

When they arrived in town, John had little trouble finding where the Fox sisters were staying—the most fashionable hotel in Cincinnati. He found their whereabouts by checking at liveries, looking for the carriage that the women had ridden in to the city. When he found the specific carriage, he asked the liveryman if he knew the sisters' whereabouts.

John met another freeman outside a bar and gave him the last money he had in exchange for the man's jacket and hat. Dressed in the more gentlemanly attire, he walked into the foyer of the hotel and straight up to the check-in desk, holding a sealed envelope. "I have to give this to Miss Leah Fox."

"I will give it to her," the stodgy, bewhiskered clerk said.

"No, I must give it to her personally. It's a matter of life and death."

The man at the desk thought a while. "Miss Fox and her sisters are out to dinner, but when they return, I'll make sure to give it to her."

John slowly released the sealed envelope to the attendant, then watched to see which mailbox he set it in, which was room 212. That was all he needed to know. "Thank you, sir." He exited, and waited for the women to return. *When they put on their show, I'll not be in the audience. I'll be in their room, takin' that chest.*

The con artist sisters returned, bedecked in the finest dresses of vibrant blue and purple, puffed out with abundant petticoats. Fashionable hats sat delicately on their coiffured hair. They swept into the hotel, and the man at the desk gave Leah the envelope in which John had placed a newspaper clipping from Fredericktown, Ohio. John, outside the hotel, watched through a window. He chuckled at Leah's confused expression. She tucked the clipping in her purse.

The evening was growing dark, and a crew of Negroes were lighting the street lamps. John was about to go to a livery and find a hayloft, when the sisters returned to the front desk. Leah spoke to the desk attendant. "If that colored man returns, get his name, please." She looked worried. "We are going to watch the 'golden trumpet orator' at the Pike Opera House."

"Yes, ma'am."

When the sisters walked out, they passed within a few feet of where John had hidden himself behind some potted plants.

"I don't understand why we have to go hear this abolitionist speak," Maggie Fox complained.

"I couldn't care less about what he has to say," Leah replied. "I want to hear the acoustics of the opera house, observe the placement of the curtains, the flooring, and the like to see if it's a suitable place for us to hold a public séance."

"Oh." Maggie frowned.

John followed the sisters at a safe distance. *I wonder who this golden trumpet is.*

Arriving at the exterior of the Pike Opera House, John could not help but notice several hundred White men and a few women milling about, many of whom wore butternut-dyed clothing. Several men and women carried baskets of fruit and vegetables. The conversations were harsh. The Fox sisters filtered in amongst the throng, seemingly oblivious of the enraged attitude of certain persons.

John had difficulty keeping an eye on the sisters. He climbed atop a wagon to watch.

Across the street, a handful of Negroes bunched together. To John, they looked worried. One Negro woman, dressed in a velvet green dress, broke from their number and crossed the street and walked, her head held high, through the crowd of White people, who stared at her in dismay. A spindly-legged, trembling doorman allowed her inside the hall, then quickly shut the door before anyone else could enter.

The crowd began shouting to be let inside. John hopped from the wagon and chose a spot several yards from the entrance. The doorman, then, before the crowd attacked him, opened the doors, and the mob flooded inside.

After the horde entered, the Negroes from across the street slipped cautiously inside, taking positions in the back of the auditorium. John followed. Once inside, he searched for the sisters. He had decided that when he was sure they were involved in watching the show, he would steal away, slip inside their room, and help himself to a handy sum from their strongbox. Creeping down the crowded aisle, he did his best not to bump anyone. The balcony seats were overflowing with angry people. Instinctively, he cringed.

Finally, he spied the sisters seated three rows back from the stage. He was about to exit when the house lights dimmed, and the stage floor lamps threw a brighter light onto the stage. A man came out from behind the curtains, stood at a rostrum, laid papers on it, and began a lengthy introduction of the "golden trumpet orator who fights for freeing the slaves."

He had barely those words before many in the crowd hissed.

John found himself gawking at the crowd, who were muttering or even growling at the man introducing the orator. The man at the rostrum stiffened with fear on his face, then stated the orator's name—Wendall Phillips, whom the man called *a national abolitionist figure*. John had not heard of him, but decided he would like to hear what he had to say.

When the man concluded the introduction, a quiet settled in the auditorium.

Wendall Phillips, a slight-built White man with graying hair around his bald pate, came from the side of the stage up to the rostrum. A few applauded. Others hissed.

A voice with a decided Irish accent called from the back, "Get your pro-secession hide out o' here! We're for the Union, and you ain't!"

Phillips paid little heed to the man's challenge. He held up his hands as if to quiet the crowd. A half-dozen men, both White and Negro, took positions in front of the stage, facing out at the audience.

When silence again resumed, Phillips rose on his tiptoes and began his oration. "My Ohioan friends, let me ask you three questions. First, how long is the war to last before we realize that the South has taken its own sordid course, and we need not follow it, nor strive to force it to rejoin our sovereign state?"

The crowd moaned. Several shook their fists and shouted epithets.

"Second!" he called.

John noticed the shrill nature of the man's voice, almost a grating alto, rather than a comforting man's tone. *Ain't no trumpet to me.*

"What will become of slavery?" Phillips exclaimed. "The bane of our land."

More hisses, mixed with boos.

"Finally," he continued in an almost mocking tone, "what will become of the Union?"

Several disjointed yells spilled out of the audience. The throng seemed to be undulating, many men and women on their feet long enough to hurl an insult.

Phillips' first remarks lauded the Union, but forsook the war. His argument was that the people of the South were too willful, too devious, and too covetous of their slaves. John could barely gather his remarks, though he strained to hear.

After a few mildly stated sentences, Phillips raised his voice. "I can tell you now. I have been an abolitionist for sixteen years, and I intend to see it through."

More hisses and boos. A tomato, flung from the balcony, splotched at the feet of Phillips.

He began reading further from his speech, often holding one arm aloft for emphasis. More vegetables landed on the stage, splattering on Phillips' pants legs. The handful of men standing as guards in front of the stage were soon dodging the thrown items.

John watched an egg sail from the balcony opposite of where he stood. The egg splattered on Phillips' right shoulder, but with a righteous conviction, he kept up his speech.

When the pavement stone crashed onto the floor at Phillips' feet, John flinched. *That man's about to be killed.* His thoughts raced as to what action to take. He wanted to get to the Fox sisters' money, but he felt compelled to keep the man alive, safe from the audience who had now become a vicious mob.

Just then, he saw the Fox sisters hasten from their seats up the aisle and out the back of the hall. The aisle then filled with people, so he could not follow them. *There's no point now.*

Phillips' voice rang stronger, rising above the shouts of the crowd. Each sentence he spoke enraged them even more. Several men ran to the side stage steps, and the handful of guards blocked them from rushing the stage.

"Put him out!" called one man.

"Tar and feather him!" yelled another.

Several walking canes clattered onto the stage. A chair was hurled from the balcony, narrowly missing Phillips' head.

Above the booing and insults called from the mob, one man yelled, "To the stage!" At that, the middle aisle cascaded with angry men and some women. John had hesitated too long. He raced to the stage and vaulted up onto it, ahead of the mob. He and three White men took hold of Phillips' arms and pushed and pulled him behind the curtain, then out a backstage door. Other Negroes had found places on the stage as well and did their best to halt the advance of the infuriated crowd, some of them taking blows to their faces and bodies.

John and the three guards continued rushing Phillips down an alley, then turned down a dark street, and ultimately through the back door of a café. There, in the kitchen, they waited, silent, save their labored breathing, listening while the mob raged through the streets for another hour.

The guards thanked John for his help, and sent him out once the mob noise had subsided. John made his way to the nearest livery, climbed up an outside drain pipe to an open loft window, slipped in and curled up in a pile of hay.

His heart raced. He began to worry about his wife and children like he never had before. It occurred to him that they may not be safe in Fredericktown. He had seen the wanton behavior of some Southern Whites, but he had not expected Northerners to behave in such a hateful manner.

Further, he ached for his wife. Having been so many years without her, he did not want to be away from her so long again. His first plan had gone terribly awry. He resolved to try once more to take some of the Fox sisters treasure. If he could not find an opportunity, he would return home.

FORTY-THREE

THE FOX IN THE HENHOUSE

MARCH 25, 1862
WASHINGTON, DC

Workman was astonished at how easily he obtained a position working at the stables of the Executive Mansion. Wearing his sharp, stolen uniform, he emptied his pockets in front of a sergeant at the front gate to prove he carried no weapon. He was allowed into the compound, directed to a captain in a tent who had him stand at attention for a long while, then to a Sergeant Stimmel stationed near a short row of tents used by the compound's guard. The sergeant, who spoke with a lilting chirrup, seemed as pleasant a man as he might ever like to meet, cordial in every respect. He was a meaty man with even meatier arms and a thick neck. When Workman mentioned to the sergeant that he grew up as a stable hand at the great horse farms of Kentucky, and that he, himself, was "old army," the convivial sergeant extended to Workman a job.

He did ask Workman why he was not serving with the regular army, for he looked fit enough. Workman then plied his skill at prevarication, holding up his right hand like a claw, and told the man he had lost use of it at Bull Run. "I can't even imagine firin' a weapon, much less actually pullin' a trigger. But the hands are fine for takin' hold of a pitchfork and tossin' the horse droppin' or totin' a burlap sack."

The sergeant eyed Workman carefully for a moment, reached over and took Workman's hand that seemed much like a chicken's claw, deformed in death. After turning it left and right, he nodded. "Start today, Corporal Workman. Go inside the house, in the first office to the left find the bursar. He'll set your pay and your hours. Now, off wit ya."

While Workman walked to the President's Mansion, wondering when he might have an opportunity at shooting the president, the sergeant began whistling "The Girl I Left Behind Me." Workman took to yodeling the tune at the top of his voice. The guards gave him a weary look when he mounted the steps and strolled unencumbered inside. *This may be as easy as shootin' fish in a barrel.*

He was told by a lieutenant standing in the hall to sit on a cushioned bench. While he waited, an elderly black woman in a clean, starched dress under a flowered apron came along, holding a vase of fresh flowers. She was humming and smiling to herself and arranging the flowers.

She broke into song. "Think I heard the angel say follow the drinkin' gourd. Follow that river 'til the clouds roll by." Workman, unfamiliar with the song, was immediately taken with the poetry. Wondering at its meaning, he sought to solve the lyrics, but was unable. The Negro maid returned to humming the melody, but he continued to consider the meaning to its phrases. In a moment, she had bustled away down the hall.

Workman was enthralled, listening to the music, fading away down the hall. He thought, *Which great prayer did the song hold? Or was it an ill-defined wish?* He spoke to the lieutenant, "Them neegroes are oft enough spinnin' yarns, and their songs seem to have a robust meanin' all their own."

The officer's reply was sharply interrupted by a woman's shrill voice. "Abraham, I need you now!"

Workman looked up and caught his breath when he saw President Lincoln stop mid-stride a few steps down the stairs. He was not wearing his jacket, just his long-sleeved shirt.

Workman raised his eyebrows in surprise watching the tall, gangly leader of the great nation wag his head wearily and trudge back up the stairs and out of sight.

While Workman continued to wait, a large number of people paraded into the home—first came men dressed in suits and top hats, then women in dresses fully blossomed with petticoats, and they seemed to flow through the hall like cream across a table; the women kept their hands in white gloves, their hair set in tight, netted buns, and some of the women were attended to by Negroes in glossy clothes of finest fabric and walking with heads held high.

Next, like a school of barracudas, frowning workers in filthy attire and carrying tool boxes clomped into the hall. They disappeared into a far office. Soon the sounds of hammering and sawing began.

Finally, some more Negroes in resplendent clothes entered, carrying various silver trays arrayed with sparkling gift boxes, and they were followed by a small, dark man in a long silk jacket with an elaborate pattern of colors and stitching. The man wore a tall turban, and at least a dozen officious attendants, also in long, silk jackets, trailed behind him.

Workman's eyes were wide from the spectacle he had beheld when the lieutenant ushered him in the office. He could officially embark on his new job, one which he hoped would end directly. *Seein' how easy it is to enter this house, I think Mr. Reeder and I will face no difficulties in dispatching the scoundrel.*

That afternoon, Workman shoveled manure, raked the shed row, fed the stables goats, combed a horse's mane and tail, walked Ted Lincoln's pony on a rope in a circle, and helped a

Patrick McGee salve a horse's weeping eye. He kept an eye on the house, watching for the president, and trying to figure a way to bring in a weapon past the guards at the gate.

He preferred to find a chance to take a shot at the president from a distance, using the Whitworth, but if he could hide a weapon inside the compound that Lucas could access during a visit, Lucas might have the only chance to accomplish their united task.

He wondered what John Wilkes Booth was planning.

FORTY-FOUR

∞

THE LECH AND
THE WATCHER

MARCH 25, 1862, EARLY MORNING
CONFEDERATE CAMP ON WHITE RIVER, ARKANSAS

Spring had finally arrived in eastern Arkansas near the
White River, and wild apple trees swayed and gyrated in
an abundant warm breeze, tossing their pink and white
blossoms high into a brilliant blue sky. Sara, still wearing the
private's uniform, lay still as a dead person on a bed of emerald
moss beneath some dense tulip bushes forty yards from where
Paul McGavin sat in General Van Dorn's campsite. She had
finally located Paul after skulking around the Confederate camp
for days.

The general's tent was located a substantial distance from
the main Confederate army, the tents unspooling for over a
mile along the bayou river. The army was daily filling with new
recruits, primarily farmers, itching for a fight.

General Van Dorn, his face flushed in anger, was now
recovered from his bout with pneumonia. He strutted about with
such zeal that his coattails flapped. He thumped the telegram
he had received from General Johnston and, in the harshest of
tones, complained of conspiracies to undo all his stratagems and

plans. Several officers sat on campstools, watching him stride back and forth.

In one of his tirades, the Federals were at fault. They had fooled the Confederate leadership east of the Mississippi into believing that they were far greater in number in Tennessee than they actually were. Then, Richmond was at fault. Loathsome philanderers had caught the ear of President Davis, poisoned his thinking, and convinced him of the lack of worth of the struggle in Missouri and Arkansas. Even the mythical fates had conspired against him.

Trying not to laugh out loud, Paul listened to the general's complaints of the multitude of machinations and saw the hilarity of them, for he considered the man as more a buffoon than a capable leader.

On two occasions since the disastrous battle at Elkhorn Tavern, Paul had witnessed General Van Dorn's womanizing. He had seen him escort a forlorn widow woman, who had lost her husband in the battle, to a tight copse of trees, supposedly to console her in her loss. He watched the woman escape the trees, more distraught than ever. General Van Dorn came forth a moment later, twirling his mustache and smirking.

The second occasion of the general's tawdry behavior occurred a day later when an unchaperoned woman with an ample bosom entered the general's tent and stayed there for what Paul considered an inordinate amount of time. When the woman finally exited the tent, her hair was mussed, and her dress collar was awry.

Finally ceasing his rants, General Van Dorn came to a stop directly in front of Paul, without a glance his way, and turned to the other officers attending his called meeting. "Our General Johnston," he announced, flicking his hand in the air to add a sort of flair to his comments, "has ordered our entah Ahmy of the West to cross the Mississippah at Memphis and to join him with all due rapidity. Whereas General Beauregard *requested* in cordial terms that we join the Army of Mississippi, General Johnston *commands* it. He does not understand the paltry conditions of these rain-soaked roads. We have made steady progress, but are beleaguered by the confounded torrential storms."

He turned to Colonel Greer. "Elkanah, gather your officers and men. You've had more than one hundred new recruits added to your regiment. Hardy men and good riders. Send more couriers down the river to obtain more river craft to meet us at Des Arc on the White River. Ten ships are not enough. We must have twenty of the fastest sailing vessels to ferry our twenty thousand soldiers down the White and then up the Mississippah to Memphis."

Colonel Greer took the occasion to expound on the proficiency of The Third Texas in his own version of bravado, replete with his own southern drawl. "I asshuah you, sir, that the regiment will be mustered and ready in a timely fashion. And with the new recruits bolsterin' ahr numbah, we shall bring glory to the South."

Immediately, the other officers decided to speak at once, stepping on each other's words. The new Brigadier General Joseph Hogg, who had replaced General McIntosh and was wearing only an overlarge civilian's jacket, spouted off with an entirely non-germane query about his needing an officer's uniform. Ignoring his request, the remaining officers joined in the discussion of the logistics of accelerating the movement of the army and of their unquenchable morale and readiness for victory.

While the group rattled off impossible questions to each other and answered with consummate confidence in the veracity of their points of view, all the while stepping on each other's sentences, Paul looked past General Price at a red-headed woodpecker tapping a tree trunk. He then watched a leaf spinning in an eddy in a narrow rivulet ten yards away. His thoughts raced away from his present situation. Was his own life spinning in circles, devoid of direction, save fighting for the cause? Had he been beating his head against a tree, searching for...something?

A Negro man standing just beyond the brook caught his eye. He stood near a tall-rooted oak with its roots in the stream with his eyes fixed forward. The young man was General Van Dorn's manservant. His features were as smooth as caramel cream, and his eyes were deep, golden pools, expressionless. He had long, slender legs, and his ankles stuck out below the ragged hem of his trousers that were gaumed with axle grease. His feet in shabby shoes. Paul deemed him a sapling, part of the forest, his dismal life's direction set, with no option to uproot itself and move away. Paul felt abject sorrow for him.

He wondered if this slave's journey through life would have been John Coincoin's fate had he not ensured the brave Negro's freedom and given him a horse on which to escape. He wondered further if John had discovered his family, and if he was enjoying some measure of self-sovereignty in Ohio. He envisioned John rejoining a beautiful family, a crew of small children wrapping around his thighs in joyous hugs, while an older son stood smiling and proud beside John's wife, who beamed at seeing her beloved husband.

Paul's thoughts, like they had so many times before, vaulted to Sara, his desire becoming more fervent daily, and if Sara did not find her betrothed Joseph alive, he would instead be her lover, then husband, and he could settle down with her in a gratifying family life. He could not shake the memory of her face, her blue eyes, the feel of her palm on his face. He admired her gumption, her drive, her femininity.

While Paul was absorbed in his reveries, the meeting abruptly broke with each officer hurrying away. Paul stood to leave.

The general took Paul by the jacket sleeve. "Captain McGavin, you've much to do. Colonel Greer will give you your orders."

Paul saluted and waded through the bushes out of Sara's sight.

Sara continued to lie still, constructing a scheme to finally catch Paul alone and share her travails with him. *I wish not to burden him, but I need his listening ear.*

∽

Four hours later, Paul was riding fast along a muddy tract, leading a second horse to trade to when the first horse tired. In his saddlebags were several pages regarding the disposition of General Van Dorn's army's numbers and timeline for fulfilling General Johnston's orders. He was to deliver the report directly into the hands of General Johnston.

Behind him about a quarter mile, Sara rode Esther, her slouch hat pulled low, the charcoal black smeared on her jaw. She worried less about being discovered than whether Esther could keep up the pace.

FORTY-FIVE

Hope Is the Thing with Feathers That Perches in the Soul

– Emily Dickinson

March 25, 1862, Late Afternoon
Eastern Arkansas

P aul slowed his dun stallion, and peeled off into the woods, leading his second horse, a steel gray gelding. He was deep enough in the trees to remain unseen from the road. Someone was following him, but the rider was proficient in staying far enough back and out of eyesight.

In a moment, he heard a horse's gentle trot, and he first caught glimpse of a sturdy roan, and a small rider in a caramel-colored jacket, with a few blond curls poking out below a slouch hat. He thought the rider might be another courier making use of the same road.

The rider was either Confederate or pretending to be, but though he felt loathe to get into a scrap, his needing to deliver the important papers from General Van Dorn to General Johnston in Corinth, he was tired of being followed. He yelled, "You there!"

The soldier pulled up and turned to look back. Seeing no one, the soldier shook the reins and began the horse's trot.

"Halt right now, Private!" Paul called. "That's an order!"

Stopping, the individual remained facing forward, away from Paul. Leaving the reserve gelding in the trees, Paul trotted his horse onto the road directly behind the potential adversary. He immediately saw the man reaching for something in a saddlebag. "If that's a gun, I would stop right there, and save your life." He aimed his own Springfield rifle at the rider's back.

Raising both hands in the air, the rider held still. "Look, mister. I'm just on an errand of mercy. Ain't no call to kill me. I ain't got no money."

Paul recognized the gentle, melodic voice. "Sara!" He stuck his rifle in the gun case on his saddle.

Sara Reeder, faux Confederate soldier, looked back and lowered her arms. "Oh, Paul!" She turned Esther and rode up beside Paul, who was smiling from ear to ear. She started to lean toward him to hug him, but stopped herself.

"Oh, Paul!" Sara exclaimed again. "I've been followin' you."

"I know that."

"Yes. Of course, you know. I knew you were on an important mission, and I didn't want to slow you down. I was goin' to come up to you when you stopped to camp."

"Isn't going to be much camping. I've got to ride all night and into the next day until I absolutely have to stop."

"Oh, my! That sounds dauntin'. But if I can ride alongside you, I'm up for it."

"I'm quite sure your horse won't be. A horse can only do so much. And Sara... I'm delighted to see you. But right now... I've got some questions for you. First, why are you dressed like a soldier? Second, I thought you couldn't hear. Were you deceiving me?"

"No, my goodness, no. I would never deceive you. My hearin' came back. It's not as good as it was. But I can hear again. All of that and more is what I must talk to you about. You see, my fiancé, Joseph… is dead." Her last words came choking across her lips.

Paul mulled over her sorrowful tidings and considered, based on when he had witnessed Joseph hanging behind to face the Yankees alone in the waning battle of Pea Ridge, that she probably spoke the truth. Seeing the despair spreading across her face, he felt immediate grief for her, but felt a cautious elation now that he might have a chance to gain her consideration and, perhaps, devotion. He was able to say, "I'm sorry for your loss."

"I loved him so, but now he's gone."

"I wish I'd known him better."

"You knew him?"

Paul cleared his throat. "I mean that I wish I could have known him. But as for you, a third question. How does that explain you being in a Confederate uniform, and you being *here*?"

Sara sighed. "I had hopes that if I could ingratiate myself into the Third Texas, I could find Joseph, but when I went to their camp, his friend told me he was dead."

"Oh."

"I have another reason for my pretense. I cannot stand that these Yankee invaders who've swarmed into our land like a pestilence and are wreckin' it, destroyin' houses, burnin' farms, puttin' good families into appalling situations in which they may likely starve, and killin' my countrymen. I've seen fine Southerners wilt and fall like corn stalks from the witherin' fire of them bluecoats. Before there was any Union, there were states, and *states* come first. Our land is ours, not theirs. So, I've decided to fight for the Confederacy in any way I can."

Paul raised his eyebrows. "Well, not as a soldier, you're not. You wouldn't fool a blind man."

"I endeavored as best I could. I can still fight, and I'm as good a shot as any man."

"I believe you are as good a shot, probably better than most, but you can also die just like any man." He rubbed his bad leg.

Then he removed his spectacles and wiped them with a cloth from his saddlebag, all the time looking at and gauging Sara's response to his last words—the blush in her cheeks, her eyes wide.

"Wasn't your leg in a splint when last we parted?" Paul asked.

"Yes, t'was. But I heal quick. It's still tender, but a darn sight better."

"That's good news. I'll stop for the day to camp. It's almost dark anyway. General Johnston may have to wait a few more hours to get these papers. And I want you to know that it is gratifying to see you are alive. I was deeply worried."

"I'm glad you're livin', too. Praise God. I need to share my many ordeals and setbacks with someone I know. Someone who'll listen. Someone who'll care. That damn Yankee woman who wants to free all the slaves is no one to share with. Frankly, I don't know how I'll go on without Joseph, unless I fight, or if you can help me find another way."

Paul considered that she was merely simpering to gain access to him and the important papers for General Johnston for scurrilous reasons. Could she be a Union spy? Despite these concerns, his heart was racing in a fashion that he could feel it thumping against his chest, and he looked up and said a silent prayer of thanks.

Maybe. Maybe.

FORTY-SIX

∞

VILE IS THE MAN WHO DELIGHTS IN HIS OWN SORDID WAYS

MARCH 26, 1862, NIGHT
A FEW MILES WEST OF ROLLA, MISSOURI

It was dark, and B.F. Richards traveled the road by listening. He was talented at operating in the dark for the things he desired. He often thought of the young blond woman who had twice escaped his grasp. Even this night, his every fiber yearned to find her and break her, but he would settle for any prey to satisfy his wanton cravings. He burned for revenge and for power. He had abandoned his two wounded cohorts in their camp behind Pea Ridge. They brought him no power. He stole one of their horses.

Now he followed a carriage. It was a lonely sound—creaking wheels, the clip-clop of hooves. No cavalry. No additional horses. He would find plunder when the carriage stopped. He hoped he would find a woman to rape. *They're stupid to travel alone at night*. He sneered.

Fifty yards ahead of Richards, Cyntha watched Ben waggle the reins of the horse pulling their carriage. She was satisfied with the progress that they were making in their journey to St. Louis.

They had passed through Springfield, Missouri, and were close to Rolla. Ben had kept the strong-muscled artillery horse pulling their carriage at a steady pace along the Telegraph Road that undulated through the high hills and low valleys. She noted that the telegraph wires had been restrung on the poles, and the wires hummed often with the telegraph messages streaking along.

Ben had a rifle and two revolvers. Reynolds, sick as he was, could still manage his big sidearm. Cyntha herself carried a small revolver—a petite item decorated with a pearl handle. It had been given to her back at Elkhorn Tavern by Anthony's wife, Jeanette.

With all their combined fire power, she still worried. The night surrounded them, and they had not come upon a single Union guard wayside camp at which to stop. An officer in Springfield had told them the road was strewn with guards whose job it was to watch for Rebel raiders or marauders who might jump the wagon trains that daily rolled along the road.

Occasionally, they passed supply wagons going the other way, accompanied by a cavalry troop, but they had seen only one camp, and that was in the early afternoon. Often, Yankee couriers coming from Rolla passed them, and other couriers overtook them from behind. The road had remained quite busy with mounted soldiers or teamsters with their wagons during the day. Cyntha had become used to hearing the trotting of horses coming either toward them or from behind their carriage.

When stars began to sprinkle across the moonless sky, Ben had achieved as far as he could drive the carriage and see the road without the aid of lanterns. "This is as much as we can do. Besides, the horse needs rest. I should have traded him out miles back, but he seemed to be pullin' the carriage fine."

"Do you want me to walk ahead with a lantern?" Reynolds offered, but he began coughing.

"No, Josiah," Cyntha said. "This is as good a place to camp as any." She bit her lip. Somewhere on the road to the south, she easily discerned the clip-clop of a horse coming at a slow walk.

The three got down from the carriage. Ben stuck a revolver in his belt, but left the other guns in the carriage and walked gingerly, always aware of his healing, painful, splinted ankle. He untethered the horse from behind the carriage and secured it to a tree twenty paces from the road in a little circular clearing that was surrounded by tall pines and brush. Next, he released the strappings from the horse that had done the pulling and tied it to another tree. "I hear a stream runnin' over yonder a ways. I'll get us water." He gathered the metal buckets from the back of the carriage and went in search of water for the horses and to cook coffee in the morning. He disappeared into the dark forest down an incline toward the stream.

Reynolds, holding a bullseye lantern and acting as stouthearted as he could, tottered about the clearing, gathering fallen branches and twigs for firewood. He was coughing, though Cyntha could tell he was trying to stifle the coughs. She brought out the sack of cornmeal, cabbage and coffee. Then the blankets, a single suitcase, and dragged the heavy cracked and soiled tarpaulin that served as their tent. She placed the store of food on a fallen log. Standing in the inky darkness, she wondered why Ben had left the carriage so near the road.

She carefully stole away several yards in behind some bushes, lifted her skirt, squatted, and relieved herself. She listened for any approaching animal, and especially harkened for snakes, though she figured she could probably never hear a snake if it slithered right under her. She started back with her hands out in front of her, for the darkness was extant. After she had walked a good many paces, she stopped. *Where is the camp?* She could not see the bullseye lantern, nor any campfire.

"Reynolds!" she called.

"I's right here, Cyntha. Come toward my voice."

She picked her way through bushes and briars that caught on her dress hem. She burst into the clearing. Reynolds was striking a match to some dry grass and kindling. He blew on the little flame, and it burst up, and the drier logs caught quickly, making a fairly tall blaze. The light from the flames flickered off the bark of the trees, revealing the flat, almost grassless, dirt clearing.

"That's a welcome campfire, Reynolds," she said, not realizing she had been holding her breath, and breathed in the pine air and listened to the crickets.

When Reynolds stood, she became aware he was standing in front of a dark bulk of a man, his face covered in the shadow of a wide brimmed hat. The man said nothing, but spat a stream of black fluid.

Cyntha gasped.

"Don't even think of tryin' anything," a foul voice from the shadows whispered intently. "I'll kill this nigger." The dark intruder's revolver gleamed in the firelight, pinned against Reynolds' ear.

"Look, mister," Reynolds offered. "You can take whatever you want. Just leave me and the lady alone."

"I'll think about it." The man was still in shadow. He forced Reynolds down upon the fallen log near the fire. "You take a seat, too, Missy."

In the dancing firelight, she saw the scar on his face that ran from the bridge of his nose and down his cheek. She saw his sneer, and she knew who he was.

Cyntha slowly sat next to Reynolds, her hands folded, and she remembered the small pistol in her reticule that hung on her wrist. *Can I get the gun out without him seeing me?*

"You travelin' alone?" the man asked. "Just the two o' you?"

"Yes." Cyntha lowered her head, but kept her eyes on the man. *Where is Ben?* Her thoughts raced. *Will Ben know? Can he stop this assailant, this beast?*

The man, wide in the shoulders, his belly protruding, came fully into the firelight. He held his and Reynolds' revolver and aimed both at them. His face reminded her of all her most horrible dreams, the unforgettable face with the scar. He spat tobacco juice again, and she knew him too well—the man whom she and Reynolds had seen back near Wilson Creek in February and who had tailed them on their journey to Springfield.

Richards straightened and looked out into the dark forest, aiming one of the revolvers in a sweeping motion. "You sure there ain't nobody else with you on this cold night, Nigger?"

"No, suh. Just us two." Reynolds said firmly. "You best state yor business and get on yor way. We ain't done nothin' to you."

"Oh, but you have, Nigger. You must be sesech tryin' to escape the Yanks. No self-respectin' White woman I ever heard of rode alone with a nigger unless he was her slave."

"That ain't true." Reynold rose. "I'm a freeman, and…"

Richards struck Reynolds on the side of the head with his revolver, and Reynolds crumpled prostrate. "Well, that was plumb easy." Richards booted the freeman in the ribs and walked closer to Cyntha. He towered over her. She took a quick glance up at him, and began fumbling with opening her reticule.

"What ya got in there, Missy?" Richards tore her bag from her wrist, felt the gun inside, and dropped the purse to the ground. He stood astride her legs, his big boots planted on either side of her legs squeezed together. "Ya know, now that it's just us in this intimate settin'." He leaned over and pitched a few more branches from the pile onto the fire. "We can have a cozy time. I ain't had a woman in days. I'll bet you ain't had a man in a while either."

She began to tremble. "I'm married."

"Don't matter to me none."

"I'm *not* going to get cozy with you. Just leave me be. If you want food, take it. Want a horse, take one. You want…"

"Oh, I'll take both horses, and then all the food, but first, I'll take you!" He stuck Reynolds' pistol in his belt, grabbed her arm and hoisted her up, then pressed against her, all the while holding his revolver to her temple. Releasing her arm, he tore at her blouse, ripping the top buttons.

She screamed.

A loud clanging sounded in the forest, the unmistakable sound of metal buckets banging to the ground and tumbling.

Richards released Cyntha and spun to the direction of the noise. "Who's that?" He growled a whisper.

Cyntha tried to run, but he caught her wrist and pushed her down onto the log. He crouched down near the flames of the campfire, trying to peer into the black wall of the forest. His eyes flashed in the direction of the metal clanging, the buckets still rolling down the incline, until they stopped against a tree. She watched him shift left and right, listening. Another noise like footsteps crunching on dead leaves sounded to the right. Richards leaned toward the sound, pulled out the second revolver from his belt and fired in the direction of the noise.

Reynolds groaned groggily. The marauder shoved his boot on the freeman's back.

An owl hoot peeled from where the original sound came. More running steps. Right, then left. Richards fired several shots into the trees.

A bullet tore through the meat of his gun arm, sending fabric and blood splattering onto Cyntha. He yowled and dropped the gun, swung up the other revolver with his left hand and fired into the night. More shots cracked, a second bullet hitting his already wounded arm. Dropping the revolver, he ripped a kerchief from around his neck and was trying to tie a tourniquet as he ran.

Three more bullets whistled into the night, one bullet hitting the marauder's knee, and he crashed face first to the earth. Cyntha leaped to her knees, keeping her body low and sweeping both arms along the dark soil, trying to locate the reticule that held her gun.

Cursing and snarling, Richards panted and tried to drag himself into the forest. When he reached the edge of light from the campfire, Ben came at a limping run at him. Just as Richards stood to hobble away, Ben tackled him, knocking him flat on his back. Ben was atop the marauder, pummeling the scarred face with iron fists. In a moment, the man collapsed, knocked out.

Ben stood and raced to Cyntha, still on her knees. No sooner had he reached her and taken her hand than Richards stood up, shaking his dizzy head. His face covered in blood, Reynolds had recovered his revolver and was trying to focus his eyes. Before Ben could react, he saw them and leveled his gun. When he fired, a dark figure jumped between him and Ben and Cyntha. Reynolds had risen, gathered his waning strength and made the wild leap, and he took both bullets in his chest.

Richards spun, mouth agape, momentarily surprised by the intercession of the Negro, but before he could shoot again, Cyntha fired her gun. The bullet pierced his skull, lodging in his brain, a black, bloody hole in his forehead. An expression of surprise in his eyes, his body slammed to the earth, its own earthquake.

Cyntha and Ben stood stunned. The awareness that the monster of a man was dead left them momentarily bewildered. Then Ben bent quickly to attend to Reynolds, whose breath came only in brief pants over timorous lips. His eyes were squinted in pain. When Cyntha knelt beside him and clutched his brown, freckled hand, she whispered, "Dear Josiah, you are still with me. My friend, my ardent life companion."

Reynolds opened his eyes and offered a feeble smile. He clenched her hand tightly, and attempted to speak, but could only cough, spitting out bright red blood.

Ben had ripped open the freeman's shirt, and was applying pressure with a cloth to both bullet holes. He pushed so hard on the bored holes that he was losing feeling in his arms. Tears spilled down his cheeks. "Don't die, Reynolds. Don't die. Cyntha needs you. I need you, too."

Reynolds looked at Ben and gave a generous smile. "You're a brave soul, Ben McGavin. I can't expect you to pay back the favor." He coughed, and his body shook. "I saved your life, but you've been a tremendous blessing...." He coughed, flinging more blood onto his grizzled beard and chest. "And a blessing to my best friend."

He looked up at the twinkling stars, the tops of the trees swaying in a swift breeze. "This is a nice place to meet my Lord."

"No," Cyntha pleaded. "Stay with us. You need to see your family again."

"Likely it'll be," Reynolds, his eyes wide in a joyous expression, spoke in a whisper, "I'll see 'em directly in parad..." His words fell off, and his head lolled to the side. His eyes closed. No more breath came from him.

"No!" Cyntha wailed, her tears bursting forth. She fell to her knees beside her old friend and clutched the lapels of Reynolds' jacket. Taking a handkerchief from her reticule, she lightly wiped dirt from his face. She looked up at Ben, her eyes fierce with anger that Reynolds had been killed by the criminal. "No, no, no," she continued to wail. "Not dear Reynolds, too. Oh, that we could escape this wretched war. It follows us like a hound of hell. We are its prey."

Ben stared at Reynolds' face, then made a few exasperated motions with his hands. "I really don't know what to do." Tears welled in his eyes. "I lose my brothers. I lose poor Reynolds."

Finally, he gently folded Reynolds' lifeless hands across his chest. He rose and helped Cyntha sit on the fallen tree. He put his arm around her, and she lay her head against his chest, like she had done not so long ago in the kitchen at Elkhorn Tavern. She remembered her feeling of loss back then, and how his nearness comforted her so.

They sat there in the dying campfire light for a long time, each deep in their own thoughts and deeper in their own hearts. Ben thought for a while about the loss he felt in Reynolds dying, but he then thought mostly about how the death of their friend affected Cyntha, and he wanted only to assuage her sorrow.

When the fire had almost died to embers, Ben rose and re-stoked it to roaring. He took a blanket and laid it over Reynolds' dead body. Ben, struggling with each step, pulled Richards' body into the brush a far distance from the campfire.

Later, Ben strung the tarpaulin between four trees and set a bed of blankets for Cyntha. After some hours, she finally collapsed onto the blankets to cry herself to sleep. Later, he heard the faint sound of wild creatures snorting and tearing at the dead flesh.

To keep Reynolds' body from harm, Ben sat all night beside it, near the fire to ensure no hog, nor other predator, nor even a crawling bug came near his friend. A slight drizzle blew in, followed by one short burst of rain. The rain that fell on Ben's face mixed with his tears. When the burst tapered off, sending up the smell of wet ground and grass, he said quietly, "I hate this war. I've lost my brothers, and now I've lost my good friend. God, if you're listenin', I ain't much one for prayin', but I can say I'd be powerful disappointed if this good man weren't up in heaven with you. Do you hear me?"

Distant thunder rumbled, so faint, it could barely be heard. Ben took it to mean yes.

FORTY-SEVEN

RESPITE IN A PLACE OF SORROW

MARCH 28, 1862
EASTERN ARKANSAS

S ara rode beside Paul in their sojourn that led first to Memphis, then to Corinth. Traveling on the slogged roads was tough, but she felt confident of her decision to support the Confederacy by whatever means, albeit not fighting. And she was pleased that Paul had allowed her to ride alongside him, using their agreed-upon false claim that he was escorting the daughter of the governor of Georgia, Joseph Emerson Brown. She worried a little that, if asked, would she remember to state her last name as Brown.

A day earlier, Sara had grown weary of wearing the Rebel uniform. Without her mentioning it, Paul realized her discomfort. They stopped in a small town where Paul bought her a calico dress and a bonnet and some women's lace-up shoes.

Struggling through rainy east Arkansas, Paul was overjoyed that Sara was always within a few feet of him. He missed her long, golden curls that she had cut off, but he could scarcely keep his eyes from her face, even though she tended not to pay him even the slightest interest. He had listened to her divulge her long tale of woe of seeking, yet never finding Joseph, but he was glad to let her tell it.

At sunset, despite slogging through mud-laden roads, they arrived at the Mississippi River across from Memphis. Sara had never seen so large a body of water, nor a metropolis with such abundant lights. The street lampposts lit, the many two-story buildings' windows softly glowing, all lined up. The buggy lamps glimmering along the streets, the trains' front beacons piercing the night. "It's like a rich woman spilled her purse full of diamonds," she said.

She walked to the edge of the mighty river, her new shoes sinking in the bank's mud. She tried to encompass its vastness and power. The water gobbled up light, so that it was ominously dark, and the rumbling current sounded like the river was being powered by a mighty engine. It was the most powerful phenomenon she had ever experienced. With its dark cloak, the moon's reflection bobbed and dipped upon the mirroring waves.

Paul located a boarding house, and they spent the night in adjoining rooms. Paul, his mind ever upon Sara's fetching appearance, slept little. The next morning, they, along with their horses, crossed into Memphis on a keelboat filled to almost sinking with sacks of corn brought by wagon and rail from Texas.

While Sara gazed, mesmerized, at the first big city she had ever witnessed growing larger as they neared it, Paul kept his eyes on her. *What is it about her? I've seen other pretty women. Just none like her.*

When they made it ashore, Sara asked to wander the shops of the downtown, and he could not say no. "A half hour. That's all."

She stepped onto the dock beside a wide warehouse. All around her, Negroes hastened to unload the sacks of corn from the keelboat to the rancorous yelling by a white boss, who occasionally popped a whip in the air like one might do to mules pulling a wagon.

Along the many streets from the wharves to the downtown, Negroes, both women and men, labored—loading wagons, shoveling the horse manure from the streets, and carrying heavy bundles on their backs. White men worked alongside them, but not in the same number. Negro servants drove carriages for White women, and, with heads bowed, they helped the daintily clad women disembark from the carriages while supporting the women's white-gloved hands with their own calloused hands.

"I can't imagine," Sara said to Paul, "how there could ever be so many Negroes all in one place. And they are all working so hard. Bless them." Sara's thoughts raced to Abram, who was her family's slave, yet she never saw him as being owned, only as a dear friend. She had never considered him as less in equality to herself and to her father, but her naivete was being swept away. Seeing a stooped, old Negress, she helped the woman, who was carrying a large bundle, to climb into a wagon seat. The woman gave a toothless smile and nodded to Sara.

"I have much to learn about this world and its...unfairness."

Paul took her arm and escorted her along the boardwalk into town. *Don't we all have much to learn.* Paul's thoughts ran to John Coincoin, who had saved his life. He grimaced, thinking he had ever thought less of John. Now he held him in highest esteem.

Reaching the downtown, Sara entered a hat shop, and she became delighted about a simple straw hat with a wide brim and blue ribbons that draped from it. Paul told her it was impractical and demanded she go get the horses. After she left with a pout on her lips, he purchased the hat with Confederate bills and gave it to her when she brought their mounts. She hugged him and gave him a peck on his cheek. She removed her bonnet and replaced it with the new hat.

"I think this will make our story about you being the governor's daughter more believable if you have a bit of fashion," Paul said.

Sara and Paul rode at a good clip for the next two days. Sara's remorse for losing Joseph to either death or imprisonment faded a little, but the shining remembrance of his face often pervaded her thoughts.

∽

Workman used every spare moment at the Presidential Mansion stables conjuring up scenarios for killing President Lincoln. He was a natural in caring for the horses' small wounds, lame legs and stomach ailments. He worked hard, cleaning the stalls and grooming the horses. Quick with a joke, the other stable hands found him a convivial companion. They thought nothing of him asking so many questions about the habits and travels of the president.

He learned that the president had taken to riding out to the Old Soldiers Home to visit the invalids or to have quiet time in the neighboring house that would soon become, as it had for President Buchanan, the summer home of the Lincolns. He took note of how wagon after wagon would arrive at the Mansion, and that Mary Todd Lincoln would often swoop outside in a glorious dress, her arms always waving.

With great alacrity, she would order the loading of furniture, vases, paintings, clothing, and a myriad of items into the wagons. Her shrill voice, that he considered to be akin to a harpy's, made it evidentially clear that the items stowed onto the wagon were to be taken to the summer home to prepare it for the family living there during the warmer weather. The Negro and White civilian laborers, some well-dressed, some in the shabbiest attire, bowed and nodded and did their best to perform every task she heaped upon them.

He had several conversations with the delicate, thin, yet matronly Maroon, Elizabeth Keckley, a free woman and Mrs. Lincoln's personal seamstress. From her, he learned of the president's wife's propensity to launch into tirades, that Mrs. Keckley called *paroxysms*, as well as bouts of severe depression.

Mrs. Keckley doted on Mary Lincoln, but, in an aside to him, she bragged that, while working as a seamstress in Baltimore long before the war, she had sewn a gown for Varina Davis, the wife of the Confederate president. She felt no animosity at all to the Southerners. "We are all kindred on this earth," she said.

When Workman happened to mention to her he had fought at Wilson Creek, she labored through the tale of how her only son had joined the Union army and been killed in that battle.

"War is war," Workman interrupted her story of woe. "A bullet'll kill a Nigger just as soon as a white man." He walked away. He could not care less about the death of a Negro boy.

FORTY-EIGHT

TO TRAMPLE THE ENEMY

MARCH 31, 1862
WASHINGTON, DC

L ucas was regularly called to man the telegraph keys. McClellan's grand Army of the Potomac was cornered on the Peninsula below the fortifications thrown up by General John B. Magruder. The messages tapping into the keys told of a vast Confederate army behind the fort that brimmed with cannons. Recent messages from General McClellan, one of which Lucas took on the key, demanded more troops and that the Rebel force was nearly twice the size of the Federal army. The Virginia ironclad sat in the James River, precluding the Union navy coming in support to bombard the Rebel fort. "All may be lost in a frontal assault against so vast a bastion," the message read. "I plan a siege with heavy mortars."

Lincoln arrived at the telegraph office a little after noon. Lucas thought, *If I had my gun, I could have killed him*. But his resolve had plummeted in recent days. He had witnessed so many runaway Negroes crowding into the city. He considered deeply the uncountable numbers who had fled from their plantation homes, and why. Washington offered them nothing but more hard labor, most of the men put to work, shoveling the horse manure on the streets or piling dirt on the fort walls. Their positions in the plantations, by Lucas' reckoning, could not have been more laborious than what they were forced to do now.

Sorrow-faced Negro mothers and skinny children huddled in shanties and tents, strung out around the city in contraband camps. They were the prize of war and had become, in Lucas's estimation, human fodder for the Union army to exploit until they used them up.

Sitting in the cavernous office, he mumbled, "Is their freedom so valuable to them to toss all their belongings aside? Every stitch of decency pitched out like a worn pair of shoes?"

He knew of Lincoln's statement that the Negro could never be equal to the White man, and that the president had often offered that all the Negroes be shipped to Africa.

Still, Lucas had spoken with several of the weakest of the families on several occasions, and each member of them said "glory hallelujahs" that they were free. Why was this freedom so cherished? His ambivalence about the tack of the war worried him. Was there a greater cause for this conflagration? Despite the incongruity of the whole Negro issue, he felt compelled to continue with his plan. *The president must be eliminated in order to preserve the Union.*

The key operators paid little attention to Lucas. He could have performed cartwheel acrobatics for all they cared. But he watched the bearded president's every move, his long legs stuck up on a desk while he leaned back in a cushioned chair, thumbing through the dispatches from the armies' officers.

While he was reading, Secretary Edwin Stanton unexpectedly bouldered into the room and up to the president, the floor creaking under his weight.

President Lincoln removed his reading glasses and lowered his legs.

"I know," Secretary Stanton began, "that you are concerned that General McClellan has not been faring well on the peninsula, however..."

"That's putting it mildly," President Lincoln responded. "He's like a cat who has given up on eating the mouse he has pinned by the tail."

All the telegraph operators chuckled. Their smile stayed until Secretary Stanton, who did not smile, continued. "Yes, well, we must press him to advance. I'm sure you are doing what you can as Commander in Chief."

The president nodded.

"But a courier has arrived. He brought a packet of reports from General Halleck explaining that all the Union armies' efforts are going extremely well in the west. These reports bear glad tidings." He clutched a number of pages in his hands. "Our army is well supplied. We own the Tennessee River with our gunboats. We will soon own the upper Mississippi. The Rebel fort at Island Number Ten will fall any day, then our gunboats will move on Memphis. And Halleck says the army under generals Grant and Sherman are positioned well in an excellent, defensible position on the west side of the Tennessee."

"I see," President Lincoln said, stretching his arms and yawning. "I apologize, Edwin, I didn't get much sleep. Mrs. Lincoln has been appraising me of plans for our summer abode at Corn Rig, beside the Old Soldiers Home."

"I understand. My own wife keeps me busy at times. But the good news continues. General Buell is moving from eastern Tennessee to join with Grant at a point called Pittsburg landing, a mere twenty-five miles from Corinth, Mississippi. The army will be so large as to be unstoppable. A hammer on the Rebels' heads. When our armies unite, we will secure their railroad crossroads at Corinth, drive to take Jackson, Mississippi, then turn on Vicksburg. Isn't that welcome news in these trying times?"

Lucas wanted to say something about the fighting spirit of southerners. *It will not be that easy, Stanton.*

"Yes, my illustrious and staunch ally." President Lincoln stood, stuck his thumbs in his suspenders and tugging them out an inch, as if her were preparing to deliver a soliloquy. "It will be good to take Vicksburg. It is the linchpin that holds the South together. But aren't there any Confederate armies to oppose our men in southern Tennessee...Where was it, Pittsburg Landing?"

"Yes. Pittsburg. Our army is in a strong defense situation with impassable streams on each flank. Grant's army could easily resist an assault should it occur. According to these reports, plus the messages you've received from Halleck and Grant, the insurgents believe only in holing up in forts with antiquated weapons. They have neither the materiel, nor the manpower even to defend a fort. General Grant has assured General Halleck that the enemy is content to stay put, hardly willing to put up a fight."

President Lincoln nodded.

"After we take the middle south," Secretary Stanton added, "then the states of Missouri and Arkansas, already in our powerful grip, will be completely secured back into the Union with new Pro-Union governments. It's a matter of a few months."

Lucas felt the blood pulsing in his temple. *Missouri in a powerful grip! Missouri never left the Union. Why are you gripping it? You bastards! You are compelled only to destroy. Both you and that monkey of a president only want to destroy.* He rose, gathered his hat and ear trumpet and left. He walked out of the War Department without speaking to anyone. He knew he had to act soon, with or without Workman's help. *President Lincoln and even his cabinet must be eliminated.*

The last thing he heard Secretary Stanton say was, "And you need to stop traveling alone, especially at night to the Old Soldiers Home. There's at least a dozen places where a man could take a shot at you."

Lucas thought, *That man to take that shot might be Workman or me.*

FORTY-NINE

THE FULL ARMOR OF GOD

MARCH 31, 1862, 3:00 P.M.
CORINTH, MISSISSIPPI

C onstance and Edward Felder arrived in Corinth by train. Edward had sold the wagon and team in Memphis for tickets, and, because he was a man of the cloth, they were allowed to ride on what had been secured officially as a train only for army use. "Our men could use your inspiring words," the young captain in charge had said.

Constance thought the officer looked splendid in his pristine gray uniform. She would not look at him though. *I'm a married woman.* Then she smiled to herself.

When the train drew to a halt, Constance could not believe her eyes. She had heard the chatter of some soldiers riding in the passenger car with them talking about the immensity of the army, but she was still surprised at the sight of thousands of soldiers. Edward and she stepped off the train onto the platform. Crates and barrels were stacked along the extent of the siding, and slaves, freemen, and soldiers labored mightily to move the boxes, barrels, and bulging sacks into waiting wagons.

Edward walked up to the captain. "How many in our army here?"

"Thirty, maybe forty thousand."

Edward gathered their few belongings. Constance took her rifle and a wicker basket of food; and the newlyweds made their way down the main street, dodging squads of soldiers and wagons. Edward twice caught sight of men urinating and did his best to shield Constance from a view of them. He spied a church steeple and took Constance's hand. "We will settle temporarily at a town church, be it Calvinist or Methodist or Presbyterian. If need be, I will adapt. Later, I believe that Shiloh Church is a little north of here."

They arrived first at the church parsonage which was locked up tight. They went to the front doors where a sign read, "Closed for the War."

"I see by your collar, you're a reverend. We're in need of a preacher." The voice came from behind them.

Turning, Edward and Constance faced an aged man and wife. The man was gray-haired and held a cane. His wife had white hair combed tight in a bun. Both bore saddened expressions.

"How do you do?" Edward said, shaking their hands. "I am Reverend Edward Felder. This is my wife, Constance." Constance nodded and smiled.

The man began. "I'm Clabe Linestock. My wife, Alma. I'll get to the point…"

"I'll do it!" Alma interrupted. "Our preacher ran off. Said he wanted to be on the winnin' side. Went north and abandoned us all." She stamped her foot. "Traitor!"

"If you'll take it on," Clabe said, "be ya Methodist, Calvinist, or any, we'll pay ya same as him. If there was ever a time we needed a man of God to give us some solace, now, with the invaders a few miles away, is the time."

A crowd of people from the town began to gather on the steps, listening to Clabe and Alma explain the position to Edward.

"Yes!" A man from the crowd hollered. "We tried to convince Reverend M. Taylor to be the preacher, but he's off to the Shiloh church, preachin' to the Yankees."

"Said he might save 'em from their treachery!" another man yelled.

"Everyone of them Yankees," a woman screamed, her voice showing terror, "is a demon from hell!"

The crowd had grown quickly and began boisterously pleading for Edward to take the position. He held up his hands to quiet them. When their pleadings subsided, he folded his hands and prayed. "Dear God, if it be your will, let me lead this flock to your peace. Amen."

Constance's smile broadened.

The crowd echoed the amen, and each one came up the steps and vigorously shook Edward's and Constance's hands. Alma unlocked the doors, and the newlyweds were swept by the enthusiastic townspeople into the church. After Constance put the women to work helping her clean the pews and walls, and while the men set to work doing odd jobs in the church, Edward made his way to the parsonage and started writing his sermon.

That evening, when Edward opened the doors to invite anyone of any faith inside to pray, the first person up the steps was Father Antonio.

FIFTY

For Want of a Windlass

APRIL 1, 1862, LATE EVENING
CORINTH, MISSISSIPPI

Riding into Corinth, Paul was amazed at the extensive earthwork fortifications. Every line of the fortifications was fronted by an abatis. The pile of stacked trees and sharp stakes would make extremely slow going for an attacking army. Drawing closer to the forts, soldiers lay in hiding amidst the felled trees like so many forest goblins, their gun barrels glinting in the sinking sun's rays. The pickets shouted at Paul and Sara, commanding they state their business. Paul hollered that he was carrying reports for General Johnston and held up the valise with the pages from General Van Dorn. Each picket waved them along.

Sara and he rode down the counterscarp ditch before a high embankment and up the glacis, then onto the road that turned and angled throughout the intricate layout of trenches, lunettes, and artillery emplacements. New cannons gleamed through the embrasures. Curious cannoneers peeked at Paul and Sara through those same openings.

Hundreds of slaves labored on the forts, their swarthy bodies glistening in the fading light. Some strengthened the revetments, pushing rough-hewn boards against the embankments. Or they piled dirt and rocks into the three-foot tall gabion baskets to reinforce the fort walls. And they sang rhythmic songs in their labor, each gang warbling a different tune.

Upon entering the town, just as the stars filtered out in a cobalt sky, Paul and Sara made their way to General Johnston's headquarters at the Rose Cottage. The general was glad to receive General Van Dorn's lengthy correspondence. While Sara waited outside the house, Paul stood inside near the general who sat perched on a couch perusing the correspondence.

"You may go, Captain McGavin." The general waved his hand.

"Begging your pardon, sir," Paul said. "I have accompanied the daughter of Governor Brown of Georgia to here. I was assigned to escort her from Memphis where she had been visiting relatives. She tells me she wants to stay in Corinth for now and serve our army, perhaps in the hospital."

"That would be fine."

"Thank you, sir."

"Wait, McGavin." General Johnston removed his spectacles. "You're a scout. Right?"

"Yes sir."

"Good. I want a fresh pair of eyes to evaluate the Federals' position. I've had plenty of reports. I need someone who has no preconceived ideas about the invaders' status to study them and give me a thorough report. Can you do that?"

"Yes, sir."

"Then go present yourself to General Beauregard. He will give you directions to meet General Forrest first. Starting tonight, I want you to scout the Federal's entire position. Stem to stern, then report back to me by the following evening. I fear we must act without Van Dorn's men, or the opportunity will be lost. If only I had a large windlass to hoist my army into position to do battle." He had a brief whimsical look. Then his expression turned dour. "Can you do the scouting? Time is short."

"I will, sir."

"And tell the governor's daughter she may sleep here tonight with the other women of the house and then go to the Tishomingo Hotel in the morning. She can sing to the men or bring them water."

"Before I go, might I trouble you to ask the good people who live here for the loan of a civilian jacket?"

"Yes. The Yanks may throw a party, and you'll need to look your best." General Johnston snickered and walked into the kitchen, and after a few minutes, returned with a drab, brown suit jacket.

"Perfect." Paul took off his uniform jacket and put on the civilian one, a ragged, forlorn item.

"My pleasure, Captain. Try not to get shot by the Yankees or by one of our nervous recruits."

Paul saluted.

With the night already fallen, Paul rode from Corinth along bleak, gloom-laden roads and narrow trails lined with wet foliage all the way up to the Lick Creek on the Confederate right flank. He found Confederate General Nathan Bedford Forrest sitting by a campfire. In their brief conversation, General Forrest pointed out that Union pickets were a mere three hundred yards away, supposedly guarding the Union's extreme left flank.

Never stirring from the camp chair on which he sat, the general handed a hand-drawn map to Paul, but avoided looking him in the face, preferring to stare into the opaqueness beyond the fire. Paul was struck by the overwhelming calm and self-possession of the man. General Forrest, with his sharp, pointed beard and severe, black eyes, seemed to possess some spiritual element Paul could not fathom. He gave Paul an eerie sense that he could somehow see into the future.

Though they fought for the same cause, Paul felt a bit of trepidation in his presence. Was the general getting even with the entire world? Did he feel gratification to toy with the enemy's lives as a cat might play with a mouse? Observing Forrest's cavalrymen preparing to ride out on a night inspection, he saw an enthusiastic esprit de corps, and that they, too, were like cats ready to prowl for mice.

Paul left General Forrest's camp and rode into the suffocating night, heading west, much of the time traveling in the forest of oak, gum and hickory trees well south of the Union camps. The trees were leafed out, and wild fruit trees' pink and white blossoms were evident in the rising moon's glow. A light breeze rustled the leaves.

By morning, the rain swollen streams had spilled over their banks to fester into wide, slimy, tarlike bogs, and he had to use considerable care not to cause his horse to step in a hole. Often, he rode within two hundred yards of the rows and rows of Federal tents, neat and sparkling white in the moonlight, and the drifting smoke of the troops' campfires. He encountered one picket, sleeping.

He saw no entrenchments, no soil tossed upon logs for parapets, no trees felled as abatis to slow an attack.

With the spears of the morning sun slicing through the trees, he stopped in a farmer's recently plowed field in full view of the blue-clad soldiers. Beyond the tents, he noticed a small log church, a simple wooden cross affixed to the summit of the pitched roof. A company of soldiers on a reconnoiter tussled their way out of a vine-cloaked stand of oaks. They were surprised to see him sitting placidly on his horse. He waved at them, and, though they at first aimed their rifles at him, but since he looked like a local citizen, they waved back and proceeded on their way.

Throughout the day, he saw Union pickets and even some Confederates hiding in the trees.

In the afternoon, he stopped to chat with the farmers in their fields. He asked their notions about the movements and disposition of the Federal troops. Most complained of the constant passage of patrols through their land, but they provided singular information about the Union regiments. He jotted notes of their observations and the regimental positions on a roll of newsprint.

One farmer, a Mr. J.C. Fraley, whose land extended along the far right of the Federal tents and whose farmhouse lay two hundred yards south of the Union camp, said there was one colonel who was regularly sending out patrols. "Seems like the skittish sort," Fraley cautioned, "like a single shadow is the entire Rebel army attackin'." He shrugged. "Wish they'd go away. Or my cotton crop won't ever get planted."

Paul thanked Mr. Fraley and rode further west. By late afternoon, he made it to where General Cheatham's three-thousand-man division was deployed across the road to Purdy. He stayed in the camp for an hour, chatting with the soldiers and sharing their fare—peppered pork, fried cornmeal sluice and burned rye coffee that was cooked on smoky fires. Twice during his stay, despite their nearness to the enemy, a Rebel soldier would shoot at some animal. A lieutenant or captain would rage off to scold the unthinking soul, but no Union patrol ever came to check out the noise or the cookfires.

"Mighty curious," Paul said to a young captain. "Do the Federals even care we're here?"

"I'm inclined to think they don't *know* we're here and don't care to find out," the captain responded.

On the night of the second of April, Paul returned to General Johnston's headquarters and shared his findings that the Union army had made no provisions to resist an attack. General Johnston had learned that Union General Buell's troops from northern Tennessee were fast approaching Savannah, Tennessee, on the opposite side of the Tennessee River from Pittsburg Landing. If that army reached Grant's troops, the opportunity to defeat the Yankees would be lost.

∽

Sara stayed in the Rose Cottage the first night, but was offered a vacant room in the upstairs of the Tishomingo Hotel the next day. She immediately began helping the doctors tend to several soldiers with various ailments: a broken a leg or tailbone in a fall from a horse, a foot run over by a cannon wheel, or a nose broken in a fisticuffs. She even tended to those who said they were "feeling poorly."

She knew that very soon a great many wounded would be arriving at the hotel doorstep.

FIFTY-ONE

DETECTIVE PINKERTON AND HIS PLAN

APRIL 2, 1862, 10:00 A.M.
WASHINGTON, DC

W hen the secretary read the letter of introduction of Joseph from General Halleck, he huffed into his beard, placed it on his desk, tapping it with his finger. Joseph waited and watched.

"Sergeant Favor," Secretary Stanton said at last. "You come heartily recommended. Either that, or General Halleck has been so busy that he really didn't give it much thought."

"Yes, sir," Joseph said.

"But now that you're here, I'm sending you to General McClellan's chief in charge of detectives and spies. His name is Allan Pinkerton. If he hasn't sailed back to the peninsula to further assist our efforts there, you'll find him at this office." He scribbled the address and an additional note on the letter and handed it to Joseph.

"Thank you, sir."

"Don't thank me, Favor. Go out and save our Union."

On his way down the hall, he stopped at the open door of the telegraph communication office and peered inside. Had he stepped into the room and looked to his right he would have seen Lucas sitting on a bench.

Turning to leave, he bumped into a tall, bearded man wearing a black dress coat and tall hat. The man clutched the tail of a shawl about his shoulders. "Excuse me," Joseph said.

"Not to worry, sergeant," the man said. "Thank you for your service."

When Joseph looked again, he realized he had just brushed shoulders with President Lincoln. He stood for a while watching the president meander about the room, chatting with the telegraph operators. His voice had a peculiar clarion ring to it when he began telling a folkish tale, a glimmer in his eye, as if he could not wait to get to the end of the story and surprise his listeners. He ended the story about a drunkard with a goat, and all the men in the room tittered. No sooner had he finished his anecdote than several telegraph keys began their rat-a-tatting.

President Lincoln took some sheets of foolscap from a desk, along with a pen and ink, and sat in a corner desk and began writing. Joseph could only guess what the president might be composing. A draft of a speech? A letter to the wife of a deceased soldier? Perhaps a general order.

When Secretary Stanton happened to step forth from his office and scowled, Joseph hurried on his way.

Joseph wove his way through the crowds on Pennsylvania Avenue, searching for the office of Allan Pinkerton. He hastened along until arriving at a brown brick building with vines crawling up one side, most of the leaves still dead. He knocked on the door. A man in a checkered suit, wearing a small cap in a jaunty fashion, opened the door.

After Joseph made his introduction and handed over the letter, the man directed Joseph to sit on a sofa, which was the only comfortable item in the room. Austere wooden chairs, a long table, laden with maps and letters, file cabinets along one wall. The man disappeared into a back office.

Joseph watched the clock tick away for over two hours. He stood to stretch and walk about the room a few times. He often heard filaments of hushed conversation from the back office, but nothing he could ascertain. Sitting still, his eyelids drooped.

The back-office door sprang open. Allan Pinkerton, a stocky man dressed in a brown suit with a vest, polished shoes, a bowler on his head, swept out of the room. He was placing a revolver in a shoulder holster and stopped short when he saw Joseph. The five other men with him halted. Joseph chuckled to himself, for they stopped so quickly, bumping into each other, they reminded him of a clown act he once saw in Memphis.

"So, what have we here?" Pinkerton spoke with a decided Scottish brogue. He sidled up to Joseph, who stood, hat in one hand, his other hand extended to shake Pinkerton's, but the lead detective did not take it.

Pinkerton plunged his thumbs into his suspenders and took on the air of one inspecting a horse for purchase, looking Joseph up and down, even circling around him. "The Southern soldier, turned Northern, from Iowa, a Unionist, an Abolitionist, now desiring to be a spy."

"Yes, sir." Joseph was surprised at what Pinkerton already knew of him.

"Put your paw there, Favor." Pinkerton extended his hand.

Joseph shook the hand, a powerful grip.

"What makes you think you can be a spy, Sergeant Favor, and do me the favor of being brief. I've no time to dally."

"Mr. Pinkerton and gentlemen." He nodded at the other men. "I don't know if I'll make a good spy, but having served inadvertently in a Southern army, I know how they think. I can ingratiate myself with the soldiers, even with the officers. I was often asked to go on special missions by the officers. And..."

"Special missions, you say?"

"Yes, sir. I had to be quite stealthy on one occasion. I was shot, but I recovered."

"Spying on a Federal army, were ya noo?"

"Unfortunately, yes. Now it's time I paid them back. I want to serve and stop the rebellion and end slavery."

"Went on secret mission, you say?" Pinkerton swiveled and winked at his companions.

"Yes, sir. Like I just said."

"Then I have the perfect mission for you. We've had a bear of a time tracking down who is feeding news to the enemy about our armies' movements. We believe the transfer of information takes place in a particular house, and we need someone who is dressed as a common soldier, as you be..." He stuck his tongue in his cheek.

"Yes. Whatever I need to do. Listen at a keyhole, make a pretense."

"Oh, no need to listen at keyholes or even make a pretense. For you, laddie," Pinkerton put his arm around Joseph's shoulders and walked him a few paces to a window. "You are to be a lonely soldier far away from home."

"I am."

"And travel to this house, make yourself at home. The folks there will be glad to see you."

"And where is the house? And what am I to try to find out?"

"It's Madam Harris's house. It's a brothel. Feel free to take advantage of the hospitality offered by the workers there. They're ever so accommodating."

"But I'm a married man."

"I don't see why that should stop you. You want to be a spy. You said so. We need to know who is visiting this establishment and giving information to the enemy. This is your first assignment. Do it well, and we'll give you something more lucrative."

"But..."

"Favor, you work for me now at the behest of the Secretary of War. Consider it an order."

"But I have no intention of taking part in the pleasures of the flesh."

"Then don't, but I'm counting on you to find out who is the rebel spy and the influencer who's feeding her or him the information. Do it your way. Stay there as long as you like. Here's fifty dollars." He handed Joseph a clip of bills. "But find out."

Joseph, placing the money in his pants pocket, shuffled to the door.

"And be careful. Our last detective who went in got himself stabbed in a nearby alley."

FIFTY-TWO

The Sojourn in the Whorehouse

April 2, 1862, 1:00 p.m.
Washington, DC

Joseph knocked on the door of a long two-story mansion on the southeast side of the city. He was wondering why the Pinkertons or the army just did not shut it down. But there he stood, going against his upbringing and entire moral code.

The door was opened by a black-as-coal Negro man, dressed in a gleaming black tuxedo with a cummerbund. His shirt sparkled white, starched so heavily it crackled when he swept his arm towards the parlor. "Do make yourself at home, sir," he said. "May I take your hat?"

"No...thank you." Joseph removed his hat and stuffed it under one arm.

"No weapons allowed inside." The Negro was firm. "I will have to relieve you of your firearm if you have one."

"I don't." Joseph refused to reveal the small revolver in his inside jacket pocket. Entering cautiously, it came to his mind that perhaps he should try to appear more confident, as if he had often frequented such establishments. His eyes focused forward, he walked through a short hall, past several urns overflowing with tall ferns. Brass spittoons squatted in many places about the extensive parlor, the floor was covered with a variety of colorful rugs with a generally red theme, and large chandeliers dangled from the ceiling. Perfume inundated the room, so much so, it made his eyes water.

"Do make yourself at home," the smiling, solicitous Negro said, giving Joseph a slight shove. "Our ladies are here to please you all."

Joseph looked around the room. Seated on the many plush, fringe-laden sofas and chairs were a half-dozen scantily clad women of various ages. Two voluptuous women clothed in lingerie perched on the laps of men wearing dapper suits, both pairs of couples laughing uproariously. Another woman, thinner, and with long brown hair, and wearing only a boa about her neck, sat reading a magazine. A fourth woman, looking to be in her forties, dumpy in girth with sagging breasts, wore a dress revealing deep cleavage. She lounged on a chair, staring out the front window. Her dimpled face, with heavy rouge, looked entirely bored.

A fifth woman glided seductively to an upright piano and began playing a classical piece. Her fingering of the intricate melody indicated a true musical talent. She was the prettiest in the face of all that he had seen so far, though her nose was hooked like an eagle. She had bright blue eyes and pouty lips, and she wore a comely red satin dress that swept to her ankles. The low-cut aspect of the dress emphasized her modest cleavage. He was feeling wildly aroused and could not tear his eyes from the enticing women.

Lastly, in a corner chair, her legs stretched out before her, one leg each on two ottomans, partially exposing her nubile, hairless slit, was a girl of no more than fourteen. Her bosom was barely budding. Her face held such a vacant expression, Joseph wanted to grab a drape from the window, fling it upon her, and carry her away to a safe home for girls.

He took a deep breath and remembered himself. Trying not to show his dismay with the scene before him, he became aware of several chirping women upstairs and men's gruffer voices. All of the intonations seemed pleased as punch with whatever was happening. The swelling piano tune, the snorting and guffawing of the men in the parlor and the cackling of the women on their laps almost made him ill. Every particle of his being longed to escape. He looked to the upstairs and saw a dowdy matron in a spangled dress studying the room below, arms crossed. She was frowning. He guessed that she may be Missus Harris.

"Hello, Sergeant." The voice was sweet, almost musical. Two dainty hands clutched his arm.

Joseph turned to look at a face as sweet as the voice. The red-haired woman in her twenties had a pert nose, large green eyes and a wide mouth with a generous smile of pure white teeth. Joseph had always admired Cyntha's green eyes, and he immediately wished he was with her. This woman's smile was kind and winsome, like she really wanted nothing from Joseph but the opportunity to chat with him. She was clothed in a modest cotton dress, the collar up to her chin, the sleeves down to her wrists.

"My name is Agnes," she said.

Joseph stammered. "Uh, Jones. Uh, Corporal. I mean Sergeant Jones. Just got promoted." He could feel his face turning hot.

"Pleased to meet you, Sergeant Jones. So nice of you to come. I'm just having tea in the next room. Would you care to join me?" Agnes lightly tugged Joseph's sleeve, leading him to a separate, well-lit dining room with the curtains drawn over tall windows. On the table, a teapot sat on a tray with cups and saucers. Agnes motioned for Joseph to sit.

He did, setting his kepi on the polished table, then snatching it back up. Agnes smiled gently, poured tea into the cups. "Sugar? Cream?" she offered.

"No thanks." He took the cup and let the tea's steam rise to his nose. He tried not to look at her comely face, but his eyes kept glancing at her until he gave in and looked at her square on.

"I'll take cream and sugar." She sat, spooned sugar into her cup, and dropped a spot of cream in as well. "You know, I knew a gentleman who said…" She ducked her head impishly. "I hope you will forgive me, but he said he likes his tea like he likes his women—sweet and creamy."

Joseph almost spit out the tea he was sipping. He managed to garner a smile.

"What a beautiful smile you have," Agnes said. Her manner and tone indicated a demure woman, not bawdy, not racy. Joseph wondered if she should even be in such a place.

After a while, Joseph's initial reluctance wore off, and they enjoyed a pleasant conversation. Joseph found himself making up stories of his wartime exploits based on newspaper stories he had read. Agnes seemed to hang on his words and offered an incredible amount of knowledge about the goings on in Washington, especially the politics. He became oblivious of the noise emanating from the parlor and upstairs, and he fairly enjoyed the conversation with her.

Occasionally, the harlots ventured through the room and on into the kitchen or to the outhouse. Joseph did his best not to look at the attractiveness of them, but found it hard not to be aroused. When the piano player danced past on her tiptoes like a ballerina, he felt his manhood swell some. He was glad when she was out of view.

Then he remembered the true purpose of his visit. He did his best to maneuver the conversation around to which woman was most friendly with single clients. Agnes did not know. He asked which of the prostitutes were more avid about taking long walks outside. She did not know. "Which of your friends here seem most interested in the Southern cause?"

She thought a moment. "That would be Madam Harris. She dearly loves all our soldiers who visit us, but she cares for the Southern men, too. She misses them. They're so chivalrous, you know. Especially the politicians." She seemed to be searching Joseph's face to see if she had answered correctly.

"Well, that is fine. You women have an important purpose to take care of all men. North or South." He could not believe those words came out of his mouth, but he was intent on finding out whatever he could. "I know you must have other... uh, clients. You may wish to consort with them. I'll just wait here and listen to the music and the...uh, frivolity."

"Don't you like my company?" Agnes's face fell.

"Oh, yes, of course, I do. You're much more than I expected." Actually, she was. He wondered what she was doing there, since all the other whores seemed so forward to any man who entered. He admired her rose-colored locks, twirled in bouncy curls. She had a small mole on one cheek that seemed to add to her attractiveness. She was not at all like he imagined a woman of a boudoir would be. "I need to use the outhouse." He stood. "You go attend to someone else. I'll look for you later."

She stood and pointed out the back to where the outhouse was. "We have a toilet upstairs, a fancy bedpan, if you wish. Running water, too."

"That's all right. I'm staying downstairs for a while. See you later." He left her standing with a befuddled look on her face.

After using the outhouse, Joseph remained for two more hours, staying in the dining room, peering into the parlor. While Agnes sat quietly, hands folded in her lap, he was trying to catch elements of the conversations of the women and the many men who came and went. He was about to leave when a robust, well-dressed, middle-aged man entered the house from the rear door and immediately ascended the stairs. He stopped at the top and handed pages of paper to Madam Harris, who stuffed whatever he handed her into her cleavage. Joseph was sure it was not folding money, nor an envelope of cash. The man exited in a rush out the front. Joseph excused himself from Agnes, who smiled demurely and brushed her hand across his, and he followed him.

∞

Keeping the man in his sights, Joseph tailed him along many turns onto many streets. The man hastened into a fashionable house surrounded by a wrought iron fence on a quiet city street. Joseph waited about ten minutes, then walked up the tall porch steps. When he knocked at the front door, a Negro maid in a frilly dress and white apron answered.

"May I help you, officer?" She held the door barely open. "Are we in trouble with the army?"

"Is Mr. McCloud here?" Joseph asked.

"No, sir. You have the wrong house."

"But," Joseph put his hand on the door facing and leaned toward her, "this is the address I was given. Who lives here?"

"The owners of this house, my master and mistress, are Mr. and Mrs. Rotter."

"Then, my apologies. I must have the wrong information." He tipped his hat and scooted off the porch and out the front gate. He had the knowledge he sought.

When he reported the incident that he witnessed and the name of Rotter to the Pinkerton's agent in the front office, he sorely hoped he would not have to return to the house of ill repute. After the agent departed into Pinkerton's back office, Joseph did not have to wait long. Pinkerton emerged, his jacket off, his shirt sleeves rolled up, and holding a tumbler of whiskey. He was joined by a half-dozen agents imbibing glasses of whiskey. With much bravado, he turned to the other agents. "This here, gentlemen, is a fine example of a sterling spy. Sterling, I tell you. Brand new on the job, and he may have solved a perplexing issue." He turned to face Joseph. "Sergeant Favor, we have had our eye on Rotter for a while. He's in the pork commodities, but something always seemed unnatural about him. I'll have McSwain, one of my best agents, pursue this."

"I don't have to go back to the brothel, do I?" Joseph asked.

"No, no. I don't think that's necessary. I think I'll send you up to the Presidential Mansion. Your job will be to listen, whenever possible, to the various visitors' conversations. I'm not sure I trust everyone who traipses in and out of the president's mansion."

"I'd like that better. Will I be staying in the president's home?"

Pinkerton laughed. "Not likely. You'll be sleeping above the stables, then standing guard during the day in the mansion itself. Try to make yourself useful to the women of the house, especially the president's good wife. What I tell you now is secret." He put a finger to his lips. "I have my concerns about the wife. She has relatives who fight in the Rebel army and many ties to Southerners. Brothers. Brothers-in-law. We need someone with a keen eye and a busy ear. Keep both eyes and both ears open." He straightened to watch Joseph's reaction.

Joseph was surprised about Pinkerton's wariness of the Mary Todd Lincoln, but he nodded his head. "Yes, sir. I'm in service to the Union."

"Good, Laddie. Now, Morton here will draw up a letter for you. Take it with you. Say, do you like Scotch Whiskey?"

"I can't say that I've ever had it."

"Then you are in for a treat."

An agent brought in a bottle of Scotch and poured a glass. Joseph took the glass, sipped the whiskey, then gulped its contents. He coughed, his voice gone.

"Ah," Pinkerton slapped Joseph on the back. "Marvelous stuff. Scotch."

Not sure what they were celebrating, Joseph found himself feeling, after two more tumblers of whiskey, a little tipsy and nauseous, so he excused himself and headed to the regiment encampment where he had been temporarily assigned.

On his way, he wondered a great deal about Agnes. What had been her intentions? Unlike the other women of the house, she had made no move nor spoken any word to motivate him to join her or any other harlot in a bedroom. She was simply pleasant company who showed him bountiful interest and a generous smile. He had paid her nothing for her time, and he found himself yearning to return to her to once again talk about whatever crossed their minds. She seemed a kindred spirit. He had been a long time without a woman, and she was more than beautiful. The thought rolled around in his mind that if Cyntha had received word that he had died, she could likely have married again. His life was all sharp corners. Nothing soft.

"Damn it!" he yelled into the night sky. "Where is my life? Tomorrow, I will ask for leave to find my wife."

FIFTY-THREE

THE MACHINERY OF WAR GRINDS INTO MOTION

APRIL 3, 1862, LATE MORNING
CORINTH, MISSISSIPPI

Under a hazy sky, the Confederate army, most of its soldiers untried in battle, was preparing to march. Every hillside surrounding the junction and every vacant lot was filled with men preparing to advance to the Yankee camp.

Every inch of railroad that filtered through town was lined with boxcars filled with kegs of salt pork, peas, corn meal, flour, and lard, all to be loaded into mule-drawn wagons and brought to stockpiles for each division.

On the Corinth-Mobile railroad line, three trains were halted, chugging, steam hissing. Hundreds of soldiers and a few civilians with their slaves slid open boxcar doors and began unloading crates of minié bullets and cannister, kegs of nails, stacks of heavy tents, coils of hemp ropes, crates of uniforms, and sacks of brogans and oil cloths.

From the single passenger car of one train, a handful of doctors and a considerable number of women from Mobile, Alabama stepped cautiously onto the platform. They stared in awe at the immensity of the army.

General Johnston, with General Beauregard at his side, briefly eyed the civilians from where he stood on the vine-covered porch of the Rose Cottage. Both generals held binoculars, each surveying the tumult. The previous week's intermittent rainstorms had left water dripping from the eaves of houses and town buildings; hundreds of puddles gleaming on the roads.

General Johnston felt frustration, with the men packing more paraphernalia than they could ever need, then rushing here and there. And officers on horseback trotting around the camp shouting orders. *Surely, by now, the army should be marching toward the enemy.* The regiments had begun preparing before the sun rose, yet none of them seemed ready to move forward away from Corinth and toward Pittsburg Landing that was a day's march to the north.

There seemed to be an incessant "preparing to march, but no forward movement." He sighed. *Ants in an ant pile.* He turned to General Beauregard. "Your plan is beginning, Pierre."

"With God's good grace, the strategy will bring about an unmatched victory."

"Yes, we will need grace." General Johnston ran his hand through his thick hair. "You know, Pierre, that new scout from Van Dorn. What's his name?"

"Captain McGavin? He's waiting in the parlor with the other couriers."

"Yes. Him. His report reinforced what our other scouts and Forrest's cavalry have said. The Federals have made no attempt to entrench. No breastworks. Nothing. Entirely odd."

"And to our advantage."

"Yes, to our advantage." General Johnston went inside the house, and he sat at a desk and began writing orders to his division commanders and to his cavalry. Fifteen couriers crowded around him while he wrote. He would hold up a page without ever looking to see who took it. A courier would step forward, snatch the page, and depart to his horse to deliver the orders.

One of the couriers was Paul McGavin. The disposition orders he clenched were for General Nathan Bedford Forrest. "It'll be the devil trying to find him," he said under his breath. "He may be the Devil himself anyway."

Paul had heard several criticisms about the acrimonious nature of the man and also heard him called the bravest leader in the entire Rebel army.

When he grasped the handle of the door to leave, General Johnston spoke brusquely. "General Forrest must screen our movements, Captain McGavin. He must hold the bridges, and let not a single picket get near our flanks!"

"Yes, sir." Paul saluted and rushed outside and past General Beauregard on the porch. He gathered the reins of his new mount, a bay mare, tied to a hitching post. Not sure where General Forrest might be sequestered, he chose to ride northeast on the Bark Road toward Hamburg, hoping General Forrest's troops would be somewhere near where they met previously.

After Paul had galloped away from Corinth to find General Forrest, General Beauregard lowered his binoculars. He handed them to one of his aides, and then leapt from the porch and jogged west down Childs Street, hopping the puddles like a happy child.

The entourage of aides and couriers followed him as best they could down the sloppy street. They reached the railroad tracks of the Ohio-Mobile Line. General Beauregard stopped suddenly, surprising his cohorts, and he peered down the tracks with hundreds of tents crowded almost up to the railbed. "All this commotion, and a great battle forthcoming to determine which army should command a set of parallel iron rails crossed by another set of rails." He renewed his jaunt to a small hillock. He once more watched in marked admiration the panoply of soldiers filing slowly up the roads from Corinth. "It is a good plan, if I do say so myself."

Beauregard's grand strategy was simple enough, designed to maximize rapid movement of the divisions along different roads, each division with a destination a mile shy of the Federal camps that were spread out two miles south of the Tennessee River landing called Pittsburg. Almost 40,000 Confederates would file out along somewhat parallel roads—the Ridge Road and the Pittsburg Road—neither byway particularly travel-worthy. On the Pittsburg Road, Bragg's corps had over 16,000 men, plus a 5000-man division assigned to him from General Polk's troops. Breckinridge's 7000 men would follow Bragg.

Hardee's and Polk's divisions took the westernmost of the roads with the balance of troops from Corinth. General Chatham would bring his 3000-man division from Purdy, Tennessee to join them at a road juncture near a house named Mickey's.

Over one hundred cannons and all the accoutrements of caissons, repair carts, portable forges, and ammunition wagons waddled along among the brigades.

General Beauregard figured that all should be in place, ready to bivouac at Mickey's tavern by evening.

Beauregard strolled back to his headquarters at the Fish Pond house. When he entered, he found General John Breckinridge reading his orders from General Johnston.

"Exciting, is it not, John?" General Beauregard said.

General Breckinridge nodded, put on his hat, and tightened the chin strap, but said nothing.

"Quite a bit different than your work as Vice President, wouldn't you say?"

"I would have to agree with you, Pierre. When I was vice-president of that wayward country north of us, I could accomplish very little. Here, fighting for our noble South, I believe I can make a difference. Bring about a better world all around, less cluttered with big government intrusion."

"I see that you are leaving already."

"Yes, some of the brigades are marching even now. I should hurry along. Good day, Pierre. See you at Mickey's this evening and a glorious victory the next day."

The Confederate army slowed to a crawl by the muddy and impassable roads. Soldiers pulled out axes to fell trees to make log corduroy roads. The army settled into bivouac several miles shy of Mickey's. The tail of the army was just outside Corinth. There would be no battle on April fourth.

FIFTY-FOUR

∞

Night—When Churchyards Yawn, and Hell Breathes Out

– Shakespeare

April 3, 1862, Dusk
Washington, DC

D red Workman stole along a shadowy alley, foot for foot with John Wilkes Booth, who led the way. The black cape of night was closing over Washington and the surrounding environs. Even as the day was shutting down, the din from every camp, every building, and every street sounded in a continuous rattle and clatter. Hooves clopped on muddy pavement while drumbeats and horn blatts sounded in the camps. A clock tower pealed. Nighthawks and crows cawed and swooped around the street lamps that the lamplighters were lighting.

Soldiers patrolled every street. Lanterns glowed in every earthen fort and camp ringing the city; and work-gangs, White and Negro, tossed up more dirt on embankments and parapets all night.

Exiting the alley, Workman and Booth crossed a narrow street, eluding the gaze of a sentry posted a block away. Booth wore a black cape with a high collar that rose past his ears, and he walked so fast, Workman sometimes found it difficult to keep up with him. Workman wore his corporal's uniform and had his Whitworth rifle slung in its cloth pouch on his back.

They were headed to the field where the balloons regularly ascended into the air, even at night. Though this night, with a storm brewing, balloon flights had been canceled.

They passed several two-story mansions, surrounded by tall trees. Rounding the trees, they spotted some hundred yards in the distance a single balloon, almost filled with hydrogen from the pumps set atop wagons. It floated, secured by ropes tied to six-foot high, heavy posts. The basket bounced up and down on the ground.

The lofty trees behind the mansions provided a natural barrier to hide the balloon launch site.

"There!" Booth pointed at the partially filled balloon. "I told you we have friends in the Yankee army."

Workman and Booth hastened out into the field, drawing up a dozen yards from the balloon.

Three Union soldiers held ropes that wrapped around tall posts plunged deep in the ground. Six more soldiers in blue managed the hydrogen gas generators housed in large crate-sized boxes on wagons. Horses that pulled the wagons were tethered several feet away.

The crates were about the size of a general's tent. The pumps sent the light hydrogen gas into the balloon that dipped and jounced in the wind of the burgeoning storm.

Booth stopped to admire the balloon engorging on the hydrogen gas. "I'll tell you how this all happens, Workman. Pure chemistry. A genius fellow named Thaddeus Lowe trained those men standing by the wooden boxes. Lowe is Chief Aeronaut of the Army Balloon Corps. I met him once. Those soldiers pour about eight hundred pounds of iron filings into a copper tank that lines the inside of each crate."

Workman was listening while checking the load in his rifle.

"Then," Booth continued, "one man pours three or four carboys of sulfuric acid into the tank, and hydrogen gas is released in a chemical reaction. Total chemistry." He looked to see if Workman was paying attention.

"Yes, yes. Go on." Workman slid his gun back into the case.

"Finally, the gas travels through that second tank over there that is filled with lime and water in order to purify and cool the gas before it travels in that rubber hose into the balloon envelope."

Workman looked at the long hose that jumped with the gas passing through it. In the ample flickering lantern light, he read *Goodyear's Rubber—Philadelphia, PA.* "I just hope them tanks don't explode."

"They never have." Booth smiled. "Look! The balloon's almost filled."

A sergeant attending the hydrogen wagon pumps waved at them. The other soldiers did not speak. The hydrogen machines chugged, but so did many other various machines throughout the city punch the air with banging and cranking.

"The noise doesn't bother me," Booth said, "it's like a thunderous applause." He took a bow to an invisible audience.

While Workman and Booth stood watching the balloon filling and tugging at its tethers, the abundant storm clouds crackled with lighting. Each time the lightning flashed, the soldiers grimaced.

Workman knew that President Lincoln took regular visits to the Old Soldiers Home, and he had recently taken to riding out in the evenings to the house adjacent to the hospital with its multiple gables, the house named *Corn Rig.* Workman had watched Mary Lincoln sending wagon after wagon filled with furniture and clothing out to the home. The presidential family would dwell there when the summer's humidity and town stench increased.

"You know," Workman said to Booth, "he'll be riding with a cavalry escort."

"Why should that matter to you, Dred? He'll be the only one wearing that infernal tall hat, trying to appear taller. An addlepated giant of ignominy!" He laughed sardonically.

The balloon began to dance in the approaching storm's wind as if hell was exhaling, yet beguiling a rider to enter into its gondola. The sturdy, woven basket dragged along the ground and came to a stop, its ropes secured to the balloon's trailing skirt. Two more soldiers gathered ropes that dangled from the balloon, wrapped the long ropes around the tall posts and held tight.

One of the soldiers crawled in the basket to check that the balloon was ready. He threw a leg over the basket and hopped out. "You're up," he said to Workman.

Stroking his mustache, his Adam's apple plunging up and down, Workman gulped several times. "Here goes." Placing one hand on the soldier's shoulder standing beside him, he hoisted himself into the basket and set his rifle in the basket floor.

He nodded for them to let the balloon rise. The hydrogen machine stopped its clatter, the soldiers handling the ropes slowly loosened their hold, and the balloon made a slow ascent. Workman clung to the basket side. Wishing he had had a little practice in ballooning before now, his grip was so tight on the basket side, his knuckles were white.

Rising twenty feet, he looked in the lit open window of a mansion where a woman was disrobing. That reminded him to take out his binoculars. He would have liked to take a closer peek through her window, but the balloon glided higher, and trees eliminated his view.

Now, the city of darkness and dirt and filth and disrepair, laden with too many people—civilians, runaway slaves, and far too many soldiers—glittered with thousands of lamplit windows and streetlights. Workman's eyes began adjusting to the nighttime view, and he was able to ascertain the road that led north out of town toward the Old Soldiers Home. The little houses and Negro shanties crowded against the road were lit like fireflies, giving a golden glow to the area. *This will be easy.* Workman felt a surge of confidence.

He took a gander at the ground below him and grew immediately light-headed. He had never been so high, except on some mesas in New Mexico where he had served before the war. There he had had solid ground under his feet. A wave of nausea washed over him.

He took several deep breaths, then raised the binoculars to his eyes. The sounds floating up from the city came together like an inharmonious symphony. Bugles were sounding chow time for the army. Horses pulling carriages and wagons neighed and whinnied throughout the city, and their hooves clopped a syncopated beat. He figured no one would even hear his gun when he took the shot.

He located a spot where the road from the president's house dipped at a break in the trees. He lifted out his Whitworth and took a careful aim at that spot. He waited. Darkness expanded. The storm grew closer, lightning zipping across the clouds, angry thunder growling.

He raised his rifle and sighted it again, twisting its sighting screw. If Lincoln rode through that juncture, he could get off a shot with ease.

"See anything?" Booth called from below, his voice sounded tiny, like a tiny piano plunking.

Workman leaned over the edge of the basket, cupped his hand to his mouth and hollered down, "Nothin' yet." When he raised back up, there was President Lincoln riding a black horse among six cavalry escorts. Another robust fellow in a black coat rode beside him. Workman figured it was Hill Lamont, the president's best friend and body guard. He aimed his rifle, finger on the trigger, then the group veered in behind tree foliage, perhaps to go around the dip in the road, and the opportunity passed. He swept his rifle to aim further down the road, looking for any sign of the president or even the cavalry.

He grabbed his binoculars with one hand and scanned up and down the road. Nothing. "Bring me down!"

The soldiers below gathered in the balloon, and in a few moments, Workman was climbing out of the basket onto the ground.

Booth saw the dejection on Workman's face. "Not to worry, friend," Booth offered. "There'll be another time."

"Not in a balloon." The sergeant walked up. His team of soldiers were already dousing the lighting and scraping the iron residue from the hydrogen tanks onto the ground. The sergeant's face was lost in the opaque night, but not his voice. "Too risky. If we get caught, we're done for. It takes three hours to get enough gas to float the damned things. Someone'll catch us, for sure. I don't want to spend the rest of this war rotting in some prison. Neither do these other fellows."

"But..." Booth said.

"Find another way to kill him," the sergeant turned and hollered over his shoulder. "Just not on my time."

The soldiers were flattening the balloon, beating on the fabric. Workman and Booth watched the balloon and their hopes collapse.

Rain, blown by the wind, began falling in heavy drops.

"He's right, you know," Booth said. "This plan is too risky."

"I'm not worried. While I was up there, I saw a perfect tree up that road that I can climb. From there, I can easily shoot the bastard dead." Workman put his rifle back in its long cloth holder. "I'll look for another opportunity."

FIFTY-FIVE

A TREE FOR
AN ASSASSINATION

APRIL 4, 1862, EARLY EVENING
WASHINGTON, DC

D red Workman located the tree he had picked out for the assassination. It lay a mere forty yards from the road that President Lincoln would travel from the Presidential Mansion to the Old Soldiers Home. He had feigned a stomachache in order to leave early from his work at the stables. He had gathered his Whitworth sharpshooter rifle from where he had hidden it before coming to work, and had sneaked through the woods behind the stables in the gray, dying dusk.

Ominous clouds hung like black, puffy drapes overhead. No stars visible, no moon. Like the night before, lightning bounced around the sky, thunder grumbling. The wind picked up.

Workman knew Lincoln would pass along the road that was lined with the runaway Negroes' hovels, their simple lights spilling just enough illumination onto the road for him to see when the president passed.

He climbed the tree with big branches that forked several times. He settled into a comfortable spot, his back against the trunk, his long legs dangling on a limb that pointed like a finger at the exact spot where President Lincoln would pass, and Workman could shoot him dead. Having recently taken up smoking, for he had heard from soldiers and civilians alike that it was good for his health, he yearned for smoke. But he dared not strike a match. His view of the road was clear for about fifty yards before it passed behind dense foliage. That would be ample time to take the killing shot.

He checked the load in his rifle. He calmed himself and listened to the ticking of his watch and the occasional croaks of a frog. A steady breeze blew, but a few heavy gusts shook the tree. The storm had settled overhead, but no rain was falling.

Imagining himself receiving a medal for bravery for killing the elected leader of the nation, and, thereby, restoring the Union, he envisioned a brass band in his head playing "Rally Round the Flag."

He had almost lost himself in fantasizing when he saw a carriage in the road. He looked down the sight of his rifle. He recognized the president's carriage. "Dang!" he said too loud. "Took the carriage instead of his horse."

Taking a slow breath, he braced one leg on the wide limb that extended toward where President Lincoln drove the carriage, alone. No cavalry escort. Workman watched, his finger lightly on the trigger, until the carriage took a slight turn that showed President Lincoln's body full on, his stovepipe hat atop his head, in clear view. When the road turned again in a few yards, the back of the carriage hood would block the view for Workman. Any shot he would take then would be guesswork.

He had a few seconds to take the shot. He drew the bead on the president. At first, he aimed at his chest. "Nah. I'll take his head off." He raised his aim to the president's head. His confidence was acute. The shot was too easy.

A blustery gust shook the tree. Workman fired. He watched the wind blast that had bludgeoned his tree also crash against the trees on the far side of the road beyond the president's carriage.

The carriage turned, the back of it toward Workman. The horses were trotting faster. Had Lincoln been hit? Was his lifeless body slumped in the carriage seat, the horses merely trotting of their own accord? Workman strained his eyes to see. He swept his gaze back to where the carriage had been when he took the shot. On the road lay a stovepipe hat.

Workman scrambled down the tree. He had to know. He was prepared to chase after the carriage to see if his shot had found its mark in the president's head. He crashed through brush, then onto the road, and reached the tall hat lying in the middle of the road. A few Negro men sat outside a hovel, smoking pipes. They nodded at him. He waved carelessly.

He picked up the hat and ran his finger through a large hole near the top edge.

He had missed, the shot went high.

He watched the carriage disappearing up toward the Old Soldiers Home. He dropped the hat and made his way stealthily back to the apartment on Pennsylvania Avenue to give the news to Lucas. He knew his friend would be sorely disappointed.

When Workman entered the apartment, Lucas saw the look of disappointment on the marksman's face. Lucas pounded his fist on his little desk. "We must have a new plan. Immediately!"

FIFTY-SIX

FORTUNE AND FOLLY

APRIL 5, 1862, LATE MORNING
WASHINGTON, DC

Joseph walked up to the guards at the gate of the Presidential Mansion compound. Attempting to appear as confident and officious as possible, he showed his letter from Allan Pinkerton to a guard, who then stepped inside the gate and showed it to a captain who examined it for over a minute. He nodded that Joseph could enter, but first, Joseph had to hand over his revolver, and the soldiers rummaged through his rucksack. They found only his change of clothes, toiletries, three books—one being on military strategy, the others recent novels—and some stationery, a pen and bottle of ink.

The captain returned his rucksack, revolver and personal items. The men saluted.

Joseph proceeded to the front doors where guards with bayonetted rifles stood.

Hesitating a little, he opened the door and walked inside. A major sat at a desk near the door. A corporal stood in a relaxed stance to the side, his rifle butt on the floor. The major took Joseph's letter and motioned for him to sit on a divan. He handed the letter to a civilian, sitting at another desk, who put the letter in a drawer and stared straight ahead.

After sitting for some time, Joseph cleared his throat. "Ahem. Major, sir. What am I waiting for?"

The major removed his glasses. "How should I know? You're the one assigned to keep an eye out for insurgents and rebel sympathizers. Do your job. And report back here before you retire to your quarters each evening."

Joseph stood at attention. "And my quarters, sir?"

"Somewhere above the stables where the grooms sleep. You should go settle in first, then go about whatever Pinkerton and Secretary Stanton wants you to do. Good day."

"Yes, sir." Joseph saluted and exited. He was perplexed about what his course of action was to be. Pinkerton's assignment for him was non-specific. *Listen and report* was what he was supposed to do. *But listen for what?*

He determined to get settled in his new living arrangements, then find time the next day to ask Pinkerton for some guidance. He located the stables, mere yards from the mansion. He asked one of the hands a few questions, who then directed him to Sergeant Smith Stimmel, who was in charge of the compound guards. Sergeant Stimmel pointed out an unused room in the upstairs barracks. The tiny room, four feet wide by eight feet long, had space only for a bed and an empty foot locker. Joseph took a few moments to settle in.

He took out pen, ink, and paper, sat on the bed, and wrote a letter to Cyntha, spelling out his deep love for her. His memories had tumbled forth like a waterfall in the days since departing General Grant on the Tennessee River. He knew why she was his life's love, and yearned for her touch. He felt fortunate that he was not off with the army facing battle once again. When finished, he sealed the letter, leaving it on the bed to be mailed later, and then he loped downstairs to the stable row.

Just below Joseph, Workman was mucking out a stall, biding his time until late afternoon when Lucas Reeder was to surreptitiously enter the compound through a hole in the fence behind the stables. Workman had wrought the hole, bending the iron bars with a crowbar. When Joseph passed, neither man saw the other.

Workman felt that they should wait until he had another opportunity to shoot the chief executive from a distance using his Whitworth rifle, but Lucas had concluded that they could wait no longer. The mechanism of war was in motion, and Lucas had decided that he must throw a wrench into the cogs of the war machine, and bring an end to it.

Joseph strolled about the entire compound, circling it twice, listening to the talk of the guards and grounds workers, then searching for any break in the fence, or a tree that bordered too close to the fence, that might allow a covert entry.

Almost hidden by some bushes, he was surprised to discover behind the stables the hole Workman had created in the fence.

That late evening, when Lucas neared the gap in the fence, he found sentries posted and alert. He retreated. It would be folly to try to enter. He would have to wait.

FIFTY-SEVEN

How Far Better is Your Love Than Wine

APRIL 5, 1862, LATE MORNING
CINCINNATI, OH

W hen Cyntha and Ben stepped off the gangplank from the sidewheeler boat in Cincinnati, she clutched the address of Reynolds' family in her gloved hand. Not only was she keen to locate her freeman friend's family, but so was Ben. Reynolds had saved Ben's life twice, the last time forfeiting his own.

Ben had sold the carriage and horses in St. Louis before they boarded the steamboat. Cyntha had taken the time while they waited for their boat to arrive to purchase a charcoal-toned mourning dress, gloves, and a simple black hat with a netted veil that she could drape over her face.

"I had refused to wear black after I received word of Joseph's death," she told Ben. "I could not face that he was gone. I loved him so much, I wanted him to see me dressed in the fine clothing he had bought for me from the money he earned by his labor and sweat. Now, I am determined to set his soul free, and for him to know I've not forgotten him."

"Yeah." Ben's response was blunt. He did not care to hear about Joseph. His heart was voracious, and he had plans of his own making—eager plans that involved capturing Cyntha's heart. Not by seduction would he win her, but his deepest longing for her.

"With Reynolds, my dearest companion, gone as well, it is incumbent upon me to mourn, and for the world to know how I grieve for them both."

Ben, in his own naïve, embarrassed way, had insisted she purchase the necessary undergarments and some new shoes with some of the money Anthony had given her. He would not hear of his spending the money on himself. When she attempted to show him the bundle of undergarments, he ducked his head, embarrassed. The thought of Cyntha wearing only the chemise or even the bone-stayed corset was too enticing for him. His mind raced to seeing her while he was unlacing the ties of her garments, then pulling her close.

After securing hotel rooms, one for each, they journeyed through Cincinnati to find Reynolds' sister's home.

The house was in the outreaches of the city on a quiet street in the section known as the Colored's Town. Stately elm trees towered over the house, and the limbs brushed the roof. The house was whitewashed, but needed a new coat. Three Negro children, all younger than ten, played in rambunctious fashion in the picket-fenced yard that had abundant, uncut grass. They stopped their play and gaped at Cyntha and Ben when they passed through the gate.

Ben, carrying a tow sack, led the way, arriving on the porch of the humble dwelling first. He stomped the mud off his boots. Cyntha followed him. She put her hand on the porch support post, for she felt she was going to faint. Finally, she stepped forward beside Ben, took off one mourning glove, and rapped on the door. While they waited, she reached out and grasped Ben's hand.

He was shocked that she had done so, but he was enamored with the softness of her palm and fingers. A surge of desire swept over him. He wanted to explore her hand, like it was a treasure to hold, to feel the sturdiness of the bones under her skin, the smooth nails, and then to lace his fingers with hers. He was drunk with yearning.

The door opened. A woman with bronze-toned skin and gray, wispy hair came out. Cyntha immediately noticed the high cheek bones and deep-set eyes, similar to Reynolds' face. She wore a blousy dress on her thin frame. "May I help you?" the woman asked.

Cyntha raised her veil, and struggled with the words. "Do you know a Josiah Reynolds?"

"Know him?" the woman's voice sang as sweetly as the bright chirrup of a nightingale. "He's my brother!"

A younger woman, her skin pale enough almost to be taken for a White woman, approached from inside the house and stood behind Reynolds' sister. Thin-waisted, she had an ample bosom in a threadbare shirt that showed her deep cleavage. "Who is it, Mama?"

"I'm to find out directly." The wrinkles at the woman's eyes crinkled, and she smiled when she saw the tears beginning to flow from Cyntha's eyes. "My name is Ida Mae Winthrop. I am Josiah's sister. This is my daughter, Elisha. That's her children, my grand babies, in the front yard. How can I help you?"

"How do, ma'am?" Ben tipped his wide-brimmed hat, his blond hair falling out over his eyes.

Her bereavement crushing her ability to prevail against gravity, Cyntha collapsed to her knees right at the door. She reached out and took Ida Mae's knobby, rough hands in hers. Looking up, she said, "Your brother, my friend, is dead."

Ida Mae helped Ben lift Cyntha from the porch boards.

"Won't you come in," Ida Mae said. Holding her arm around Cyntha, she helped her to a plush sofa in the parlor. All the other furniture in the house was crudely made, simple chairs, a writing desk, some lamp stands. Not even a mantel on the fireplace. A few, simple framed paintings adorned the walls. The floor was swept clean and polished.

"Elisha," Ida Mae commanded, "make these fine White folks some tea."

"Yes'm." The woman of about twenty-five years left to the kitchen and began lighting a fire in the stove.

Ida Mae sat slowly in a wooden chair opposite Cyntha. She said to Ben, "You may sit, too."

"My name is Ben McGavin. Late of Texas." He plunked down on a second wooden chair.

Ida Mae gave him a head motion for him to sit beside Cyntha, which he did, clumsily. He held his hat in his hands.

"It's nice to meet you, Mr. McGavin," Ida Mae said. She turned to Cyntha. "And you are?"

"My name is Cyntha Favor."

"I figured as much," Ida Mae said. "Josiah wrote many letters which I'm sure you know, and he always spoke highly of you. I know you have lost your husband in a battle. I'm terribly sorry."

"Oh, yes." Cyntha dabbed her eyes with a kerchief from her sleeve. "It's been many months. I miss him... but I guess I've grown used to him being gone now. However, I'm not here to talk to you about my late husband, Joseph, but to tell you about your courageous brother, Josiah."

"I would imagine that he acted bravely. He always did so, even back when we was on that plantation in northern Mississippi. He weren't afraid of nothin'. If a bull broke loose and was makin' mayhem, he marched right up to that bull, grabbed the ring in its nose and led it back to the pasture." Ida Mae looked up, a smile across her face. "I remember him like it was yesterday."

"Well," Ben said. "He was ridin' with us to come see you before he died of the consumption."

"Yes, he spoke of his lungs ailin' him in a letter."

"He did not die on our way here from tuberculosis," Cyntha said, her words choking.

Ben stood. "Your brother took two bullets in his chest whilst savin' mine and Cyntha's lives! He's a hero." He handed the tow sack to Ida Mae. "These are some of his things. His hat and shoes, his Bible and watch. He really didn't own much."

"Oh, my!" Ida Mae exclaimed. She dropped the bundle. "Someone shot him. What for?"

Ben, with some reluctance, explained the details of their sad encounter with the marauder on their way to St. Louis. He also explained how Reynolds had saved him after his wound at Elkhorn Tavern, then lied to the Union officers, so that he would not be hung as a spy.

After Elisha brought in tea, which she poured into dainty cups, Cyntha, Ben and Reynolds' sister and niece shared memories of Josiah well into the late afternoon.

Elisha cooked a dinner of collard greens, a little pork roast and some fresh bread. Halfway through the meal, the children were making such clever comments that everyone was laughing.

"Where are your menfolk?" Ben asked. "If you don't mind me askin'."

"My husband's been most dead for ten years," Ida Mae said. "Elisha's husband done went off to help out the blue soldiers."

"Blue soldiers?" Ben said.

"The Union boys. Bertram, her husband, tried to join a Colored regiment. They had a flag and everythin', but the police tol' 'em this was a White Man's war, and Negroes ain't allowed to fight."

"Mm, mm." Elisha interjected. "So, he still wanted to hep dem army boys, so he's off somewhere in Tennessee, drivin' a wagon. That's all dey let 'im do to hep."

"Oh," Ben replied.

"Don't make me no never mind," Elisha said. "I don't miss 'im anyways."

"Hush that talk, Elisha!" Ida Mae turned a demanding eye at her daughter.

Elisha ducked her head a moment, but then gave Ben a flirtatious look, and tugged slightly at her blouse where her cleavage was evident.

Ben had experienced enough young ladies making eyes at him that he was not unaware of her suggestive behavior. He had had some young women approach him from time to time, at a barn dance or party, and, to him, they acted fully ready to give away their treasures completely. He had always politely excused himself. He did not want to face the wrath of his older brother, Asa.

When she continued to make eyes at him, he concentrated his gaze on his plate of food.

The majority of the evening, whenever he could, he kept stealing glances at Cyntha, hoping she did not see the seductive behavior of Elisha. Cyntha, this adamant abolitionist woman, so different from him, had robbed him of his emotional wherewithal. He could barely keep a straight thought sometimes, especially when she stood or sat close to him.

Once, on the riverboat ride up to Cincinnati, he had stolen into her room and watched her sleeping. He was enamored at her soft inhalations, the slight rising of her bosom under her heavy wool nightgown. He never meant any disservice to her. He slipped away, glad that he had had the private moment to fully admire her beauty.

Cyntha noticed the forwardness of Elisha toward Ben and how Ben was doing all he could do to ignore her. She smiled.

After the dinner, Elisha cleared the table and huffed away into the kitchen from whence she made a point of causing considerable clattering and clanking of dishes and pots. Ida Mae escorted Cyntha and Ben into her front room again, where they continued their talk.

When the day's light began settling into gray, Cyntha thanked Ida Mae for her hospitality. Cyntha hugged Ida Mae, Elisha and the children. When the children hugged Ben around his knees, he did not quite know how to react. His face reddened, but he bent down and hugged them. Suddenly remembering, he dove his hand in his pocket, dug out some horehound candy and gave it to them. They cheered, "Hurrah for Ben!" Then they skipped away into the kitchen, sucking on their treats.

Ben blushed even more. Ida Mae came up close to him and looked into his eyes. She extended her hand, and he shook it. She leaned to his ear and whispered, "You stay with this woman, Ben McGavin. There is no finer woman on this earth. Hmmm mmm."

"Yes, ma'am," he whispered back. "I love her."

"I figured as much."

When Ben and Cyntha turned to go, Ida Mae asked, "What was the reason for your comin' up this way besides tryin' to get Josiah home?"

"Well," Cyntha sighed. "I have it on good account from two mediums that my husband's soul is lost in the oblivion, and he needs me to reassure him that he may continue on to Heaven. We were heading to New York. Supposedly, the most renowned mediums of our day live there. They are excellent at contacting specific deceased loved ones."

"Who are they?"

"The Fox Sisters."

"Well, you don't have to go all the way to New York to find them. They're stayin' at a hotel here in Cincinnati."

Surprised and pleased, Cyntha could barely contain her joy. They said their goodbyes and returned to the boarding house in central Cincinnati. After Ben and Cyntha settled into their separate rooms in a boarding house, Ben took a stroll to look at horses in the livery. He came back an hour later, grinning. He could not stop smiling when Cyntha asked him why he seemed so jovial, but he did not tell her the cause of his glee.

FIFTY-EIGHT

Murderers Are Punished, Unless They Kill in Numbers to the Sound of Trumpets

– Voltaire

April 6, 1862, 4:00 a.m.
One mile south of the Union encampment at Pittsburg Landing

The dark of early morning extended through the forest as though a black fabric had been stitched to the trees. The advance elements of the left flank of General Johnston's Southern army were moving stealthily into position in a forested section, south of a fallow farmer's field. Through the trees, the house's windows glowed with lantern light. The farmer was up early. Paul watched their advance and remembered whose farm it was—Mr. Fraley's. He felt a pinch of remorse for the families in the area who would soon be surrounded by battle. *Can't be helped.*

From where he sat on a fallen hickory tree, he saw the waves of soldier shadows skulking through the crowded trees. These were Colonel Wood's Regiment. Colonels Claiborne's and Schaeffer's regiments straddled Wood's men. Somewhere in the shadows, officers whispered orders to close ranks and not to make a sound. He snickered at the comical notion of thousands of marching men ever being able to keep totally quiet.

He had not slept much since they stopped and bivouacked at midnight, and he was remembering his recent dream about Sara. He smiled, entertaining wishful thoughts of a life with her. Then he shook his head, certain that he had no chance with her. She had a calling to help heal the sick and wounded. *She has no room for me in her life.*

Lost in his thoughts, one company of Brigadier General Wood's Regiment came up so noiselessly through Paul's bivouac that he jumped from where he was seated to get out of their way.

He edged up next to his horse, already saddled. He tightened the cinch strap, then checked the loads in his three revolvers, feeling the bullets in the chambers with his fingers. The mare nickered when Paul patted its neck. "Steady, girl." He eased the horse a few steps back, then forward to prepare the horse for riding. *Never just jump on a horse that's been sleeping.* He had learned that early in his horse-riding career.

The crimped line of faceless soldiers, mere bulks of flesh, crept along with their rifles' bayonets occasionally gleaming in the spare moonlight.

Paul heard one soldier whisper, "When we gonna see them blue bellies?"

No one answered. Then they vanished into the somber obscurity.

In another minute, a regimental band trod through where he had been seated with their horns, concertinas and fiddles tied up in burlap sacks draped on their backs. They were softly whistling "Dixie" in harmony while they marched to their own private drumbeat. In a moment, they were lost in the forest gloom.

Paul had been assigned as a temporary adjutant to General William Hardee, the gentleman-soldier from Alabama, the former Commandant of Cadets at West Point, and author of *Rifle and Light Infantry Tactics,* called *Hardee's Tactics* by most who read it. Paul had learned that Hardee had published the tome in 1855, and it had quickly become a required study before the war. Paul thought the gray-haired officer akin to a sprightly, banty rooster, who was admired by his corps and whose admiration for his men showed. He usually thanked his couriers and staff for even the slightest effort.

Paul led his horse to General Hardee's tent, the only one allowed, for the men had slept on their arms. A faint glow shone through the tent fabric, and silhouettes moved inside.

The night had been filled the continuous clanking of the soldiers' accoutrements, the accidental banging of drums, even occasional gunshots. Paul worried. *Surely, the Federals would guess we're coming.*

When the lamp in the tent suddenly shuttered, the dark was all consuming. For a moment, he wondered, having seen so much of the glory of God's creation in his life, the travesty of having his eyes torn from their sockets in battle.

He folded his hands. "Dear Lord, I don't know how to pray. I guess ... thanks for letting me live so long. Keep me and men on both sides as safe as ought."

"Who're you talking to, Captain?" General Hardee exited his tent, holding a bullseye lantern, the light beaming out. Behind him, men wrapped in darkness began dismantling the tent, pulling stakes, the center pole, and folding the tarp.

"Uh, praying, sir."

"Good idea. It is Palm Sunday, after all. I've sent a few requests to God myself. I hope our prayers get heard better than the ones the Yanks are prayin'." He turned to the men dismantling the tent. "Thank you, gentlemen."

An aide brought General Hardee his horse. The general rose in the saddle. "Mount up, my kindred," he said to his personal surgeon and staff officers. "We'll have us a battle, I imagine, before sunup."

In a moment, Paul, General Hardee and his staff arrived within yards of the farmhouse of Mr. Fraley. They halted shy of the tree line. The house had gone dark. Paul guessed that Mr. Fraley knew battle was forthcoming. Beyond the trees stretched a barren field.

General Hardee held his lantern to a map spread across the pommel of his saddle. He looked up. "We have artillery in place, the Arkansas and Alabama troops in the lead. We've made enough noise and commotion over the last few days, I wonder if the Yanks are setting a trap."

"Day before yesterday, some of our artillery did fire on a group of pickets who had meandered close to our lines," Paul said, "but I didn't see any response in the Union camps. It's like they think we're a mirage."

"A mirage? Maybe so."

Looking out over the dim, plowed field before them, Paul could just make out a black line of about a thousand Union soldiers, by his estimate, emerging from the far forest. They were arrayed in a broad skirmish line. Some Northern officers had figured something was up.

A few anxious Confederates, still hiding among the trees, fired at the snaking black array. Union officers called orders into the vast obscurity. Immediately, bursts of rifle fire erupted along the Union line. Confederated replied with a brief volley.

The firing between the line of blue soldiers and the gray, standing about two hundred yards apart, increased. By a quarter after five, the battle was in full evidence.

∞

APRIL 6, 1862, EARLY MORNING,
ONE MILE SOUTH OF PITTSBURG LANDING

General Johnston sat in his tent scribbling dispatches. The increasing level of firing caused him to stop his writing. He turned to an aide. "Please make note of the time, sir."

"It's 5:14 a.m., General Johnston."

"The battle has begun." He rose and handed the pages of orders to several couriers. "Ride hard, gentlemen. Time is our friend or our foe, depending on how we use it."

The couriers sped away. General Johnston walked out of the tent, looked up at the star-laden sky, and mounted his horse he had named "Fire-eater." He had not ridden but a few paces before he encountered General Beauregard, riding from the opposite direction, holding a bullseye lantern in one hand. The generals and their aides halted.

General Beauregard removed his hat and ran fingers through his red hair. "General Johnston, sir, I must reiterate what I stated yesterday. We've had too many delays. Surely, the enemy is well-entrenched and waiting to cut us to shreds. We must pull back and save our army from certain defeat."

General Johnston looked everywhere except at General Beauregard. A hammered pewter pre-dawn sky was creeping out from the east. Squads of soldiers hurried past them in the direction of the firing. Finally, General Johnston said, "I wonder if there's any coffee. I could sure use some now." His finger tapped his saddle horn, waiting for General Beauregard's reply.

"Sir." General Beauregard rose in his stirrups. "Surely, you can take my admonitions seriously. I drew up the plan. I admit I am at fault for not allowing for delays. Their earthworks will be bristling with guns. I entreat you to call it off."

"Dear General. I admire you, and I do not fault you for the delays caused by rain and bad roads. But ... as you can hear ..." General Johnston pointed toward the burgeoning noise of rifle fire. "The battle has opened. It is too late to halt the attack!" He cupped his hands to his mouth and shouted, "Tonight, soldiers, we will water our horses in the Tennessee River!" He galloped past General Beauregard toward where General Hardee's troops were engaged.

FIFTY-NINE

TO RIDE DOWN
THE PATH OF DEATH

APRIL 6, 1862, SUNRISE
A FEW HUNDRED YARDS SOUTH OF SHILOH MEETING HOUSE
THE LEFT FLANK OF THE CONFEDERATE ADVANCE

Riding close to General Hardee, Paul watched the vast gray and brown tide of Rebel soldiers roll forward. *How could so many men be packed in so tight together?* The thousands, row upon row, following in close order, seemed to him like a writhing behemoth, a Goliath of immense proportions, devouring all in its path.

Many Confederates fell to their knees in the boggy land and struggled up again. Some tried to run and leap the rivulets and gullies. All the soldiers dodged around trees and bushes. Some landed in bogs up to their waists and floundered there, slogging their way through, cursing. Their world was water and mud and men and smoke. And confusion. At regular intervals, officers would have the men stop, re-form the line and fire a volley.

The racket of the Rebels' insidiously ear-piercing yell, a cross between the yipping of a fox and the screech of a banshee, rose in volume even above the growl of gunfire and artillery.

Spears of light from the morning sun glanced through the trees.

Beyond the army of gray, the Yankees fell back piecemeal. Barely dressed, they would fire a volley, then flee, most abandoning their firearms. Union attempts to stop the Confederate onslaught were futile.

When Paul topped a small rise, he saw a few Yankees who had been tedious in their retreat being impaled with bayonets by the Rebels. One man, in particular, caught Paul's attention, his face showing, at first, surprise, then agony, then hopeless fear of his impending death. Paul had never witnessed that method of killing, and it sickened him. *Shoot the man in the head. Don't force him to die a slow death.*

Paul trailed General Hardee and his staff, the group halting occasionally to offer encouragement to some soldiers who were lagging. Many of those Rebels had the blankest expressions on their faces, as if their ability to reason and even their life spirits had escaped them. Yet, they followed the admonitions to buck up and hurried to draw alongside the larger multitude of men.

In a moment, Paul and the general and his staff were riding through areas where large numbers of men, primarily Union, lay wounded, or dying, or dead. Paul looked at the face of one prostrate man who appeared to be praying, his hands folded, his eyes toward heaven, but then he perceived that the man was gone, his stare piercing eternity.

He came upon another Yankee who had been thrust though with a bayonet. The man was writhing, clutching his bloody stomach. Paul felt an inordinate desire to leap from his saddle and render aid. But, maintaining his sense of duty, he turned his horse and rode on.

In short order, it became evident that the avalanche of Confederates had ground to a halt. They had reached the outer line of the Union's camps. When Paul and the general's staff rode into the middle of the tent rows, Confederates were running about in a sort of wild abandon, and almost every common soldier was stuffing his mouth with the Yankees' freshly-cooked breakfasts. Or they were plundering tents, their arms filled with treasures of blankets, weapons, clothing, camp stools and desks, framed photographs and bundles of letters. A few soldiers had seated themselves and were reading the letters.

"Hey! Look what I found," one soldier hollered, opening a wooden box filled with jewelry.

The gunfire had stopped, but the celebratory despoliation of the tent cities by the rowdy, victorious men was voluble.

Paul laughed at the joy of the soldiers picking their way through the camps and filling their arms with whatever they could carry. He realized how correct he had been in his assessment of the Union encampment. The surprised Federals had made no attempt to entrench or prepare a defensive ring around the camp. *How foolish could the Yankees be?*

Above the din, he could just make out about a hundred yards to the north the tinny sound of fifes and bugles, then the rat-a-tat of drums. Yankees were being mustered into formation and were regrouping. He mentioned as much to one of General Hardee's staff, who nodded, then yelled in the general's ear.

The general gave a fierce directive to the staff. "Get this army moving! Drive the invaders back to their dens!" The staff galloped away to every officer they could find with his orders.

Paul was amazed how quickly the melee of pillaging was being halted by mounted officers, shouting orders for their soldiers to re-form their lines. He watched a major raise his booted foot and plant it squarely into the back of a private whose arms were laden with food stuffs and a sword. The man tumbled into a firepit and rose with a sleeve of his jacket on fire. He beat it out, shoved the sword he had gathered into his belt and jogged to join the new files of Confederates spreading like the great wings of an eagle for a new charge.

Plenty of soldiers were still pilfering through the camps when General Johnston rode in on Fire-eater. He trotted the big horse along, his booming voice rolling out into the camps. Again, and again, he entreated his soldiers to cease their looting and strive for victory.

He stopped a dozen feet from where Paul, his binoculars to his eyes, was watching the Union army form a line of defense. Paul lowered his binoculars in time to watch General Johnston lean from his horse to a camp table and pick up a tin cup of coffee. He swished it around, gulped its contents, and shouted, "This is all the plunder I will take. Carry on, my brave soldiers. Defeat the invaders!" He waved the cup around and galloped with his staff officers and personal physician in close pursuit. He rushed past General Hardee, then stopped when he saw several wounded Yankees lying in a group. He turned to his personal surgeon. "Doctor Yandell, stay here and render aid to these men."

"But, sir," Doctor Yandell said, "these men are the enemy!"

"They were once. Now they need our attention. It is our Christian duty."

"Yes, sir." Doctor Yandell dismounted and carried his bag with him to the wounded.

General Johnston headed east toward the center of the Confederate advance.

General Hardee looked straight at Paul. He gave a nod of his head for Paul to follow General Johnston. "McGavin! Keep me informed. Find me again with news of our other divisions' progress!"

"Yes, sir."

General Hardee and his staff turned into an enveloping smoke of renewed fighting. Paul galloped after General Johnston.

SIXTY

OLD FRIENDS FOUND

April 6, 1862, 6:00 a.m.
Corinth, Mississippi

The lanterns in the Hotel Tishomingo glowed bright in the dark morning.

Sara moved briskly in the foyer that was filled with cots and mats in preparation for receiving wounded soldiers. A hundred or so soldiers who had fallen ill or were injured filled the upper rooms of the hotel. When she stopped and leaned over to wipe a wet cloth on a fevered soldier's head, she heard the initial rumble of cannons, like distant thunder. She knew it was not a new thunderstorm. This sound was more uniform, a series of regular poundings, like a giant hammer was striking a vast muffled anvil. A deep uniform thumping.

She stepped onto the porch of the hotel and listened. Not a cloud in the pearl-colored new morning sky. The distinct concussions of cannon fire plowed through the wind and set the tree leaves to shaking. She hated the sound. The doctors, male nurses and a considerable number of women who had taken on a role similar to hers joined her on the porch.

"That's cannons firing, I do believe," one of the women stated the obvious.

The men took the break in their efforts to light a pipe or cigar. A few women lit pipes as well. Soon, tobacco smoke inundated the porch. Sara watched their faces, all of them contemplative in appearance. Each one's visage seemed somber, but not fearful, reflecting about this momentous event that they could not see, but knew was historic for either victory or defeat.

Thump. Shrieking whistle. Whack. Thump. Rat-a-tat over and over. The battle was expanding.

Many soldiers still rushed about the streets of Corinth on various errands, but all were quiet. No generals were present in Corinth this day. War had marched to the town's outer reaches, but the gray army had marched forth to strike the wolves who prowled at the gate.

"Let us be about our duties, gentlemen and ladies," Dr. Caldwell, the lead surgeon, said. "I know that before this day is over, we will have many wounded to attend to." He turned to his male attendants. "Gird your loins, men. It will not be a pretty sight." Next, he faced the women. "You ladies, be prepared, but if you cannot bear the sight of blood and carnage, I bid you adieu. There is not enough smelling salts to revive you all. You can find plenty else to do; rolling bandages, gathering buckets of water, washing sheets, and the like in the neighboring homes. In fact, go out and borrow as many cups and pots and as much coffee as you can. Be quick about it." He stalked inside and joined a handful of other doctors.

The soldier nurses returned to their duties inside while the women left to knock on doors.

Sara stayed on the porch. She had seen carnage, and seen such butchery that the doctor's term of *not a pretty sight* did not meet the caliber of what they were about to witness.

Her thoughts rushed to Joseph's face and his blond hair, and she wondered what his last moments had been. She had saved his life once on the battlefield at Wilson Creek. For so long, she had sought him, following a trail that became thrice lost and vanished again at Pea Ridge. She believed now that God in His wisdom did not deem her desire for Joseph meritorious enough. *Your will be done, Lord.*

Before she walked into the hotel, she noticed a man in a brown robe, cinched with a rope about the waist, striding toward her. "Father Antonio!" She ran to him and embraced him.

He smiled broadly. "Bueno, niñita. Muy bueno. It is so good to see you again, young lady. I recognized your mare tied to a tree in the back, so I knew tu esta aqui. You are here."

"Father, what are you doing here?"

"I will soon ask you the same question, my amiga. But I am here because my Cherokee family found sus amigos y las casas in Alabama. They are home with their family and friends. And here around Corinth, I have been going about helping where I can. I try to do the Lord's work. Gracias Adios. I helped a family rebuild a barn that the Yankees burned. I helped a man get back his cow that a Rebel stole. I interceded for some soldiers who were very drunk to *not* get shot for desertion. The Lord's work. Gracias Adios. I see you cut your long hair. Pobrecita. Sad young lady. Now digame, tell me, why you are here, so near the war?"

"I'm here with a friend who brought important papers for General Johnston. Since I'm here, I figure I can lend a hand. At least for now."

"Hay muchas personas que requesta ayuda in Corinth."

Sara blinked, not sure what the priest had said. Then she fathomed his meaning. "Oh, Father Antonio. Yes, there's always plenty of folks who need help, if we just look."

"Si, you and I must attend the service at eight o'clock at the protestant church in the middle of town. I do it as a favor to the minister and his wife. I have no congregation here. And it is, after all, *Palm Sunday.*"

"Oh, my. I had forgotten. I would like to attend a service."

"I have met a most interesting protestant minister, a Reverend Felder. After some malo verbos—bad words—contentiousness.

That is the word he used. We have since become amigos—good friends. Working together at his church."

Sara gawped. "Revered Felder here? He's the pastor from Springfield. He's a fiery, God-fearing preacher. I will definitely join you to hear his sermon."

"Es verdad. It is true that he is a passionate preacher. And he knows his scripture. But I must go now. A Catholic woman in town seeks confession." Father Antonio started to leave.

"Wait! Father."

"Yes, my child."

"Father. I don't know how to put this. I want to know if my presence here is somehow causing war, if it's my fault, when all I really want to do is stop it."

"What do you mean?"

"When I lived in Wilson Creek, the battle began in my front yard. When I came north looking for Joseph, an ammunition warehouse exploded, almost killing me and making me deaf for weeks. When I kept trying to find my fiancé, the battle started in a field of a kind farmer who had taken me in. Is my being here going to bring war to the town?"

"No, Sara. That is far from God's will. I know this war is not His will either. Sometimes, misfortune finds us, and it can make us stronger if we pray and trust."

Sara sensed the intensity of his advice and felt relief.

"Here is another pregunta—a question. Did you find your fiancé?"

"No, Father." Sara stared down at the tattered hem of her dress, her scuffed shoes. "He was killed in battle. At least, that's what I was told."

"Lo siento—I am sorry. God has a plan. You will find someone else, I assure you. Another man to love you."

"I hope so, Father. In the meantime, please remember me in your prayers."

"Si."

"And pray for a soldier named Paul. He is my best friend now, and he's off at the battle."

"I will." Father bowed his head and prayed ardently in her presence.

Just before eight o'clock, Reverend Felder's church bells rang. A few dozen townspeople came to the service. Reverend Felder delivered a stirring sermon on forgiveness, even while the concussions of battle shook the walls and pews and sent plaster sprinkling from the ceiling.

Sara sat in the back pew beside Father Antonio. When they were leaving, she hugged Reverend Felder, but then she saw Constance, standing to his side. Both women embraced and smiled and hugged again.

"So sad," Sara told Constance, "that we should re-meet here, with war so close by."

"I figure it's God's providence to let me meet an old friend."

When Father Antonio joined Reverend Felder for coffee in the parsonage, Sara and Constance found a bench, and, for three hours, despite the ceaseless reverberation of the distant battle, they shared their stories of sorrow and joy. They each cried at times, sometimes for their sorrows, sometimes tears of joy.

"I ain't never believed I could find a man like Edward," Constance said. "I feel loved every day, and he's teachin' me the good book, though I'm a little addled about them big words and all that history."

"I understand your frustration," Sara said. "The Lord didn't plan it to be simply a lark to understand His teachings, so we have to spend a lifetime studyin' it. But He made it easy to find Him if we just take the time to look."

Constance clucked her tongue, looked away, then turned back at Sara. "I must tell you that I missed my time of the month. I'm pretty sure I have Edward's baby. Our baby." She rolled her hand on her belly. "I can't wait until I feel the quickening."

"That is wonderful news. Congratulations."

Constance's face turned sad. "But what about you losin' your fiancé in battle?"

"He was never really my fiancé. I do have hope though for another man I can love."

Violent cannon roars of the far away battle shook the peach trees under which they sat and spilled blossoms on them.

"This battle sounds far bigger than anything I can imagine," Sara said. "Must be a whole lot of dyin'. I pray God finds a way to end this war soon."

"Gotta be up to Him. Ain't no men gonna figure out how to end it."

They rose and went to the Tishomingo Hotel to prepare to receive the wounded.

SIXTY-ONE

∞

AMBIVALENCE

APRIL 6, 1862, MID-AFTERNOON
WASHINGTON, DC

L ucas sat on his bench in the War Department telegraph office, waiting for an assignment, wringing his hands in worry. He had twice surreptitiously brought a revolver into the telegraph office and had planned to shoot President Lincoln then and there, despite the fact that he would certainly be caught, tried and hung. But those two days, the president did not show up. This was the third day he had brought the revolver, but the sun was going down and the president had not appeared. His previous plan to sneak into the Executive Mansion compound through the hole in the fence had been thwarted. *Perhaps it is the will of God that I not shoot him. Perhaps it is the will of God that he not be killed at all. Maybe I am wrong.* His thoughts swayed back and forth.

Gathering his ear trumpet, he rose from his seat and paced into the hall. Striding to its end, he spoke under his breath. "I know there are enough Democrats in the Congress that once Lincoln is dead, they will pressure his successor, Vice-President Hamlin, to surrender their heinous cause of invasion and let the South go its way. Then they will send emissaries to see if they can assuage the South's issues of slavery and tariffs, and the South will have to reconcile. The Southern planters need the Northern mills as much as the mill owners covet their cotton. Probably in only a few months, the nation will heal itself, better than before." He beat his hand into his palm and again checked his small revolver in his pocket.

He suffered from a divided opinion. Since the war had begun, he had never felt so sure of a course of action. It was no longer a pipe dream to kill the loathsome Illinois lawyer who had wronged his friend, but an urgent calling to set the nation right. Yet, on the other hand, though he had been a soldier, he was never a man of unprovoked violence. He had grown to oppose slavery and wished it gone from the nation's soil. And he knew Lincoln was the abolitionists' candidate. He somewhat admired the way President Lincoln had interacted with the telegraph operators and with citizens on the streets. He further appreciated the cordial nature with which he had spoken to him.

As far as the newspaper editorials and political cartoons, Lucas usually disagreed with the editorial analyses of the president that persisted in the press. The newspaper's editorial cartoons typically drew him as a buffoon or an ape.

Lincoln means well, but he must know his very presence is the cause of the bloodshed. If only he could see it.

Lucas grabbed a newspaper that lay on a nearby table. He read the article that essentially outlined everything that General McClellan was doing on the Peninsula east of Richmond. Lucas had looked at enough maps to know that it was a short march up to Richmond. If the Confederate capital fell, it would bode badly for ever healing the wounds of the war. The article and editorials harangued about McClellan's inaction before the Southern defenders led by General Magruder below Yorktown.

Who is this General Magruder of the South? The Southerners call him Prince John. Is he a genius? Well, bless this prince's efforts if it stalls McClellan, let him squander away his time and his army.

Lucas had fought in the War with Mexico. He knew a land fort could not stand long against a concerted siege effort. If the Rebels failed to hold General McClellan's vast army at bay, then all was lost.

That's it. I have to act. I will go to the President's Palace tomorrow. Tonight, I will plan with Workman.

.

SIXTY-TWO

TWO WARS, ONE SKY

April 6, 1862, Late Morning
Pittsburg Landing Battlefield

Paul raced his horse to catch up with General Johnston, who was headed east, threading in behind the advancing Rebels. Everywhere, loud volleys cracked and cannons caused the whole land to tremble, the trees to shake, the leaves cascading like rain. It was as though both armies had dug up monsters from below the earth. At no time was there silence, the air constantly filled with the hum, snip, patter, and thudding of bullets. Then there was the agonizing yells of men who had been shot, clubbed, or bayonetted. Often, he had to halt, because the smoke was so dense in the trees, tangled with vines, that he could not see his way forward.

Half a dozen times, he witnessed a melee of men of both armies, dozens of yards from any organized brigade, soldiers in blue fighting hand to hand against soldiers in butternut or homespun, all of them grappling, shooting at pointblank range, stabbing with Bowie knives and clubbing with rifle butts.

It seemed to Paul as if these waifs of war, these hopeless souls, were in their own private war. For them, there was only one sky, but two wars.

There was the larger war that had engulfed the nation, and there was their private war against someone they did not know, and who, in another situation and time, might have been a good friend who would join them for a drink and a toast.

Constantly, Confederate companies crossed his path in wavering lines, slopping through the mire to shore up the advance of those in front of them. The throngs slowed his progress. He grew frustrated that he could not find General Johnston to keep up communication with General Hardee.

At length, he made his way through the dense foliage and gained a road. He guessed it was the Hamburg-Purdy Road that ran east to west.

He arrived near Colonel Stephens' regiment at the edge of a line of trees facing a wide, grassy field that stretched in front of a peach orchard about three hundred yards away, the pink blossoms glittering even in the billowing gray smoke. Amongst the trees were Union massed artillery and thousands of soldiers.

All around Paul, thousands of Confederate soldiers crowded into a ravine beside the road behind a ragged rail fence. In the meadow beyond them, hundreds of Rebel soldiers lay still—dead or near death. Some of the wounded in the field crawled, flung their arms about, or cowered behind the corpses. Their wounds were severe enough to cause excruciating pain, but not enough to make them lose consciousness.

For the soldiers crouching in the ravine, they engaged in a long-range sniping fight with the Federals in the orchard. Many of the Confederates had already faced death several times in futile charges at the emboldened Yankees, and death's long scythe was awaiting them at the next charge.

Paul took a moment to examine the faces of some of the privates and corporals. Some wore dazed expressions, others showed abject, immobilizing fear; but a substantial number showed a vaunted courage, a sort of bravado and anxiousness to get it over with.

Behind those men, officers conferred. Couriers raced away with urgent messages. Other brought new missives to the officers.

He recognized a few of the officers he had briefly met—one of them he knew by name, Colonel Statham, under Breckinridge's command. He realized he had made his way to the far right of the Confederate line. These were Bragg and Breckinridge's troops. He pulled out his pocket watch, flipped it open. It read almost one-thirty.

He rode up to the group of officers, jerking his mount to a halt. "Who is that Yankee division in that orchard halting our advance? And what is its strength? I'm Captain McGavin, a courier for General Hardee. I need to give him as much information as I can."

"We're sure that it's some of Brigadier General Prentiss' Michigan and Missouri troops," Colonel Statham said. "The Yanks we've captured are kindly disposed to tell us anything we ask them." He pointed at a crowd of Union prisoners squatting in the rear, under guard.

Next, he pointed at the peach orchard. "Several Iowa flags over yonder. Some of General Wallace's brigades, maybe, on their right. Illinois boys, too. Hurlbut's right in front of us. They're massed pretty tight. We can't mount another attack. Everything we've tried so far has been completely thwarted. My Tennesseans are tired."

"Thank you, sir. One more question."

"You'll excuse me, Captain. I've got to get Rutledge's Tennessee battery to give those Yanks some hell. And if you've got any gumption to move my Tennesseans to charge one more time, I'd appreciate it. I have the Governor of Tennessee, Isham Harris, here with me, and he can't get them to budge. They think they're done. But one more charge, and we'll have 'em." He started to leave.

"One more thing, please."

The colonel turned.

"I'm tasked with finding General Johnston. Have you an idea of his whereabouts?"

"He rode down this road twenty minutes ago headed to our extreme right. He wants us to turn the Yank left flank away from the river. Then they can't get support from their riverboats."

"Thank you, Colonel Statham." He galloped past Governor Harris, who looked as miffed as a man could be. He gained the road, ignoring the rifle fire of the Yankees in the orchard.

He had not ridden one hundred yards before he met General Johnston and his staff riding toward him. Accompanying the general were a half dozen couriers, some junior officers and his brother-in-law, Colonel William Preston. Paul turned his mount and fell in with the entourage.

General Johnston and his group arrived behind Statham's troops just as General Breckinridge rode up.

"Sir," General Breckinridge stated in a tired monotone. "We've been charging that Yankee position for hours. We need a new strategy or a miracle. These men won't budge." He pointed at Statham's brigade cowering in the ravine, a few men occasionally popping up to take a rifle shot at the Union line.

When General Breckinridge stated his complaint, the entire brigade turned almost as one, and seeing General Johnston, let out several hurrahs and waved their hats.

"Who else do we have here on this flank?" General Johnston asked.

"Let me see." General Breckinridge rubbed his whiskered chin. "On our right, there's Jackson and Bowen's brigades. To our immediate left is Stephen's."

"Ride with me, General," General Johnston said.

Paul and the staffs followed the generals.

"See those Union troops falling back over there." General Johnston raised his field glasses and pointed. Paul noticed that the general still held the tin cup he had picked up earlier in the morning in the Union camp.

Paul and every man in the group watched a substantial number of bluecoats retiring in orderly fashion from the field.

"They must have run out of ammunition," General Breckinridge stated.

"Precisely," General Johnston said. His tone changed to emphatic. "Now is our chance to turn that tidy retreat into a rout. We'll pound their left flank and drive them back." His face was flushed. He kicked the haunches of Fire-eater, causing the stallion to rear up, flailing legs in the air for several seconds. "Now is the time!" he bellowed.

With every one of his aides in tow, he trotted along the front of Statham's men in the ravine. He hollered, "You men must do the work! Soldiers, those invaders from the North are stubborn. Therefore, we're going to have to give them the bayonet!"

The soldiers stood, cheering. Johnston halted his steed at the center of Statham's brigade line. "Come, hearty men of the South. Follow me! I will lead you!" He trotted his stallion forward.

The convulsing line of men surged forward, the general's offer to lead them causing in them a perceptible tremor of joy. Screaming their fox yip yell, they charged at a run alongside General Johnston. The brigades on either side of Statham's, catching sight of their general, swept up also like a crushing ocean breaker. The soldier's piercing howls spiked high above the sound of Union rifle and cannon fire.

General Johnston, his entourage and Paul rode along just behind a company of Rebels who were advancing on the far right. They were clothed the same odd uniforms, whitest wool.

"They look to be attired in their grave clothes," one of the aides remarked.

"You there." General Johnston stopped a captain who had been loading his gun while walking just behind his company. The man stopped. "What regiment is this?"

"This is the valiant Second Texas, just arrived a day before we marched. But here we are, whippin' the Yanks." The captain continued loading his revolver.

"Texans! Good." General Johnston called to the man above the roar, but his eyes were watching the advancing Rebel line. "What's your name, Captain?" he said, still surveying the attacking Confederates.

"Captain George Washington Fly, sir." He saluted.

General Johnston turned to look at Captain Fly. "George Washington. Your parents endowed you with an honorable name. What happened to your hand, Captain? It looks burned."

"That it is, General Johnston. We didn't get a full ration before we marched, so when we chased the Yanks from their camps, we were all substantially hungry. I dove my hand into a pan of bacon fryin' and grabbed some to eat. My hand isn't hurt bad. If it's to your liking, sir, I need to attend to my company."

"Proceed, Captain Fly."

The officer raced ahead to catch up with his troops who were storming ahead.

General Johnston smiled. "It's men like him who will help us win the day."

In short order, the blue line collapsed, hurried and harried. Paul kept close behind the line of Confederates. General Johnston's aides rode back and forth, encouraging the soldiers. Ultimately, the last of the Rebels surged past General Johnston, who had halted in the open field. Bullets were still flying from the retreating Yankees. Several zinged past Paul. One struck his horse's shoulder, but when he examined it, the wound was just a graze.

Another shot clipped his boot heel.

In the whirl of smoke, Paul turned his mount and galloped up to within a few feet of General Johnston. Paul was going to ask what message to give to General Hardee, but the general was watching through his binoculars. The Federals were regrouping in the orchard and along a sunken road. Hundreds of the very men in gray who had so boldly attacked were now slinking back from the new withering fire of the re-established blue line beyond the orchard.

"My, dear God. The Yanks are stubborn," General Johnston growled. He turned to his couriers and aides. "All of you, go! Stop those men from retreating. Tell them we must press the attack. We can't have victory if we keep running away. Go! I say."

All the couriers and aides raced toward the retreating infantrymen, save Paul and one other aide, Colonel Preston. General Johnston watched the battle developing, his eyes intense. In minutes, the couriers returned, one by one, with their reports, and he sent them in new directions to encourage other soldiers to halt and regroup for a renewed assault.

While Paul and the general watched the men in gray re-forming new lines, General Johnston turned to Paul. "What can I do for you, Captain McGavin?"

"What message for General Hardee, sir?"

"Ah, yes, let me think." General Johnston's face suddenly blanched, all color sloughed from his face, his brow beaded with sweat. His eyes became glassy, his expression at first worried, then vacant.

Governor Harris rode up at that moment. "My, God. What is wrong with the general?"

"I'm not sure," Paul said.

"Are you wounded, Albert?" Governor Harris asked General Johnston.

"Yes, and I fear seriously."

Governor Harris took hold of the general's shoulders, propping him up in the saddle. Paul grabbed Fire-eater's bridle and led the horse down into a gulley away from gunfire. A small stream babbled nearby. The general, though his eyes were open, made no effort to speak.

With more couriers and aides arriving, the group lowered General Johnston onto a patch of moss and clover by the stream. Governor Harris tore open the general's coat and shirt, examined his thighs, then his neck and head. He found no wound.

Each man in the little group regarded each other in confusion and shock. One aide brought his canteen to General Johnston's lips, but he did not attempt to drink. Another aide rubbed his arms vigorously, while a third listened at the unconscious man's chest. Paul stood holding the reins of Fire-eater and the mounts of the other aides. He felt helpless.

"Where is Doctor Yandell?" Governor Harris asked.

"The general sent the doctor to care for the Federals' wounded," Paul said in a whisper.

The aides leapt on their horses and galloped away in search of any doctor. Colonel Preston arrived. He knelt beside the dying general. "He's still breathing." Then he drew closer to General Johnston's face. "Johnston, do you know me?"

At that moment, General Johnston took his last breath. His pupils dilated and fixed.

"Look at his pants leg!" Paul said, pointing. General Johnston's right pants leg above the top of his tall cavalry boots had turned maroon.

Colonel Preston gently pulled off the boot, turned it over, and blood flowed freely out of it onto the ground. The sock and lower pants leg were swathed in blood. Ripping open the pants leg, Colonel Preston saw the artery that had been struck by an errant bullet and the last trickle of blood.

Holding his wrist against his forehead, his tears flowing, Colonel Preston said, "We must quickly inform General Beauregard, but keep this from the men for now. No one who does not need to know should hear of it." He turned. "Who can go inform Beauregard?"

"I'll go now," Paul said.

Several of the couriers and aides who had just arrived said the same. In a minute, the couriers and some of the aides had departed to spread the word in secret. Paul decided to travel along the Hamburg-Purdy Road that he had originally traversed. It was not a good decision.

SIXTY-THREE

So Near to Victory, Bound for Defeat

April 6, 1862, 3:00 p.m.
Shiloh Battlefield

A n errant shot, or perhaps one shot by a sharpshooter like at Pea Ridge, struck Paul and he tumbled to the side of the road, blood pooling rapidly around his body.

The minié bullet tore through the meat of his right arm, missing the bone. He fell from his mount onto his long-injured leg and gun-shot arm into a pile of wet, moldy leaves, pungent, and icy cold. The immediate pain caused him to swoon. In a moment, he woke and had enough cognizance to pull a cloth from his jacket and wrap a tourniquet around his arm, and then sit in the vile mire beside the road, the pain in his leg being far worse than his arm. His horse had run away into the smoke and trees.

Scanning the wide meadow before him, he saw the peach orchard, barely visible in the distance. Many soldiers' bodies lay still in the grassy field in front of it. The meadow was blemished with so much blood that much of the grass had a maroon tone. A number of nurses of necessity, generally older soldiers and musicians, were gathering the wounded up onto drays and wagons and taking them east, far away from where Paul sat. He yelled at the men, but they never indicated that they heard him. He guessed those retrieving the wounded would take them down the Hamburg-Savannah Road, and thence to Corinth. He was not in their line of sight.

The battle continued to rage far beyond where Johnston had fallen. Though the Rebel army had forced the Yankees to fall back, like the general had stated, those Northern men were obstinate.

He was able to drag himself to lean against a white oak tree. He was quite thirsty, but his canteen was on his saddle, now lost. All the while that he was waiting in his private cove hoping someone could help him, the concussion of the artillery off in the distance to his right mounted to a steady, unending roar. The ground shook like he had never before felt it. Nothing at the battle of Pea Ridge had matched this din. His heart grew heavy in sorrow for whoever was being pummeled by the cannons.

After an hour, the battle slid farther north. All the sound of gunfire, cannons, and men, wailing in pain, faded. The battle clamor to the west was also moving north. Paul realized the Union right was collapsing faster than its left.

When night began to cloak the battlefield, the battle continued, now with the heavy booms of the Yankee gunships on the river firing their huge cannons. Dense rainclouds began gathering in bulbous bubbles, like dark cotton bolls. A few raindrops sprinkled on Paul just when a short haycart with high board sides and pulled by a single mule churned up the road. A lantern swung from the mule's neck by a tether. The cart was driven by a skinny, ancient man with a caved-in chest, wearing no hat, balding. His stringy chin whiskers fell to his bare chest. Paul hailed him, and he stopped and crawled down from the cart. Smiling cordially, he took a brief look at Paul's arm wound, clucked his tongue to indicate it was fixable, then helped Paul limp to the back of the cart. When Paul reached the tumbril, he saw three wounded Confederates and a Union soldier shoved up against each other;

two of the butternut-clad men were out cold. Paul had to sit on the end of the cart, dangling his good leg off the edge.

"I'm takin' ye back to Corinth," the bewhiskered man called, "and let them surgeons fix all y'all up." His words whistled through the few teeth in his mouth.

The Yankee, his shirt glistening in blood, raised a weak arm and pointed at Paul. "We're gonna whip you flea-ridden insurgents tomorrow."

"Not likely," Paul said in retort.

When the land was like a lightless coalmine, save the bright artillery flashes to the north, a wild gale swept in while the cart moved tediously along. The battle continued into the night on all fronts, but it echoed more than half a mile from where Paul had been shot. Shivering from the cold, Paul watched the flashes of cannon fire glow through the trees and into the clouded heavens. The firmament became electrified, lightning dancing in a disjointed wedlock with the blasts of cannons. The temperature plummeted to near freezing.

The rain that had begun as a sprinkle began to pour. The cart ended up behind a long, serpentine line of wagons, drays, and the walking wounded, all of them slogging through rain-drowned roads.

Paul looked at his arm wound and was astounded to see the wound and skin around it had taken on a luminescent green tint.

∞

In the pitch-black night, nearing midnight, the torrent of rain poured on the Union line on the ridge beside Pittsburg Landing. The Yankees had been laboring for hours, some men shoveling dirt entrenchments, and others battling several Rebel attempts to scale the heights. The attacks were beaten back. At last, the shooting stopped except for the roar of the Federal gunboats on the river lofting heavy caliber shots into the Confederate lines.

General Grant sat on his haunches at the back of the ridge under a tree that provided partial cover from the downpour. He was soaked. Deep in thought, he was trying to keep a cigar lit while he smoked it. A lantern sat by his feet.

General Sherman rode up to a skidding stop in the mud. His aides arrived shortly after and halted. Sherman dismounted. "Oh, there you are, Ulysses."

"Yep." General Grant puffed vigorously on his cigar. He finally stood and shook hands with General Sherman.

Sherman winced, his hand wrapped in a bloody cloth.

"I heard your hand was injured, Will."

"Yes, Ulysses. When we were surprised this morning, a bullet went through my palm. A different bullet pierced my aide and killed him. Our army was completely taken by surprise. But we slowed 'em down plenty. Always regrouping to make new stands."

"Sadly, not of all of 'em hung around to fight. We had so many men trying to escape and jumping in the Tennessee, the sailors had to knock them off the boats with oars. Hundreds of men in the water, scared for their lives. Thousands more crouched behind trees like scared birds. No glory there."

"At least, we have all of Buell's men arriving. We'll have thousands of fresh troops in the morning. General Lew Wallace finally found his way here with his division, too. Said he had a bad map and went the wrong way."

General Grant nodded. "Hell of a thing. Them Rebs attacking us. Never saw it coming."

"It was the devil's own day."

"It was. We'll lick 'em tomorrow. Let's get to my tent where we can see the map. General Buell should be here soon. Half of his troops are here already. The remaining ten thousand should have crossed the Tennessee on our transports before morning."

The Union generals strode to General Grant's tent and began planning for the next day's battle.

SIXTY-FOUR

∞

DESPAIR, NEGOTIATION, HOPE

APRIL 6, 1862, 6:00 P.M.
CINCINNATI, OHIO

C yntha and Ben braved the crowds at the Opera House to see the Fox Sisters put on their final show before they returned home to New York state. The event was a wild one. First, outside the Opera House, a dozen women and men held placards complaining of the sisters as sham artists, decrying their ill-gotten gains from the sorrow and despair of widows and orphans. They shouted and shook their fists.

Then, inside the showplace, several who had paid for a ticket were also making disparaging remarks, hooting at the stage, calling for punishment of the sisters, even as far as tar and feathering. They were obstreperous enough that uniformed policemen took them by their collars and escorted them out.

Ben and Cyntha had located seats off to the side, but near the front. Roughly twenty minutes after the official start time, the curtains parted. Leah Fox, matronly, clad all in deep maroon, save a broad pink collar on her dress, stood with her hands folded, looking up in an attitude of prayer.

One more fellow hollered a cursing insult, and the police handily pushed him outside. The white policemen and some Negroes wearing suits took up positions at the back doors and at the bottom of the stage. The magnesium footlights blazed.

Leah finally looked out into the audience and smiled a generous smile, then winked. "I have a surprise for all of you. Can you imagine?" Leah walked back and forth across the bare stage, pointing at the paying customers and asking if they could guess. None of the patrons guessed the answer she sought.

Cyntha did not know what to think about this attempt at jovial revelation. She leaned to Ben and whispered, "What could be so cleverly intriguing? I would think the event would be more somber."

When stagehands brought out and set down a round table with three chairs near the front of the stage, Leah gave an astonished look. "Oh, my," she said, "my sisters are already prepared to speak to the deceased. Our dear loved ones, our boon companions, our husbands, brothers, parents, even grandparents. And here is the surprise I hoped you would guess." She leaned toward the audience like a carnival barker might do. "Here, before your very ears, my sisters, Maggie and Kate have informed me that they have been in contact with none other but the president's own departed mother!"

Numerous gasps went up from the crowd, followed by murmuring in private conversations.

"That's right! Mrs. Lincoln will join us tonight. She has much to say about her son and about the war!"

The crowd's enthusiasm grew. Ben even felt some exhilaration, though he had remained dubious of the entire séance and the concept of speaking to the dead. Not his curiosity but his admiration and devotion to Cyntha were the reasons for his attending. Had he not cared, he could have escorted her to the event and waited happily outside.

The evening events began with a bang when an elderly woman in somewhat shabby, worn dress apparently spoke with her deceased husband and her brother with the aid of the two younger sisters. After the initial thumps and snaps that echoed against the floorboards of the stage where the woman asked particular yes or no questions, each sister had comments to add, all of which the woman verified as true statements, and that no one, save she, had known these details before the sisters revealed them in the first séance by speaking with the dead men.

After the woman returned beaming to her seat near the front of the stage, Leah went through their usual charade of demonstrating that the table was bare, free from any noise-making contraption. She invited three women to come up and check the dresses and hairdos of Maggie and Kate. The thoroughly believable *guest investigators* found nothing askew.

Leah then invited the chief of police, who had been seated in the back, to come forward, and he vouched in a rich baritone that no contrivance was used to fool the audience. He even held up a document saying as much that he handed to Leah. She rolled up the page and placed it in her dress pocket while the prominent constabulary took his seat.

Throughout the rest of the performance, Leah asked for volunteers to come forth and participate in a séance, all of whom came away satisfied that their deceased loved ones had spoken with them. Maggie and Kate sat still as statues at the table the entire time, though often yawning between bouts of displaying their spiritual conversational skills. Several times, a sudden wind blew the dresses of the séance participants, even though all doors were securely closed.

The episode where the sister mediums spoke to President Lincoln's deceased mother brought thunderous applause, though no one could argue whether any of the statements that the sisters offered were in any way true.

Each time Leah asked for a volunteer from the audience, Cyntha stood, waving her arms, shouting, and sometimes leaping to gain the woman's attention, but to no avail. "I'm here. I came from far away!" she yelled.

After two hours, when Maggie tumbled from her chair, Leah abruptly announced that the episodes had been too taxing on her sister's health, and the show ended, the curtains were drawn.

With some minor grumbling, the majority of the audience appeared pleased with the results of the show and chattered like magpies while exiting. Cyntha sat, depressed, unable to rise. She looked up at Ben, who was standing. "Whatever shall I do, Ben? I don't believe I can travel all the way to New York. I don't have the will. How long must I bear this burden of my husband's soul being lost in eternity?"

Ben took both of her hands in his. "Don't give up, Cyntha."

"But I must give up. I cannot move on in my life, knowing his soul is unsettled."

"Maybe..."

"Maybe what? There's nothing I can do. The show is over, my chance lost!" Tears flowed down her cheeks.

"Yes, but maybe there's something I can do. Come with me."

Cyntha took his hand and followed him as he limped up the stairs onto the stage. A Negro guard stepped in front of them.

"Don't try to stop us," Ben ordered. "This here is the Fox sisters' cousin."

Before Cyntha could even show surprise, and the guard stood in a flummoxed state, Ben pulled her behind the curtains. In the shadows, they saw dressing rooms, a few stagehands, coils of rope, and two large fans at least a yard square and with long handles leaning against a wall. Ben wondered, "What could be the use of such things?" Not seeing the Fox sisters, he bolted out the rear door, yanking Cyntha with him. They arrived in a very narrow alley, dimly lit by the glow from streetlights at each end of the affair. The alley was strewn with stage paraphernalia, wooden crates, and torn posters of previous shows at the Opera House. Rats scrambled about the boxes.

The alley was too narrow for a carriage, but Ben caught sight of a landau parked at the end on the street, the horses pawing the pavement. Ben figured that the carriage was for the sisters.

"We'll wait."

"What are you going to do, Ben?"

"Some Texas-sized negotiating." He grinned. "I've got a trick I learned from my brother, Asa."

Like he had guessed, twenty minutes later, the Fox sisters exited, accompanied by two bulky guards, each wearing a stovepipe hat. Leah carried a bag of money. The guards immediately strode forward as if to push Ben aside, but he pulled out a revolver that he had kept secured in the back of his belt and hidden under his dress jacket.

"Gentlemen," Ben said, "why don't you take a walk to the end of the alley. You can come back in a short while."

Both men held up their hands and walked cautiously to the end of the alley and stood under the streetlamp.

Ben winked at Cyntha. She whispered to him. "Ben, what are you doing? There are police everywhere. They'll arrest you."

"Naw, they won't. Watch." He pointed the gun lackadaisically at the sisters.

"Surely, you don't mean to rob us?" Leah clutched the money bag to her breast.

"Nope."

"Please don't harm us," Leah stated, pulled her shawl tight about her shoulders. The younger sisters shrank behind her.

"No, ma'am, I have no such intention of robbing you or harming you. That is, unless you harm this woman here." He gestured toward Cyntha.

"We would never harm another human being," Leah protested, joined by Maggie and Kate, nodding agreement.

"Well, that's what I wanted to hear. You see, if you don't have a séance for my dear wife," he nudged Cyntha, hoping to keep her from protesting, "then y'all will be causin' harm that ain't even been heard of. Ya see, she's been searchin' for you ladies for most of a year, been through battle, had all her life's savings stolen, been taken advantage of, and all she wants to do is put the soul of her dead husband to rest. Now, that ain't hard, is it?"

"You want a private séance?" Leah gave a smug expression. "That's out of the question."

"Why?"

"Because it's not easy to summon the dead, especially the right ones."

"Does it cost money?"

"Well, of course." Leah stepped forward, the revolver near her stomach.

"How much?"

Leah eyed Ben and Cyntha thoughtfully, then arrogantly, now that she knew what he wanted.

"More than you can afford." She turned her back on him.

The guards made a move of a few feet toward the arguing group. Ben twirled, fired a shot that blew the hat off one of them. They stopped short and retreated. Ben walked closer to Leah. "How much?"

She turned toward him. Continuing her smug countenance, she announced, "Fifty dollars."

"I'll give ya one hundred." Ben pulled Cyntha around the waist close to him and squeezed hard.

"One hundred! Where would you have that kind of money? You talk like a country rube."

"Don't you worry. I've got the money. And I know you've lost some money lately. I talked to the policeman who you reported it to. Now, where do we meet?" Ben shoved the revolver into Leah's ribs.

"You know about our stolen money?" Leah's smug look fell. She was beaten.

"Where for the séance?"

"At the Cincinnatian Hotel, tomorrow afternoon, three o'clock."

"We'll see y'all then." He lowered his revolver. "And if y'all want to see the whole hundred, I wouldn't be involvin' no lawmen." He tipped his hat, and walked as steady as he could on his bad leg to appear as strong as possible, Cyntha close to his side. He waved at the guards who hurried back to the Fox sisters. They made no effort to follow Ben and Cyntha.

When they had walked the few blocks back to their own hotel, Cyntha stopped Ben in the lobby. "I appreciate you trying to get a séance for me, but, Ben, how will you pay them one hundred dollars? I only have about twenty dollars to my name. And ... why would you do something so foolish?"

"I would do a hundred foolish things for you."

Cyntha gasped, then her face flushed. In the past weeks, Ben had sloughed off much of his rough demeanor in their journey from Elkhorn Tavern. He had taken care of the horses, cooked the meals, cared for Abram while he was alive; then, when they arrived in St. Louis, he sold the horses and wagons to pay for their travel on the steamboat. He doted on her, helping her with every matter that had come up.

Cyntha opened her mouth to admonish him, but stopped, unable to find words.

Ben leaned close to Cyntha to whisper. "I met an old acquaintance when I went for that walk last night."

"Oh?"

"He was an escaped slave that my brothers and I helped when we drove our herd to Fort Smith. Well, actually, I didn't help him at all, but my mind has changed toward the Coloreds. The shade of skin doesn't make the quality of a man. I learned that from Reynolds. So, I happened to run into John Coincoin. That's his name. We get to talkin' old times, and it comes up about the Fox sisters, and he tells me he done stole some of their money, actually, a lot of their money. He's done paid for his wife and children to come to live with him in Cincinnati. He told me he was worried about carryin' so much money, that it didn't look right for a black man to have even a little wealth. So, he just up and gave me four hundred dollars in gold coin and bills. Wouldn't take no for an answer." Ben jingled the coins in his pants pocket. "That's only some of it. The rest is hid. I figure some of it is for your séance, the rest to help us set up a business."

Cyntha smiled, admiring this man, whom she found so problematic, and, yet, she so much desired him. "But you were still foolish. Firing your gun at those men. And scaring the sisters."

"If I'd meant to shoot one of those brick-heads, I wouldn't a'missed. And I don't think much of anything ever scares that Leah Fox. If them sisters can speak to the dead, let's get this done. And for that extra fifty, they're gonna talk to my dead brothers for me."

Cyntha stepped closer to Ben. "You said we could set up a business. Like a mercantile?"

"Yeah, I figure we could start us a general store here about." He turned to point out the window.

When he turned back, Cyntha had put her arms around his waist and gazed up into his eyes. He took her in his strong arms, and they kissed for a long time. Each kiss more deep, more passionate. Their tongues briskly racing around each other's lips, until each tongue touched in joint delight. Both their hearts raced, both feeling the relief of so many trials, so many losses, but all of that behind them.

When they at last released their embrace, Ben said, "If after the séance, you are able to release Joseph to go to Heaven, then I figure we might take a little of the remaining money and pay for a marriage certificate. It might be another foolish thing, but I want to spend the rest of my life with you."

Cyntha hugged him, tears of joy flowing down her cheeks. She thought of her lost husband, *Oh, Joseph, I do so want you to be released, but I also want to move on with my life.*

The next day was the séance, three o'clock.

SIXTY-FIVE

THE THIRST THAT FROM MY SOUL DOTH RISE

– BEN JOHNSON

APRIL 6, 1862, EVENING
CORINTH, MISSISSIPPI

When the wounded men began arriving in wagons, or on mule or horseback, or almost running despite their wounds, Sara was prepared. She made many encouraging comments to the handful of women who were new to the exacting toil of caring for the piteous soldiers. In the space of a half hour, she watched three men die under the surgeon's knife. Another soldier, not older than sixteen, clung to a fragment of a Union stars and bars flag that he had wrested from a Yankee like it was his magic talisman needed to survive. She knew the wretched black and burgundy hole in his stomach would lead to his death. She came back an hour later and wondered how he still lived. One of the young women, her dress spoiled in blood, sat stroking his forehead and hair. She sang a tune softly to him, and Sara heard the words. She thought it an odd tune to be singing to him—"Oh, Sinner Man."

One tune at this time of your life is as good as another, I reckon.

When soldiers were lighting lanterns strung on ropes throughout the city, Sara stepped outside for some fresh air. The men's wounds had not yet festered to a stench. There had not been enough time, but the salty iron pong of the blood irritated her. She longed to smell honeysuckle, like at her old home in Wilson Creek Valley.

While she stood on the porch of the hotel, watching the steady stream of wounded being carted into the camp, she thought of Paul, and her emotions churned. Her soul was thirsty to know him. How had she been so callous to him when he had always been so gallant? She vowed to show him more consideration after the Confederates won this battle.

She leaned against a support post of the porch. The wailing inside the hotel seemed to fade, and she watched the last of the stars swept away by the racing storm. *Who are you, Paul? Why do you suddenly have a hold on me? I was betrothed to Joseph.*

She shook her head. *I was never, ever, ever betrothed to Joseph. He had someone else he loved. I spent these last months foolin' myself. I ain't no future bride of Joseph Favor. Now Paul is another story. I can tell he fancies me, but doesn't know how to tell me. Perhaps I fancy him, too. Perhaps more than fancy him.*

The doctor came out on the porch and called her for assistance. "You're the only one that knows a decent stitch. Get your dainty little paws in here and help me save this boy!"

SIXTY-SIX

THE SÉANCE

At three o'clock, Cyntha and Ben sat in the Fox sisters' dark hotel room, the heavy curtains drawn. Leah Fox, the only sister in the outer room, had lit a minimum number of candles in strategic points. Ben noticed that the rug that should have laid on the wood plank floor had been rolled up against a settee. Their packed bags and trunks sat near the door.

"Maggie and Kate will join us soon," Leah announced. "Having had so many seances lately has left them exhausted." She held her lips tight.

The clock ticked. Leah stood stock still. Ben fidgeted in his chair. His ankle hurt more when all he could do was think about it.

Cyntha had trouble breathing. Her heart would not calm despite her efforts to command it to do so. Her hope of finally being able to set Joseph's soul to rest in the bosom of Abraham, to be one with God in Heaven, was possible within the next hour.

When Maggie and Kate entered the room barefoot, in simple long, white gowns that stretched to the floor, their faces were expressionless. They stared straight ahead and seemed to be gazing into the netherworld. Neither looked at Cyntha or Ben, nor acknowledged their greetings.

"My sisters have been preparing for this séance as they always do, and it takes a toll on their bodies and minds. So, I hope that you will be courteous of them and their discourse with the spirit world. Now, I believe there is the formality of the fee. We expect payment in advance."

"Not this time." Ben dropped a bag on the table, the gold coins spilling a little from the opening. Cyntha noticed that neither Kate nor Maggie flinched when the coin bag plunked against the wooden table.

"There's your fee and more." Ben was cross. "But you get it when your sisters reach the dead. I ain't satisfied until I'm satisfied." He folded his arms.

Cyntha placed her hand on Ben's shoulder. She whispered, "Dear Ben, let them do their work. We needn't worry. We've seen their methods were successful in the grand séance at the opera house. It is time now. Then we may begin our lives anew."

Ben unfolded his arms and gave her a glowing smile.

"Let us begin," Leah said. She placed a single candle in a cup at the center of the table, then set about blowing out all other candles in the room, plunging it into gloom. Cyntha could hear the passage of horses and carriages outside the hotel. A fly buzzed somewhere in the room.

"Join hands," Leah whispered. "Close your eyes and concentrate on your loved ones you wish to contact."

Ben took Kate's hand, then he took Cyntha's and squeezed it several times. Cyntha took Maggie's hand, and Maggie held Kate's. Leah sequestered herself into a dark corner.

In a moment, almost in unison, Kate and Maggie began low moans. After they had done so, Ben said, "I want to see if my brothers Asa is in Heaven and if Paul is still alive."

"So that we may find their souls," Kate said in a monotone. "What is their last name?"

"McGavin."

"How did Asa die?" Kate asked, almost imperceptibly.

"Went down in quicksand." Ben wanted to ask why they did not know that detail.

"Yes, yes. I believe I have contacted him." Maggie spoke.

"Where is he, sister?" Kate said.

"There by the big tree of life." Maggie swayed, limber as a spindly sapling.

"Yes, I see him now. And do you see the quicksand on his clothes?"

"Yes, sister."

"There is a glow about him."

"Asa, can you speak to us? Tap on the wall. Once for yes, two taps for no."

Immediately, a loud crack against wood bounced off the walls.

Kate began mumbling, then her voice grew louder in a deep tenor tone, "What is your want, little brother?"

"I want to know if you made it to Heaven?" Ben asked.

"Yes, I am in the eternal bliss now." Kate growled, "I want you to know I'm sorry for anything I ever said to you that was mean or cruel."

"Asa." Kate sucked in her breath several times. "Don't leave us."

Now, Maggie moaned. "Asa, tap once if you forgive him. Twice for no."

A second loud crack.

"Must you go so soon, Asa?" Maggie asked the air.

Crack.

"What shall I tell your little brother?" Kate paused, tilting her head as if she was listening. She guessed correctly that Ben had opened his eyes and was watching. "I will, Asa."

Kate snapped her eyes open. "Asa is gone. He had an urgent task with the angels to stop some Indians raiding a farm. But he said he will always be looking out for you, Ben."

When Ben began asking questions about Paul, Maggie took up the contrived conversation. She asked many questions, and Ben explained the shootout at Elkhorn Tavern.

Ben, frustrated, blurted out, "Look! I just want to know if he's dead and where I can find him if he's not." He opened his eyes in his fury.

"Close your eyes," Leah called from the dark.

Ben reluctantly shut his eyes.

Maggie began mumbling. "Speak, oh, Spirits. Tell us about Paul McGavin." She made a gurgling sound, followed by a high wail.

"What's she doin'?" Ben complained.

"The spirits are searching for your brother," Leah, invisible to those at the table, explained.

Of a sudden, Maggie stood, and flung down Kate's and Cyntha's hands. "He's not dead. Paul is alive." Then she sat and began mumbling.

"What? What?" Ben was halfway out of his seat.

"Sit, young man," Leah commanded.

Maggie ceased her mumbles. "Open your eyes, everyone."

They all stared at her. "Paul is not dead. I've been assured of that. But he thinks you dead, Ben. But do not search for him now. You have a greater task." She turned toward Cyntha, took Cyntha's hand and placed it in Ben's. "You needn't worry about your brother. You have plenty of life left to find him at a later time."

Ben's mouth was wide open. He turned to Cyntha. "I just got good news, Cyntha. Very good."

"Yes." Cyntha smiled at him. She knew in her heart she wanted Ben in her bed, to have his hands on her body, but she had a more urgent task ahead of her. She must help Joseph be freed from his sojourn in a lost horizon.

SIXTY-SEVEN

ONLY THE DEAD HAVE SEEN THE END OF WAR

– PLATO

APRIL 7, 1862, JUST BEFORE DAWN
WASHINGTON, DC

Lucas Reeder had slept only in spurts, twisting and turning in dreadful nightmares. He awoke in the dark, lit a candle in the dismally cold room and looked at the clock. A little after five in the morning. *Today is the day I will save the Union.* Late into the night before, Workman and he had hatched the stratagem to kill President Lincoln when he returned home to the President's Mansion from the War Department. Killing the president in his own home would be more dramatic, and Lucas had reached the point in his frustration with the progression of the war and the deaths of so many good men that their new course of action was precisely what he deemed best.

They would follow President Lincoln inside the Executive Mansion grounds and look for the opportunity to dispatch the *ogre* of the nation. For their escape, Workman had found a new hole in the compound's fence behind the stables. He would secure two fast horses, and hire a boy to hold them, ready to ride. *Shoot the demon man, escape through the hole in the fence, and ride away.* Lucas was determined. He lay back on his bed and tried to settle his racing heart. He listened to Workman snoring, seemingly unperturbed by their impending peril.

∞

Before the sun's early beams sliced the air, Joseph lay in his bed, feeling as low as he ever had. He had fought for the very army that stood against his ideals. His current appointment to eavesdrop on Presidential Palace visitors seemed to him as inconsequential and petty as any task he could imagine. He was thrust into the background of the war, play-acting as a spy, sure that nothing he did mattered. He was resolute to perform his task well, but it was only a perfunctory routine. There was no honor in his duty. *At least, let me fight. If I can't see my wife, let me die in battle with honor.*

He rose, dressed and trod with heavy steps down from his room above the stables. The grooms were already tending the horses. When they paid him no heed, he trudged, head down, like a forgotten soul, to the Mansion front doors. The odor of pork frying wafted out the kitchen windows on a stiff breeze. With his new duty, he could eat his fill of the fare offered him by the kitchen staff. He was not hungry today.

When he was about to place his hand on the brass knob, President Lincoln burst out the door, his face intent, a crumpled telegram in one hand, his other hand brandishing a large cane that looked akin to a shillelagh. He watched the president rush down the walkway and out to the street, headed to the War Department. *Something is awry.* He raised his eyebrows.

In the handful of days at his new duty of eavesdropping at the president's house from dawn until the Lincolns had retired to bed, Joseph had settled into the mundane task, monitoring the staff, the hired workers, and even Mrs. Lincoln.

Spending most of his time inside the house worked best for listening for any suspicious comment. He bantered with the kitchen staff and house servants and stood nonchalantly outside a few closed-door meetings of Mrs. Lincoln and her male cohorts.

He had made quick friends with the young Lincoln boys who, when he was sure no officer could see him, often engaged him in a game of tag.

More often, he listened to the various guards thumping their chests about their heroic exploits, or others' complaints about inaction. He could not share his occasions of battle or about spying for the Confederates. He could only hope to do something heroic. *I would give my life for the Union.* He could never bring himself to say that out loud.

He had a few opportunities to catch the prattling of Mary Todd Lincoln, though he made no attempt to talk with her. The temperament of the president's wife and her natters with the maids and butlers and occasional government officials indicated she had little, if any, interest in the war effort. He immediately noticed that Mrs. Lincoln was totally enthralled by any man who beamed at her and complimented her with the most bald-faced flummery. The more avid a male sycophant's preposterous approbation, the more she glowed.

She held meetings with a set of *tawdry-seeming* gentlemen. No ladies were allowed in her closed doors meetings with these less-than-noble visitors. He had gathered the names of the men who traipsed into the Mansion's dining room for her gatherings, and he had reported as much to Detective Pinkerton. At the end of each day, Joseph handed his notes to a courier who took them to the detective's office.

On this bright, blue, spring morning, cherry tree petals floated about the yard. Joseph decided to spend time outside. He skipped breakfast, choosing to meander around the compound, paying considerable attention to the talk of the soldier guards about recent reports of Grant's army out west being trounced badly by the Rebels. Their discussions ranged from worry to anger. He then knew the reason for President Lincoln's earlier haste.

Joseph made his way back to the stables, talked at length with the grooms and spent time viewing the horses.

Absent from the stables was Dred Workman. Though Sergeant Stimmel made no mention of his absence, Joseph, since his arrival, had never seen him there. Both men were oblivious of the other's presence at the compound.

He took a break at midmorning, went to his quarters above the stables and wrote a letter to Cyntha and gave the letter to the postal courier. At noon, he went inside the mansion and settled into gazing at the many paintings throughout the nation's main abode.

What a lonely post I have. If only I had my wife, with me. My true love. Don't forget me, Cyntha.

SIXTY-EIGHT

DEATH'S KNELL
TOLLED LOUD

APRIL 7, 1862, 4:00 P.M.
WASHINGTON, DC

At three o'clock, President Lincoln abruptly left the War Department telegraph room. "I've seen enough for today," he said to the operators. "Pray that our men may be victorious somewhere." He stormed out and down the stairs, clacking his large cane on the marble stairs.

Lucas had not shown up at the telegraph office. He had waited the whole day alongside Workman in the park across from the War Department. When President Lincoln came down the steps, Workman and he followed at a careful distance. Lucas held his ear trumpet in one hand, a leather valise in the other. When they arrived at the President's Mansion gate, Workman was as cheerful as always with the guards. He explained that "his friend" was largely deaf, and carried important papers from the War Department. The guards still indicated by hand motion that Lucas was to show he had no weapon. Lucas undid the buttons of his jacket and turned around. He lifted his pants legs to show no weapon in his shoes. The sergeant waved him inside.

While President Lincoln chatted with some congressmen on the Presidential Mansion front steps, the pair of assassins made their way to the east side of the mansion. The stables stood several yards to their left. They stopped beside a spreading elm with a wide trunk. Workman strolled over to the stables and talked a while with the grooms. All laughed at Workman's ribald jokes. Lucas heard nothing of the remarks, but figured that Workman had put those men at ease. He watched Workman amble out in front of the mansion to a stack of arms and lightly lift one of the rifles.

He strolled back to Lucas with the gun held in front of him, out of sight of the front gates guards. Using the ramrod, he dropped it down the barrel to check that the gun held a load. It did. He placed a firing cap on the nipple and lowered the hammer. The gun was ready. Lucas opened his valise and found the revolver buried under papers, and checked again that it was loaded. Now they only had to wait.

Joseph was standing at the top of the main stairs, gazing at a painting when President Lincoln entered through the front door. His boys, who seemed to appear out of nowhere, gathered around him, hugging him and chattering about their day.

"Mother!" Lincoln called.

Mary Lincoln came from a room not far from where Joseph stood. She held a needlepoint piece in her hands. "What is it, Father?" she called down to her husband.

"I am going for a ride to think. I shall return within the hour."

"That is fine, my dearest."

"What's for supper?" The boys had vanished down the hall, cavorting with make-believe wooden swords, dodging in and out of the servants who had come forward to greet the president, but primarily to nod at him and smile.

"The cook is preparing some venison."

"That's good."

Joseph watched through the wide-open door. Mary Lincoln returned to the room where other women in her cohort giggled and threw smiles at her. "That husband of yours," Joseph heard one of the women say, "he's so unsophisticated. He thinks he has to ride a horse in order to think." All the women sniggered. Then Mary Lincoln closed the doors.

Joseph decided to follow the president. He had not had a chance to actually speak with the man and hoped he would be able to do so. It would be a good story to share with Cyntha. No sooner had President Lincoln started out the east door than Ward Hill Lamon, heavily armed and carrying his banjo, joined him. Joseph hurried after the men.

When they exited, the door slammed in Joseph's face, and he almost turned around. He decided to forge forward and, at least, introduce himself to the president. Stopping just outside the door beside a tall, dense, green shrub, he thought about which words to choose when speaking to the leader of the nation, strongly considering saying something about the plight of the Negroes. While he watched the president and Lamon come to a stop while the president searched for a stick to whittle, he decided on the content of his conversation. He would espouse about slavery.

President Lincoln bent over and picked up a sturdy twig, then took out his pocket knife, and commenced to whittle. Lamon and he stood chatting some thirty yards beyond where Joseph watched.

Just as Joseph started out from behind the shrub into the open, he collided with Dred Workman who was striding forward with Lucas by his side. Both men stumbled but regained their stances. At first, each man glared at the other.

Then Joseph recognized his old acquaintances. "Lucas!" he exclaimed. "Dred!"

Both men turned toward him. Lucas' face first showed joy at seeing Joseph, then sank into disdain when he saw him dressed in the Union uniform. "Shame on you, Joseph," Lucas blurted.

Joseph was taken aback, but frowned seeing that both men were armed, guns pointed forward. "Dred, what are you trying to do?" His mind raced for the meaning of what these friends looked like they were prepared to do. "And you're in a Union uniform. What's going on?"

Workman swung his rifle around to point at Joseph's ribs. "Stay back, old friend."

"Why are *you* in a Yank uniform?" Lucas asked Joseph, his eyes darting to the president and back at Joseph. "Surely, you're not a traitor." Lucas held his trumpet to his ear.

Joseph was quick to respond. "Because I've always been Union. Workman misled me and everyone else into thinking I fought for the South. I detest my involvement with them. In fact, I detest this whole war!"

"Keep your voice down," Workman ordered. "We've got work to do!"

"What work do you have to do?"

"Don't you see?" Lucas barked. "You hate the war. So do Dred and I. We're here to put a stop to it. Eliminating Lincoln is the best way to stop the war." His face contorted, and he dropped the ear trumpet that clattered on the stone pavers. He clutched his chest with one hand, his other hand tight on the revolver. With marked steps, he strode toward President Lincoln, who was now heading to the stables. Lamon, unaware of the commotion of the three men, still stood where the president and he had been conversing. He was tuning a string on his banjo.

Lucas hastened his step to a jog. Workman pushed his rifle barrel harder into Joseph's side. "Lucas has the pleasure of killin' that no-good president. And I intend to dispatch his bodyguard." He raised his rifle away from Joseph to aim at Lamon.

"No! Stop!" Joseph raced after Lucas. The stable grooms, aroused by the shouting, rose from the hay bales and stools. President Lincoln turned toward Joseph's call. Workman rolled his aim toward the running target—Joseph.

Twenty paces from President Lincoln, and facing him, Lucas raised his revolver. "Be gone, demon!"

With speed born of months of training, Joseph pulled his revolver from its holster and shot Lucas exactly where he aimed—in the back—the bullet spinning out near his heart. Lucas slumped to the ground, first to his knees, then prone, as if he had grown weary of a useless toil. When Joseph knelt beside his old friend's body, Lucas looked briefly at him and choked one final word, "Why?" and his soul fled.

Workman fired.

The bullet pierced Joseph through the arm, then entered his chest, and lodged there. He pitched forward, falling lengthwise beside Lucas's body, gasping for breath, blood seeping out his throat over his lips.

Lamon was immediately on Workman, both grappling and slugging like angry bears. Lamon landed a blow to Workman's chin, and the tall traitor tumbled to the ground. In no time, Lamon was securing him in a firm grip, turning him over, and forcing him face-down onto the ground. He planted his boot on Workman's buttocks and pointed two revolvers at him. Guards who had heard the shots arrived in seconds.

The guards took ahold of Workman, raised him up and shoved him against a tree, rifles at his throat.

"Look," Workman complained. "I had to stop them from killin' our president." He kept espousing his fabricated entreaties while Lamon joined President Lincoln, who already knelt beside Joseph.

The blond soldier who had started out a Yankee, then became a Rebel, and finally a Yankee spy, was panting and choking up blood. His fiery blue eyes shone, but were growing dim. "Sir, I…"

"No need to talk, son." President Lincoln looked deep into Joseph's eyes. Across the widening pupils, he saw the reflection of the brightest azure sky with long, white clouds drifting. "You saved my life. I am grateful beyond measure. Now, you lie easy."

Lamon called for the house doctor, and a corporal ran in search. Mary Lincoln and her ladies appeared at the east door, all a flutter. Seeing her husband, Mrs. Lincoln ran to him, and flung herself about his neck.

"President Lincoln." Joseph strained to get the words out.

"Yes, friend, whom I do not know well yet, but I intend to. What can I do for you?"

"Sir, please..." he gasped, his lungs flooding. "Set the Negroes free."

"I intend to, friend. I just have to figure out the best way."

Joseph did not hear the president's answer. His breath and heart had stopped. Lamon reluctantly set his fingers on Joseph's eyelids and closed them.

Workman was hauled away while he continued his admonitions that he was the innocent one trying to save the president. Lamon had him locked up.

Lamon threatened everyone in the compound, including the president's wife, not to ever speak a word of the event.

SIXTY-NINE

A New Beginning

APRIL 7, 1862, LATE AFTERNOON
CINCINNATI, OHIO

A t 4:45, according to the clock on the mantel, though the windows and drapes hid the sunlight, a light breeze brushed through Cyntha's hair. She placed her hand where the breeze had tossed her tresses, smoothing them. Listening to the Fox sisters thump the floor with their toe knuckles cracking, and then their chanting, followed by their comments about searching the spirit havens for Joseph, she almost felt she had gone elsewhere, leaving the world below. She closed her eyes, feeling as if she was drifting, and, after so many months, finding peace in a warm glade by a pleasant, clear stream.

"Yes," Kate said, "your husband has been lost. He needs your assurance in order to proceed to Heaven. Speak to him, Cyntha."

"Dear Joseph," Cyntha, her eyes remaining shut, barely whispered. "I love you and I miss you, but we both must move on. Go forward, dear, to Heaven."

The room was quiet, save the ticking of the clock. Occasional noises in the street.

Maggie suddenly leapt from her chair, trembling and wailing, "Oh my! Oh, my Lord. Dear me! Oh, Oh!" Leah moved quickly by her side, then struck a match and lit a nearby lamp. Maggie continued to shriek and babble. Leah rushed to the windows and flung open the drapes, bright daylight flooding into the room. Kate, her eyes wide, went to her sister.

Leah returned to Maggie, whose body was shuddering next to Kate. Maggie bawled into her hands.

"What is it, sister?" Leah asked. "Are you hurt?"

"I might as well be," Maggie lamented. "I *saw* him. I *actually saw* him."

"Who?" Leah demanded, her tone indicating she was trying to minimize this unexpected disturbance and departure from their protocol.

"I saw her husband, Joseph. I am certain." Maggie walked unsteadily to Cyntha's side and stooped beside her. "Cyntha, I've never had this happen before. We could not find your husband in the abode of the dead, because he had not yet died. He had been knocked out in a battle and lost his memory. And I don't know why I know this, but somehow I know."

"What?" Cyntha could barely contain herself. "Is he..."

"But he has just now died, moments ago." Maggie allowed these last words to sink in to Cyntha's understanding. "I am as sure of it as I am here kneeling beside you. He is definitely dead, but he did something brave, denying his own safety. He spoke to me as he departed that he wants you to know he always loved you, and he is happy now in Heaven."

"This is all horseshit." Ben rose from the table. "We already know he was dead. The colonel wrote her and told her. This is just some fancy idea of yours to get more money. For that, you get nothing." He grabbed the bag of coins, took Cyntha by the arm and led her to the door.

Cyntha, too, doubted the extravagant display Maggie had performed. She could not help but feel that the entire séance was contrived just for the money. *My husband suddenly dying while I am seeking his soul. What a sham! They are a family of shysters.*

Maggie called after them. "Joseph said you should marry this man who loves you so. I'm very happy for you both."

Ben tossed two ten-dollar gold coins on the table, and Cyntha and he departed and made their way downstairs into the hotel lobby.

Leah went up to Maggie and pinched her arm hard. Maggie ignored the pain, and barely flinched when Leah slapped her face.

"How dare you ruin our chance to make a hundred dollars," Leah complained.

"Isn't it all just an act, anyway? I thought if I played that right, we'd get more money. It's all just an act." Maggie walked into the bedroom and closed the door. "I need whisky."

In the lobby, before strolling into the sunny afternoon, Cyntha turned to Ben and put her hands lightly on his strong chest. "Dear Ben, I've known for a long time that my husband is gone, and that I have to move on. You have helped me to see that there is a bright future beyond the life and love that Joseph and I had."

She tilted her head, closed her eyes and drew close to the wild, but tamer than he used to be, Texan. He took her in his arms and kissed her passionately. She did not hold back, but allowed herself to be enveloped in his love, and kissed him ardently.

When they paused their kisses, they continued to embrace, gazing into each other's eyes.

Ben smiled. "Come on, our new carriage and team is waitin' at the livery. Let's go wherever you wanna go and start that business."

The day was unclouded and sundrenched, with a delicate breeze. The walk to livery was not far.

Cyntha could not stop smiling. *I am finally free. Joseph's soul is at peace. I'm in harmony with life again.* She tore off her mourning hat and tossed it to the street. "I am finally reconciled."

SEVENTY

TO BRING SUFFERING
AND CHARITY
INTO CONSONANCE

APRIL 7, 1862, LATE AFTERNOON
CORINTH, MISSISSIPPI

Sara walked out of the Tishomingo Hotel with a bucket of water in one hand, a corncob-stoppered bottle of turpentine spirits, a syringe and scissors in her bloodied apron, and a long roll of bandage under her arm. She was determined to go to every wounded soldier who lay in the muddy streets, offer them water, squirt a syringe of the turpentine spirits in their wounds and rebind them, and offer support. Her short blond hair was matted with sweat, and the cold April wind made her shiver. It was her third trip out into the rows and rows of wounded men, sprawled on house lawns and every avenue. Hundreds of soldiers were twisting in pain and moaning, for the surgeons could not get to the sheer number of wounded and dying men in a timely fashion. Other soldiers lay, contorted in death's throes. But most endured various treatable injuries and were dealing stolidly with their pain. Sara found herself dodging the many civilians and dozens of unharmed soldiers who were rushing on singular errands of mercy.

Even as she offered support and a drink of water to the men who sat or lay in the streets, wagons brought more wounded. Negroes bore the task of unloading each casualty as cautiously as possible. Sara noticed the thoughtful care the Negroes showed each man. The drivers then turned their wagons to return to the battlefield.

Whole regiments of Confederates arrived in a steady stream. They were not wounded, but were retreating in an orderly fashion. Though exhaustion showed in their entire being, their spirits were undaunted. They joked, swore and bragged. They laughed and crowed about the great prowess of comrades in battle. Numerous ones were so tired, they plopped down wherever they found a stretch of grass in the house yards.

Nearing the railroad station, Sara came upon a wagon bed with its wheels removed to replace broken wheels of other wagons. Three men lay inside the wagon bed asleep. Then she saw the man she had longed so much to see. Leaning against the sidewall of the wagon on a patch of grass was Paul McGavin.

"Oh, Paul." She ran to him, almost spilling the water bucket. "You're not supposed to be hurt." She kneeled beside him and brushed back his black locks from his tired eyes.

He brightened when he saw Sara. "Well, I've been hurt a few times before." He snickered at his own comment.

"Let me see to your wound."

She deftly removed the wrappings from his arm. "Your wound is green."

"Yes, I'm not sure why. But when I was brought in here last night..."

"You've been here since last night? And no one has seen to you?"

"No, but that's all right. The wound's not that bad, Sara. When I arrived in the early morning, I saw a number of men had green wounds, and the wounds glow in the dark."

Sara gave him an incredulous look. "Here, let me pour some turpentine on it."

"I'd prefer you not. I know that you, being a good Christian woman, believe in miracles. Well, here's one before you. It seems to be healing on its own. I've checked it to see if any pieces of the bullet were left in it. There's not. But I would like some water."

Sara ladled the water, and he gulped it.

"I heard some men saying we won the battle, some saying we lost," Paul said. "Do you know?"

"I can't say. Someone will write a history about it sometime. Let them decide. What's most important is that you're alive and that I'm here to help you."

"I'm very glad you're here, too."

"I heard they're gonna start shippin' the wounded to Mobile and other towns south beginnin' in the mornin'."

Sara looked at his right leg for the first time, the pants leg torn open. Paul's knee was swollen and reddened. She gasped. "Oh, Paul. I'm so sorry."

"Don't worry. It's swole up before. An old bronc-busting injury. It will subside." He paused and reached his palm to her cheek, touching it lightly. "You can do me a favor."

Sara closed her eyes and let her cheek rest in his hand. "Anything."

"Come with me on the train to Mobile."

Sara did not have to reflect even a moment. She opened her eyes. "I will."

Paul gazed into the most beautiful face he had ever known. She looked back at him, deep into his eyes, and became lost in them. She held her hand to his stubbly-bearded cheek.

After a long moment, Paul said, "You have beautiful freckles, Sara Reeder."

Sara said nothing, but laid her head against his chest. "I will be with you on the train. I can think of nothing better. And we'll get your leg and arm better."

"I'm sure you will. No one could be a better nurse, or maybe a surgeon someday."

Sara giggled. "There's a wild thought. A woman surgeon. I think I could be if they'd let me."

"We'll see. You know, the reason I want you to come with me isn't so much that you're a great nurse, but that... I love you."

"I know. I think I've known a long time, but was mystified by my own folly. I'm fairly fond of you, too." She snuggled closer to him. *God has amazing plans, far better than mine. He has given me this man who loves me.*

Father Antonio and Reverend Felder ambled up to them.

"Hello, Sara," Father Antonio said. "This must be Paul."

"It is," Sara said, rising to greet them.

Though Paul remained seated, the men shook hands and exchanged pleasantries.

"Sara, we can't talk long," Reverend Felder said, "We're needed back at the church. We've opened it up as a hospital. But Antonio and I," he patted Father Antonio on the shoulder, "had a deep theological discussion about the question you asked him yesterday."

"Yes," Father Antonio said. "You asked if your presence was somehow bringing war to wherever you went. On the contrary, your very presence has brought comfort y paz, peace, to so many. Constance told us of your sacrifice at Wilson Creek and at Elkhorn, and here, caring for the wounded, even saving lives. Based on our study of scripture..."

"We have determined," Reverend Felder added, "that beyond a shadow of a doubt, your presence, like many other good people that sacrifice for others in times of great evil, is perhaps helping reconcile the guilt of this land. We are in consonance on this. Total agreement."

Sara and Paul both gaped.

"At any rate, niñita," Father Antonio said. "We really don't know the mind of Los Dios—God. But keep doing the good you are doing. Muchos milagros. Many miracles."

"Father and Reverend Felder," Sara said, "I'll be going to Mobile on a train. I need someone to watch my horse, Esther."

"Si, el caballo." Father Antonio stroked his black beard. "I was planning to go to Mobile later. Let me watch your horse, and I will ride it in a day or so to Mobile. I hear it is a ciudad bonita, a pretty town with many pretty churches."

"Can you ride, Father?" Sara asked.

"Si, mi amiga. I have ridden since I was child. I will take care of your horse. I will bring Esther to Mobile for you."

"Thank you, Father. Muchas gracias." Sara hugged the priest.

"Si, mi amiga. Sara, take care of Paul. Buena suerte. Good luck."

"I'll be taking Constance to Mobile, too," Reverend Felder said. "This war is no place for a woman with child." He pulled on Father Antonio's sleeve. "Come, my friend. My wife needs our help in the church. Let's see how many we can save—body and soul."

The two servants of God departed, talking together like they had known each other their entire lives.

∞

By evening the next day, all the talk among soldiers and civilians alike in Corinth was of how General Forrest, in a rearguard action in a portion of the forest with fallen timbers, had charged a regiment of Federal soldiers far ahead of his own regiment. Firing his pistols and swinging his saber, he charged into the midst of forty Yankees. One of their number shot him pointblank in the ribs. But rather than falling from his horse or surrendering, he jerked that Union soldier up behind him onto his horse to keep from being shot again when he turned his mount and rode away. He escaped and still lived.

The story of his wild ride was a morale booster for the defeated army. Sara felt that she must have heard the story thirty times while caring for the wounded on the streets of Corinth.

Paul, still lying by the wagon, enjoyed watching General Beauregard, standing not ten feet from him, giving orders almost non-stop. The general was already commanding the Confederates to bolster the defenses surrounding Corinth. *We may have lost that battle, but we ain't licked yet.* Paul slept most of the day, and his wound was healing.

That night, Edward, Constance and Sara rode as nurses in the boxcar with Paul and two dozen other wounded men on a train, slowly winding its way to hospitals in Mobile. With the side door shoved open, a warm wind ebbed and flowed through the boxcar. Constance sat, leaning against Edward's chest, their legs stretched out toward the door. Edward held his hands on his wife's stomach, smiling about the new life she bore. They watched the moon and the stars in the deep cobalt sky and the soft gray landscape sliding by like mercury.

With the gentle rocking of the boxcar, the train chugging along, Paul slept, his head on a pillow on Sara's lap while she softly hummed "Dixie."

REAL HISTORICAL PERSONS
IN *RECONCILED*

Part of my decision to write *Reconciled* was to build in as much REAL history, not politically correct history, and show people on both sides of the conflict in as accurate a fashion as research would provide. Aside from obvious persons like President Lincoln, here are other real individuals serving in their actual capacities.

- **Colonel Elkanah Greer:** First colonel of the Third Texas Cavalry. Full of energy and admiration for the South.
- **General Earl Van Dorn:** Appointed by Jefferson Davis to bring the divided factions of the Missouri army together. Arrogant, cocky, and overly prided himself on being a lady's man.
- **The Fox Sisters (Leah, Kate, and Maggie):** Spiritualists who made a fortune off of fooling bereaved persons that they could speak to the dead through séances. They were some of the most famous, though they never held a séance for Mary Todd Lincoln.
- **General Ulysses S. Grant (who's real name is Hiram Ulysses Grant):** Grant was against slavery, but unwilling to push for emancipation since his wife's family owned a number of slaves.
- **General Albert Sydney Johnston:** Commander of the Army of Mississippi, the army of Southerners gathered at Corinth. Many of the comments made by him in the book are his actual recorded comments. His actions before and

during the battle and his death happened very closely to that described in *Reconciled*.

- **Ward Hill Lamon:** President Lincoln's close, personal friend and bodyguard who stayed with him throughout the war, though sometimes Lincoln eluded him to go his own way alone. Lamon was rugged, and he played the banjo quite well.

- **Generals Bragg, Breckinridge, Hardee, and Beauregard:** All generals under Johnston and portrayed as close as possible to their true character.

- **Charles Colchester:** A shyster spiritualist who actually held séances for Mary Todd Lincoln. A close friend of John Wilkes Booth, later in the war, his foolery was discovered at the White House. He had a small drum attached to his leg underneath the tablecloth.

- **Edwin Booth:** John Wilkes Booth's older brother, also an actor, who was mentioned in the story. After his wife died, Colchester held private séances for Edwin.

- **Wendall Phillips:** The Golden Trumpet orator for Abolition of Slavery. The event told in *Reconciled* mirrors an actual event that took place in Cincinnati.

- **Captain Thomas Eckert:** A telegraph specialist who was appointed to the War Department in charge of military operations. He was later promoted to major.

- **Secretary Edwin Stanton:** Secretary of War for President Lincoln. His demeanor is set to copy the general attitude he actually possessed.

- **David Bates and other telegraph operators:** They worked at the telegraph office and interacted with President Lincoln when he made his regular visits there.

- **Sergeant Smith Stimmel:** The officer commanding the security guard at the President's Home.

- **General Albert Pike:** Commanded the Confederate mercenary Native Americans. He wore buckskin and rode in a carriage to the battle because of an injury. His statue is the only Confederate general placed in Washington, DC.

- **The Cox family:** Polly and her children and daughter-in-law lived in and ran the Elkhorn Tavern (more a stagecoach waystation than a tavern.) Her husband, Jesse, was away selling cattle to the Union army at the time of the battle. Obviously, Cyntha and Anthony were not real cousins. During the battle, the Cox family actually hid in the cellar, and blood really did drip through the floorboards.
- **General Curtis (Union commander of the Army of the Southwest):** Stuffy numbers man who alienated President Lincoln because he sought to free the slaves before Lincoln did.
- **Union Colonels Carr, Dodge, and Osterhaus:** involved in the battle of Pea Ridge/Elkhorn Tavern. Colonel Dodge went on to become General Grant's head of spies.
- **Confederate Colonel Frank Armstrong:** General Ben McCulloch's staff aide. He later was promoted to general.
- **Confederate Colonel Louis Hebert:** Third in charge, after McCulloch and McIntosh.
- **Confederate Major Will Tunnard:** In charge of the Third Louisiana Pelicans.
- **Thaddeus Lowe:** Mentioned in *Reconciled*, he was the inventor of the hydrogen gas-making tanks used in *Reconciled* and head of the Union Army Balloon Corps.
- **Doctor David Yandell:** General Johnston's personal surgeon whom he sent to tend to Union wounded soldiers, and thus Yandell was not near Johnston and might have saved his life. Dr. Yandell ordered tourniquets given to all soldiers. General Johnston had a tourniquet in his pocket when he died. It could have been used to save his life.
- **Confederate Colonel William Preston:** General Johnston's aide and brother-in-law. Preston was a cousin of General Breckinridge.

- **Farmer J. C. Fraley:** His farm is where the battle began.
- **Union General William T. Sherman:** Commander under General Grant who led the army at Pittsburg Landing and refused to believe reports that the Confederate army was near and forming up for battle.
- **Lt. Colonel Walter Lane:** next in charge under Colonel Greer in the Third Texas Cavalry.
- **Confederate Colonel Winfield Statham:** Third Brigade of the Army of Mississippi.
- **All of President Lincoln's cabinet secretaries** are fashioned to mimic their personalities.
- **Detective Allan Pinkerton:** Scottish immigrant who made a name for himself protecting the president, and establishing the Union's spy effort. Pinkerton Detective Agency lasted long after the war.
- **Governor Isham Harris of Tennesse:** Present at Shiloh and at General Johnston's death.
- **Captain George Washington Fly:** Organized the Gonzales Invincibles at the beginning of the war, part of the Second Texas Infantry Regiment. He served throughout the war.

ACKNOWLEDGEMENTS

I wish to thank all the good people in the Woodlands Writers Guild, in Houston Writespace, those members of Daughters of the Confederacy, Sons of Confederate Veterans, Sons of Union Veterans, and The Third Texas Cavalry reenactors. I wish to specifically thank Dyson Nickle, Bob and Sue Mennell, and all my friends around Texas and the nation who have been so supportive. A great deal of the historical accuracy of the book is because of their generous guidance.

I offer sincerest thanks to Becki Kinch, who did initial editing of *Reconciled*, and to Sandra Timm, whose editing and ongoing support is incredible. Special thanks to my publisher, Mindy Kuhn and to her staff. Mindy is always there to answer a question or find a quick solution.

Finally, I thank all of my supporters. Let's keep history alive—particularly among our youth.

Subscribe to Curt's blog at www.curtlocklearauthor.com
Follow Curt on Twitter @CurtLock

If you would like for Curt to speak to your group,
please contact him at Curt@curtlocklearauthor.com

Download your complimentary MP3 album at
www.reverbnation.com/splinteredsongsofthecivilwar

Please go online to Amazon and Goodreads and leave reviews.
All reviews are helpful to spread the word. Thanks in advance.